MW00696461

BROADWAY REVIVAL

BROADWAY REVIVAL

LAURA FRANKOS

SWALLOW'S END PUBLISHING

Copyright © 2021 by Laura Frankos

Table of Contents

Chapter 1

"One Foot, Other Foot" —Oscar Hammerstein II

From the diary of David W. Greenbaum, July 14, 2078

I buried Ramon today, after losing him last week to his Tantalus 3 addiction. Strictly speaking, I lost him to the drug two years ago, but this time there'd be no more bouts of recovery, no more heartfelt promises of clean living, no more battles. The pews were jam-packed. His parents were there, of course; his mother tearfully embraced my nieces and nephew, the closest things she'd ever had to grandkids. My brother Nate and his wife, Isis; Chan Ho Chen, Ramon's long-suffering agent; even his grade-school dance teacher. A few of his Tantalus 3-crazed cronies, sallow-faced and maybe wondering what their funerals would be like. That bitch, Shanta Gholkar, who seemed to have kicked her own addiction, though she kept dealing the shit. And, naturally, many of the people Ramon had performed with over the years, including half the cast of the centennial production of _Follies,_ where we first met, seven years ago. I played Young Ben and he was one of the dancers, and we wound up in Loveland. For a while, anyway.

I survived the services without much trouble. Religious rituals and the theatre have enough in common to make them interesting, even to a nonbeliever. I'm a secular Jew, and Ramon was a lapsed Catholic, but he had insisted on the whole church bit, mostly for his mother's sake.

His other deathbed wish was for "an old-fashioned Irish wake for a Mexican-American." That was a lot harder to take. Not the stories and songs about Ramon; those were wonderful, and I'm glad Isis was filming them. No, it was the way everybody kept asking, "How are you, David?" I automatically replied, "I'm fine," all the while tossing back Ramon's favorite drink, Bronx cocktails (a concoction from the early twentieth century that he researched during a Jerome Kern festival; when Ramon got into a role, he really got into a role). I wasn't fine, but at least the gin and vermouth flooding through my veins made me fairly numb.

I was scowling at that bastard in the coffin, still handsome despite what he'd done to himself, when my niece, Rose, sidled up. *No, no, no. Don't you start, too. I thought you knew me better.*

But Rose, a sweet sixteen-year-old, who inherited her dark complexion from her Jamaican mother and her obsession with musicals from her uncle, looked down at Ramon and softly said, "Well, he is looking purty and nice. But he always did."

I resisted the temptation to take her cue and start singing. Maria Abarca accepted the fact that her late son was a gay chorus boy, and there *had* been many show tunes sung during the wake. But "Pore Jud is Dead" probably went over the line in her taste.

But not Ramon's. He would have loved the joke, and Rose knew it. I compressed my howl of laughter into a more decorous guffaw—yes, I am an actor, ladies and gents—and hugged her. "You're swell, kiddo," I whispered in her ear.

She pulled back, studying me with her dark eyes. "What now, Uncle David?"

"I'll think of something." I kept my tone light. I couldn't tell her my plans.

#

Rose once remarked that the nickname of the multinational time-traveling program, the Rippers, was inaccurate. It came from Washington Irving's Rip van Winkle, who fell asleep and woke up twenty years later. But Nate says that although the best brains of many nations have been working on time travel for longer than Rip's nap, they still haven't figured out how to go forward in time. Backward, yes; forward, no. Or, as Ramon quipped, "They're still stuck in *Merrily We Roll Along,* with the action unscrolling in the past." I called them "Winkles," which Rose and Ramon thought was hilarious, but Nate didn't.

As a Ripper (or Winkle) veteran, Nate had a part in that Oscar-winning documentary about the program, "Traversing Through Time." He was the chubby guy in the 1890s top hat and tails, the one with the dark brown mustaches. Even Rose had a cameo; she waved good-bye as Daddy, whiskers and all, trundled off into the SlingShot, the time-machine capsule. Millions more people have seen Nate in that two-minute scene than ever watched me on stage or heard my songs. (Who's jealous? Not me!) Maybe billions, since there are bootlegs of "Traversing Through Time" in China. The Chinese government has opposed the whole concept of time travel, even fictional treatments, for decades. Nobody's allowed even to think of a time when it might have been nice to live in a less oppressive China, which naturally makes stories and films even more popular, especially anything about the Rippers. I once asked Nate if he thought the Chinese, despite their denials, actually had built a time machine of their own. He gave me that classic, "God, you're a moron, little brother!" glare.

No, Nate wouldn't talk about the Chinese, and he wouldn't talk about "Traversing Though Time," either, except to say that it showed as much as the participating governments wanted the public to know. Implying, of course, that there's more to it. We're not as bad as the Chinese—we haven't had to put down two bloody uprisings in the last forty years—but I suspect the secrecy is more due to the massive investment in the program than anything else. To say nothing of not wanting the average Joe off the street to use time travel for his own nefarious purposes. Like me.

People have daydreamed for centuries about what they'd do if they could go back in time. Ramon was no exception. We hadn't been together very long—*Follies* was into its third month—when I told him about my family.

"Your brother's a Ripper?" Ramon stopped in his tracks on Hudson Street, spinning about with a dancer's grace and grabbing me by the shoulders. A heavyset fellow following behind us had to sidestep around him, and nearly got hit by a speeding z-bike that had strayed out of its designated lane. Ramon ignored his curses. "Oh, we got to work on this guy, get him to take us along. Think of the shows we could see! Everything from Harrigan and Hart to George and Ira Gershwin! Bock and Harnick! Sondheim and Prince! Estévez and Pappadakis! Moonrise Johnson!"

"More than that. How about original Shakespeare or Sophocles? But Nate says we'll be old men before they'll let tourists go sight-seeing through time. Assuming we could afford it. It'll cost a fortune. Nate's always bitching about funding. Might as well be Broadway."

"Unh-unh. I can't wait. I'll charm my way on board for the chance to see Michael Bennett's original choreography for 'Who's That Woman?'" He bounced on the balls of his feet, ready to knock on Nate's door and start coercing him *now.* He gave me that look—and it was a good thing I wasn't in charge of anything just then, because, like Lola in *Damn Yankees,* whatever Ramon wanted, Ramon got. It took me years to learn to resist it. In those early days, I was stupid, crazy, goofy with love.

When Ramon did meet my family a few weeks later, Nate, happily married to Isis, proved immune to his charms ("Sorry. No civilians in the SlingShot."), but clearly liked his wit and humor.

After dinner, Isis hugged me in the kitchen and murmured, "Good one, Dave. Don't fuck it up."

Rose, then nine, showed off her latest dance steps; Ramon promptly taught her a new one. Five minutes of watching him had Rose accurately concluding, "You're a better dancer than Uncle David."

No arguments, though I'm the better singer and a songwriter-librettist with several shows under my belt. Little Hannah and Bertram, seven and five, enjoyed learning Ramon's Southwestern version of "Greasy Grimy Gopher Guts." A first-rate first meet, in other words. Ramon always got on beautifully with my family. Maybe too beautifully. He liked Nate's kids so much, he always avoided talking about us having kids of our own. Not that I mentioned it much in the last few years, either. Tantalus 3 addicts don't make good parents. Or good spouses.

I remember one other thing from that dinner. Although Nate brushed off Ramon's initial comments about time travel, my lover was persistent. He tried again as we were leaving, with containers of leftovers in our arms.

"Are you sure you can't save us a couple of seats in that time ship of yours?" Ramon said. "I'm in a Harold Rome mood, so I really want to see *Pins and Needles.* 1937."

"Hmm." Nate pretended to consider it. Out of the corner of my eye, I saw Rose grab her Ally and start muttering into it, looking up Harold Rome. A fourth grader then, but already nuts about Broadway.

"Maybe I can swing a single passenger," Nate said, shifting into teasing-brother mode. "But where does that leave David?"

"Where? 'Alo-o-o-one, all alo-o-o-ne! Al-o-o-o-ne amidst eight million souls!'" Ramon sang. I couldn't help smiling; the tune was from a wretched flop from 2050 called *Dateline: Hong Kong* that we both loved as kids. Nothing says soul mates like a fondness for the same flop musicals. That silly verse became a catch phrase between us. I suppose a shrink could read subtle, hidden meaning into it, since Ramon was constantly leaving me all al-o-o-one among millions while he ran off to blink in a Tant-house. But really, it was just another snippet of a show tune, part of our daily dialogue. Sometimes we had whole conversations in song fragments.

So that was one reason I decided I would hijack Nate's time machine: going to those long-ago shows Ramon had fantasized about. But it wasn't the main reason. I couldn't save Ramon Abarca from himself. However, so many other talented men died too damn young...and I might save them. George Gershwin. Cole Porter. Kurt Weill. Vincent Youmans. Jerome Kern. Lorenz Hart.

It would to take a hell of a lot of work, but it would be the role of a lifetime.

#

August 18, 2078
Rose Greenbaum had been to enough plays to know to bring a sweater against the slings and arrows of outrageous

6

air conditioning. She stepped out of the Music Box Theatre into the sticky August heat and shed her cardigan. Her best friend, Zanzi Stubbs, did the same as they headed for an early dinner before going home to Brookline on the evening train.

"Two hours of my life I'll never get back," Zanzi said, tossing her waist-length blond hair. She rummaged in her purse for her Ally. "You and your Noël Coward."

"Hey, you can learn plenty from an unsuccessful show. Pay attention to its flaws, and stay away from them in your own productions." Rose ticked her fingers: "Murky lighting. Poor pacing, especially in the first act; Coward's dialogue should fly, not trudge. On the positive side, old Anne Hathaway was a wonderful Madame Arcati."

"She was pretty lively for somebody in her mid-nineties. And the guy playing Charles was definitely 'lish. Mmmmm." She waved her Ally at Rose; she had already accessed the man's C-page, and his baby blue eyes gazed soulfully from the screen. Rose didn't have the heart to tell Zanzi that Uncle David said the actor was a first-class prick. "But, Rosie, you got to stop talking about 'my productions.' You may end up on stage, but I'm going into law. Who'll have a nicer house in thirty years? No offense, but I've seen your uncle's place. Every time I've been there, something else is broken." Zanzi wrinkled her nose.

"It's historic," Rose said. "Greenwich Village reeks of history."

"Your uncle's plumbing reeks. I want old stuff, I'll go to the museum." The Ally pinged in her hand, and the actor's mug morphed into a transportation alert. "Shit! There's a huge wreck on our line. It's gonna take us forever to get home."

"We could go to Uncle David's, if you're brave enough to spend the night in a hovel built in 1960."

Zanzi made an exasperated noise. "I'm never going to hear the end of that. Are you sure he won't mind?"

"I've got a standing invite for any time I'm in New York. Even got a key. Let's grab dinner and text him."

The girls could have got dinner anywhere, but they automatically headed for Katz's, the oldest deli in New York. Though she looked like a blond supermodel, Zanzi knew Jewish deli food as well anybody on Rose's dad's side. The Greenbaum connection to Katz's allegedly went back decades. Family legend had it that one ancestor, Mort, worked at Katz's where an accident with the slicer killed his career as a jazz pianist. Uncle David claimed that was the source of the family's musical ability. Ramon always said it was just an excuse to eat pastrami, to honor Mort's aborted career.

I miss Ramon, Rose thought, picking at her cole slaw. *I hope Uncle David's okay. Maybe a visit from us will cheer him up.* She pushed aside her plate and texted him. **HEY UD STUCK NYC CAN Z&I STAYW/U**

The reply didn't come for nearly five minutes, an eternity as far as Zanzi went. "Maybe we should take the bus."

Hey, Rosie, Zanzi. I'm stuck, too, in romantic Trenton, until six. If you don't mind a huge mess, you can stay. BUT DON'T TOUCH ANYTHING, ESPECIALLY THE BOXES.

"That's weird."

Zanzi leaned over to look. "That your uncle uses proper punctuation and spelling, or that you have a SJ-Ally 26? It's two years out of date."

"Quit insulting my unit. I've been texting Uncle David all my life, and I've never seen him use all caps or give orders like that. And why is he in Trenton?"

"A job, obviously. Maybe he's got something he's working on and he doesn't want teenagers fucking it up. Tell him we're coming, and let our folks know we're staying there, so they won't panic."

David Greenbaum's apartment was on 12th Street, close enough to Christopher Street that Rose kept singing snatches of *Wonderful Town* and *Stonewall* until Zanzi smacked her. Rose's key worked, though the temperamental door needed a hefty shove from both girls. Zanzi staggered in, muttering.

Rose followed, then stopped in her tracks. "God. He wasn't kidding about the mess." The place looked like a sea of boxes. "What *is* all this?"

"Whatever it is, we promised not to touch it." Zanzi collapsed on the lumpy, vomit-colored couch.

While her friend glued to her Ally, Rose shuffled about the apartment. Something else seemed odd. Murky lighting, as in the play she'd just seen! The late-summer sunlight should have been coming from the study, but it wasn't. She went to investigate.

The shelves had been cleared of Ramon's tchotchkes, books, and photos. The small closet was empty. Six boxes stacked on the floor had sticky notes on them: MARIA, LUIS, VERACRUZ, T3 AID. A cheap vinyl tablecloth covered the desk, with three shallow plastic trays on top of it. Several large plastic bottles stood next to the trays; a thin rope stretched from the bookcase to the wall fixture, with small clips attached to it. One glance at the window explained the strange lighting: black cloth covered the panes, with tape sealing the edges.

Rose had a horrible, fleeting thought that somehow Uncle David was cooking up drugs. Then she picked up one of the bottles. Photographic solution. *The kind of photos that need cameras and film and special paper, like those*

Civil War pictures in our textbook last year, she thought. *Matthew Brady, that's the guy.*

The apartment suddenly shook as the door banged open. Rose heard her uncle greet Zanzi, so she hurried out to the front room.

"Hi, Uncle David. We brought you cheesecake in lieu of rent. Thanks for bailing us out." She gave him a quick hug. He was sweaty, and definitely needed a shower. *He looks tired... and fat. Cheesecake is the last thing he needs. How much weight has he gained since the funeral?*

He also looked as if he were barely controlling his temper; his hazel eyes seemed much darker. "Were you in the study?" he snapped.

"Yes," she said. *What's wrong with him?* "I noticed the blackout curtain, but don't worry, I didn't touch anything. So you've taken up photography! My fifth-grade teacher was good at it. Her pictures were beautiful."

His shoulders relaxed, and he ran a hand back over his wavy brown hair. "Yeah. Something to do, so I don't mope about here. I'm taking a class at NYU extension."

That sounds more like my uncle. "Could we see your pictures?"

"Wait till I get better at it." An idea seemed to occur to him. "But I'll practice on you, if you don't object. I've got a shot in mind, to go with the old-fashioned medium." He rushed into the bedroom and returned with a boxy-looking camera. "This isn't a real antique; it's just made to look like one. It works like an old camera, which is the point. Maybe I'll get good enough to want a genuine model. First, I'll take one picture of you both on the couch... like so. I'm using black-and-white film, so the wretched color won't matter. And now I want just Rose in the kitchen, in front of the famous Abarca tiles."

The kitchen was cramped but cozy. Mexican tiles in vibrant orange, blue, and white covered the back wall. They had belonged to a great-aunt of Ramon's whose old house near San Diego was damaged in a fire. When she redecorated, Ramon rescued the tiles and installed them in the kitchen.

Uncle David moved the table and positioned Rose in front of the tiles. "Wardrobe!" he called, then frowned in mock exasperation. "Where ees zat woman? A great artiste like moi should not have to do every little thing! *Zut alors!*" He stepped back into the front room and returned with the box marked MARIA. "I'm sending Ramon's stuff to his mom, his cousin, and the family in Veracruz," he said, abandoning the silly French accent. He rummaged in the box. "Aha! This mantilla belonged to his aunt; Ramon was always crazy about the delicate lace work. All hand-made. Here. Put it on … stand right there … head up. The mantilla covers most of your blouse, and your jeans aren't in the shot. That makes you timeless." He stepped back a pace and kept looking in the little window. A click, a flash, and it was done. He adjusted her pose for a second shot: "In case I botched the first."

"When can we see them?" Zanzi asked. "Can we watch you turn them into photos?"

"This roll of film isn't used up yet, so I can't develop them." At the girls' blank expressions, he explained further: "There are twenty-four exposures on this roll, and I've used seven. If I develop the roll now, I'm wasting expensive film. I'll take some more after I get my next assignment. Now where's that cheesecake?"

For most of the rest of the evening, Uncle David seemed like his usual self, with one brief exception. Rose convinced him to let them see the things he was sending to Ramon's family, arguing, as only an impertinent teenager could do, that he "shouldn't do anything hasty."

"We knew Ramon was dying for months, so it's not really that quick, Rose. Besides, I'm keeping the things that mattered. But take anything you want."

That led to a predictable sniffle-fest. The girls pawed through the boxes, taking some of Ramon's outrageous cufflinks, a tiny stuffed sea lion from San Francisco, several scarves and ties, and the old mantilla. But when Rose began to open a box near the recliner, he barked, "Not that one! That's mine!"

The bad temper had abruptly returned. As far as Rose could tell from one glance, the box held nothing but papers and books, with an advertisement from Trenton Piano Movers and a letter from San Marco Hospital in Mexico City on top. "Sorry, Unk. I didn't know." She gave an uncomfortable laugh. "I think the last time you yelled at me was when I asked to you to read lines with me in ninth grade for *Romeo and Juliet* and I was 'woefully unprepared.'"

He rubbed his chin; all the Greenbaum men had thick beards. "Ah, you deserved it then, but I'm wrong now. I apologize. It's...a work in progress."

Zanzi, ever one to defuse a tense situation, pulled a hideous eye-searing sweater from a box. She squealed in horror. "Tell me Ramon never wore this!"

"He didn't. It was a gift from his grandmother, who had poor vision and worse taste. Ramon kept it as a joke. That's the box going to charity, right? Abuela's gone, but I guarantee the family would recognize it."

When Rose got home at lunchtime the next day, her parents asked her how David was doing. She thought hard. "He's getting pudgy, but not as pudgy as you, Dad. Yet."

Nate looked pained, but Bertie snickered. "Bet his agent hates that!"

"He was grouchy, too," Rose continued. "He blew up like Mount Vesuvius because he thought we were messing with some stuff. Does that sound like Uncle David to you? And he hasn't written any new songs, either. I can't remember ever visiting him and not hearing a new song."

"Sweetie, he's been through a lot," Nate said. "Losing Ramon was tough in itself, plus the stress of the last months. I hope he gets a job soon, to get his mind off things."

"Well, he has taken up old-fashioned photography and he's got some personal private project he wouldn't even explain to his own niece." Rose couldn't hide the hurt in her voice.

"He needs to grieve in his own way," Isis said, giving her eldest a quick kiss on the head. "I'm sure he'll tell you about it when the time is right."

"But isn't it too soon to box up Ramon's things? Even the pictures from the study walls are gone!"

"Survivors have to deal with their lost ones' leftovers eventually. Some drag their feet, others do it quickly," Isis said. "Another brownie, anyone?"

With a glance at his stomach, Nate loudly declined, but Bertie made a production of taking three.

"I still think Uncle David's acting weird," Rose muttered.

"Of course he acts weird!" Bertie said through a mouthful of crumbs. "He's an actor!"

Rose stomped off to her room. "Nobody ever listens to me around here!"

\#

From the diary of David W. Greenbaum, August 19, 2078
I did not cover myself with glory last night with my niece. I was a total jerk about what I've taken to calling "the Broadway Revival Project." What makes it worse is she's the

13

one person who would understand what I'm doing. God, I'll miss her.

Preparations for the Revival occupy me from waking to bedtime. I keep thinking of more things I need to know to survive in 1934 and do what I need to do, and I despair of ever learning enough. I thought I'd scream when Rose started mucking with my boxes of research materials.

The only good thing that came out of the evening was the photo. I had realized I couldn't display my contemporary photos once I went back in time, and that depressed me, since I love surrounding myself with photos of family and friends. Like Irving Berlin, I'm a sentimental guy. Then I had the idea to take my favorite pictures, blending faces into genuine old pictures with PhotoArtist, and using my imitation Kodak to snap the results. The shot of Rose in front of the tiles is perfect as is; there's no hint of the 2070s about it. The only pictures of me and Ramon that were already suitable for time travel were our opening night gifts from *Versailles,* a musical about the 1919 Paris Peace Conference. Ramon played a doughboy and I was John Foster Dulles, one of Wilson's aides. The producers brought in a professional photographer who created lovely sepia-toned portraits of the cast. I loved that show, got great notices, but it's tainted. Ramon resented my success and moved out, haunting the Tantalus 3 dens and screwing anything that held still long enough. Until, of course, he got sick. Again. And again.

Enough moping. Back to work for the Revival, though I'm kind of at cross purposes: I'm learning to move pianos, which makes me hurt in muscles I didn't know I had, but at the same time I'm on a high-calorie diet, so I can impersonate my brother. Ramon would have loathed the extra pounds I'm carrying. I hope they won't be hard to lose once I'm back in the 1930s. How did people diet and exercise back then? More things to research, on top of my three main concerns: Medicine, Survival Gear, and New York in the Thirties.

#

From the diary of David W. Greenbaum, October 4, 2078
Shanta Gholkar wasn't expecting me during her office hours in the Columbia English department, but she hugged me and made sympathetic noises about Ramon. She certainly didn't expect me to plunk a piece of paper on her cluttered desk. She read it, ticking a sparkly red fingernail against her node—a habit that's irked me for years.

"Dave, I can't help you with this," she said. "No way. Get out of here. I'm not getting involved in anything illegal."

"You've been up to your ears in illegal shit. You trusted Ramon too much, or maybe you thought he was too addled to remember. One night, when you were both blinking, you shared your dirty secrets, and he blabbed them all to me. The scam with your cousin. The tax dodges with those investments. And, of course, your career as a Tantalus 3 dealer."

Shanta sputtered, "I haven't used or dealt in months! You can't blame me for his death!"

"He was responsible for his actions, but you made it so easy to relapse again and again."

She looked again at the paper. "I don't even know what these terms mean. Something about tumors?"

"You don't need to know. Your dad's a doctor. He can get what I need. He'd better, or his darling daughter will wind up in jail."

"You're crazy, Dave. Why are you doing this?"

"It's a mission of mercy. I couldn't save Ramon, but I know a young man in very difficult circumstances who *will* die without those drugs." *Strictly speaking, Gershwin got his brain tumor in his late thirties, and there's no guarantee that this particular immunotherapy will even work, but I have to try. I can pick up the more ordinary meds myself, but the cancer treatments need a specialist's approval.*

Clearly, Shanta didn't believe me. But I must have projected enough determination that she sighed. "I'll talk to my dad. I assume you this has to be done quickly?"

Actually, no. When time travel's involved, deadlines don't mean much. "Apparently, it's a slow-growing tumor, so it doesn't have to be immediately. Say, two months max. I'll contact you, since I'll be in Mexico for a while."

"Is that where this guy lives? Is he one of Ramon's relatives?"

"No and no, but he doesn't live in this country." *That's sort of true; America in 1934 isn't the same as America in 2078.* "Look, Shanta, I'm not telling you any more. You do your part and I'll keep my mouth shut. Unlike you, I'm good at it." I stood up to leave, gathering my scarf and umbrella.

Shanta jabbed a long red fingernail at the paper. "What's to stop me from telling the cops you're threatening me?"

I had expected that. "The usual precautions. Anything with the police, and this goes public. Ditto if any of your Tant-head pals jump on me."

That rocked her. She disliked me—the feeling had always been mutual—but she never wanted to hurt me. Maybe it had never occurred to her until now. Her glare indicated she wouldn't mind if I dropped dead on top of her Milton manuscripts right in front of her. "Obviously, I set myself up for this"—she grimaced—"since Ramon and I talked about everything together. Everything. You wanna know what he really thought about you, asshole?"

Resentment faded, at least mine. A wave of sadness washed over me. "Oh, Shanty. Do you think I haven't heard it all before, straight from Ramon himself?" I closed the door behind me with a quiet click.

#

Shanta's dad came through with the cancer drugs, and plenty of questions, none of which I answered. I did promise Shanta she had nothing more to worry about, at least where I was concerned. Somehow, I got the feeling she didn't believe me, but it's true. Four weeks from now, I'll be long gone. If I were the bastard she thinks I am, I'd spread word about her before I step into the SlingShot. But she was close to Ramon for years and got me what I needed, so I'll keep quiet.

According to my research, the best way for George Gershwin to survive his brain tumor would have been convection-enhanced delivery. That pumps drugs through a catheter straight into the tumor—drugs specifically tailored to match the genetic profile of the cancer. Unfortunately, short of bringing him to a modern hospital, I can't do that. I needed other options, so I took several trips to Mexico City, where I spoke to several doctors in a strictly hypothetical way about Gershwin's possible prognosis. It was nice to play a part again; the neurosurgeons were eager to help "Dennis Bradshaw" research his Gershwin biography, especially since Dennis was paying for dinner. They suggested a broad-spectrum combination of vaccines and antibodies designed to attack the tumor's surface. Oncolytic immunotherapy has had some amazing breakthroughs in recent years. That made the list I gave to Shanta. I promised the oncologists and neurosurgeons acknowledgments in the biography. Sorry, docs.

The other drugs were easier to get. I picked up the tuberculosis treatment in Mexico (Minarcin, the stuff that defeated that superbug pandemic when I was a kid); the hypertension meds in San Bernardino, using a false ID; and flew to China for the last item. The Chinese have developed something called "the Boost," which reduces side effects of many harsh drug treatments. There are plans to release it in the States in two years, but I don't want to wait. In Hong Kong, "all alo-o-o-one" with piles of cash, it was easy to score. The worrisome part was getting through customs, but my looks are generic enough not to get me profiled. Not many drug mules carry the Boost—recreational drugs are more profitable. I did wonder if the stuff would kill me if the plastic bag ruptured. That might have led to a very strange obituary.

I had what I needed, though no guarantee of success. Obstacle One: could I get close enough to the great songwriters to administer the doses? Obstacle Two: it would be years before some of these treatments were needed. Would the drugs stay potent? My parents used to squabble over the expiration dates on their medications; Dad ignored them while Mom chucked bottles when they hit their due date. I hoped Dad's theory was right; government studies seem to back him up.

With the medicines in place, I completed my Survival Gear. This included my carefully constructed assortment of photographs; two SJ-Allys—fully loaded with music and books that hadn't been written in 1934; eight thousand dollars of contemporary cash, purchased from puzzled coin dealers; and three custom-made extension cords. Obviously, I couldn't run the Ally on batteries, and 1930s' electrical outlets are incompatible with modern electric plugs. Modern ones have three pins for grounding, so I went to an electrician and concocted a story about traveling to a back-country village in Central America, to a house equipped with primitive two-pin sockets—the kind used in the thirties. She gave me a funny look, but did the job.

I needed a new identity, too: meet Joseph David Cohen, born March 22, 1905 in San Francisco. In the classic musical, *Damn Yankees,* Joe Boyd's false persona, "Joe Hardy," comes under suspicion because there are no records of him in his alleged hometown of Hannibal, Missouri. But there's a reason Mr. Cohen has no birth records: they were destroyed in the earthquake and fire of 1906! And all his relatives died in the 1919 flu epidemic, poor guy.

And finally, my contingency plan. Nate once described a trip in the SlingShot to me: standing in a little box, the blackness, the roaring, the intense headache on arrival. A few technicians run the whole procedure, since it's become fairly routine. The hard part's finding the funding. I was counting on my acting skills and my resemblance to my brother to fool the techs, but in case they caught on, I had a duffel bag full of … persuasion.

One month to go.

#

January 18, 2079
Rose's high school had a staff day scheduled for the nineteenth, so she asked her parents if she could take the train to New York. "I want to see some films at the Paley. Maybe I can narrow my options for my audition numbers."

"Have you talked to your uncle about them?" her mother asked.

Rose poked around her cereal bowl. "Of course. He's been very helpful."

Isis put down her washcloth and went into Analyst-Mom mode. "You're still upset because he didn't automatically say yes to your living with him if you got into Juilliard or NYU."

"No!" She smashed another bran flake. "Well, yeah. I know it was rude, and I know I haven't even been accepted yet. But Ramon always said…"

"Ramon's gone. David didn't say no, either. He just said, wait and see."

Which is grown-up for "Not very likely," thought Rose.

"Did you tell him you're coming to the city? Maybe you can have lunch."

"Like he needs lunch these days! But I'll text him. It would be nice if we could just chat. When he was here for Bertie's birthday last week, all he wanted to do was talk to Dad about time travel. He said he's thinking about revising *Second Chances,* which seems strange."

"He's the author. Maybe he's got some new ideas. Anyway, you know time travel was a running joke with your dad and David and Ramon for years."

Rose finished her cereal and brought the bowl to the sink to wash. "I don't know. It just seemed different. Not jokey; he was getting all technical. I can't see how that works with the libretto…"

"My kid, the dramaturg! Speaking of your dad, give him his good-luck kiss tonight. He's scheduled for the SlingShot tomorrow at noon, and you know he wouldn't want to leave without it."

"Of course! It's the kiss that makes it work. Without it, who knows when he'd end up? Some heathen era with no musicals!"

\#

Rose took the early train to New York, at home among the commuters, clutching her coffee and her Ally. She *was* fairly confident no one else in the car was listening to twentieth-century show tunes. "Summertime" or "Rose's Turn" for her audition? Or maybe "Reparations" from *Versailles*—though that would be an unusual choice for a girl. She couldn't wait to discuss them with Uncle David. He'd finally answered her text, but warned her he might have to go out. So Rose, against her nature, got up at the ungodly hour of five-thirty. *Better a little time with her Uncle-the-Broadway Actor than no time at all, especially when it came to college auditions!* Besides, she was bringing his favorite chocolate-cherry coffee cake, in case she did rouse him.

It was sleeting when she left Grand Central Station and took a podcar to the Village instead of the subway. Her parents and uncle remembered a Manhattan teeming with hundreds of thousands of personal cars ("most of them gridlocked," Dad joked), but the construction of the ziplines and the corresponding astronomical increases in car registration fees helped lead to their near extinction. Emergency units and delivery trucks were exempt, and some gazillionaires continued to drive, not minding the cost or being viewed as pariahs. For her part, Rose loved the sleek, speedy podcars, and wished all cities had them. Z-bikes, on the other hand, were less attractive and often dangerous.

When she reached Uncle David's apartment, she pelted up the stairs to the third floor. Bursting out of the stairwell into the green and yellow hallway, she was startled to see her father emerging from Apartment 5. *Impossible! He was still in bed when I left. And he's scheduled for the SlingShot today. Wait...* "Uncle David!"

Her uncle started and nearly dropped his keys. Rose took in many things at once: the dark brown wool coat and hat, the old-style leather suitcase, the close-trimmed haircut David didn't have last week, and, above all, the two moles on the left side of his neck that he also didn't have last week, but her father did. Everything about his attire screamed 1930s except Ramon's FC Barcelona duffel bag.

And there was the look of pain and dismay on his face.

"Uh, hi," she stammered. *Please tell me you've been cast in a Clifford Odets revival. Please. Because I don't like where my imagination is going right now.*

Uncle David's mouth twisted—and Rose saw he had added a pale scar on his chin, just like the one her dad had, the result of a childhood fight. He grabbed her arm, kicked the suitcase back inside, pulled her into the apartment, and slammed the door. He shoved her into a chair and ran his hands through his hair.

"Now what am I supposed to do?" he howled, more at the heavens than at her.

#

From the diary of David W. Greenbaum, January 19, 2079
"I don't understand, Uncle David," said my beautiful and far too smart for her own good niece. But she did. Of course she did. I saw her piece it all together—the clothes, the make-up, the way I look now, and the fact that Nate was scheduled to time travel today. It reminded me of when she was ten, and I took her to a production of *Sweeney Todd*. She figured out who Beggar Woman was before the big reveal, and kept muttering, "Oh, no! Oh, no!" under her breath as the second act approached its grisly conclusion. Now I felt like saying it.

"Yes, you do," I finally said. "The Greenbaums don't raise dummies."

Her dark eyes filled with tears. "But *why,* Uncle David? It's like suicide, and I'd never have expected that from you. Ramon, maybe, but not you."

"I'm not killing myself. I'll still be alive, but in 1934. I...have to do this. For Ramon."

She wasn't buying it. "How can this help Ramon? He's *dead.* Going back to 1934 won't stop his addiction."

"Going back even four years wouldn't have stopped it. I was there then, and I couldn't do a damn thing. I can make a difference this way, and I mean to go through with it. Whatever it takes." I zipped open the duffel bag and let her glimpse my contingency plan: plastic explosives, a timer, a mass of wires. Props, of course, but I wasn't about to tell Rose that. "Nobody—absolutely nobody—is going to stop me. The detonator's on my belt, and I'll use it if I have to. Now, I'm going secure you here somehow, and I'll text my landlord to let you out in a few hours. That's the best way."

"No, it isn't!" she blurted out. "Take me with you to the SlingShot. The techs all know me. I've practically grown up there, watching Dad take his trips. I can distract them. Then no one will get hurt."

#

January 19, 2079

Her uncle was looking kind of wild-eyed, since Rose's early arrival had deranged plans he'd been making for months. His expression, and that first peek into Ramon's old duffel bag did scare her, but only for a moment. Fakes. Unquestionably fakes. Uncle David was obviously desperate, but she would never believe he'd hurt or kill anyone. Not ever.

What's he saying? Leave me here? Hell, no! "No, it isn't! Take me with you to the SlingShot. The techs all know me. I've practically grown up there, watching Dad take his trips. I can distract them. Then no one will get hurt."

He didn't answer right away, and his hesitation crushed any doubt she might have had. David Greenbaum would never put his favorite niece—sorry, Hannah!—in danger. "Uncle David. Listen. I don't understand why you want to leave us, but I won't stand in your way. Your disguise is good, but you need me to get past the techs."

"No, I don't. That's why I've got that." He pointed at the duffel bag.

Ramon's favorite duffel, the one he took to his auditions. I'm supposed to believe you'd stuff it full of explosives. Ha. "You won't need that. Not with me along."

He rubbed his chin, shaped so like her dad's, thinking hard. "You have a point. You know the routine, and I don't, which means it's less likely I'd need that bag. But I'm taking it anyway." He held out his hand. "Give me your Ally; we'll leave it here. I don't want your folks suddenly seeing your location as 'New Haven' instead of 'New York.' Good thing we Greenbaums haven't gone in for implants. Use the john. It's a long drive, and we're not stopping."

The word "drive" stopped Rose in her tracks. She'd been contemplating options like jumping off the zipline, something some of the idiot boys at her school did for thrills, or, once they were out of the city, bolting from the train car; getting word to her dad or the cops, in spite of her promise not to stop him.

"Yes, I said drive. Got a rental car in the garage."

"Expensive."

"I won't be here for the bill. Your Ally, please."

She handed it over, used the bathroom, which Ramon had decorated with framed Playbills, and wondered what to do next. Uncle David gripped her arm when she came out, not hard enough to hurt, but firmly, and guided her through the hall and into the garage. A 2076 Toyota MinuteVan, the Tricentennial model, was parked close to the stairwell. They both climbed in, and he drove off.

It was the weirdest trip Rose had ever taken—the first time she'd ever felt uncomfortable with her uncle. She tried probing, but he wouldn't play. "We can talk about anything except what I'm doing and why I'm doing it. I need to disappear, that's all, and I'm going to disappear into the 1930s. Got it?"

So they discussed her upcoming auditions. David made plenty of suggestions, which Rose hoped she'd remember later. Her mind was more on what would happen after they got to Yale, not on what would get *her* into Yale. Or NYU. Or Juilliard.

Uncle David parked without a permit in a lot near the Rippers' lab, not caring for the consequences. He shut off the engine and looked at her, his face worn and pinched. "I don't know what I was thinking, Rosie. I can't get you involved in this. Can you—would you—stay here until it's over?"

"What's to stop me from running to the University cops?"

"I'm asking you not to."

She opened the car door and got out, tempted to run like hell. But his expression shook her. *Like he's lost everything in the world.* She banged on the roof. "Come on, Uncle D. You're not doing this alone." Some color rushed back into his cheeks, which pleased her. He jumped out of the van, grabbing his coat and bags. "The blonde tech is Maxie, the other's named London. The student who helps you into the 'Shot is Danny or Kimia. Danny's cute."

"I suspect in this guise I'm not his type."

"Too true. When's the departure?"

"Three o'clock."

That stopped Rose cold. "You're almost an hour early! That will make them suspicious. Dad's never early."

Uncle David snorted. "Nate the Late. I'm counting on that. It's the biggest gamble of all. If we're both here at the same time... well, it gets harder."

Your phony bomb, thought Rose. *Oh, Dad, don't be on time!*

They walked into the Casterwell Building, named for the first Ripper to lose his life in the early days of time travel, and quickly passed their first tests. The security guard greeted them with a cheery hello; a grad student, whizzing by in a wheelchair, called out, "Safe trip, Dr. G!"

All too soon, it seemed to Rose, they reached the Rippers' lab.

#

From the diary of David W. Greenbaum, January 19, 2079
I'll never know why she decided to help me, but she was right. It would have been rough without her. The techs—Maxie and London—*did* remark at "Nate's" early arrival, but Rose breezily claimed credit for that. They seemed happy; something about a complicated 'Shot to seventeenth-century Japan scheduled next, one involving detailed programming. Danny, the student, prepped the capsule without saying much. He was good-looking, in a boy-band way, despite the shaggy sideburns. Rose caught my eye and mouthed, "See, I told you!"

Danny mumbled, "New suit, Doc?"

"Clothes make the man," I said. I didn't want him looking too closely at me.

"Uh-huh. Got your boots? Long walk ahead of ya. Might be snow, too."

Boots? Clearly, I should have them, but don't. In my bag," I said. Danny gave me a funny look, but went on with his work.

Rose saved me again as the techs went through their checklist. London called out from behind her console, "Remember your Zobrist, Doc?" *Zobrist? What the hell was that?*

My niece ad-libbed like a pro when I dried on my lines. "Of course he did. If he didn't, he'd be shaking and puking his guts all over Yosemite. I reminded him to take them at breakfast. Right, Dad?"

"What would I do with you, kiddo?" I said gratefully. The Rippers keep mum on the details of SlingShot launches; no matter how much I pumped Nate, he never told me much. I should have interviewed Rose. Thanks to her, I now knew I'd have vomiting and tremors along with the migraine. And I knew my destination. I had expected it to be remote, just not how remote. It made sense, though. The Rippers wouldn't want their arrivals noticed, and Yosemite, if I remembered straight, was one of the first national parks.

The launch prep kept the techs so busy, they paid scant attention to me. After all, Professor Greenbaum had gone into the past many times. Danny motioned to me, and I stepped into the SlingShot, trying to seem blasé. Rose came over to say good-bye, unshed tears in her eyes.

"I'll never understand this," she said in a low voice, "and I'll miss you like anything, but in a weird way I'm glad I could help."

"Rose, missing you grow up and become a brilliant actress is the hardest thing about my little project here, but, as the Bard says, though this be madness, yet there is method in't."

She squeezed my hand. "At least I had this one chance to play a scene with you. I think I was pretty good." She flicked a glance at the duffel bag, which I had unobtrusively placed by the door. "That bag's just a clever prop."

"You knew?" I could barely speak.

"Since the start." She kissed my cheek. "Godspeed, Uncle David."

I swallowed hard. "If I had my say, you'd get the Tony right now. Break a leg, my very dear, in all your performances."

She shook her head. "Say the other one. What you and Ramon always said to each other before a show."

"As Noël told Gertie: a warm hand on your opening!" I kissed her back, and she stepped away from the capsule.

Danny came forward to seal it, but before he did, Rose called out once more. "Hey, in there! See some shows—just for me!"

"Oh, I will. Yes, I will."

The doors shut with a thump and pneumatic hisses. The interior had a cool, blue light, but only for thirty seconds or so. A dull, roaring noise filled the velvety darkness. My head began to throb…and I remembered nothing else until I woke up, lying on my back on a boulder.

#

January 19, 2079
Rose turned away from the SlingShot, surreptitiously wiping her eyes. Maxie and London checked their monitors. After several minutes, London announced, "Successful contact. He's away."

Rose swallowed hard. She wished she could leave before Dad got there and pretend that she, like the techs, had been fooled by Uncle David's performance, but she knew her family would never believe it. "Um, everybody, I think you should know…"

Shouting and thumping feet penetrated even the thick doors of the Rippers' lab. With a crash worthy of her little brother's Bash'em Robots, her father and the very pissed-off security guard charged into the room. They looked around wildly. The expressions on Maxie, London, and Danny's faces were beyond belief. *How Ramon would have roared,* thought Rose. *He loved pranks.*

"…that wasn't my dad in the 'Shot. It was my Uncle David."

#

March 20, 1934

I hadn't taken that damn Zobrist, so the moment I regained consciousness, I barfed up my breakfast. Then I had the dry heaves for an eternity, and, as Rose foretold, horrible shakes, too. The glare from the watery sunlight seared my eyes. At least I managed not to puke on my coat or shoes—more than a small mercy, though I would have traded my Moonrise Johnson autographed playbill for something to rinse out my mouth. I felt ghastly, but I wanted to make tracks, and fast. Somewhere buried in the rock was the sensor a brave, pioneering Ripper had placed to establish the link between eras, and I had no idea how to disable it. Nor did I know how long the SlingShot took to reboot. Hours? Days? No time at all? Or maybe I was fretting over nothing. While Nate was closed-mouth about giving details about the practical aspect of time travel, he had mentioned "anomalies in targeting." Pressed for a translation, he would only admit, "It's not easy to pick an exact date and time. Of course, if we arrive early, there's always stuff to observe—carefully. But it's bad to get there late, especially if it's something your backers want you to record. We're better at it now than when we started, but still not exactly precise."

But how often did they send one Ripper straight after another, to the same era? Maybe the complicated coordinates for the next trip were gumming up the SlingShot. *Time for me to leave this nest.*

The Rippers had chosen their landing place well: a cozy niche in a cluster of granite boulders, with only a narrow gap for an entrance. I could easily imagine Bertie turning it into a fort. A twenty-first century graffito, bright red letters on the rock wall, said ROAD TO OAKHURST—14 MILES, with a cheery arrow to help disoriented time travelers. I squeezed through the gap, carefully removing my coat, for fear of losing buttons. *If Nate gets any fatter, he'll have to climb up the sides to get out.* I looked back at the vomit-scented landing pad. Unless one were looking for a geologic hidey-hole, no hiker would think anything of this clump of rocks, and no animal would use it, since it was open from above. *Good thing, too. It'd be horrible to come all this way through time, only to get eaten by a bear.*

But there were no bears. No people, either. Just one raven giving me a suspicious stare from the lower branch of a sequoia. "Oakhurst?" I asked it. "Nevermore?" The bird said nothing. I set off in the direction the arrow had pointed.

Chapter 2

"I'm A Stranger Here Myself" —Ogden Nash

From the diary of Joseph D. Cohen, March 20, 1934

For the moment, my luck held out, thanks to Franklin Delano Roosevelt. After finding a small stream to rinse out my disgusting mouth, I began tramping along Route 125. It wasn't long before a heavily laden truck rumbled past me into the park. The driver slowed as he passed, no doubt wondering why a lone man was on the road, but my spirits soared. My first glimpse of the natives! And where there was one truck, there might be more going the other way! Sure enough, not ten minutes later, a coughing engine disturbed the silent wilderness. I looked back over my shoulder: a battered black Ford pick-up was rattling towards me. Summoning my courage, I stuck out a thumb in the time-honored tradition. The truck ground to a halt.

A skinny man in his thirties leaned out of the cab window. "Well, friend, you ain't Claudette Colbert, but whutthehell. Jump in."

"Thanks." I scrambled in, noting the stark steel interior and the leather-covered seat, stuffing erupting from splits and holes. Functional, but not comfortable or attractive. "Um, Claudette Colbert?"

"Ah, you ain't seen her new movie yet? Clark Gable's tryin' to hitch a ride, but the cars don't stop till she sticks out one of the prettiest legs you ever did see. Hoo! I'd pull over for her any day. You, now, you look like something the cat drug in. Where you headed?"

Of course! It Happened One Night. *Oh, God, my first cultural reference—a film that would sweep the Oscars—and I flunked it.* "Anywhere out of Yosemite. I've had all the natural beauty a man can stand."

The driver laughed. "Buddy, that ain't all a man can have too much of! Take it from me, lay off the booze. Ya got crud in your hair and your eyes look like cherry tomaters. I'm heading to Fresno for another load, to say nothing of better grub than at the work camp. Maudie brews good java, too."

"Wherever you're going, I'm with you. Whatever you're having, it's on me." I didn't mind being taken for a lush. It was easier to explain my appearance as a hangover than time travel. Plus, Fresno would have better bus and train connections than tiny Oakhurst. "What's this work camp you mentioned?"

"You musta been way off the road if you didn't notice all the action! The BPR's building new roads in the park, and the CCC's putting up new bunkhouses, cutting trail paths—some of 'em'll cut a new stairway up Half Dome. Busy as hell. I helped build the Wanona Road last year; first job I'd had in months! Thank you, PWA! I tell ya, I'm voting Democrat to the end of my days. Hoover didn't do nothing like this."

I recognized the alphabet soup as New Deal programs.

The driver continued, "You're lucky I'm headed south. If we were going back to the camp, I'd put *you* to work." He chuckled at my quizzical look. "See, I'm picking up

32

dynamite. The sticks get tied down in the truckbed, but I gotta carry the caps in a box on my lap. Sure would be nice to let someone else hold them."

"Eeep," was all I could manage, which made the driver laugh even more.

We reached Fresno in about an hour. I tried not to stare like a yokel. The street looked like a period movie set. Nearly everyone wore a hat, the clothes had an odd, heavy look to them, and the cars seemed ancient, but were, of course, perfectly contemporary. The advertising looked peculiar, too. As in the 2070s, ads were everywhere, but instead of the uniform modern look, flashing from ever-changing digital screens, handmade and local signage clashed with recognizable corporate logos. Besides the ads for Kellogg's Corn Flakes, Old Gold cigarettes (with Mae West!), Gillette razors, and Coca-Cola—the last one looking completely unchanged—there were billboards for San Francisco Floral, Fresno Brewing Company, Aki Hardware, and a small hand-lettered card for George Lauck, Baker. The truck driver led me to an honest-to-God greasy spoon, with DON'S painted loudly in yellow and red. He wasn't kidding about Maudie's coffee, either: it was strong, hot, and reviving. After searching the menu for items containing potassium, I ordered chicken noodle soup and a banana split, and treated the driver to a patty melt, fries, and apple pie. "Good luck with that dynamite," I told him, "and thanks for the lift."

The driver raised his mug in salute. "Any time, pal. Stay off the hard stuff. It'll kill ya."

"I don't expect to get bombed that way ever again," I said. "Not ever."

#

33

Landing in Yosemite worked well with my plans, since I needed to be on the West Coast before heading to New York. While my new persona had no surviving birth records, thanks to the 1906 earthquake and fire, I hoped to create a backstory with my acting talents and ephemera I'd bought from antique dealers. First, I needed some contacts in the city by the bay.

I took a bus from Fresno to San Francisco, arriving late last night. I'd visited there twice with Ramon, so it wasn't a city I knew well. I had only a vague notion of which areas got devastated in the quake of 2042, so I couldn't tell how different this city looked from the one of my era. The oddest thing was the way San Franciscans of 1934 left the lights on in the office buildings—a fantastic waste of energy. My own reserves depleted and my head still aching, I found a cheap hotel on Kearny Street, had a dish of scrambled eggs, ground beef, and spinach at a restaurant called New Joe's (a peculiar, if tasty, combination, recommended by the waitress), and slept for ten hours in my underwear.

Today I ventured out. I bought a second suitcase, pajamas, underwear and socks, and several changes of clothes at the Emporium department store on Market. A simple task, but one that scared the hell out of me. Who knew thirties salesmen were so...personal? I just needed some shirts and pants, not an interrogation! And wouldn't that guy have been surprised to see what I really did have in my BVDs? Several thousand dollars...The time it took also dismayed me. I had liberally tipped the Filipino bellhop and maid (and addressed them in Spanish, which pleased them) and had left the Do Not Disturb sign on my room, but I still felt uneasy leaving the meds and most of the cash behind, hidden under the bed, while I shopped. Seeing the room undisturbed when I came back with my parcels made me woozy with relief.

Unless, of course, shakiness was another side effect of time travel. I'd planned to start dieting right away to lose the Nate-waist, but calories seemed to fend off the wobblies, so I chowed down on spaghetti carbonara at New Joe's before setting off on my mission. Except for the truck driver, who'd offered a ride in the middle of nowhere, everyone I'd met thus far in 1934—waitresses, bus and taxi drivers, hotel staff, the eager clothing salesman—had been in a standard service-customer relationship with me. As I'd found at the department store, though the details had changed, the parameters between seller and buyer were close enough to mine that I managed fairly easily. This next encounter would be require improv skills.

I climbed halfway up Telegraph Hill, weaving my way through the side streets. As with Greenwich Village, this area had attracted its share of intellectuals in the twenties, but I wasn't looking for bohemians. In a mostly residential neighborhood, I turned a corner and found a nondescript, pale blue building: Temple Beth Ami.

I adjusted my hat. It still felt peculiar, though I'd worn plenty as costumes. But this was no costume; this was real life. Taking a deep breath, I approached the Temple. A plump woman in a dove-gray dress was pulling weeds in the flower bed along the brick walkway.

"Mrs. Epstein?" I'd seen this woman's obituary picture from 1957, but had no trouble recognizing her younger self; Shirley Epstein would age very well into her eighties.

"Yes?"

"I'm David Cohen. You won't remember me, but you and Rabbi Epstein were very kind to my family back in 1904, and helped them find a place here in the city. Samuel and Ruth Cohen." I had researched the Epsteins; they had spent their lives assisting Jewish immigrants to the Bay Area.

She struggled to her feet; I hopped over the low wall to give her a hand. "If your father was as good-looking as you, I'd remember," she said, surveying my long frame. "But if I had a dime for every Cohen I've met, I could order prime rib at the Palace."

"Of course." *Why else did I pick that name?* "And we didn't stay here long. I'm told we had a place on Gough, where I was born early the next year, and then..."

"I know what came next. Plenty of folks left after the quake."

"Hey, Shirl! You trading me in for a new model?" Rabbi Epstein, puffing away on a cigarette, looked over the side gate.

"Mr. Cohen, my better half, Michael Epstein. Mike, we did a *mitzvah* for this boy's family thirty years ago, and he's come to pay his respects."

"*Nu?* Let's be respectful over tea. It's freezing."

"Sissy," Mrs. Epstein said with affection. "I'm from New York, but Mike's from Florida. He thinks San Francisco is the North Pole."

"Well, Mark Twain agreed with me," the rabbi countered, leading led the way to the rear of the temple's social hall. Mrs. Epstein bustled about the kitchen, brewing tea and heaping cinnamon cookies on a plate. "So, what happened to your branch of Cohens?"

I launched into my fictional background—father working as a tailor's assistant; the quake and subsequent moves ("Lompoc, Los Angeles, Chicago; usually connecting with cousins; that's why you two were so helpful. No cousins here."); the death of most of the family in the flu of 1919; a year studying music at City College in Chicago, now shuttered by the Depression, which I hoped would make records harder to track; and finally working in theatres and nightclubs in Southern California, Veracruz, and Mexico City ("A good friend in Chicago taught me Spanish.").

As I spoke, Mrs. Epstein's face lit up. "Tell me, was your mother short, with dark brown curly hair, and a stubborn streak a mile wide? And a wonderful baker?"

How many Jewish mothers fit that description? "That sounds like Mama, yes."

"Now I remember her! But forgive me, I thought her name was Edith, not Ruth."

I grabbed this like a drowning man after a life raft. "Ruth was her legal name, but the family called her Edith, since she looked like an aunt by that name. It's funny. I also don't go by my real name. I'm Joseph David, but when everyone died in the flu, the cousins who took me in said I couldn't be Joseph any more, or the angel of death would find me." *This way, I can still be David, even if the ephemera I've dug up say "Joseph David Cohen."*

This confirmation sparked stories from Mrs. Epstein about the Edith/Ruth Cohen she remembered from 1904. Even the rabbi began chiming in about the long-lost Cohens, though he had thought Samuel had worked at a laundry. ("Well, something with clothes, anyway.") I absorbed every detail, later writing it all down in my notebook. Like a carnival fortune teller, I played up on remarks the Epsteins made.

"I loved her *hamantaschen;* I miss them every Purim," I said, and was pleased to see Mrs. Epstein's reaction.

"Such delights! Most ladies make prune and poppyseed fillings, but she conjured up apricot with almonds, raspberry with raisins. And her kugels—perfection!"

The chatting continued, with references to the Cohens' origins in Munich, Sam Cohen's limp, and an older sister, nicknamed Tootsie for her tiny feet, who had streaks of red in her hair. "You're darker, more like your mother," Mrs. Epstein concluded.

As I sipped my tea, I thought, *Now, if I ever have to establish my background, the Epsteins will vouch for me. I won't get caught out, like Martin Guerre or Shoeless Joe Hardy.*

When I drained my cup, I rose and reached for my wallet. "There's no way to repay you for your kindness, but please take this for some other family in need." I handed the rabbi twenty dollars.

"There's always someone in need these days," Epstein said. "But what of you, son? Can you be so generous? Not to be insulting, but you don't look too great."

"I'm on the mend." I grinned. "What I've got can only be cured by Broadway. I leave for New York tomorrow."

#

January 19, 2079

The lab exploded into chaos. Rose was not used to grown-ups yelling, but they all started screaming at the top of their lungs. She was center stage, getting it from every direction. Her father grabbed her by the shoulders, sweat beaded across his forehead, despite the lab's air conditioning. He pulled her to his chest. "Are you all right? When Joba said he'd already seen you … and *me* …" His voice cracked.

"I'm fine, Daddy, really." *Just got to keep playing this part a while longer.*

"We need to get all the departments in here," Maxie said. "To decide what to do. A mass message, or they'll bitch about seniority." She looked off to the right, with that abstracted look people use when accessing an implant, then looked up in dismay. "I don't even know where to begin! Or how to contact all the Ripper Council members!"

Handsome Danny fingered his sideburns, pondering. "I thought something was squiffy today! He seemed uncomfortable in prep, and you're always smooth, Dr. G."

"What about the cops?" the security guard said, looking around the lab, maybe for clues. "Like, what can we charge him with? Kidnapping? Impersonating a professor? Using time travel illegally? How do you catch a criminal who's gone into another century?"

Nate gently relaxed his embrace. "Let's hear what Rose has to say first. Sit down. Somebody record this, even if it is unofficial. Maxie, before you make any calls, start reprogramming to match David's trip."

"But, Dr. G!"

"Do it. Now start talking, Rosie."

Sitting on a hard plastic chair, she began the tale, keeping more or less to the truth, but she hadn't anticipated the reaction when she said she went with Uncle David "because he said he had a bomb in that bag, and I got a peek inside. It did look like there were wires."

Her father went white; the moles on his neck stood out in stark relief. Everyone stared at the blue and red FC Barcelona duffel bag. Maxie and London froze at the console. The Rippers' lab, so noisy only minutes before, became deadly still.

"Shit!" the guard said, his voice barely above a whisper, as if he thought volume could set off explosives. "We gotta get out of here! Evacuate the campus!"

"I don't think it's gonna go off," Danny said, lounging against the SlingShot. "He can't detonate it from 1934."

"But if there's a timer?" London squeaked.

"Would he blow up his own niece?" Maxie asked. "Well, Doc, would he?"

Rose had been watching her father. Maxie's words made him look as if he was wrestling with himself. He turned that hazel gaze, so like Uncle David's, back on her, and Rose felt a quiver of worry. *The Greenbaums don't raise dummies, Nana always says. I think Daddy's coming to the same conclusion I did. Oops.*

"We can't take that chance," Dr. Nathan Greenbaum said. "Joba, sound the alert. Let's clear out."

Everyone scrambled for the exit. Sirens began wailing. People started flooding out of offices, heading for the open space on New Haven Green. Her dad steered her toward a bench. "Sit here. Don't move. Call your mother."

"I can't. Uncle David made me leave my Ally at his place."

Nate made a low, rumbling noise. "All right. Just sit."

Rose suddenly remembered how Bertie once stepped on an ant hill a couple of summers ago, visiting Nana in Tampa. With malice aforethought, his sandal smacked down on the bugs. *That's the way everyone looks right now. Like those frantic bugs, but without the background noise of Bertie yelping when the fire ants got their own back.*

Swarms of police, including the bomb squad. Enterprising news vans. Dozens of nosy citizens, not content to get feeds on their own units or implants, but perhaps hoping to add their views to the WorldStream. Some senior Rippers showed up relatively quickly, perhaps from their campus offices. They huddled with her dad, the techs, and Danny. Dad and Danny obviously wanted to get right back in the lab; but the cops insisted that nobody go inside until the bomb squad checked the duffel bag.

Dad said something, and Rose heard the exasperation in London's reply: "Even if we can reset it to those coordinates, there's no guarantee you'll match his arrival time. We can't even do that under normal circs. You'd probably end up there weeks afterward. And who's gonna *pay* for it, Doc?"

"Don't you see, every minute he's there, he could be doing some horrible damage!" Nate kicked the bare ground of the green, nearly slipping on the slush.

He's a composer, an actor, a writer. What kind of damage is Uncle David going to do?

Just when things couldn't possibly get any weirder, a guy in full samurai armor, swords and all, stomped over. "What the hell do you mean, my 'Shot is canceled?" he bellowed. "I'm gonna kill whoever's responsible!"

Whereupon several of New Haven's finest took him to the ground.

#

From the diary of Joseph David Cohen, April 6, 1934
I've spent most of my life in Greenwich Village, so it was only natural that I settled here. Some parts seem eerily familiar, others wildly different. I have the preservation societies to thank that I recognize any of it at all. I spent my first weeks battling cockroaches at 46 East 8th Street, a five-floor walk-up for $35 a month. If anything is going to rat me out as a man from the future, it's keeping a straight face at these prices. In another year, I could share that address with Jackson Pollock, but I really needed better digs, one with room for a piano.

My new address is 11 Cornelia Street, the "Seville Studios," tucked away in a quiet corner near Bleecker and 6th, near where I lived in the 2070s. I remember walking past this building with Ramon and admiring the sign shaped like an artist's palette that gave the building its name, and the small relief molds of parrots and galleons. It seemed sunny, Latin-flavored, intimate yet welcoming. It reminded me of Ramon.

It was nicely spruced-up, too, in the late twenties version of gentrification. Italian immigrants and African-Americans once dominated this neighborhood, but many (not all) were forced out when landlords spruced up the nineteenth-century brownstones for middle-class tenants. My apartment boasted a new refrigerator and gas range, beamed ceilings, and a beautifully tiled bathroom. I ordered a new bed, not trusting the "sanitized" claims of secondhand dealers, and scavenged for a nightstand, dresser, and kitchen table and two chairs in the Sunday markets on Hester Street. I intended to spend as little as I could until I got established. Then I had plans.

I also put a punching bag in my bedroom, as boxing is an acceptable form of exercise in this era. So are jump roping and jogging, especially in Central Park. Thanks to generations of city fathers (and mothers), Central Park looks the most like its 2079 counterpart. The layout's nearly identical, though there aren't as many memorials; it seems odd not to see Strawberry Fields and the fountain for the Father's Day Massacre of '52. The park is full of sailors, many of them definitely on the prowl. One ginger-haired fellow with a cleft chin jogged alongside me for half a mile, sending out not-so-discreet feelers. I sent him packing, especially after I saw him scratching himself. My antibiotics have Vincent Youmans' name on them, and God knows where that sailor had been.

I could also run in Battery Park. Now *that's* something I can't do in my own time, unless I jog underwater. Nothing like time travel to show you global warming.

After hanging the punching bag, I used a toolkit and a hacksaw to cut out hiding places in my apartment for my goodies from the future. I'm no skilled carpenter, but I had consulted various DIY 'loads and practiced a lot. The holes for the Allys, painstakingly chiseled out of one of those ceiling beams, took hours, but were worth the blisters. This is a decent neighborhood, but I can't take chances.

The other thing I wasn't taking chances with was smallpox, which still kills thousands here. My great-grandfather died of COVID before the vaccine was available; I never knew him, but I was thinking of him when I found a doctor and got the smallpox vaccine.

Much as I wanted to start changing musical history right away, I knew I had to take things slowly. In some cases, my targets were out of reach. George Gershwin was just back from a concert tour and working on *Porgy and Bess,* but would move to South Carolina for much of the summer. Cole Porter was finishing a film score. Then he'd head to Europe, where he'd start writing *Anything Goes* for the fall. Kurt Weill was in France, having escaped the Nazis. He'd arrive in the States soon. Richard Rodgers and Larry Hart were in Hollywood, but would be back for a spring visit. Vincent Youmans was also just returning from California. He'd soon have a devastating TB attack that sent him for a Colorado rest cure. I didn't need to fret about Marc Blitzstein for decades.

From the medical standpoint in 1934, Youmans was the most seriously ill. If, as I hoped, Gershwin's tumor was the slow-growing kind, it was only just developing. I needed to find a job—with luck, one connected to Broadway—and begin getting to know all about them, as Oscar Hammerstein had Anna tell the royal children of Siam.

#

From the diary of Joseph David Cohen, April 10, 1934
No luck on the job front, though it's still early days. Anyone would think there was a Depression. Not much to see on the boards, either. Last week, I caught the astonishing Helen

Hayes in *Mary of Scotland,* but aside from *Tobacco Road,* just into the first of eight long years, no hits were running. I bought a radio today, to keep up with pop culture. Gershwin's twice-weekly show is part of my homework.

I was on my knees, twiddling the dial of this alien technology and contemplating dinner. Should I investigate more of the delicious Village eateries, or be a good boy and wash down carrots and celery with some mineral water? The doorbell interrupted my thoughts.

I opened the door to find a smiling quartet—well, three-fourths smiling. A schoolage boy, gripping a casserole dish, scowled up at me, blatantly wishing he were elsewhere. His beaming Italian mother, however, had grabbed his left shoulder to prevent escape. A young couple in their late twenties stood directly behind the pair, also bearing bundles; he had wavy auburn hair and a lithe frame, while she was short, swarthy, and buxom. The mama, a take-charge type in her thirties, announced, "Welcome to the Seville Studios! I'm Frannie Spinelli, and this is my son, Leo."

Leo, prompted by a squeeze, mumbled, "'Lo," and shoved the dish at me.

"And we're Adam and Mabel Finkelstein," said the young man. "We're your neighbors on either side, and wanted to make you feel at home." They both raised their baskets; they smelled divine, far better than celery sticks.

Leo muttered, "Yeh, an' snoop on ya, too," but even if nosiness helped motivate them, I was still flabbergasted by the friendly gesture. I knew a few people in my building in 2079, but would I show up on a new tenant's doorstep with dinner? Nope.

I nearly asked if they were the Welcome Wagon, since I knew there were such things, but since I wasn't sure when that began, I waved them inside. "Come in, and thank you so much. I'm Joseph Cohen, better known as David. Please, won't you join me in this feast? I've got some wine, but not enough plates, I fear. And there's nothing in the fridge for Leo. Here, kid." I tossed him a dime. "Make like an Olympian, and run to the A & P for a soda. Keep the change." The Olympics had been held in Los Angeles in 1932, but I couldn't conjure up any athlete's name. Jesse Owens would dominate Hitler's Games, but that was two years off.

Leo's scowl vanished. "Thanks!"

I didn't have enough chairs or forks, either, but Adam brought some from his place, and no one minded using glasses and coffee cups for the wine. Leo drank his Coke straight from the bottle. The Finkelsteins brought a loaf of crusty bread, a pie, and a tsimmes, rather like one my grandmother made—a casserole with a small piece of flank steak smothered in carrots and potatoes. Knowing the cost of meat, I served Leo the biggest piece and took a sliver for myself.

Frannie's casserole contained some kind of pasta; she looked at me, suddenly concerned, as she took the lid off. "Mabel doesn't keep the kosher house, but maybe you do, Mr. Cohen? Because this has parmigiano cheese." I told everyone to call me David, assured her I adored bacon, and we all began to eat and talk and laugh.

It was so nice, so normal, it reminded me achingly of dinners with my brother's family, right down to Leo sticking his finger through a slice of bread, his boyish glee so like my nephew's. I had to swig a second glass of the wine to keep the lump in my throat from rising.

"So, David, what do you do?" Mabel asked, clearly ready to begin the "snooping" part of the evening.

"I'm a composer and a pianist, though I've done some acting, too, in California and in Mexico City. Hoping to crack Broadway someday."

"No kidding!" Adam exclaimed. "I'm a dancer! Adam Flint, since that sounds better than Finkelstein. Just a suggestion, pal, but if you might want to drop the Cohen."

"Could be Cohan," Frannie said, "but, funny, he doesn't look Irish!"

The impromptu dinner party roared, and I joined in, but Adam was right. For all my months of searching for a common alias and digging up period documents with "Joseph Cohen" on them, I'd have trouble working in show business with that moniker. I frantically ran through names in my head, trying to come up with something.

Mabel didn't help as she began ticking off Jews with changed names. "Asa Yoelson to Al Jolson. Hyman Arluck to Harold Arlen, Israel Balaine to Irving Berlin."

"Berlin" might have been just a typo on an early songsheet. Songs! Yes! I have it! "Of course. My stage name is Joseph Taylor, Junior. Uh, Joseph D. Taylor. It's got a double personal connection: my father was a tailor, and my mother was a Schneiderman." *And it's the lead character in Rodgers and Hammerstein's* Allegro, *which won't be written for another fourteen years. But it's the first name that popped into my show tune-filled noggin.*

Frannie looked puzzled, but Adam mimed scissors. "'Schneider' means 'tailor' in Yiddish. You should learn that one, Frannie. You're a seamstress yourself."

As we talked, I learned Frannie's husband was a steward on a liner, doing the tourist runs between New York and Bermuda, that Mabel was a bookkeeper ("She's got her C.P.A., but the big firms won't hire a woman!" her spouse complained), and that Adam was washing dishes at the Hotel Lafayette, since shows were hard to come by. He shook his head at me. "Really, David, you should have stayed out west, maybe try the flicks. The Great White Way's not so great."

"'The fabulous invalid?'" I said. "Well, they've said Broadway's been dying for a long time. They'll probably keep on saying it for a long time." *You have no idea!* "I'll take my chances. I may even help revive it; got some money saved."

Mabel's mouth opened in a horrified O, rimmed in crimson, the same shade as her nails. "You want to invest in a play? Are you *meshugge*? Better you should use your dollars to scrub your floors—you'd at least have clean floors!"

"We gotta crazy man for a new neighbor," Frannie said. Leo had taken refuge from grown-up talk. He was sitting in a corner with a comic book. Now he eyed me carefully for signs of madness.

I spread my hands. "It's something I've always wanted to do. Besides, even if the show fails, I'll make some good contacts. Speaking of shows, Adam, what have you been in?"

He reeled off some titles, most of which I'd only heard of because of my research. But one in particular caught me. "You were in *Through the Years*? I love Vincent Youmans!"

"Howzat? You know about that mess? Folded in three weeks."

"But some great songs! The title tune, 'Drums in My Heart!' Tell me, what was it like working with Youmans? Hey, maybe I can use *you* as a contact!"

Adam snorted. "You think the great man paid attention to a boy in the dance chorus? Now if I'd been a chorus girl... " He batted his eyelashes and simpered.

"And you so cute, too," Mabel teased. "Just broke your heart, I know."

"You bet. But, seriously, Youmans' music was grand, but he was a pain in the keester. Cranky cuss, drank like a fish."

"I'd still love to meet him," I said, spooning up the last of Mabel's lemon meringue pie. *It's why I'm here.*

"He's in Hollywood now. After a hit like *Flying Down to Rio,* the studios must want more."

They did. But Youmans made unreasonable demands, even by Hollywood's standards.

Frannie began gathering the dishes; Mabel, humming Youmans' "The Caricoca," rose to help. I got to my feet, too, but Adam waved me back down. "It's obvious you're a bachelor. That's women's work, bud."

"We know what we're doing," Frannie said cheerfully. "And let me say, it's a pleasure to have you here. May you write many songs in your new home."

"That reminds me," I said. "I'm buying a piano. I hope it won't bother anyone."

My neighbors assured me music was not a problem. Mabel said, "There's a would-be opera singer in 4G, a fellow that plays gypsy violin at Lupowitz's in 3B—a riot, since he's Swedish—and a geezer with an accordion almost as big as he is up on the fifth floor. A piano would be welcome."

"You play any jazz, Mr. C?" Leo asked, piping up at last.

"Some. I play a little of everything," I said.

Adam was halfway out the door with one of his kitchen chairs when he caught that last exchange. "Gee! That gives me an idea. I'm pals with the cellist for *Through the Years.* He'll know how to reach the show's music director, a joe who's been doing shows for years. He might be able to help you out."

"That's great!" I picked up the last chair. "What's his name?"

"Bill. Bill Daly. I'll write to my friend tomorrow, if you like."

I was glad I was clutching the chair, because I definitely needed to be holding on to something. "Yeah, that sounds wonderful. Thanks ever so much."

We put the chairs away; the Finkelsteins' place looked so much more homey than mine, with knickknacks, books, and papers everywhere. I thanked everyone again, and we all retreated behind our various doors.

And then I did an insane happy dance that would have convinced young Leo I was indeed screwy.

William Merrigan Daly wasn't just Vincent Youmans' m.d.. He'd worked on many Gershwin shows, even toured with Gershwin, playing second piano to George's on "Rhapsody in Blue." They weren't just colleagues; they were close friends. In the spring of 1934, as the Gershwins and DuBose Heyward were starting work on *Porgy and Bess,* Daly helped out. If Adam's friend could get me in touch with him, I'd be that much closer to George Gershwin.

I have a feeling I'm not going to sleep much tonight.

#

From the diary of J.D. Taylor, April 16, 1934
Item 1: Like my new handle, Dear Diary? Anonymous and non-Jewish, and I can still tell people to call me David. I'm not sure how I go about legally changing it. Frannie Spinelli's brother is a lawyer; maybe he can help.

Item 2: I've got a job! I'm playing piano for the lunch and early dinner crowd at the Golden Eagle. Still getting used to it; more on that later.

Item 3: Best news of all! Adam's friend wrote back with Bill Daly's address, and I've written to him, inviting him to lunch tomorrow, which happens to be my day off. Where else but Sardi's?

#

Daly had asked me to bring along some of my music for
him to evaluate. This presented some problems, as topics
for musicals of the 1930s and the 2070s...differed. Most
of the songs from *The Best of These Are Shadows,* my
NetShow about ghosts in a theatre, would pass without
much confusion, but I had to heavily revise the lyrics for a
ballad from my show, *No Heroes Here,* about two families
struggling in the ruins of San Diego after the Comic-Con
disaster. Textual specifics aside, it remained a good ballad
about the will to survive, a theme Depression-era listeners
understood. I included two numbers from my moonbase
mystery, *Eclipse,* figuring that thirties audiences knew
pulps and Buck Rogers, however strange such material
would seem for a musical. Finally, I added the title song for
Second Chances. It stood on its own as a love song, with no
references to the time-travel plot.

I got to the restaurant early, and was pleased to see the
exterior closely resembled the Sardi's of the 2070s. The
interior was much the same as well, though darker and
more cramped. The counter where a pretty redhead took
my hat would vanish in the intervening decades, along with
the hats. The later Sardi's survived largely on tourist dollars,
but in 2064, the owners tried to recreate the Broadway
camaraderie of old by fostering a club for members of the
theatre 'Net communities. Ramon and I both joined the
Sardi's Club early in our careers. I smiled, remembering the
party here after the off-off-Broadway debut of *No Heroes
Here,* and especially what happened after the party.

One other thing stayed unchanged through time. The
caricatures on the walls, celebrating famous Broadway
denizens, were Sardi's most distinctive feature. In 1927,

50

owner Vincent Sardi wanted to make his restaurant more popular with the theatre crowd and hired Alex Gard, a Russian artist, to do sketches of celebrities for the sum of one meal per drawing. After Gard died in the late forties, other artists kept up the tradition. Bert Lahr, Eddie Cantor, Fanny Brice, and Tallulah Bankhead looked down on me as I waited. Ramon always swore he was going to doodle a picture of me and stick it up with a thumb tack, but he never did. Who knows? Maybe I'll get my face up there yet!

I was so busy staring at Jerome Kern's likeness that I jumped when the waiter, Carlo, came up behind me. "Mr. Taylor? Mr. Daly is here."

Carlo motioned to a lanky man in a rumpled checked suit who was chatting up the hat-check girl. William Daly had a big pouf of reddish brown hair, thick glasses, and an animated air. He winked at the girl and hurried over. "Hey, Carlo," he said, "I'll have a sidecar and the moules marinières. I'm sorry, Mr. Taylor, but I'll have to eat and run. Duty calls. Do you know what you're having?"

"The bouillabaisse. And coffee, please." Carlo led us to a table, passing Rudy Vallee—the man and his drawing—on the way. Daly groaned; the caricatures above the booth included one of George Gershwin.

"I'll be seeing him soon enough," Daly complained. "Geez, Carlo, you have no heart."

Carlo bowed with great dignity and floated away. Daly rubbed his temples. "Not enough hours in the day. So, Mr. Taylor, let's see your songs."

I opened the briefcase I'd bought that morning (secondhand, Hester Street) and passed over the sheets of music. Carlo brought the beverages, and I soon wished I'd ordered something stronger than coffee. Daly peered at the pages for a solid fifteen minutes, occasionally gulping at his drink. Even after Carlo came with the meal, Daly didn't pick up his fork until he'd finished reading all six songs. I felt like I was back at Juilliard, getting evaluated by my advisor.

"Well, Mr. Taylor, you've written some extremely interesting songs. You certainly don't stick to the rules, and I, for one, like that. I don't know how such songs will do with the general public, though. Irregular lengths, unusual rhyme schemes, and the subject matter! Not a cheery walk in the park, some of them. One can't exactly imagine der Bingle crooning 'No Air.' The average listener is going to be confused or depressed. Or both."

I had to ponder "der Bingle" before realizing that Daly meant Bing Crosby, legendary crooner. I mustered a defense: "Maybe I'm loopy, but I was thinking of the shows and the songs' context before their commercial potential. My story ideas are out of the ordinary, but musicals can be more than just boy-gets-girl fluff! Why not take on serious subjects? It worked with *Show Boat:* forty years of history, miscegenation, discrimination, and divided families, yet audiences ate it up. Even in comedies, like the Gershwins' *Of Thee I Sing,* the songs worked best when they served the story and characters. As for structure, well, sometimes a song just demands a certain length. There's this composer I knew whose credo was, 'Content dictates form.' I hold by that, too."

"I like that! What's his name?"

"Uh, Esteban Ria Nido. I worked with him in Mexico." *Which just happens to be a Spanish pseudonym Stephen Sondheim once used.*

Daly plunged into his lunch, eating quickly and glancing at his watch. The mussels in wine and cream sauce smelled heavenly, but all I could think of was how it was clogging the man's arteries. I wanted to scream, *Don't eat that! You're going to have a heart attack in 1936! Damn, it's like being in a triage unit: I have to decide who I can save and who I can't.* I did manage to comment, "Your mussels look tasty, but I'm trying to lose weight myself these days." I patted the Nate-waist, still there, but smaller.

Daly shrugged. "I've never been fat. I just like to eat. And drink. Carlo, another, please?"

We spent some time talking about my background—I was getting good at these lies—and analyzing my music. Not surprisingly, Daly knew his onions, as the locals put it. My formal training was good, but composition seemed second nature to this man, even though Daly had begun his career as a writer and editor.

"May I take these?" Daly asked. "I'd like to show them to some people I know."

"Of course. And if you know anyone who needs a rehearsal pianist or a pit player, I'd be grateful."

Daly immediately reached for his wallet. "Are you skint, David? These days, too many folks are flatter than a Child's pancake."

"No, please. I invited you! I do have a job, at the Golden Eagle on West 9th Street. But it's part-time, and while I love the Village, it's not Broadway."

"I spent more time in the Village when George and Ira lived there. Of course, Ira's father-in-law, Papa Strunsky, is still the best landlord in those parts. If you don't believe me, just ask him."

I filed that away. A Gershwin connection for a landlord could be valuable. "I'll keep that in mind, but I like my place."

"Wait until that subway line goes through," Daly warned. "Property values will skyrocket, and so will your rent."

I knew that. Not from my homework, but from *Wonderful Town,* set in Greenwich Village in 1935—though it wouldn't be written until 1953. For that matter, I didn't know if Ruth

McKenney, who wrote the *New Yorker* pieces on which the musical was based, had even moved to the Village yet.

A middle-aged Italian man approached the table as we were finishing. "Everything fine, Mr. Daly?" The answer was obvious, as we'd both cleaned our plates.

"How could it be otherwise here? Mr. Sardi, this is Mr. J.D. Taylor," Daly said. "A fine young songwriter, just come to New York."

"Welcome," Mr. Sardi said, "though it's not the best of times to break into the business."

Oh, it's absolutely the right time for me. "So I've heard."

Daly stood up. "I really must dash. David, it's been a pleasure. You've got interesting notions, and I like your attitude. I'll see what I can do. No promises, mind."

"No, sir," I said. "I'm simply grateful to be here."

#

From the diary of J.D. Taylor, April 27, 1934
My hand is shaking so much, I can hardly hold this pen—and let me go on record as loathing these fountain pens! I bought a good one, a Waterman's Patrician for a whopping ten bucks, but I still keep blotting my shirts and tablecloth. When do they invent ballpoints? Excuse the smudges, I'll try to make this account as complete as I can.

Here's what happened. My shift at the Golden Eagle runs from 11:30 AM to 6:30 PM, when a jazz combo takes over. I keep thinking how Ramon would have flipped, since this place is steeped in gay history. In the twenties, it was Paul and Joe's, a drag cabaret and speakeasy. Its clientele inspired Mae West to write *The Drag,* a play so controversial, it was banned from Broadway. In the future, renamed the Lion, it would become a gay mecca again, where Barbra

Streisand (who lived across the street) won a talent contest and her ticket to glory.

In 1934, it's a comfortable spot serving Italian and French fare. There are some gays around, but plenty of Village locals, too, including families. It even has a resident pet, a de-scented skunk named Petunia, who makes her nest in the hollow wooden footrest that runs the length of the bar. Mostly, Petunia does what she wants, but Jimmy the barman will "sic" her on drunken oafs who don't realize she's weaponless.

My piano's shoved way in the back of the room, on a small stage, with tables crammed on all sides. I don't sing unless requested; lunch is considerably quieter than dinner, and nobody dances on the postage stamp-sized floor unless they're really boiled. The day manager, Karl Sundgaard, is handsome in a Nordic way. I'm pretty sure he's gay, though I'm not rising to the bait, so to speak. Too much at stake. Besides, I'm still losing this gut, and I look disgusting.

Being surrounded by the Golden Eagle fare, loaded with butter and oil, doesn't help my weight. Neither do my new arrangements with Frannie Spinelli. I give her some money each week, and she cooks up Italian meals which I try to eat in moderation. Still, she obviously needs the iron, as they say here, and it's good to see Leo putting on some flesh while I try to lose mine. The other deal: she does my laundry and I give Leo piano lessons. He's eager, and I enjoy teaching, though it will be a while before he can tackle Duke Ellington. He reminds me of Bertie so much.

One of my difficulties at work is not playing any songs written after April 1934. I've compiled a repertoire of safe tunes, which I practice every morning. The lunch crowd doesn't usually chat me up, but I keep having nightmares about somebody asking me to identify a melody, and suddenly realizing it wouldn't be written for ten, fifty, or a hundred years. Thus, my safe sheet.

Today, I was midway through Schwartz's "Dancing in the Dark," stuffing it full of flourishes and mugging at an elderly couple at the closest table. Her white-haired head cocked to one side like a bird, she conducted my performance with her fork, while her spouse beamed at her. Hopeless romantics. I had decided to play some Kern for them next, maybe "Smoke Gets in Your Eyes" from last year's *Roberta,* when a hubbub started near the front door.

Tucked in the back, I couldn't see a thing. It couldn't be a raid, though the joint had been hit several times during Prohibition. Besides, the patrons' murmurs sounded excited, not frightened. The old man dropped a dime in my tip jar, jerked a thumb at the front, and said, "Something's going on!"

Then young Hank Ito, our Japanese busboy, who looked like a round-cheeked bobble-head doll, bounded up to me and hissed, "*Gershwin's* here! Mr. Sundgaard says, 'Play Gershwin!'"

I was never so scared in my life. Not entering the SlingShot. Not staggering through Yosemite after jumping through time. Not auditioning for Juilliard. Not my first time on a professional stage. Not asking Ramon—glorious, dazzling, popular Ramon—out for our first date. Not singing Sondheim or Estévez or MacGugan or even my own songs in public.

George Gershwin. Within earshot of my piano. I was frozen. Then Hank, bless his chubby cheeks, smacked my arm. "You deaf? *Gershwin!*"

"*Arigato,*" I said, which always weirds him out. White guys in the thirties just don't know Japanese. I launched into "Someone to Watch Over Me," "Fascinating Rhythm," and "The Man I Love."

The oldsters had figured things out. "Do you sing, young man, or just play?" the dame asked. "Sing 'I Got Rhythm.' Do you know it?"

Do I? Well, maybe. While this song, the one that shot Ethel Merman to fame, has since been rendered by thousands of gay men mimicking her clarion tones (many of them under this very roof), I sang it as myself. David W. Greenbaum. Joseph David Cohen. J.D. Taylor. All of the above. I invited the diners to join in on the second chorus.

At the conclusion, Karl worked his way to me through the tables, a slender, dark-haired man just behind him. Karl addressed the diners, "Ladies and gentlemen, the Golden Eagle is honored today by the presence of Mr. George Gershwin!" Loud cheers, applause; I nearly blistered my hands. Gershwin gave me a nod, and at Karl's wordless invitation, stepped onto the stage beside me.

"Thank you," he said. "Bill Daly showed me some songs written by Mr. Taylor here, and I liked them well enough to pay a visit to the Village."

"Would you play something for us, Mr. Gershwin?" Karl asked, practically salivating.

"Sure, if Mr. Taylor doesn't mind."

I gurgled and slid off the bench so fast, I scorched my ass. Gershwin played "Strike Up the Band," "Do, Do, Do," and "Who Cares?"—songs I knew were among his personal favorites. The place was silent while he played: no clinking silverware, no clatter of plates, no pots banging. Hank stood with an empty dish tray; chef Mario came out of the kitchen, his arm around his daughter, Tessie. The Eagle erupted again when Gershwin finished, the regulars slapping themselves on the backs for choosing this joint for their minestrone or osso buco. *Hey, guess what I had for lunch today? Pasta fazool and Gershwin!*

But just when I thought it couldn't get any more surreal, Gershwin winked at me and started playing again. I didn't recognize my own music at first, not until he played the lead-in vamp again and quipped, "Any time you want to join in is fine by me!"

Which is how I came to sing "Second Chances" to my idol's accompaniment. Thank God for my training; I didn't blubber like a baby and I remembered the revised lyrics. The originals referred to a gay love affair, and if Bill Daly thought lyrics about dying on a moon base were tough for a 1934 consumer to accept...well, let's just say the 2077 edition had different pronouns. The revised version made a decent, wistful ballad, with a nice descending chromatic shift. It's also a bitch to sing and uncommonly long, so between my nerves and lack of a proper warm-up, it wasn't my best.

No matter. Gershwin radiated approval, and the customers gave us a great hand. Karl bellowed, "The Golden Eagle's own, J.D. Taylor!"

Gershwin rose, pulled out his wallet, and stuffed ten bucks in the tip jar. That was outrageous, but not with his budget. He leaped from the stage and spoke to Karl: "I realize Mr. Taylor's on the clock, but could he have a short break? I'd like to talk to him."

"Of course!" Karl couldn't agree fast enough. "Want something to wet your whistle, Dave?"

"A Bronx," I said. *It's what Ramon would have ordered, and one of the most popular drinks of the decade.*

"Anything else for you and your party, Mr. Gershwin? No? Jimmy! A Bronx for Mr. Taylor!"

Gershwin led the way to a table where his brother Ira and Bill Daly sat, the Eagle's dim light reflecting off their glasses. Daly was wearing the same wrinkled blue suit as when we met at Sardi's, Ira had a green v-neck sweater and a yellow-speckled bow tie. "You know the Irishman," Gershwin said, "and this is Ira."

"Mr. Gershwin," I said, "I'm a tremendous admirer of your work. Uh, of you both." *Snap out of it, Greenbaum!*

Ira smiled, putting me at ease. He was shorter than George, with a slightly dumpy frame and a rounder face. Both brothers seemed happy, but while George's pleasure seemed near incandescent—especially while he was at the piano—Ira's cast a warm glow.

"Thank you. Do call me Ira. We were impressed with the songs you gave Bill, Mr. Taylor. George was playing them all morning, ignoring his own work. Myself, I especially liked 'The Actor's Lament.' Clever work, that."

The thrill of having Ira Gershwin praise my lyrics wrestled with a feeling of dread that my songs distracted George from composing *Porgy and Bess.* Damn! Was I already affecting musical theatre history, but not in a good way? Fortunately, Karl materialized with my drink, from which I took a healthy swig. Jimmy hadn't stinted on the gin, bless him.

"I usually answer to David," I said. "I'm quite flattered, but I certainly didn't meant to take time away from your own work."

"Ha!" said Daly. "Ira's usually the lazy one. Pincus always gets done what needs doing. It's a measure of the sophistication of your material that he messed about with it for so long. That, and he wanted to get through 'Second Chances' cold, the big show-off."

George reached into his pocket and took out the sheets he hadn't needed to look at. He waved the folded papers around nearly knocking over his bowl of vanilla ice cream. "Hey, it took some time to get it right; there's a helluva lot of music here—108 bars. What kind of screwy length is that,

David? Still, it's a pip of a song, especially these shifting harmonics." His long fingers noted several lines.

I hadn't finished that cocktail, yet Gershwin's comments created a buzz as if I'd downed three in rapid succession. The song's length…yes, it was long, especially by thirties' standards. Nor could I resort to Cole Porter's huge hit, "Begin the Beguine," which was the same length, for my defense, as it wouldn't be written for another year. "Well," I managed, "it just seemed the right length for the material, especially given where it fits in the libretto."

"I like that," Ira said, raising his mug of beer in toast. "For theatre songs, anyway, the closer they're tied to the story, the more effective they'll be. We're doing that with our new project."

"But David's not putting on a show—yet!" George noted. "I think, though, with a little work, he could sell this baby on its own to Dreyfus. Change the lyrics so a girl could sing it. I hear Ruth Etting in my head."

We discussed the song in some detail, and I marveled at their combined insights. George and Daly made some suggestions on the release, while Ira hummed the refrain and commented, in his mild fashion, that one line had too many silibants. "That works in poetry, less so in songs." My sports-crazed nephew would have said this was like getting batting lessons from Hall of Famers Mike Trout and Al Awane.

Wrapped up in his study of my song, George finally noticed his ice cream had melted. He waved to Karl, who had been keeping an eye on our table. "Another dish, please. It helps my composer's stomach. Another beer for my brother and a sidecar for Pincus. Never fear, we're nearly done with Mr. Taylor. In fact, I think I'll help him out with one more song myself before his next set." Karl spluttered agreement and ran off to the kitchen. George laughed. "That'll hold him. Tell us about yourself, David."

I spun out my phony yarn again, though what I said about my hopes and dreams was real enough. "I'm concentrating on music now, but I once had aspirations of being a triple threat, like Cohan or Coward or Novello ... " *Or Lin-Manuel Miranda or Ellie MacGugan or Dave Malloy or Moonrise Johnson or T.K. Singh, only they're not born yet.*

"A trifecta of acting and composing and playwriting?" said Ira. "Not easy."

"Plenty of joes can act," said George, tossing his spoon in the bowl with a clink. "Few can make decent songs. That señor in Mexico taught his pupil well. You can go far with such talent, as long as you've got *chutzpah,* too! Like Gershwin!" He thumped his chest. "Now that you're here, you should meet our crowd. Good people to know." He handed me a business card. "We have a little festival most Sundays. Light grub at Ira and Lee's, then music at my place—very casual. Come by, if you can."

"I can't thank you enough," I said, swallowing down a lump in my throat the size of a grapefruit. "For a man of your stature to take an interest in a nobody like me ... "

"The music's what matters! Besides, once I was just a song plugger at Remick's. Irving Berlin helped me. So did Jerry Kern, though it took me years before I got the gumption to speak to him. Even then, I ignored his advice! So I do what I can for other songwriters. Besides, I'm selfish. I just *had* to meet you after seeing your songs. Gee, you never know what you'll find playing piano down in the Village! A couple of years ago, Howard Dietz dragged us to this joint above a deli at Waverly and Sixth. That's how we discovered Oscar Levant."

Daly growled into his sidecar. "Some things are better left undiscovered."

George mock-punched his friend. "You got to admit, Irishman, that Oscar can play. One of the finest interpreters of my work, and he's a card, too."

"Yeah, he should be dealt with," Daly said.

Ira put out his hands as peacemaker. "Boys, don't quarrel. It's time to meet Frankie at the station. George, you want to finish up?" He motioned in the direction of my piano.

The younger Gershwin got to his feet. "Yes, Mama. What shall we give these good folks, the blues number?" He turned to me. "It's a number from this show we're working on with DuBose Heyward."

"Porgy and Bess!" I blurted out.

The trio gave me odd looks, and I wondered why. What mistake did I make? The show wasn't a secret; there had been talk of a musical version ever since Heyward's 1925 straight play. Hammerstein and Kern had considered it; Al Jolson proposed playing Porgy in blackface! Gershwin himself had been interested in the property when he first read the 1924 novel, *Porgy.* Oh...

"Yes, *Porgy,"* Ira said, pointedly stressing the single word. "From DuBose's novel and play." Was it my imagination, or was he staring at me? Hard to tell, with those glasses.

"Huh. *Porgy—and Bess. "* George seemed to be savoring the title, like an unfamiliar dish.

"Like *Tristan und Isolde* or *Samson and Delilah, "* said Daly.

"It's correct in the operatic tradition," George admitted. "Let's suggest it to DuBose. Pity he had to go back to Charleston so soon. *Porgy and Bess* might be useful in case the Guild thinks people might mistake our show for a revival of the play." He tossed bills on the table and bounded back to the small stage.

His energy and athleticism were so plain it almost hurt to watch him. I wouldn't let that light, that genius, be snuffed out. I had the medicine, hidden in the Seville Studios, and now I had met the man himself. All I had to do was figure out how to give it to him in the next few years.

George addressed the crowd. It now included the Eagle's owner, Peter Terracino—Karl must have phoned him—and its press agent, Shep Henkin, who were clearly thrilled by the celebrity guest. "Like to hear another, folks? This one's new. It's called the 'Jasbo Brown Blues.'" He launched into the piano hall tune which I knew had been considered as the show's opening number, but would be cut in favor of "Summertime."

I didn't want to take my eyes off Gershwin, especially his phenomenal left hand—really, it didn't seem humanly possible to play like that—but Daly nudged me, and pointed at Ira, who was beaming at his gifted brother. "They're a pair, eh?" he said. "I think Ira would do damn near anything for Pincus."

From my vantage point of nearly a century and a half, with a wealth of books and literature stored on my Ally, and months of study before I made this crazy trip through time, I knew a helluva lot about the thirties, New York, and especially musical theatre history. But there were odd gaps in my knowledge.

"Bill, why do you and George call each other 'Pincus'?"

"Private joke, goes back years." Not much of an answer, but all I was going to get, since Gershwin was finishing the number to loud cheers.

"I leave you in Mr. Taylor's capable hands," he said. Ira handed him his fur-lined overcoat. "I hope we see you Sunday night, David," he told me as they headed to the door. I saw Mr. Terracino and Shep fawning over them as they left.

I sat on the piano bench, still warm from George Gershwin's posterior, which may have been the single hardest thing to comprehend yet. Sitting where Gershwin just sat, I stared at the keys, wondering what to play. Wondering if I could play. I waved to Hank. "Another Bronx, please."

"Okie-doke." Hank grinned at me, his chubby cheeks crinkling his eye-folds. "You hear what *he* say to the boss? No? He say, 'That Taylor is golden. Golden!'"

"Hank. Tell Jimmy to make it a double."

What did I play? What else but "'S Wonderful"?

Chapter 3

"Mountain Greenery" —Lorenz Hart

From the diary of J.D. Taylor, April 29, 1934

When my shift at the Eagle ended at six-thirty, I hurtled up the stairs to the sidewalk, eager to make my way to the Gershwins' gathering at the northern end of Manhattan. Mario told me how to get there, since, as Daly had mentioned, the subway connecting the Village was still far from finished. I barreled down 9th Street—smack into a small bearded man. The man, his hat, and a battered, brown cardboard portfolio went flying.

"Fuck," I muttered, and then instantly hoped I'd hadn't additionally offended his victim. While many New Yorkers here could swear just as fluently as their descendants, it depended on the social status of those talking, and whether ladies were present. This fellow might be a bum, a janitor, a middle-class lawyer at the nearby courthouse, or a gent on the social register sampling Village nightclubs.

"Who'd you think you are, Bronko Nagurski?" the man asked in a harsh nasal twang. He glared up at me, red rheumy eyes in a pinched, dirty face. A Village vagabond, maybe even the same one I'd spotted on Cornelia Street the day I moved in.

I had no idea who Bronko Whoeverski was, but I spluttered apologies and helped the man to his feet; easy, since he weighed next to nothing. He scooped up his portfolio, clutching it to his chest while he gave me the once-over. *He's figuring out how much he can touch me for, in exchange for steam-rollering him.* I couldn't tell how much damage I'd done, since the guy was uniformly filthy and bedraggled. At least he didn't look so furious any more.

He cleared his throat—a wretched, hacking process. "Sir, I deserve some recompense for your actions. And if you make a living felling honest folk, kindly cease practicing on me!"

"Of course. I'm extremely sorry for my clumsiness, but I'm late for an engagement. I play piano over there." I pointed at the Golden Eagle. "Tell Mr. Terracino that J.D. Taylor sent you, and that Mario should fix you the special."

"Ah, the Eagle. I recall when it was a notorious pansyspot before the big raid in '24. Perhaps I could have something to wash that special down?"

I pulled out three half-dollars, plenty to cover the meal and drinks. The fellow tucked them inside his oversized coat, and put out a grimy hand to shake. I took it, reminding myself to wash ASAP, and grew alarmed when the little man didn't let go right away. He clung to me with a mighty grip for his size; his red-rimmed eyes took on a glazed look. Just when I thought he might be having a seizure, he came back to himself. Once more, he scrutinized my long frame, sizing me up again, but differently.

"If I may introduce myself, I am Joseph F. Gould, Harvard Class of 1911, last of the bohemians, and resident of this city for nearly two decades. But you, Mr. Taylor, you are *not* from around here."

A statement, not a question. In the month I'd been in 1934, I'd had some folks remark on my accent. It's not a regional effect, but temporal. Languages evolve. I grew up speaking an English nearly a century and half removed from the one used here. In general, there are more distinct vowel sounds here; by 2079, a lot of them have sort of merged, and more have shifted forward. Thank God for my dialect coaches, who made me stand for hours in front of mirrors, watching my lips and concentrating on my tongue. I'm conscious of how different I sound, and I'm trying to pattern my speech more like the natives'. It's not a big issue, since in New York, every other guy is from somewhere else. Nobody hearing me would declare, "Aha! A time traveler!" as they might if I ended up in medieval England, trying to pass my talk for Middle English.

But I had a creepy feeling Gould wasn't basing his comment on the little I'd said to him. I gave my standard response: "California, with some years in Chicago and Mexico."

"And farther away than that, I believe." He adjusted his hat. "Ask Mr. Terracino, you said? I shall. It has been some time since I had even a rhombozoidal meal. I subsist on air, self-esteem, cowboy coffee, fried egg sandwiches, and ketchup. I thank you, Bronko. A pleasure bumping into you." He bowed, cackling softly, and made a beeline for the Eagle.

I wiped my hand on my pants and ran for the bus stop, trying not to run into any more derelict bohemians.

#

The doorman at 132 East 72nd Street had no idea who I was. That wasn't the case for lanky George S. Kaufman, who had immediately preceded me into the building. The noted playwright-director was waved through with a cheery greeting. I, a "nobody in New York," to paraphrase the guys from *[title of show]*, had to present Gershwin's card. Even then, he telephoned upstairs for approval. He said, "Yes, Mr. Ira," so I passed muster. I'd read that Ira often screened George's visitors, keeping undesirables from wasting his brother's time.

A pimply-faced elevator boy gave me the eye as I approached the car. "Mr. Gershwin's, please."

"Yessir," he mumbled, but continued to watch me. *Trying to figure out if I'm famous. Sorry, kid.*

The elevator opened into Gershwin's fourteen-room apartment. Unlike his earlier residence on Riverside Drive, which had a distinctly modern decor, this was stylish, but not off-putting. The walls were gray, and covered with artwork: some collected by Gershwin, some his own fine work.

The valet stepped forward to take my hat and overcoat. "The bar's over there, Mr. Taylor. Please make yourself comfortable."

I could hear music ("Of Thee I Sing") and singing. There was a big crowd in one corner; obviously, that's where Gershwin was. The knot at the bar included the newly arrived Kaufman; his writing partner, young Moss Hart; and composer Kay Swift, who was laughing at something Hart had just said. Kaufman looked deeply into his highball, seeking who knows what? Perhaps a second act curtain?

I stood in the foyer, wondering how deep over my head I was. Ramon could have played this part without breaking a sweat. He'd have sauntered over to the bar and introduced himself to that illustrious trio, or added his pleasant tenor to the happy mob at the piano. I'm no wet blanket, and I have a healthy ego—what actor doesn't?—but I'm not wildly extroverted or a heavy drinker. These masters of the Great White Way, with whom I'd be spending the rest of my life, really liked to party. The social scene was crucial for business. And I hadn't even met the real night owls like

Porter, Youmans, and Larry Hart, those Broadway babies who won't say good night until early in the morning.

Fortunately, Ira jolted me out of my stage fright, his pretty wife Leonore on his arm. "Lee, this is David Taylor, the fellow who wrote those songs George keeps playing."

"Oh, like the one about the trapped man on the moon! So gruesome, yet I haven't been able to get it out of my mind since the fellas sang it. We must get you something to drink."

I let her steer me towards the bar. Ira trailed after, his usual smile on his face and a beer in one hand. I took a bottle of Pabst Blue Ribbon from a huge silver bowl loaded with ice. Luckily, Moss Hart handed me the opener before I looked like a moron trying to twist off the top.

"I'll tell George you're here," Ira said. "He was so hoping you'd come."

Leonore introduced me, but aside from polite greetings the trio took no notice of me, which was fine. I sipped my beer and listened to Hart tell Swift about his recent trip with Kaufman to Palm Springs, where they'd been working on a new show. I realized he meant *Merrily We Roll Along,* which would open this fall and flop, then flop again in 1981, despite Sondheim's brilliant score. It had been years since I read the original, but one of the characters was modeled on Gershwin.

Then someone clapped me on the back so hard, I nearly staggered.

"So! This must be the great J.D. Taylor! The pride of Greenwich Village!" A short, pugnacious man with yellowed teeth and big ears, a cigarette in one hand, leered up at me. Oscar Levant—pianist, composer, actor, writer, wit, and close pal of Gershwin's. His words seemed friendly, but his gaze was harsh and appraising: *Who are you, punk, attracting the attention of the all-powerful Gershwin, pounding the ivories in a Village joint? And what's more—do you have designs on my position as George's acolyte?*

I took a pull from my Pabst and answered as mildly as possible: "No claims to greatness here. I'm just getting started. This is all very new to me."

"Oscar Levant." He stuck out a hand, almost belligerently. Was he going to see who could squeeze harder? I hate that macho nonsense. He looked pissed enough to want to, but perhaps my size changed his mind. The shake was perfunctory; the old Village bohemian had a firmer grip.

"David Taylor."

"Interesting songs you wrote, Davey. Mighty interesting." No praise, and a belittling diminutive. I will answer to Davey, but it depends on who's using it. As Ramon always said, "You can call David lots of things, just don't call him late for dinner." *Oh, Ramon. I wish you were here. You could trade barbs with this putz.*

"I'm glad you think so," I replied. "I'd hate to be boring and repetitious." We exchanged hostile looks; Levant clearly assumed I was digging at him for his numerous (and admittedly brilliant) performances of the "Rhapsody in Blue." He'd done it so many times, even his own mother complained, "Again with the 'Rhapsody!'" Was I baiting him? Not really. It was more like poking my brother. A thing you do for the reaction. Out of the corner of my eye, I saw Kaufman watching everything, and I half-worried that our head-butting would show up in one of his plays. Besides, however aggravating Levant could be—and that's saying a lot—the world should be forever grateful to him for the way he kept Gershwin's work alive.

Then George called out, "David! Get over here!"

I drained the bottle and set it on the bar. "Excuse me," I said to Levant. A royal summons like that trumped anything.

George, seated at the piano in his shirt sleeves, introduced me to the others as "a treasure Pincus found in the Village," which wasn't exactly right, but I wouldn't quibble. "Show them what you've got," he ordered, and accompanied me on "Second Chances" and "The Actor's Lament," which went over well with everyone. Almost everyone. Levant leaned against a bookcase, scowling.

He needn't have worried. I had the spotlight for only those two numbers, then Gershwin called Swift over for a duet. I strolled back to the bar and got an approving nod from Kaufman. Fortunately, Gershwin didn't give any details about the songs' context, or I would have fretted that "The Actor's Lament" might subliminally influence Kaufman and Hart's 1938 flop, *The Fabulous Invalid.* Like my show, *The Best of These Are Shadows,* it featured a haunted theatre.

The gathering broke up around ten, which surprised me. Gershwin closed the lid on the piano, and Leonore began herding guests towards the door, where the valet doled out coats. "I've still got work to do," George explained when a pretty brunette pleaded for just one more song.

"He's got to plug the air waves for Feen-a-mint, the world's best laxative chewing gum," Levant said. In falsetto tones, he chorused, "Oh, Feen-a-mint! I'm feeling so keen-a-mint! 'Cause you make my shit turn green-a-mint!"

George ignored the teasing. "Laugh all you want, Oscar. Feen-a-mint is paying for *Porgy.*" He nodded at me. "Glad you could come, David. We'll stay in touch."

I sure hoped so, since I had two bottles of drugs I needed to get inside him in the not-too-distant future. Our paths probably wouldn't cross again for a while, though. He'd be leaving for South Carolina soon, to study the music of the Gullah blacks: research for *Porgy.*

A promising start for my first month.

January 19, 2079

Rose told her story to the authorities over and over; fortunately, ever since that middle-school *Romeo and Juliet,* she'd made a point of knowing her lines. They weren't really interested in her, anyway. Uncle David, now beyond their reach, was the criminal. The Ripper project, however, had no protocol for unauthorized use of the SlingShot. It did what bureaucrats do when faced with the unconventional: called a meeting. A representative, hastily dispatched from Washington, took the title of Event Coordinator, and told everyone to come back tomorrow, when the Council would convene. The academics at Yale, including Dr. Nathan Greenbaum, fumed.

Nate packed up his unused gear and his daughter, and drove home in near total silence. "Your mother needs to hear this. No point in yapping now." He had phoned Isis earlier, giving her a sketchy outline, enough to keep her from worrying too much.

Rose was the worried one now.

When they walked into the house, it didn't help that Bertie was banging off the walls. "Uncle Dave hijacked the 'Shot? That's so t.o.s.!" Rose had never learned what that stood for, but it was high praise in a twelve-year-old's vocabulary.

"You're not part of this, Bertram," Nate said. "Security. Go upstairs. You too, Hannah."

"Aw, Dad!" Bertie squawked.

"We'll decide what you can be told later."

Bertie clumped up the stairs like a thundering herd of buffalo, while Hannah trailed behind in silence. She stopped halfway, looking down at her parents and older sister. "Will we ever see him again?" she asked, her voice barely a whisper.

"I very much doubt it."

Rose felt a pang at the way Hannah's head drooped. Nate didn't notice. He yanked open the fridge for a beer, while Isis put water on for tea, fetching two mugs in response to Rose's nod. Rose's special mug was from the 2069 revival of *Carnival,* the first Broadway show she'd seen with her uncle, who took her backstage afterwards. She still cherished it, even if its logo had faded with repeated washings.

Her dad threw himself into a kitchen chair. "You knew that bomb was bogus, didn't you?" he asked.

She nodded. "Uncle David would never hurt anybody."

Nate sighed. "Sweetheart, there are other kinds of damage besides blowing up New Haven."

"What, he's going to change history?" Rose snorted. "Can you picture Uncle David warning the Navy about Pearl Harbor or building the atom bomb early? That's silly. He'll go to classic Broadway shows, and maybe he'll be happy again."

Isis took her daughter's hand. "It's not so simple. Your dad and his colleagues train for years, not just to fit into the past, but to observe without changing anything. A Ripper's *presence* is dangerous."

"Think about it," Nate said. "David will need a place to stay. Somebody else—Mr. X—should have been living there. Maybe history doesn't change because Mr. X lives on a different street, but it *could.* That's why Rippers in modern eras stay in hotels with lots of vacancies if they can. Next, David will get a job. Will Mr. Y survive without that job? That's just the start. Every time he interacts with the people of 1934, like taking a taxi that should have gone somewhere else, he's potentially changing history."

"But Mr. X and Mr. Y wouldn't be world changers, like FDR or Einstein."

Nate drained his beer. His eyes were red and had dark circles under them. "You're missing the point. Mr. X and Mr. Y might be nobodies in the thirties, but what about their descendants? By having different homes and jobs, they could end up with different spouses. Their offspring— who never existed in our timeline—will have more kids, and so on. Odds are, the original descendants of X and Y are not the Great Men and Women of history, but their combined contributions are likely important. The *lack* of those contributions could change the timeline."

The tea suddenly tasted bitter in Rose's mouth. "So he could create a different world? Like that old movie about the teenage time traveler and his disappearing family?"

Her dad pitched his empty bottle in the recycle bin. "Rest your mind; we're not going to disappear. What I'm going to tell you is classified, but you're already in this up to your ears. David's presence will almost certainly generate a splinter world, one parallel to our timeline. We've done it twice by accident, and once on purpose. Our man in Reformation Germany had been there many times, when all of a sudden the tech had two sets of coordinates, both for September 1524. We still don't know what exactly he did, but there seems to have been some minor changes in the history of the Fürstenbergs, an aristocratic family in that area."

"That's it?" Rose seemed incredulous.

"Hey, it took three years to find that out, and a lot of truly brave Rippers, who took the 'Shot into totally uncharted coordinates! And getting the backing for those trips was nearly as much fun. We still haven't figured out the change in the other Splinterverse, except that it started in England in 1796. Either we're missing it, or the ramifications haven't happened yet. The Splinterverse for January 2079 seems identical to here."

"And the 'on purpose' one?" Isis asked.

Nate ran his hands through his hair. *Just like Uncle David did, when he got so upset at seeing me,* thought Rose.

"The first two Splinterverses have existed for five years and seemed stable," said Nate. "So six months ago, the Council voted to alter history deliberately—an extremely controversial decision, backed by tons of French money. It always comes down to money. They stopped the assassination of Franz Ferdinand in 1914. Well, let's just say it's a different world." He ran his finger along the edge of a placemat, not meeting his wife's eyes. "I've been applying for a 'Shot there, right from the start."

Isis sat back in her chair. "And you never told me?"

"I would have, if I'd got it. That will never happen now."

"They'll blame you for your brother's actions?"

"Who knows? If they have any sense, they'll send me after David, because we have no idea what can happen if changes in a Splinterverse continue, as they will, the longer he stays." At Rose's stricken look, he reached out and smoothed her hair. "If I can find him, I'm sure I can convince him to come back."

"You wouldn't hurt him?" There was a catch in her voice.

"No, no. I wouldn't." He smiled reassuringly, but Rose suspected he wasn't telling her everything. Nate stretched his long legs. "So, Rosie. Tell me about Broadway in the thirties, since that's where my dumb kid brother likely is."

\#

From the diary of J.D. Taylor, April 30, 1934
Mr. Terracino pounced on me when I got to work. "You are the limit! One week, you get George Gershwin to come

75

through our door. Swell! Then you go the other way, and Joe Gould shows up, on your say-so! Just as bad as the other was good!"

"Who? Oh, the little guy I trampled. What's the harm? I gave him enough to cover his grub." I hung up my overcoat and went behind the bar for a glass of water.

Mr. Terracino gesticulated as only Sicilians can. "You gave him money? That pipsqueak swindler said you told him to put it on your tab!"

Hank looked up from laying out silverware. "He scratches and smells worse than a skunk. No offense, Petunia." Petunia, curled up on a bar stool, didn't answer.

"David, Joe Gould is a notorious Village mooch," Terracino said, smoothing his thick black hair. "I don't want him here. And he'll be back, that's the rock-bottom truth. Once he gets some booze and a meal out of you, he's certain to tap you again for contributions to the Joe Gould Fund."

"As bad as that?"

"Worse," Karl called from the kitchen. "Get some gin in him, and he'll start talking seagull."

Before I could get that remark translated, the door opened, letting in watery sunlight and a small, shuffling figure. "Speak o' the divil," Jimmy announced from behind the bar.

"Ai!" Hank began scooping up ketchup bottles from every table, stuffing them in the steel pan he used for collecting dirty dishes.

Gould sniffed audibly as Hank clanked and rattled his way from table to table. "Spoilsport. Now how can I partake of the fine free tomato soup here? Ah, Bronko! Score any touchdowns since last night? Thank you so much for the superb spaghetti and meatball. But I regret to inform you that I've discovered our encounter last night has irreparably damaged my best trousers." He waved a grimy hand at his pants leg.

I'd bet money those shabby brown wool pants had had those very same rips before, each mended with different colored thread. *This guy's a pro.* Mr. Terracino drummed his fingers on the bar, impatient to boot the bum before the lunch crowd arrived.

"I'll pay for a new pair, Mr. Gould, but I don't have that much on me. Perhaps you could meet me at my home—"

"You're meeting your neighbors for dinner tonight, right?" Karl interrupted. "Joe could meet you *outside.*"

"Yes, that would be better," I said, realizing my mistake. I didn't want Gould haunting the Seville Studios. "The Bamboo Forest at eight."

Gould nodded his small head, causing a cascade of dandruff. "Very well. But perhaps I could—"

"Good-bye, Joe," Mr. Terracino said, opening the door behind Gould. "I haven't forgotten what you did here last year."

"You haven't, but I have!" Gould laughed. "Oh, well. I look forward to talking more with you, Bronko. You have an interesting manner. I'd like to record you in my Oral History." Before Terracino could stop him, he scooped two handfuls of peanuts from the bowl on the bar, bowed with great dignity, and left.

"Oughta fumigate," Jimmy muttered, pitching the remaining nuts in the trash. "I wouldn't feed these to Petunia now."

Something Gould had said worried me. "What's this Oral History?" I asked. It wasn't anything I'd read in my exhaustive research on the period.

"Gould's been scribbling in school notebooks for years, calls it the Oral History of the World. I know a guy that's seen a bit and claims it's mostly gibberish." Terracino shook his head. "The Lord tells us to be charitable to the poor, but I think even St. Francis would have had trouble with Joe Gould. Ah, hello, Miss Martinis, you're looking well today. Right this way, please."

I drained my glass, refilled it, and took my place at the piano.

#

Sure enough, Gould was waiting outside the Bamboo Forest, a Chinese place on MacDougal, where I was meeting the Finkelsteins and Frannie's brother for dinner. Mr. Williams, the owner, was keeping an eye on the little bohemian. His irked expression matched the one Terracino wore earlier.

"See," Gould was saying, "here's the young man. He will recompense me, and I shall no longer disturb the serenity of your establishment." He swayed slightly.

Mr. Williams looked heavenward and swore softly in Chinese. He turned to me. "You're welcome here, Mr. Taylor, and your friends are already inside." The look in his eye said, *And Joe Gould had better not be one of them.*

"Here, Mr. Gould, two-fifty for some new trousers," I said, pressing the money into his grimy hand. "Good luck." Feeling ill at ease, I hurried inside with Williams.

This dinner was a business expense; Nick Santino agreed to help me navigate the legal waters in changing my name, though he furrowed his bushy black eyebrows over the destroyed records in the San Francisco City Hall. He brightened when I mentioned Rabbi Epstein and his wife, and muttered about affidavits. I'd naturally invited Frannie, too, but she was home with Leo, who had the chicken pox. (What a horrible disease!) I told Yang Williams, one of the owners' adopted sons, to fix some take-out for the invalid.

The Chinese food of this era isn't as varied as in my time, but the Williamses were true old China hands. Their stuff was tasty.

At the end of a delightful meal (chop suey, what else?), we lingered by the roaring fireplace, sipping jasmine tea, and watching the light flicker on the red lacquered walls. Nick seemed like a good fellow, and I always enjoyed the Finkelsteins' company. Mabel's competent, practical air reminded me of Isis, and Adam seemed like an older, male version of Rose, but with his show biz dreams already tempered by reality. He'd just lost a spot in the dancing chorus of a new operetta "to some fella named Jack Cole." I couldn't tell him Cole would become one of Broadway's greatest choreographers.

Then I had a brilliant notion, one that might help us all. "Know what I'd do, if I were filthy rich?" I asked.

"Vacation in Paris?" "Publish your songs?" "Stuff it in a mattress?"

"Mabel's guess was closest," I said. "Remember the night we met, how I said I'd like to help back a show? Well, one day, I'm going to do it. I want to be a producer." Somehow, I managed not to sing that line to Mel Brooks' melody. "Of course, I'd need an office. I'd hire you, Mabel, as head of accounts, since *I'm* not afraid to hire a woman. You for legal, Nick, and Adam, when you hang up your taps, you can manage it. How about it, gang?"

Adam waved his hand at our hostess. "Hey, Ma Williams! What did you put in Mr. Taylor's cup? He's gone clean loco."

"I'm serious!"

Mabel smiled "It's nice to have dreams. They keep you sunny inside when the world's gray. I'd adore being in charge of your firm's accounts, whenever you start it."

"Ay, there's the rub," said Adam. "I'd be game, too. Dancers' careers aren't long, God knows."

"And I'd love to leave my uncle's firm," said Nick. "But, David, where's the pot at the end of the rainbow?"

"David's getting closer to it," Mabel said, "meeting Gershwin and all."

"It will happen," I predicted. "I guarantee it. My fortune says: GREAT FORTUNE COME YOU WAY."

They were dubious. But that fortune cookie wasn't wrong. I knew which hits to back. But more than that, I planned that Taylor Productions would invest in the shows that would be written because I changed history.

#

From the diary of J.D. Taylor, May 14, 1934
I met Vinton Freedley today. With his partner, Alex Aarons, he backed the Gershwins' early hits in the twenties, and built a splendid theatre on West 52nd Street, the Alvin— named for the first syllables of their first names. But the Depression hit them hard, and Aarons left for Hollywood. They lost the Alvin to the Shuberts, who let Freedley stay in his old office on the second floor of the building he once owned. A kindness from the boys from Syracuse? Perhaps. Or maybe they were sticking it to Freedley for the rent.

In the spring of 1934, Freedley was trying to claw his way back to Broadway, looking for backers for his new show. I intended to be one of them. Freedley didn't know it yet, but his fall offering would be one of the biggest hits of the decade.

I got there on time, smartly dressed in my best brown suit.... and was forced to wait fifteen minutes by a harridan in a gray bun. The message was clear: Mr. F. was a very busy man. Busy checking his watch, more likely.

When the door dragon passed me in, Freedley, a careworn man in his early forties, didn't rise from his seat behind a gigantic desk: he was in a wheelchair. "Been a little under the weather," he said as we shook hands. My research said he'd either had a minor heart attack or stroke; whatever it was, he'd reach his seventies. I sat down in a scuffed, hard-backed chair that creaked. The decor was stark and dreary: a battered filing cabinet, a stained red divan against the wall, and the usual yellowish nicotine tinge on walls and curtains. Maybe J.J. and Lee Shubert had confiscated the good stuff.

"What can I do for you, Mr. Taylor?" he asked. His voice was high-pitched, squeaky like a rat's.

"I understand you're producing a musical this fall, and I'd like to join the bandwagon. It sounds promising."

"We're calling it *Crazy Week,* a light-hearted, rollicking comedy, good for taking folks' minds off the headlines." He lit a cigarette, offered me one, and put the pack away when I declined. "I came up with the scenario myself, on my yacht in the Pearl Islands last winter."

Hiding from your creditors.

"A ship-board comedy, book by Plum Wodehouse and Guy Bolton, who are meeting in France next month to start writing. Cole Porter for the songs," he continued.

"Porter's quite talented. And the cast?" I inquired, ever so mildly.

"How do Merman and Gaxton sound?"

"Terrific. Are they signed?" I knew they weren't, not yet, and that Freedley would lie to each about signing the other before getting those contracts inked. I could hear Ramon giggling, *Oh, you bitch, David! Be nice to the poor producer!*

Freedley's "hail, fellow" grin faltered. "Mere formalities. But, uh, we're not releasing anything to the papers until everything's aces. Do keep that under your hat."

"Naturally. You've convinced me," I said. "I'd like to invest five grand." Two-thirds of my stake, but it was worth it. I'd recoup the investment, plus, as an investor, I was guaranteed to meet Cole Porter. We spent some time drawing up papers—Freedley was a little surprised to learn I was a lowly key-banger in a Village joint, but money is money. But by the time I walked out the door, I was a Broadway backer—on my way to becoming a producer. In honor of the occasion, I bought myself a new hat, like Leo Bloom. Maybe I'd eventually feel comfortable wearing it.

#

From the diary of J.D. Taylor, June 16, 1934

My first target in the Broadway Revival Project was Vincent Youmans, who would move to Colorado in July for the mountain air, but I had no idea how long I might need to get close to him. Youmans, in the midst of testy contract talks with RKO Studios, wasn't exactly broadcasting how sick he was. So, though I had enjoyed playing at the Golden Eagle, I went to tell Mr. Terracino about my intended departure. "I don't have many relatives, but there's a cousin in Colorado Springs that I'd like to see this summer, before it's too late. I'm grateful for the chance to have worked here."

Terracino's angular Sicilian face softened with compassion. "My Auntie Lena is a lunger, too. She's leaving tomorrow for Denver with my no-good drunkard nephew … Hey! David, you're coming back here after it's over with your poor cousin, right? Tell you what. If you take Lena out west, I'll find some college boy to fill in for you till you get back, whenever that is. And I'll keep your cousin in my prayers. You can have Gino's ticket. I trust you a damn sight further than that lout. Plus, I'd like to keep you. You're good for business—Shep's been making hay out of Gershwin's visit in the papers for weeks. What say?"

The combination of a free ticket and continued employment was tempting, though it meant I'd be cooling my heels a while before Youmans got settled in his own place in July. Well, Colorado's supposed to be pretty. "When do we leave?" I asked.

#

From the diary of J.D. Taylor, June 23, 1934
I've now been on two cross-country train rides. This journey was far more enjoyable than the one in March, when I was suffering from time-travel-induced migraines and a weird sense of dislocation. I've grown more used to the pace of the 1930s, and especially to losing the Internet, with its instant connections, answers, and details. In my era, every American, whether through a device or an implant (the Greenbaums were still wary of implants' potential medical issues) was a click or a tongue-tap from practically everything. 1934's information sources—newspapers, magazines, the radio, movie newsreels—were far more limited and harder to search. The first few weeks here, I kept checking my Ally, but I've weaned myself of that. My current reading material consisted of *Goodbye, Mr. Chips* and the latest *New Yorker.* I was fitting in, little by little.

The old lady was frail, though pleasant. My Spanish skills let me converse with her in broken Italian, which she loved, telling me, *"Basta, basta!"* because I made her laugh too much. She spent most of the trip sleeping while I watched the country pass by.

When we got there, we checked into a hotel; a relative would pick her up in the morning. We had grilled rainbow trout for breakfast, the freshest I'd ever tasted, then I took her out front to wait for Cousin Paulie. The bellhop was nowhere to be found, so I dashed back inside for her bags...and promptly tripped over the doorsill. Mr. Terracino's basket flew open, and oranges bounced in all directions. One skittered across the veranda and off the steps, where a bearded man on the sidewalk lunged for it, making a shoestring catch before it hit the ground. His friends—a mob of them, even shaggier—whooped and applauded.

"Nice catch, Snake! Keep it up this afternoon, when it counts!" one said, white teeth glinting in his dark whiskers.

Snake laughed. "I'll surely try. You okay up there, sir?"

"Only my dignity's hurt," I said. "I can dance, you'd think I could walk out a door." I scrambled to my feet and straightened the basket. "All the way from New York, and I spill everything at the last minute."

"That's life for you," Snake said, jumping up and helping to reassemble the basket. "So you're a...dancer?" His tone had changed slightly, and he was clearly appraising my appearance.

"These days, I'm a songwriter and piano player. J.D. Taylor."

"Jack Spivey, outfielder." Spivey looked relieved. "I didn't *think* you were one of those gigolos. You look too decent." He retrieved the last orange from the far corner of the porch. "Hey, this one's an inside-the-park job."

"Thanks for the help. Here." I tried giving the young man a quarter, which he wouldn't take until I said it was a lucky two-bit piece from New York. "I had this in my pocket when I met George Gershwin. Maybe it will bring you luck in your game."

"Gershwin? Yea, bo!" one of the other beards said. "Take it, Snake!"

But Spivey hesitated. "A man needs all the luck he can get nowadays. Don't you want to keep it for yourself, Mr. Taylor?"

"Nope. I believe in spreading luck around. Besides, I've got that memory of meeting him up here"—I tapped my head—"and nothing can take that away from me." I grinned, but more to myself, for paraphrasing lyrics Ira hadn't written yet.

"Well, thanks!" The ballplayer waved genially, and the furry crowd continued down the street. The hotel waiter had said there was some kind of baseball tournament going in Denver. Nate and Bertie, the family sports junkies, would have loved this encounter: bearded ballplayers! Maybe a cult or something. *I haven't seen that much facial hair since the late 2050s, when beards got trendy again. Or maybe when I played Perchik in my high school production of* Fiddler.

Minutes later, I waved *"Ciao!"* as Zia Lena drove off in Paulie's Chevy Mercury, then caught an afternoon train to Colorado Springs.

#

From the diary of J.D. Taylor, July 14, 1934
I'm staying at a "Mountain Greenery" known as the Antlers Inn, waiting for Vincent Youmans to get settled before I visit him with antibiotics in my pocket. It's been a profitable delay. The Inn is festooned with turrets and animal horns, and its rooms are full of honeymooners. Their obvious happiness has spurred me into writing a new song, my first in months. It's called "Paintings on the Sidewalk," in honor of the Greenwich Village art expositions. The thirties feel of the melodic line pleases me, though the lyrics have more bite than most numbers of this era. I'll also need help with orchestrations—maybe I'll see Bill Daly about lessons when I get back. If only Ramon and Rose could hear it...

Back to my Project. Youmans, accompanied by his parents and a nurse, was staying in a rented house on Beverly Place, with lovely rustic views. As if there were any other kind here. His doctor, the famous James Webb, had limited visitors, so today I sent him a letter, saying I had overheard in the hotel lobby that Youmans was here for treatment, since it wasn't truly public news. I said I was a fellow composer, a big fan, and played up the truthful, if tenuous, connection with my neighbor Adam ("who worked in Mr. Youmans' *Through the Years*"). Could I please, please, with sugar on top, pay my respects to the invalid? Then I crossed my fingers.

#

From the diary of J.D. Taylor, July 17, 1934

July 15, 1934
Dear Mr. Taylor,
   Thanks for the kind words, which Dr. Webb has passed on to me, though I'm dismayed to learn that gossips are bandying my name in public. I confess I'd like to forget about Through the Years, *except the title song, one of my personal favorites. Webb says I may have a visitor for an hour Thursday or Friday afternoon. Come if you wish.*

Vincent Youmans

Not cordial, but I was in. I assembled a basket like Zia Lena's, but without the Lambrusco and Chef Mario's amaretti: fruit, chocolate, cheese, bread. Youmans' place was only two miles from the Inn, but I had a taxi drop me off close by. I didn't want the candy—or me—to melt.

   The small, white wood-frame house nestled far back on a quiet street overlooking a ravine with a creek running through it. As I approached the door, a doe and her fawn watched me suspiciously from the hillside before bounding away into the brush. A jay squawked, a vulture wheeled in the sky, and the towering Rockies seemed close enough to touch. A long way from the bright lights of Broadway.

A beefy blond nurse answered my knock and immediately looked at her watch. "One hour. Don't tire him." Youmans' mother, behind her, was more welcoming. She took the basket, practically pulling me into the front room. "How kind of you, Mr. Taylor. I'll fetch some lemonade; it's so warm. And here's Vincent."

Well, yes. That was obvious. The composer was semi-reclining on a floral couch, with books and magazines piled around him. A piano was wedged into one corner, a radio rested on a table within his reach. His dad sat on the remaining piece of furniture, a mismatched loveseat. Youmans senior rose, folded his newspaper, and nodded briefly. His wife bumped him in the doorway, coming back with the promised lemonade. "We're going to the market. Have a *lovely* little chat." With a fond look at her son—one that wasn't returned—she retreated to the kitchen.

I wouldn't have recognized him. His beard was growing out during his convalescence, nothing like the weird baseball players, but more than customary for the thirties.

He must have noticed my gaze, for he put a self-conscious hand to his face. "I look like a medieval French monk. But I can't go out, so why bother shaving?"

"Looks piratical to me. You need a gold earring and a spotted kerchief," I said, trying to keep my voice light. His pallor, the sick glitter in his dark eyes, the pink-tinged hankies on the floor had shaken me. I knew Youmans would last until 1946, but the last man I saw who looked this awful was Ramon. "It's an honor to meet you, Mr. Youmans."

"Vincent. Thanks for the treats. Maybe I'll work up the appetite for them soon. Doc says I'm improving—a very light case, and not communicable."

Wrong on all three counts.

Youmans frowned: a common expression on him, as I would find. "You didn't happen to notice who was wagging his tongue about me? Lousy gossips, no respect for privacy. Ah, what the hell. What's new on the Rialto? I've been away since the spring."

While Youmans mocked the local gossips, he could dish dirt himself, especially about his peers. "So Harold Arlen's doing a revue? Good chap; he was my rehearsal pianist for *Great Day.* A new Porter comedy this fall? Cole can turn out some gems. Trouble is, he'd rather play—and how! Yeah, I'd heard about George's Negro folk opera. Can't work up any excitement for it. I'm still furious with him for stealing the melody of 'Tea for Two' for his 'Looking for a Boy.'"

He bitched about RKO's shabby treatment in Hollywood, and his doctor's ban on booze. "If I'm a good boy, I can have a beer in August. That's a long dry spell, let me tell you!"

But when I commented on the books by his side—elementary French, trigonometry, music theory and nautical texts—he got as excited as a kid. "While I'm here, I intend to improve my mind," he said, tapping *Principles of Navigation* with a long, gaunt finger. "Can't wait to get back on my yacht, the *Carioca,* but this break is good for me."

Since I don't sail or speak French, and my math skills are nil, the sheets of music sticking out of *Harmony and Counterpoint* were my only chance. "A new project?" I said, feeling like Dot in the finale of *Sunday in the Park With George.*

"Got the makings of two good songs already, even though Dr. Webb won't let me sit at the piano. That's not really a handicap, since I tend to whistle a melody first, and wrestle the bass harmonies with both hands. Say! Would you play them for me? My parents aren't that musical."

"Sure!" I looked them over. One had definite Caribbean rhythms; the other was a fragment of a bluesy torch number. I played the first, stumbling twice and feeling self-conscious, but Youmans applauded, and some color returned to his face.

I'd just started the second when Nurse Ratched banged open the door and announced, "Time's up. Doctor's orders."

Youmans scowled, but I held up my hand. "Perhaps Dr. Webb will let me visit again. I'll be in town for a while." I flashed a dazzling smile on the nurse. "For now, I'll just finish this piece—one Mr. Youmans himself wrote—and slip out the door, without another word. That can't be considered 'visiting.' I'm merely providing musical accompaniment for the patient. No doctor could object to that…" And before she could say anything, I went back to playing. The glint in Youmans' eye came from enthusiasm, not fever.

#

From the diary of J.D. Taylor, August 2, 1934
At first, Dr. Webb allowed three short visits a week. Youmans finished the two songs, with me at the piano as his avatar. He worked slowly and carefully, replaying a phrase or a passage over and over before deciding it was right, a contrast to Gershwin's speed and fluency. However they did it, both men knew how to write music. I also attended a family dinner, where I met Youmans' girlfriend, Mildred Boots, a stunning, tall former *Follies* girl, destined to be his next wife. "Boots" was staying with a friend in nearby Broadmoor, making not-so-secret visits that the town gossips really did chew on.

Since Youmans disliked talking about his condition and didn't get along with his mother, my best chance of getting the antibiotics in him was Boots, who was clearly worried about her lover. Youmans' spirits remained high, but he wasn't improving. Dr. Webb canceled all visitations, disappointing everyone, especially the randy composer.

Claiming I had to return to New York and had something for Youmans, I invited Boots to lunch at the majestic Broadmoor Hotel, a late-Victorian rival of the Antlers. I had a "western sandwich," which was something like a Denver omelette on bread. Boots picked at her pot roast à la mode. "I'm too upset to eat," she said, sipping her coffee instead. "He's not getting any better. That doctor's pie-in-the-sky hooey!"

"Well, that's what I wanted to talk about," I said, seeing an opening. "During my time in Mexico, I met this rather unconventional doctor, who's compounded a supplement for lung cases—vitamins and extracts. It peps them up, so they respond better to treatment. I've hesitated suggesting it. I didn't want to seem presumptuous, and I know his doctor wouldn't approve if he knew." *On the other hand, this era's really obsessed with vitamins, extracts, laxatives—you name it. From monkey glands to iron tonics, they'll try anything. That's in my favor.*

Boots put the cup down, all business now. "Is it safe?"

"Safe as houses. I'll take one myself, if that's what it takes to prove it, but I'd rather he gets the full dose. There can be some effects: stomach ache, a touch of diarrhea, but it's usually mild." I reached into a bag and put a brown glass bottle on the table. For verisimilitude, I had covered a paper label with hand-written Spanish instructions, which I glued to the bottle. "In case you don't read Spanish, I've translated it here, on my business card. The most important bit is that he finishes the entire bottle, even if he starts feeling spry before they're all gone."

Boots studied the little pasteboard for a moment, then grabbed the bottle and stowed it in her handbag. "I'll *make* him take them. I've got powers of persuasion where Vince is concerned." She winked shamelessly, every inch the show girl. "And we won't say a word to Dr. Webb."

"Good idea. American doctors tend to think anything from a less developed land must be suspect."

"He's a Brit."

"Even worse!" I laughed. "I'm confident these pills will help perk up Vince in no time. Perhaps you could write and let me know how he's doing. I know what it's like having a sick loved one. Especially when he's in denial." Boots looked confused, and I corrected the anachronism. "When he can't admit how serious his condition is."

"Of course. Thank you, David." She pushed aside her pot roast and waved for the waiter. "I hear their strawberry parfait is simply marvelous."

#

September 16, 1934

Dear David,

Those Mexican vitamins are tip top! Vince didn't want to try them without consulting Webb, but I got around him. Hee hee. I do believe he was feeling stronger by the second day, and he truly seems his old self again. He's finished the bottle, and is letting Webb and the mountain air take full credit. We're coming back to the East Coast next month. Can't thank you enough!

Boots

Chapter 4

"Nice Work If You Can Get It" —Ira Gershwin

From the diary of J.D. Taylor, September 22, 1934

Having completed the first phase of the Broadway Revival Project, I settled into a comfortable routine of shifts at the Golden Eagle; orchestration instruction with Bill Daly; giving Leo Spinelli his piano lessons; going to shows, parties, and nightclubs (major highlight: sixteen-year-old Lena Horne at the Cotton Club!); and composing new songs. I've been to another "festival" at the Gershwins' after George came back from South Carolina. Gershwin also kept his promise, and introduced me to Max Dreyfus at Harms. As the composer predicted, the publisher balked at my unconventional approach.

"These songs haf no verses!" Dreyfus thundered.

"They don't need verses!" Gershwin roared back. After some haggling, Dreyfus bought "Second Chances" and "Paintings on the Sidewalk." I was now a published songwriter, over a century before my own birth. I couldn't wait to get the sheet music, so I could frame them by the family photos, right between the ones of Ramon and Rose.

On this Saturday morning, I was giving Leo his lesson. Plenty of kids hated the idea of studying piano, but Leo was enthusiastic, practically haunting my place. "How much longer until I can play like Duke Ellington?" he wanted to know.

"Leo, nobody plays like Duke Ellington. But maybe I can work up some simplified versions of his songs for you. For now, let's—" The telephone rang—a shrill metallic sound. I much prefer the customizable ring tones.

"Hello?"

"Mister Taylor? My name's Earl Busby. I'm the music director for the new Porter show, *Bon Voyage*. Bill Daly says you're keen to be a rehearsal pianist. Interested? Ten a.m., on the eighth." He gave the address of a rehearsal hall in Hell's Kitchen.

Interested? Damn right. I've got five grand in this show, even if it does keep changing its name! I swallowed and found my voice. "Yes, I'd like that very much. I'll be there." I hung up the receiver, which still feels funny in my hand, and turned to Leo, who was pecking out "The Wabash Cannonball."

"Hey, Leo, I've got a new job—on Broadway."

#

January 20, 2079

"Where's the likeliest place to find Dave?" Nate asked Rose. "New York is hella big. You know musical theatre history. Is there any one specific must-see, one he couldn't resist?"

Rose frowned. "I'm not an expert, like Uncle David. Mm … *Show Boat* was 1927. *Oklahoma!*'s 1943."

"Too early, too late. What about 1934?"

"Let me look, Daddy." She huddled over her Ally while Isis made more tea and Nate munched on granola without paying attention to what he was eating. "Wow, there's not much happening on Broadway; I guess it's the Depression. Something called *Caviar* ran only two weeks. Wait! *Anything*

Goes, November twenty-first, huge hit! Uncle David would never miss this. It's Cole Porter's first show with Ethel Merman."

"Think he'd be at opening night?"

"How could he not? This says it was the event of the season. Besides that show, there's not much on Broadway until 1935. You know how obsessed he is with Gershwin; he's sure to be at *Porgy and Bess.*"

Her father dismissed the suggestion. "Let's stick with the other one." Nate stood up and stretched. "I'm going to try to sleep, or I'll be in no shape to make the 'Shot. Assuming the beancounters let me go. Meanwhile, do some homework for me. Put together an outline of whatever you think is relevant about *Anything Goes* and Broadway in the thirties."

"Maybe I could come, too?" Rose said.

"No!" her parents yelled with precision timing.

"One relative lost in the past is too many," Nate said. "Your concern is your *future.*"

#

January 20-21, 2079

The Yale department heads had convened during the night, and the Council linked with them through the morning. Budget woes dominated the discussion. A contingent of Council members from India complained that every visit to a Splinterverse drained resources from original Ripper programs; the deliberate change to World War I never would have happened without backing from French corporations and the Ministry of Cultural Affairs. Who would pay for this unscheduled jaunt to 1934, a possibly fruitless search? So what if there were now four Splinterverses?, they argued. Let the first two go their merry ways. We've wasted enough time and money on them. Aside from minor German nobility, SV-1 1525 had changed very little and the change in SV-2 1796 still wasn't clear. The French could keep paying for the trips to their 1914 playground. Chalk up SV-4 1934 to lousy American security, and get back to real history. As always with discussions of the Splinterverses, the Indians took the unstated moral high ground that all these distortions of history had occurred in Western timelines.

But the Americans, led by the Yale faction, countered that David Greenbaum was a criminal, and that Nathan Greenbaum, as his brother and as a Ripper already prepared to travel to 1934, stood a reasonable chance of finding him. What's more, their hard-working, fine-print-reading lawyers gave them an out: the lab's insurance policy covered a multitude of mishaps. While hijacking a time capsule wasn't *explicitly* listed, the legal eagles felt thought they could soak Lloyd's of London for a good chunk of David's trip. Or spend years in court fighting about it.

With that news, the Council narrowly approved sending Nate on his original mission, making trips to New York to look for David whenever he could.

All the lab techs and their superiors had been checking the coordinates since the lab reopened after the bomb threat. They were dismayed to learn that David began affecting history almost from the start: the dreaded double coordinates indicating a Splinterverse appeared by mid-April 1934, though in a weird, fluctuating pattern no one had ever seen before.

"All this means my data will have a big, fat asterisk, like Roger Maris' home-run record," Nate complained as he readied himself for the SlingShot on the morning of the twenty-first.

"What do you mean, an asterisk?" Rose asked. She had come along to give him his good-luck kiss. It seemed freaky to be in the lab, just two days after David's escapade. She kept glancing towards the door, half-expecting to see Ramon's duffel bag.

"Maris broke Babe Ruth's record in 1961, but some people didn't regard it as legitimate since he played a longer season than Ruth. Some folks will bitch everything I learn in SV-4 1934 is tainted, even though it's unlikely my idiot brother is affecting anything I'm there to record. What does he know about strikes? Or the death of John Dillinger? Oh, well, he can't change the weather, so the Project Haboob team won't mind our runaway's presence."

Yale was backing Nate's own studies of labor relations; New Line Cinema had funded his filming of Dillinger's death (they had wanted him to film the ambush of Bonnie and Clyde, too, but that was deemed too dangerous); and a multi-national group was researching the Dust Bowl in an effort to fight the increasing dust storms across northern China and the American southwest. So Nate's schedule was jam-packed. Finding time to go to New York after his fugitive brother would not be easy.

He kissed his wife and daughter, knowing they would see him in a day or so, but he wouldn't see them for months. "Be careful, Daddy," Rose said.

"I'll try," he said. "Let's go, Danny." He climbed into the SlingShot and set off for this new, altered past.

#

From the diary of J.D. Taylor, October 30, 1934
Oh, Ramon, if only you knew what I've been doing for the last three weeks. This much fun should be illegal. And I get paid, too—fifty bucks a week. I'm back in a Broadway show, with the familiar chaos, sweat, late hours, all multiplied more than usual, since we're days away from the tryouts in

Boston without a finished libretto. As Vinton Freedley told me back in spring, Guy Bolton and Plum Wodehouse were doing the script, but Freedley hated what they came up with ("It's hopeless!"). Both of them were still in Europe, Guy recovering from an appendectomy and Plum burdened with tax concerns and new projects, so Freedley had director Howard Lindsay and press agent Russel Crouse overhaul the mess. They're still hard at it; just last week, I overheard someone ask Crouse how the second act would end. "Damned if we know," he replied.

Ethel Merman has been a huge help with the endless rewrites. When she's not onstage, the former stenographer sits with the creative staff, taking down changes in Pitman shorthand. Then she goes home and types them up on multiple carbons (no xeroxes or scanners here, alas!) for the next day.

I got up the nerve to compliment her, the lowly rehearsal pianist addressing the star. She fixed a gimlet eye on me. "What's the big deal? I type sixty words a minute." She's a marvel, always prepared and professional.

Though it's thrilling beyond words to meet a gay icon like La Merm, my target, of course, is composer Cole Porter. It's been ... interesting. Unlike many of his contemporaries, Porter comes from the Midwest, his family loaded with money and status. Where George and Ira and even Youmans took an active interest in me, the aloof Porter clearly views me as his inferior. But that didn't stop the snob from scoping me out, head to toe and all parts between, when m.d. Earl Busby introduced us on that first day of rehearsals.

Frankly, his explicit attention kind of unnerved me. Aside from a few visits to some Russian steambaths and gay bars in Harlem (I'm avoiding those in the Village and Times Square), I've spent six months suppressing my sexuality. There is a vibrant gay culture here, largely under the radar, but the Project comes first. Porter's status lets him be more flamboyant; I don't dare have a pejorative label wrecking my mission.

In the drafty, ramshackle hall, I stood by the piano, meeting the cast and staff. I had dressed for the part of the eighty-eighter: a black felt hat perched jauntily on the back of my head and a warm plaid flannel shirt. I miss the heating systems of the future. They really heat.

The chorines' chatter stopped when the diminutive Porter stepped through the door, dressed in a smart gray suit and blue shirt and holding the score in his long, elegant hands. Busby ushered him over to the piano and introduced me. "Well, Dave, you're a long, tall drink of water," he said in his reedy Indiana accent. "Earl says you're good. How good?"

"Good enough for the job, I hope," I answered. He handed me the score, letting his fingers brush mine. Tempting, yes, but this was not the time for that—if it ever would be. I'd read Porter went for tall athletic types, like his current lover, muscular architect Ed Tauch. I certainly fit the bill. At six-two, I towered over him, and I was trim and fit, the Nate-waist long gone. But no—I needed to impress him in other ways.

So I acted as if I didn't notice his gesture and took my place at the piano. Big, bluff Howard Lindsay assembled the cast, and we began rehearsing. As any musical fan knows, this score has some of the greatest standards of all time: "You're the Top," "I Get No Kick from Champagne," "Blow, Gabriel, Blow," and more. Songs I've known my whole life. I even knew the obscure ones, since I did the show at Juilliard. I breezed through the music, hesitating only over the numbers destined for cutting in Boston.

My facility attracted Porter's attention. As I would learn, though he loved cavorting and practical jokes (so like Ramon!), his attitude towards music was as serious as Gershwin's and Youmans'. His interest in my piano-playing trumped my physical attributes; he wasn't a smooth pianist himself and had trouble transposing keys. "Say, you *are* good!" he said, leaping up from his folding chair when Lindsay called the first break.

"Dave's been studying with Bill Daly," said Busby.

"It's as if you knew the songs already, like magic. You must be some kind of wizard." Porter tilted his brilliantined head to one side, trying to figure me out.

Keep a low profile, Greenbaum! I answered, "Thank you, Mr. Porter," words I'd been mentally saying for decades, in gratitude for all those great songs. Then I went out for coffee with some of the ensemble, including that little pixie, Vivian Vance.

That was how we started. There's been a lot of coffee guzzled since then, usually in quart containers. 1934 coffee is *terrible*. Oh, for the smoothness of Kona, the rich notes of Kalossi Celebes, and the glory of Jamaican Blue Mountain! This swill's only virtue is its strength, which helps us cope with rewrites and endless song changes. William Gaxton, the male lead and a truly funny guy, couldn't handle the high notes on "Easy to Love," and began muttering about going back to Hollywood. Merman, stalking around the chilly hall in a white fur coat, beefed about the naughty lyrics for "Kate the Great." Surprising, since Ethel could swear like a longshoreman. But she found the song "durrrrrty," as orchestrator Hans Spialek put it. The accommodating Cole shelved those tunes for later use ("Easy to Love" would give James Stewart trouble in a few years), and quickly wrote new ones.

But Porter's best moment was coming up with the title number.

We had just moved to the Alvin. Lindsay and Gaxton were discussing the timing of Gaxton's entrance when the actor threw up his hands and said, "In this kind of a spot, anything goes."

I was eating a triple-decker sandwich (pastrami, roast beef, swiss—say, can you believe some people don't know what pastrami is in 1934? It's true. Talk about primitive ages!). Pausing mid-bite, I turned my head in time to see Porter leap out of his seat in the front row, as if zapped with a cattle prod. "Say again, Bill?" he said. "'Anything goes?' Howard, Russel. I've got an idea to work on at home."

The next day, the show had a new title (its fourth) and a title tune, which everyone needed to learn in a hurry, except J.D. Taylor, rehearsal pianist.

#

March 28-April 1, 1934
Nathan Greenbaum arrived safely in SV-4 1934 Yosemite. He noted, with savage *schadenfreude*, the fossilized remains of David's vomit. That was the high point of his day. It was just past dawn, with an icy wind blowing, and the long road to Oakhurst was covered in slush. Nate stumbled soon after he started out, ripping his pants and spraining his ankle. It was horribly swollen, turning ugly rainbow hues, when he finally limped into the Oakhurst Diner. The waitress and local customers fussed over him and telephoned the g.p., Doc Anderson. That grandfatherly man drove over to the restaurant, wrapped the ankle in an elastic bandage, and gave Nate some codeine. He also sent the diner's dishwasher down the street to buy some crutches for Nate, drove him to the Oakhurst Hotel, and didn't leave until he was settled in his room.

I'd never get that kind of attention in 2079, Nate thought. *On the other hand, I'd have Vicodin, ultrasound treatment, and a referral for physical therapy. Trade-offs.*

"Stay off that foot," Dr. Anderson said, plumping pillows. "It needs rest, and so do you."

"Thanks, Doctor," said Nate. *Fat chance.*

The hotel was modest, its young receptionist tripling as bellhop, waiter, and janitor. Wishing he were in an era with mini-ice machines, Nate gave him a generous tip: "Keep those buckets of ice coming, son. Bring some beer, too."

Nate's cover story was that he was an FBI agent looking for a Red radical. The residents, starting with the ones in the diner, never doubted him. These small town residents didn't like Communists one bit. He hobbled around for two days, showing David's picture everywhere in vain.

He could have hitched a ride, maybe to Fresno. I got lucky with a delivery van like that two trips ago. Well, I need to go there, anyway.

Fresno had more connections than tiny Oakhurst, and Nate got his first bit of luck at the station. "Yeah, I think I saw this joe," said the ticket seller from behind his iron grill. "Heh. Looks like your twin."

"Remember where he went?" Nate wobbled on his crutches. *Is it a lead? Is it?*

"Bus to Frisco. I remember thinking he seemed sick as a dog."

San Francisco? What the hell?

Nate thanked the man for complicating his life. He knew nothing about the San Francisco theatre scene, if David was searching for jobs in his old line of work. On the other hand, his brother could do other things: nightclub work, music lessons, radio. Hell, even tree trimming. That was how he'd paid his student loans; he said it was healthier than bartending. This period's tools weren't as nice as modern ones, but the techniques were similar.

I don't have time for San Francisco! Nate urgently needed to place his monitors throughout the Dust Bowl states before the huge storms of April and May. The next stop was Toledo, for the Auto-Lite strike in May. That was crucial to his own studies, and might be dangerous—two people died and hundreds were injured—though he'd promised Isis he'd stay on the mob's outskirts. Then he'd go to Minnesota, for the summerlong general strike there, with a side trip to Chicago in July to record Dillinger's death. The rest of his trip would have him bouncing between Minnesota and textile factories in New England and the South for strikes there.

Did he have *any* chance to go to San Francisco? Rippers needed to be flexible, but within limits. However much he itched to follow David's trail while it was hot, those micro-monitors came first. The Dust Bowl funding helped make his research possible, and had its own scientific value. He might be able to go west between the Auto-Lite strike and Dillinger. The West Coast waterfront workers would be striking until July, which would lead to the unionization of the western ports.

I'd lose days in Minnesota, but in a good cause. I nearly included those dockworkers in my original itinerary... So— San Francisco in June. And maybe I'll find David there. Maybe not.

"I need a ticket to Amarillo, Texas," he told the agent, who blinked at him in surprise.

"Not going after that anarchist in Frisco?"

Nate looked at his brother's smiling face before shoving the photograph into his coat pocket. "Unfortunately, I got other things to do first."

#

From the diary of J.D. Taylor, November 22, 1934—6:00 AM
Good thing I'm from the future, and knew this show would be a smash, because you wouldn't have thought so from the

102

trouble we had in Boston. Lindsay and Crouse managed to finish the finale on the train north, though the score's order kept shifting. The cast grumbled: Merman wanted another song; comic Victor Moore bitched his numbers were "humiliating." Somehow, it all came together. Beantown loved us, building momentum for opening night on November twenty-first.

The Great White Way hadn't been this showy in years, people said. Standing with the boys and girls, I peeped at the VIPs togged to the bricks in white ties, furs, orchids, long dresses, and diamonds: Edna Ferber, Oscar Hammerstein, Fiorello La Guardia, Marilyn Miller, Elsa Maxwell. Tickets were going for an unbelievable fifty bucks apiece. As rehearsal pianist, I didn't rate any, but as a backer, I sure did. Funny thing: Vinton Freedley had seen me playing at rehearsals for weeks without recognizing me as the young investor from the spring. He looked completely flabbergasted when I asked for those passes. I gave them to Adam and Mabel and promised Leo and Frannie I'd treat them later in the run.

Earl Busby handled warm-ups for the whole cast, while I did some individual work with Gaxton and played for the dancers. Mostly, I hung around backstage, pitching nickels at cracks with the boys. I lost twenty cents to those sharpers. The Merm passed by, all business, and a chorine (the one who'd never heard of pastrami) said, "I'm a-quiver! Ain'tcha nervous, Miss Merman?"

"Why should I be nervous? I know my lines," she said. Moments later, she nailed "I Get No Kick from Champagne." I watched from the wings, and the applause was almost palpable. I felt oddly warm, too, as if someone were standing right next to me. The spirit of Ramon? Or was it just that the Shuberts had cranked up the heat now that we had actual patrons in the cavernous pastel blue and gray Alvin?

I did earn my keep at the party afterwards, playing the whole score again and again. Not at Sardi's, as you might think, but at the Waldorf Astoria. Sardi's didn't become the destination for opening-night bashes until late in the decade. The leads ignored me, but I got hugs from the ensemble, including perky Vivian, who was destined for a bright future.

Best of all was Cole himself, wandering by with a drink in one hand and a cigarette in the other, listening appreciatively to his own work. "It is good, isn't it?" he said, knowing the answer.

"Doesn't get much better," I agreed, finishing "You're the Top" for the third time.

"You've got a way about you, Wizard. Maybe we can work together again."

I couldn't help myself. I broke out into what Ramon called my "killer smile." "I'd be honored, Mr. Porter," I answered. *Aw, ya-whoo!, as my nephew would say. Porter's 1935 musical is* Jubilee, *a forgotten show with great songs!*

Porter beamed back at me, just as an attractive, dark-haired older woman appeared at his side—his wife Linda. I won't speculate about their relationship; it's not my business. Linda's first husband abused her, and Cole was the original gay blade, but they obviously cared for each other. She was more to him than just a beard. But, while she didn't object (much) to his longtime paramours, she disliked his chasing boys in public. And an opening night party was pretty damn public. I think she took my killer smile as something other than enthusiasm for Porter's music.

"Darling," Porter said, "this is our wizard, Mr. Taylor, the chap I told you about." *See, Linda, it's work, not play.*

She delicately coughed, part dismissal, part real; Linda Porter had health problems all her life. "Of course, how nice. Coley, look, it's Irving and Ellin." Without another glance at me, she sailed off to meet the Berlins. Cole's dark brow furrowed in his elfin face: not at Linda, but at me, for I'd started playing "All Through the Night." Good, keep him guessing.

The night wore on with a succession of highlights. The eighth time I played "Anything Goes," Tallulah Bankhead joined in, fueled by God knows how many old-fashioneds. I swear, her voice is deeper than Gaxton's. Bill Daly, hanging out with Hall of Fame orchestrators Hans Spialek and Robert Russell Bennett, clapped me on the back and called me a good pupil. Then the papers came in with the reviews.

I knew they were raves. I knew *Anything Goes* would run for over four hundred performances, phenomenal for the period. What thrilled me beyond any kick from champagne was this tiny notice: "Composer Vincent Youmans will perform his new composition, 'Caribbean Concerto,' at Orchestra Hall in Chicago on February 16. He is also in negotiations with Twentieth Century Fox Studios for an operetta, with a tentative release in January 1936."

I've done it.

#

June-July, 1934
Nate once again walked into the Oakhurst Hotel, this time on two good ankles. The receptionist-bellboy recognized him and joked, "Need more ice, sir?"

"Just a room for the night," Nate said. *If I were younger, I'd do this in one day, but I'm too damn tired. I'll dump everything in the bank tomorrow, then head to San Francisco.* The Rippers kept a safe-deposit box in Oakhurst, stocked with emergency cash. That would be welcome indeed after all his travels. The box also stored precious data, in case anything happened to a Ripper. Nate had recovered all the

Dust Bowl micro-monitors for Project Haboob. They'd go in the box, so would his footage from Toledo.

I got some terrific material there: those interviews with the Auto-Lite strikers, their families, city officials, and the teenaged National Guardsmen. But Isis will be furious when she sees the "Battle of Toledo." He had filmed nearly everything: the picketers improvising slingshots of inner tubes and using them to fling bricks at the Auto-Lite plant; their repeated attacks on the building; and the National Guard's escalating responses, from fire hoses and gas bombs to bayonets and gunfire. *If only I could edit the parts where that rock clipped my ear and I was blind and puking from the gas. Oh, well.*

The next morning, after a greasy breakfast at the Oakhurst Diner, he put the monitors and the Toledo files in the bank, and hopped a bus to San Francisco. The town was boiling with strife. Nate began haunting the waterfront as a reporter, interviewing striking longshoremen and sailors, as well as shopkeepers and businessmen. Many people sympathized with the strikers, but everybody felt the pinch because the port had been closed for so long. He even talked with two salesmen from competing chemical firms, each eagerly supplying the authorities with free samples of tear and nausea gas. *You bastards, have you ever "sampled" your products? Nah, too busy making money out of civil unrest.*

Those interviews, despite their historical value, irritated Nate no end. His next, though, was deeply moving. It followed a raucous meeting of the International Longshoremen and Warehousemen Union on June 17. Nate stood with nearly three thousand men who roared their rejection of a proposed settlement. The union president, Joseph Ryan, had signed the deal without the members' approval. He tried to talk to the crowd. The workmen, all in black jeans and waving their white caps—"West Coast Stetsons"—booed him off the stage.

"Some fun, eh?" yelled a man in Nate's ear.

"I'll say!" *This drama rivals anything on Broadway.* "Hey, since it looks like this shindig's over, I'll stake you a beer in exchange for an interview. I'm Nate Newton, reporter."

"Sure thing! I'm Howard Sperry."

Rippers have to roll with the punches, but Nate found it hard to stay cool interviewing Sperry in a noisy dive close by the Civic Auditorium. *This is his final testament. This poor guy'll get shot about two weeks from now—shot in the back by the cops. Damn, this job is hard sometimes.*

On July 3rd, Nate took his place on Rincon Hill with thousands of strikers and spectators. He leaned on a wooden railing, recording the action as the warehouse owners tried using scabs to move goods at Pier 38. They were getting desperate; they'd been losing money each day the port was closed. When the strikers blocked the trucks, the police tried clearing the way with clubs. Nate slipped off before the cops began hurling tear gas and the strikers, bricks and railroad spikes.

Both sides took the Fourth of July as a day of truce. Nate used the quiet to set up a wide-angle minicam on a tall fence post at Rincon Hill and another at the union soup kitchen on Steuart Street. He didn't know "Bloody Thursday" as well as the Battle of Toledo, but he did know those areas would be so crazy, no Ripper had any business near them. The cops would fire on the crowd at the kitchen, while Rincon Hill would look like revolutionary Paris, with the strikers building a barricade of rubble and repelling three assaults before dispersing.

The next morning, he wandered the Embarcadero just after dawn, looking for a safe spot from which to record other conflicts. Two burly men with stout clubs stood in front of a shuttered dry goods store with a sign in its window: "CLOSED UNTIL THE BOYS WIN." Nate remembered them; he'd interviewed them the week before. For a dollar, they let him up onto their roof.

"I know you're not yellow," one said, pointing at Nate's still-healing ear. "Not after getting clobbered in Toledo. Don't blame you for wanting to keep your distance when things get hot today." He thumped his club in his palm. "Me and Doug gotta protect our place, though."

"Good luck."

His vantage point gave him a clear view of Pier 30, where scabs, strikers, and police battled through the day: fire hoses, gas canisters, fisticuffs. He glanced at his watch around one o'clock and spared a thought for Howard Sperry and Nick Bordoise, a volunteer at the union kitchen, who were dying only blocks away. The city was a war zone.

When the sun began sinking into the Pacific, Nate made his way down the fire escape. Doug was still standing on guard in front; his partner was inside, wrapping a bandage around his arm.

"You okay?" Nate asked.

"I'm tired, but whole," said Ewan. "Got cut by a damned gas bomb, but after it banged off me, Doug chucked it back at the cops." He grinned at the memory. ""But, Mr. Newton, it's not safe on the streets. There's goon squads, and the Governor's sending in the Guard."

Because sending in nervous, armed teenaged Guardsmen worked so well in Toledo, thought Nate. "It's only a mile to my hotel, and there's still daylight."

Ewan rubbed his chin. "You're welcome to bunk with us, have a bite."

Nate considered it, then agreed. Despite his regular self-defense training, the roving thugs worried him. He paid

Ewan fifty cents for his snack and Coke and stood watch outside for a while, letting the men get a nap.

He made it back to his hotel near City Hall just after dawn, recording the signs of destruction along the way. In the days that followed, he retrieved his minicams and filmed the massive funeral procession for the victims and the general strike that followed it. On July 17, he prepared his files for the Oakhurst box, feeling pleased with his work. *If only I could find any sign of David. I'm not getting any sleep, doing interviews on the waterfront in the day, and covering theatres, clubs, and bars at night.* He had two pictures of David, both photoshopped to 1930s standards: one adapted from a Yale security camera, one from an older photo. Most people said the fatter David looked like Nate. Eighteen identified the slimmer David as Cary Grant. Nobody'd seen him. Nate even telephoned every Greenbaum in San Francisco, though David had probably changed his name.

Rose is right: he must be in New York. Well. After Dillinger, I'll start hunting there.

#

From the diary of J.D. Taylor, November 22, 1934—10:30 PM

When I first met the Village bum, Joe Gould, Mr. Terracino warned me about his skill at canvassing for his personal Fund. He didn't exaggerate. For months, Joe would pop up in my path with a happy, "Hi, Bronko." I've learned it's a football player's name, a tribute to our first violent encounter. Joe even noticed when I went to Colorado, since it meant a drop in his weekly income. He bitched about it, like Reb Nachum, the beggar in *Fiddler.*

Usually, he approached me for a hand-out, but today I reversed things. I was walking down Sixth Avenue, feeling happy after the glorious opening night and the even grander news of Youmans' concerto, when I saw Gould stuffing newspapers (always the *Times*) in his oversized clothes to ward against the chill.

Feeling generous, I started singing Youmans and Caesar's classic, "Tea For Two." I pointed at Alice McCollister's, a tearoom that was coziness itself, with lovely open fireplaces, warm red tile floors, and tiny rustic wooden furniture. I loved it, even though my knees don't fit under the tables. What's more, it was a place that welcomed Joe. Many Village folks genuinely liked the filthy scrounger.

Joe started conducting with a rolled up paper. "Bronko! Delightful to hear your dulcet tones. But maybe something stronger than tea?"

I stopped singing. "I'm asking you to tea, Joe. Do you want it or not?" He nodded. Better free muffins and tea than nothing at all.

I pulled open the heavy, bronze-edged door, and we settled by the first fireplace. Alice herself brought us a floral-patterned teapot and a three-tiered tray full of toasty English muffins, little cakes, and those crustless sandwiches. I welcomed the tea, since my headache from last night lingered. When he wasn't stuffing himself (he ate almost a full jar of marmalade), Joe prattled on about his Oral History and his enemies, the "radicals" at the Raven Poetry Circle. I had tuned him out, reliving last night's triumphs, when he unexpectedly leaned forward, and hoarsely whispered, "The radicals say I don't belong. Maybe I don't. But you'd know about that. You don't belong here, either, Bronko. Misfits, both of us."

"Excuse me?"

Joe blinked his rheumy eyes and leaned back in his seat. "More tea?"

This guy is screwy, as the locals say, but I wish he'd stop singling me out like that. It's creepy. He doesn't talk that way to anyone else.

Alice brought us the check—decorated with a little drawing of a robber holding a gun on a man, and captioned THE BAD NEWS. Joe squinted at it and rasped, "Bad news. Bad news. Bad news. Yes, bad news." He coughed horribly, or he might have kept saying it.

I was regretting my charitable impulse. Still, I flipped him a quarter. "Go to a real flophouse tonight, Joe. Don't use this for gin, then sleep in a doorway. Promise?"

"Yassuh, Massa. Whateber youse say." He trumpeted his nose into a napkin and headed out the door, his portfolio tucked under his arm.

Smiling ruefully, Alice picked up the money, but she pitched the napkin in the fireplace. I headed for home, where I wrote this up before grabbing a taxi to the Alvin.

#

November 21, 1934
After filming John Dillinger's gruesome death from four angles—including the disgusting images of people dipping cloth in the pool of his blood—Nate spent the summer and fall bouncing like a ping pong ball. He interviewed hundreds of striking textile workers throughout the South and New England, and narrowly dodged arrest when Georgia Governor Eugene Talmadge declared martial law, throwing picketers into an old World War I prisoner-of-war camp.

Whenever he could, he went to New York. He walked for miles in areas he thought David might favor: the theatre district, Greenwich Village, Russian and Turkish steambaths, and countless nightclubs. The gays he encountered were friendly—sometimes too friendly—but decidedly uncooperative.

They don't believe my cover story about Reds; they think I'm after David because he's gay, and they don't want to give up one of their own. One flamboyant fairy in a red tie admired the slim David: "I'd remember *him,* dearie. I'd like to lay my hands on him, too. Drop a line if you find him. I'm Miss Peg. Don't be vague, ask for Peg!" He threw his arm around Nate and planted a wet smack on his cheek.

"Thanks, Peg. I'll be in touch."

I'm not getting anywhere with this hit-or-miss approach, Nate thought, riding the bus back to his cheap hotel in Brooklyn. Unfortunately, his schedule handcuffed him; he could rarely spent more than a couple of days at a time in the city, not enough to set up a search pattern.

The only extended stay he had in New York was in mid-August for the United Textile Workers' special convention, where they set forth their demands to the factory owners. Nate ran a picture of David in several newspapers, captioned HAVE YOU SEEN THIS MAN? With his hotel's phone number. The quality of the reproduction was wretched. So were the responses. Teenagers called his number with giggling, silly prank answers, ranging from FDR to King Kong to Lou Gehrig. Miss Peg called, too, and made shameless suggestions. Only one fellow seemed convincing, a ticket seller from Grand Central Station—a call that came in just as Nate was packing for Alabama.

"Saw this guy in early summer," the man said. The line made his voice crackle, but he sounded sure of himself. "He was going to Denver with this little old lady, a real lunger. Italian, right?"

"Italian?" Nate asked.

"Yeah, they were talking Italian. He called her Zia Lena—Aunt Lena—and he was teasing her, real sweet-like. She kept saying, *'Basta, basta!'* I know that means 'Enough!' because my neighbor yells it all the time at her husband."

"Do you remember if it was a round-trip or not?"

"One way. Don't know about the tall man, but Saint Peter will punch Zia Lena's next ticket."

"Okay. Thanks for the tip." Nate hung up the phone, pondering. *That man sounded so certain, but why would David be taking an old lady with TB to Colorado? Does he even speak Italian? Maybe with his Spanish? And Denver's not exactly a hot spot for entertainment. Nah. The fellow must be wrong.*

The search stretched into November, to the 21st—Rose's hunch about the opening night of *Anything Goes.* Nate ran into trouble as soon as he got to the Alvin Theatre. His press credentials weren't the right ones for the roped-off photographers' section. The veterans jeered at his chutzpah; they'd earned their spots. Nate slunk over to the public area, where scores of fans had taken positions for the best views of the red-carpet area. His only advantages were his height and his determination. For appearances' sake, he brought a Leica, but mostly he scanned the crowd for his brother. The minicams in his Ripperglasses recorded everything.

Hundreds of well-dressed types swept their glamorous way inside, but David wasn't among them. The crowd broke up then—the fans heading for home, the press for nearby bars. Nate followed the Fourth Estate into Gallagher's Steak House, next door to the theatre.

A more genial photographer tried chatting him up at the crowded bar. "You're new at this, Mac. I can tell. You spend more time fiddlin' with your glasses than taking good shots. Trust your instincts. Just press that shutter."

"What's it to you, pal?" Nate scowled at the man. He tossed back his whiskey sour, and began elbowing his way to the door.

"What a sorehead! Can't take a bit of friendly advice? Well, up yours!" the photographer said.

Nosey bastard, thought Nate. He reclaimed his spot near the lobby entrance, and stood there, shivering, until the happy audience exited at the play's end. No sign of David, even though he hung around until the house manager— who gave him a funny look through his wire-rims—locked the Alvin's doors.

He scooped a crumpled playbill from the sidewalk. *At least I can grab this for Rose, so this evening wasn't a total loss.*

#

From the diary of J.D. Taylor, November 23, 1934, 1:00 AM
Got to stay calm and write this as it happened. Though my contract ended with the opening, I went to the Alvin last night. Two reasons: to see the show from the house and to find my favorite scarf, which I'd forgotten. Frannie had knitted it for me in a nice dark green, and the nights were getting colder.

"Hey, Big Mike," I asked the guard at the stage door, "have you seen a green scarf?"

"Mr. Jenkins has the lost and found box," said Mike. "Geez, the things the big wigs left behind."

"Thanks." I made my way to the Alvin's austere lobby, all polished black marble, and through a door to the house manager's cluttered office. Spofford Jenkins, a short, fussy type with wire-rimmed glasses, beamed at me. The *Anything Goes* family was in a terrific mood. That's what hits do.

"Your scarf, Dave? I found it with one of Mr. Porter's cigarette lighters. See?" The silver lighter was engraved: STOLEN FROM COLE PORTER.

I laughed. "Well, I hope he keeps better track of the case his wife gave him last night—solid gold and covered with jewels. Not for the likes of us, brother!"

"Brother! That reminds me! Do you have one?"

"What?" I paused while folding the scarf. "No. A sister, died in 1919."

Jenkins sat on the edge of his desk, knocking over a stack of receipts. "There was this fellow outside last night, looked like a relative of yours. He had a great camera, a Leica, and was taking pictures of the swells."

Nate! I broke into a sweat, though the Alvin was chilly as usual. "There is this one, um, unsavory relative. Wrong side of the sheets, you know." I laid a finger on the side of my nose—a silly gesture, but I'd seen enough locals do it to adopt the mannerism for keeping something secret. "Always trying to put a touch on me."

The manager nodded. "Aw, hell. He needs dough, let him pawn that camera."

"It's sad, but I really don't want to have anything to do with him. Enough's enough." *Sorry, Nate.*

"Say no more," Jenkins said. "That mooch won't find you through us. I'll tell the front of house staff and Big Mike. What Mike knows, everyone knows."

"Thanks." Feeling uneasy, I abandoned my plans to sit in the house and took refuge in the wings, safe with my theatrical family. Ethel Merman sang, but all I heard in my head was Joe Gould chanting, "Bad news, bad news."

#

From the diary of J.D. Taylor, November 23, 1934

I'm feeling better this morning. Maybe Nate's here. Maybe not. If he is, good luck finding me in sunny Mexico. No, I'm not running away. This is part of the Project. Gershwin would travel to Mexico in late 1935, after *Porgy and Bess* opened. He hoped the country would inspire him, since an earlier jaunt to Havana resulted in his "Cuban Overture." He didn't find enough indigenous Mexican music for another composition, but this trip will be different. I'll be there.

Since Joseph David Taylor is supposed to have spent years in Mexico, I'd better familiarize myself with the thirties' version of the place. I'm fluent and already know the geography. What's more, Ramon taught me a bit about regional musical styles, so I know there's more to *son jarocho* than "La Bamba." So I'll scout ahead, plan some good stuff to show George next year.

After Thanksgiving (I'm invited to the enormous Finkelstein bash in Brooklyn!), I've booked passage on the *S.S. Siboney* to Veracruz. First class.

Hey, it's homework.

Chapter 5

"Children and Art" —Stephen Sondheim

November 27, 1934

Nate continued his stakeout of the Alvin Theatre, night after freezing cold night. More than once, peering into the black marble lobby, he made eye contact with the manager in the wire-rims, who frowned at him. As the last patrons left on November 27th, the manager followed them and planted himself in front of Nate. He was only five-five, but he had backup; a broad-shouldered galoot hovered behind him.

"What's the story, bub? Got some reason for hanging around here, or do you just like the view?" Specs said.

"I'm, uh, investigating a man. Seen this guy?" Nate fumbled in his pocket for the photos of David.

Specs and Galoot leaned over to look in the glow from the Alvin's marquee. "Haven't seen him. What's he done?"

"He's a Red, a fanatical Commie."

Specs snorted. "So's my brother-in-law. I'm not crazy about it, but it's not illegal. Loitering is. Clear out. Mr. Freedley thinks you're making the patrons nervous."

Nate was cold, tired, and depressed. Part of him wanted to argue, to flash his forged credentials, to show these men he really was indeed after a criminal. But the rest wanted to go back to his crummy hotel room and crank the radiator as high as it could go. *Anything Goes* would run for hundreds of performances. If David was here, he might not come to see it for months.

The pair waited for his answer. The galoot tapped his large booted foot, as if he were itching to kick something, like maybe Nate's keester. Another gust of icy wind blew through him. He pulled his coat close and muttered, "Fine. I'm going."

The pair watched him hail a cab. Big Mike turned to Mr. Jenkins. "Do you think Mr. Taylor's a Red?"

"I've never heard Dave talk about anything but music. He's got money in the show. That doesn't sound like a Commie to me."

"Should we tell him this clown was here?"

Jenkins pondered for a minute. "Nah. Not unless he comes back. We put a flea in his ear, that's for sure."

#

From the diary of J.D. Taylor, December 1-5, 1934, at sea
Sitting in the veranda café, sipping coffee while Havana recedes through art-deco windows—a guy could get used to this. No wonder people spoke of "the romance of travel." In first class, with servants catering to your every need, life was pretty damn good. And there are other kinds of scenery besides tropical islands; specifically, a steward named Alberto, whose handsome face lights up every time I spoke Spanish to him.

But all I do is look. Only two years ago, the poet Hart Crane made a pass at a crewman on the *S.S. Orizaba,* the *Siboney*'s sister ship on this same route. Crane got brutally beaten up, jumped overboard, and drowned. *Alberto, you're an eyeful, but not for me.*

There are other kinds of fun. I've danced every night with the women tourists. I played enough piano in the lounge to attract the attention of Sidney, the stout, excitable cruise director, who had me teach the ship's band songs from *Anything Goes,* and got in some fierce rounds of deck golf with Amelia Küster, a fourteen-year-old whose bright smile reminded me of Hannah's. Amelia was heading for her father's vanilla plantation with her grandmother, Helga, after stays in London and New York.

Amelia turned into a valuable contact. After I escorted her on the daylong excursion to the Uxmal temples near Progreso ("Visit Maya-land!"), Helga gave me the name of the family's manager during our final dinner at sea. "We have many small houses in Mexico. Plenty of room, Herr Taylor, much nicer than the hotels. Tchah! Such a country. Conrad should sell everything and join his brother, growing fruit in Anaheim. That is in California, you know."

"Near Holly-wood!" Amelia said. She was a rabid film fan, which had helped her English. I think I'll send her some of those movie photo-magazines once I get back to New York.

I glanced over at the bandleader. "Amelia, go ask Jack to play a foxtrot for us." When she was out of earshot, I said, "Frau Küster, your offer is generous, but I'm Jewish."

Her pale blue gaze didn't alter. "A concern elsewhere, but this is Mexico. You have been good to the child. I could not climb the hills to those temples, and she did wish to see them. A kindness for a kindness."

"She's a darling," I said, meaning it. We drank tawny port as Amelia skipped back from the bandstand—a gaudy structure shaped not like one of Cortés' caravels, but a Viking ship. Damned if I know why. I'm surprised Sidney didn't put Jack and the boys in horned helmets.

"Frau Küster?"

119

"Hmm?"

"Keep after your son with that California idea. The climate's better than Europe's—and I don't mean sunshine. Come on, Amelia! Let's dance!"

#

December 11, 1934
Nate went back to the Alvin several more times, all in vain. The first time, he bought a ticket, and sneered at the house manager as he entered. He recorded the show, knowing Rose would appreciate it. Maybe Yale could make a deal with whoever owned the rights. *Corny, but good music. Amazing how loud that actress is without a mic!* The other visits, he watched the patrons from the safety of Gallagher's Steak House to avoid another run-in with Specs and Galoot.

The search was wearing him down and costing much too much. He'd had to resort to the time-honored time-traveler's method of raising instant cash: betting on sports. Not outrageous amounts, nothing that would draw attention to himself or bankrupt any bookies, but enough to cover expenses. Following the NFL and the college football games was easy for a sports junkie like Nate.

It also led to the best fun he had all fall: the historic NFL championship game at the Polo Grounds. A night of freezing rain had turned the field into a chunk of grassy ice, making it hard for either team to score. At halftime, the Giants cleverly switched from cleats to basketball sneakers. Better traction helped them trounce the Chicago Bears in what became known as the "sneakers game." Nate enjoyed himself, cheering with the rowdy Giants fans, getting drunk, and filming every minute. *This is great! And I bet Yale will be able to sell this footage to one of the sports-nets for big bucks. I never would have stayed in 1934 this long on my*

original mission, so I guess I have David to thank for this.
He hates football. Ha.

Two days after the game, he woke up with a horrible cold—a gift from his pals in the bleachers. He staggered to the window of his dingy hotel room in Hell's Kitchen. A lovely view of freight engines, chugging along Eleventh Avenue; warehouses covered with snow; a glimpse of the gray Hudson. He'd picked the place because it was cheap and close to the theatre district and the waterfront. When he wasn't looking for David, he interviewed longshoremen about their work conditions. Sighing, he grabbed his towel and clothes and hustled down the icy hall to the tiny bathroom. He showered in the moldy shower stall—at least he had warm water this time—and shaved in a spotty, poorly lit mirror. He blew his nose. His reflection stared back at him. "I want to go home. How about you? Yeah, that's what I thought. This is the last day."

Oatmeal, coffee, and watery orange juice at the diner down the street didn't improve his mood. He bought some aspirins at the Rexall, dry-swallowed two, bundled himself against the cold, and set off for Greenwich Village. Given David's lifelong love of the area, Nate suspected he'd live there, given the choice. He'd searched six times in vain; was this the lucky seventh?

It didn't look promising. The weather kept people off the streets, and those who were out didn't want to stand around answering questions. He did get a couple of nibbles—vague "Yeah, I mighta seen him around" responses that could mean anything. But when one of those nibbles turned into, "He looks like the guy in the Mae West movie, only more Jewish," Nate suppressed a groan and moved elsewhere.

He haunted Washington Square, interviewing anyone who stopped to admire the Christmas tree. He popped in and out of cafés on Bleecker, where he'd warm up with

121

coffee and show the staff David's photo. He tramped along countless side streets, passing rows of dormered houses with latticed windows. *Where are you, David? Are you hiding on the other side of one of those white doorways— cozy and warm and content in 1934? Shit. The Village looks so small on a map, but it's packed with stupid dinky streets. Goddamn Dutch colonists and their cowpaths.* Nate peered down Gay Street: two young women, clearly sisters, laughing as they hustled along. *Follow them or get lunch?* He sneezed. *Lunch, something filling and hot.*

The Pepper Pot on West 4th Street was nearby. Its menu boasted of their "real Southern chef" and fresh eggs, straight from the owner's farm in New Jersey. Inspired by that combination, Nate ordered chicken-fried steak and eggs. *Isis can scold me about my diet soon enough. I'm eating what I want today.*

The Pepper Pot's rustic interior was as dark and gloomy as his mood. The other patrons, however, seemed to be having a grand time. A man in his early thirties in a pale yellow sweater was carving chunks from the globby, two-foot tall wax candle on his table. Every table had a similar mammoth candle. Once, they'd been wine bottles with single candles in them. Scores of candles must have melted over the originals to get them that thick. The artist's companion giggled and offered suggestions: "I don't think giraffes have ears like that, Willem."

"Mine does," he said, displaying his work. "He's listening for lions."

Two men were playing chess at a small table. "Checkmate!" one announced. "Pay the tab, Bob. I need to meet Lynn uptown."

"See if I write another play for *you* any time soon," the loser groused, but he was smiling as he spoke. "Ta, Alfred."

Nate resented their having a good time. He resented David's stealing the SlingShot and fucking up his life. He resented the dim light in this creaky old building and the stupid monster candles on every table.

But the steak and eggs were grand, one of the best things he'd eaten anywhen. He paid his check, donned his coat and muffler against the chill, and headed back into the fading afternoon light. *I'll walk to Christopher Street. If I come up empty, I'll call it a day.*

As he expected, he got the usual noes from the people he stopped on his way west. A game of ringolevio on Cornelia Street proved a happy distraction. He didn't interrupt the play, figuring David was unlikely to have anything to do with a bunch of street urchins. One dark-haired skinny kid in a knitted green cap had the making of a fine general, with far more captured prisoners on his side. *Bertie would be good at this, if only they played it 140 years later,* Nate thought. *I miss him, even his snarky remarks.* He kept on walking.

In his own era, Sheridan Square, the small triangle of land at Christopher and Seventh Avenue, was a pleasant, fenced-in public garden, carefully tended by locals. In late 1934, it was a litter-strewn traffic island, with three delivery vans illegally parked next to a stack of wooden crates. A small, shabby man sat on one of the crates, feeding pigeons from a paper bag.

"This one's for you, Anna," the man said, chucking a piece of bread. "Fiorello's already had two."

Aw, why not? "Excuse me, sir. Have you ever seen this man?"

The man raised a grubby hand. "Wait. Anna Pavlova keeps losing her meal to the predatory actions of Fiorello, who sheems to think he's William Howard Taft today. Feathered pig!" He rose to get a look at the photo, but teetered and abruptly sat back down. Alarmed, the pigeons retreated to the safety of the parked vans.

"No need to get up, sir." Nate shoved the photo under the man's snotty nose.

A smile split the bearded face. "Of coursh I know him! Thatsh Bronko Nagurski. Very fine fellow. He bought me these pants. Hello, Big Bosom! Did you follow Fiorello here from Washington Square?"

Disappointment clobbered Nate. *A Village drunk. Obviously delusional. I just saw Nagurski lose to the Giants on Sunday. I doubt he buys trousers for bums.*

But then the little guy continued: "Yes, Bronko's lovely. Sings like an angel.'" He began singing "Tea For Two." The birds listened to his rasping melody, but kept their beady eyes on the heel of stale bread in his hand.

He seemed to recognize the photo. He says "Bronko" can sing. Does this mean anything at all? Nate tried probing further. "Have you heard him sing many times? Does he sing around here?"

"Squawk skree skree!" the man addressed the birds, shredding and scattering bread. He beamed at Nate. "I speak fluent seagull, but the pigeons can translate a bit, especially Einstein."

"This man," Nate persisted, "have you heard him sing?"

"Of coursh I have! And he took me for tea. And muffins." His face fell. "But not now. He got the Bad News and he's gone away, away, away."

"Away? Where?"

The drunk began drumming his feet on the crate. Several bugs, disturbed by the vibrations, skittered out onto the curb. "La cucaracha, la cucaracha, ai, ai, ai! Bronko's gone to Mexico!"

Nate didn't know what to think. Points in favor: a possible ID, a connection with music, David and Ramon often went to Mexico. Points against: a highly unreliable witness, David wouldn't have a sports nickname, maybe the bum only mentioned Mexico because those cockroaches triggered the song in his addled brain. *Shit.*

"Well, thanks for your help." Nate turned to go. The sot clutched his sleeve.

"You're not from here, either, like m'buddy, Bronko. But if I *have* helped you, you should contribute shomething to the Joe Gould Fund." He stuck out his hand, waiting. He happily accepted a dollar. "Yes, indeed, this will come in handy!" He dipped his head and headed towards the brightly lit windows of Stewart's Cafeteria.

Nate watched him go, then noticed a policeman patrolling the opposite side of Christopher Street. He jogged over. "Excuse me, officer, but do you know that short man in the brown coat, the one staggering into Stewart's?"

The cop, whose florid face revealed his Irish origins, chuckled. "Indeed I do. That's the li'l Professor, Joe Gould. A regular souse, but harmless. Though he's been known to nick things now and ag'in, small stuff."

"So I shouldn't put much faith in anything he says?"

"Depends on how sozzled he is. Joe's not stupid; he's a Harvard grad. But he's a sponge."

"I see. Thank you, Officer." Nate pulled out the photo. "I'm looking for this guy. Joe seemed to recognize him."

The policeman studied the picture. "Looks a bit like you, if I may say so. But you know how the fortune teller in the carny works? When she tells you what you want to hear, you pay her more. If Joe thought he could squeeze you by saying he knew this fella, well, he'd say this was his best buddy."

"Thanks."

Screw 1934. I'm going home.

*From the diary of J.D. Taylor, December
5-28, 1934, in Mexico*

Helga Küster didn't waste time. On my second morning at
the Veracruz Hotel, Juan Guzmán, the Küsters' manager,
called for me in a battered Ford truck. "Señora Küster says,
get your bags. I'll take you to one of their best houses."
We rattled along the road to Santa Elena, a small village
sixty miles north of Veracruz. He brought me to a modest
pink and yellow house with a resident housekeeper-cook
Delores Hernández, short, stout, smiling, and a cousin of
Juan's. I explained I didn't want the usual tourist spots, but
the more remote areas with unusual music. The cousins
looked at each other and spoke as one: "Señor Taylor,
you must meet Victor." Victor was Dolores' son. He played
the guitar, knew the countryside, and had two horses. I
promptly hired him, though I was antsy about horses. Big,
scary beasties, but necessary evils in a place where even the
best roads were lousy. Well, I knew Gershwin rode horses
on his Mexican trip. I guess I should use the future tense:
will ride. If George could do it, so could I.

In the end, we traveled by every means possible: horses,
mules, motorcycles, river barges, autos, and on foot. I
ached all over while riding Pegaso, but Victor kept saying,
"Come on, *Profesor* Taylor!"—everyone's convinced I'm an
academic— "It's only a little farther!"

And we'd get to another village. Three hours later. *Oy.*

But it was worth it. Santa Elena made a good base camp,
from which we visited different areas. I took notes on the
Afro-Caribbean-flavored *son jarocho* near Veracruz, the
pulsating rhythms of the drums and flutes of the Totonacs,
the fiddle and guitar trios of the Huastecs. I spent pesos like
water, and brought the Indians gifts from the States—small

medical kits, pocket knives, aluminum saucepans for cooking. Everywhere I went, I told the people of these desperately poor regions that I'd be back next year, with a good friend, a musician even better than I was. Then the entire village, mobbed me, calling, *"¡Sí, sí, Profesor Taylor! ¡Hasta la vista!"* It happened so often, you'd think they'd rehearsed it.

Victor and I also spent five days in Mexico City and Taxco—two places Gershwin would visit, so I needed to get a feel for them. The Mexico City I remembered had been built on the ruins of the 1985 and 2057 quakes; weirdly, many of the old buildings from the colonial days survived those (and older) disasters. Maybe because they weren't so tall? Well, I'm no engineer. Victor had never been to the capital, and its size overwhelmed him. "You think that's big, come to New York," I told him.

In Taxco, I bought a silver belt buckle for Victor and a brooch for his mother, in return for their good care. The silversmiths there, so famous in my time, were just getting going in the thirties. The prices were ridiculously low. I bought souvenirs for my neighbors, and gifts for the Küsters, too.

Before I left Mexico, I visited the Küsters' ranch near Jalapa to thank them for their generosity. Helga accepted a pair of candlesticks with a slight sniff, having seen better goods in Europe, but Amelia loved her charm bracelet.

"Write to me," she said, shaking her spangly wrist. "I wish to improve my English. You can be my pen pal. The girls I knew in London had many pen pals, all around the world. Some collect the stamps in beautiful albums."

"If it is permitted," I said, looking toward Conrad Küster, a wiry, angular man with dark circles under his eyes. Business woes—the invention of vanilla extract had devastated cultivation of the plant. The Küsters had other ventures around Veracruz, including a sugar mill, but the Depression had hit them hard.

Conrad nodded. "A good idea, improving the English. We welcome your return next year."

Something told me the Küsters might be in Anaheim by then. In California, you know, as Helga remarked. I'd miss seeing Amelia next year, but Juan and Dolores and Victor and all those musical Indians would still be here. And George Gershwin would meet them.

#

From the diary of J.D. Taylor, January 3, 1935
While tramping around the Mexican back country with Victor, I began letting my beard grow out. Vincent Youmans' beard made him look like a French monk. With my coloring, I look more like a Russian revolutionary. It's not as fuzzy as the ones those crazy ballplayers in Denver had, but this era doesn't favor facial hair. At that final dinner in Jalapa, Amelia made her preferences clear. "Before, you look so handsome. You have the nice chin. Now…" She stuck out her tongue. My neighbors didn't approve of the beard, either, though they loved their Mexican gifts (silver from Taxco, rum, vanilla beans, serapes, and a sombrero and jumping beans for Leo).

But that's not all. Today, I went to an optician for a pair of glasses. The Greenbaums tend to be nearsighted, so we all get our eyes fixed in our teen years. I told the man I wanted glasses with plain glass. He stared at me. "You nuts, pal?"

"Trying to look more intellectual," I explained.

Ever see pictures of early twenty-first century hipsters? That's what I sort of look like, except I have a real fedora, not one with a cheater brim, and my scarves are wool, not cashmere. But I bet if I put on a v-neck t-shirt and skinny jeans, I could pass for my own grandfather.

What's behind this makeover? Simple. If Nate is lurking around Times Square, I don't want him recognizing me right away. I can't do anything about my height, unfortunately. Thank goodness for hats, including real fedoras.

#

From the diary of J.D. Taylor, February 28, 1935
No sign of Nate. Jenkins at the Alvin hasn't seen him, either. Maybe it was a false alarm. I think I'll keep the beard and glasses, even so.

I'm at the Golden Eagle again. Mr. Terracino likes me, so after my replacement got in a fistfight with Jimmy, he took me back. He knows that the next time Broadway calls (this fall, if Porter remembers his promise), I'll be off once more.

"Hey, that's show biz. I get it," he said. "But you're popular. The customers like you. So does Petunia."

I'm still giving Leo lessons; he's coming along well. I've been taking him to shows, too. Last fall, he howled at Bert Lahr and Ray Bolger in the revue *Life Begins at 8:40*, with music by Harold Arlen and lyrics by Ira Gershwin— Ira keeping busy while George orchestrated *Porgy and Bess*. I took him to *Anything Goes* twice, including stops backstage, where he blushed at the half-dressed girls, and the pit, where he played "You're the Top" on the piano after the house emptied.

He liked plays, too, especially ones by Clifford Odets. He told me he'd seen friends' families forced onto the streets, like the Bergers in *Awake and Sing*. This month, we saw *Waiting for Lefty* at the Civic Rep on 14th Street. It had him riveted. Like many in the audience, he joined in the

"Strike! Strike! Strike!" chant at the end, kicking his chair for emphasis. Amazingly effective theatre: you could feel the house falling under the playwright's spell.

But seeing these original Odets productions had me glancing over my shoulder, worried my big brother would suddenly turn up. Nate's specialty is labor history, so he knows plenty about agitprop. When I was doing a seminar on Depression drama in college, he was a newly minted PhD, and gave me tons of research material. All these years later, I'm still proud of that damn seminar paper.

Yet it wasn't the stirring (but manipulative) ending that fascinated Leo. Walking home through a light snowfall, we chatted about the show.

"Know what I liked best, Mr. Taylor? When the actors talked straight at the audience."

"That's called 'breaking the fourth wall.' Actors on a stage are surrounded by visible walls on three sides and a fourth one, separating them from the audience. When an actor delivers his lines as if he's addressing people he shouldn't be able to notice because of that wall, he's breaking it."

Leo stopped, right on the sidewalk of Sixth Avenue, chewing on that. "I liked it. It was *keen.*"

I doubt Clifford Odets ever got more sincere praise.

#

From the diary of J.D. Taylor, March 10, 1935
Last month, Vincent Youmans performed his "Caribbean Concerto" in Chicago to mixed reviews. He recorded it the next week, and I've just bought a copy. It's got flaws—he bit off more than he could chew—but it's popular. I've put a special case in my place to hold the records and sheet music that come from my presence in the past. My two songs (one

written in 2073, the other in 1934) should be the first items, but I don't rank with the greats of this era.

Youmans' film deal with Fox fell through. I don't know the details. I suspect he was being, as my nephew would put it, a total-absol-butthead. I cured his TB, but I can't cure his buttheadedness.

Nor his alcoholism. I saw him tonight, at the Gershwins'; he and George have made up their quarrel. I was playing ping-pong with Oscar Levant, and losing, as usual. Over the past year, Oscar has decided I'm not Public Enemy Number One, but he's still not exactly warm and cuddly. And he plays cutthroat ping-pong. After dropping three games, I put down my paddle in surrender.

Levant flashed his snaggly grin. "C'mon, Davey, I'll get you a drink, if Vince has left us any."

We made our way to the bar. The Gershwins were noshing and chatting with George Kaufman, Youmans, Boots, and composer Vernon Duke. There was meat on Youmans' bones, which pleased me, but it looked like he was working on his third gin rickey. Oscar and I opened cans of Krueger beers, listening to another young songwriter, Burton Lane, at the piano. Levant waggled a finger at Lane. "Maybe when Burton's done, I'll do my famous musical fortune-telling act. I'll predict when Davey here will sell another song or Vince will get a movie deal. Only it's *so* hard to see that far into the future."

I ignored the snide comment as typical Oscar-noise. But Youmans thumped his glass on the bar and began to rise from his stool. Boots shoved him back down. It didn't take much—he was that wobbly and Boots is a big gal. She also promptly changed the subject.

"Great to see you again, David." She turned to the others. "David visited us in Colorado last summer. He had the most amazing vitamins from Mexico. Vince said they made him feel like a new man."

In a sense, that's true.

"Swell!" George said through a mouthful of Ry-Krisps. "You were looking awful puny last year, Junior." He and Youmans were born a day apart; Youmans called George "Old Man."

"Mountain air, Mexican vitamins—a good combination," and Youmans. "I'm fit as a fiddle now." You could barely hear the booze, but it was there.

"That's grand!" said George. He glanced over at the piano. "Hey, Burton, let me in there for a spell."

Kaufman coughed. "Play some Chopin, George. For variety's sake."

"Nope. Gershwin's what you get," George said, punctuating each word with a thumps of his left hand in right palm. He crossed the room and began singing, "It Ain't Necessarily So."

"George should be careful," Kaufman said. "He's played so much of that score, when *Porgy* does open, it'll be a revival."

The others laughed, but I just smiled. Kaufman's joke was familiar to me from my homework. Besides, even with the Gloomy Dean cracking wise, I couldn't concentrate on anything but that music. Something happens every time George plays. I don't quite know how to describe it. The air itself becomes charged, like when there's a lightning storm nearby. When Boots touched my arm, I expected a zap of static electricity. That's how powerful George is.

She pulled me away from the others. "We're not sending announcements yet, but if you can keep May 18 open…"

"Oh!" *Wake up, Greenbaum! You're being invited to a wedding!* "Congrats!" I looked over at Youmans and raised my beer in toast. A slow smile on his face, he lifted his glass.

"I wish you both the very best," I said, knowing that, in my timeline, Boots would divorce him in 1946. She stuck with him through bout after bout of illness, but finally couldn't stand the drinking any more.

What would happen now that I'd dosed Youmans with Minarcin? I didn't know, but I wished them well.

#

January 24, 2079

One part of her dad's job always disturbed Rose. Dr. Nathan Greenbaum spent large chunks of his life in another century. She'd kiss him good-bye, he'd get in the 'Shot, but when she saw him the next day (the lab alternated between arrivals and departures), he wouldn't be just one day older. He'd have weeks or sometimes months under his belt. The time away from his family, he'd never get back. Rippers called it an occupational hazard. Dad and Mom had discussed the issue at length, and Dad had begun cutting back on his missions. He planned to take just one short trip a year after his actual age reached fifty. But now this mess...

How long is he spending in 1934? Has he found Uncle David? What's happening? Her teachers noticed her distraction. Ms. Edison excused her from the afternoon rehearsal of _The Serene Ones:_ "Rose has got some family business. Mira, you read the role of Lavinia." If she weren't so worried about Dad, she would have appreciated the croggled look on Mira O'Toole's face.

She got home before there was any news. The whole family hung around in the den, waiting, waiting. When the phone finally rang; everyone crowded around the screen. Dad looked terrible—circles under his eyes, and yes, some new gray in his hair.

"Well?" said Isis.

133

"I couldn't find him. Danny's driving me home."

"Hey, Dad, you look—ow!" Bertie glared at both his sisters. Rose had smacked him, while Hannah had kicked him.

"How long, Nate?" Isis asked in flat tones. She didn't mean before his arrival home.

A pause. "Nine months, and no baby to show for it. See you soon." He cut the connection before Isis could respond.

She pursed her lips and set down the remote with a sigh. "Well, no matter what, we've still got to eat. Hannah, can you give me a hand?"

While they cooked, Rose began outlining a paper on the Industrial Revolution, even though textile mills were the furthest thing from her mind. Bertie fidgeted. He kicked the couch until Rose snapped at him, then jumped up with the elasticity only boys have.

"I'm *glad* he didn't find Uncle David. So there!" he yelled, and stomped upstairs.

Rose watched her brother's neon blue sneakers disappear from view. *I'm glad, too, bro, but it's not the thing to say. Unless you're a tactless kid.*

Two hours later, the door opened and Nate trudged in. Danny hovered behind him, just long enough to make sure he'd delivered his charge, then flipped his hair in farewell. Nate collapsed on the couch, where Isis handed him a Sam Adams Classic and his family gathered around. Bertie's eyes were suspiciously red, but Rose had no urge to tease him.

"The verdict is that everyone's disappointed," said Nate. "Well, not everyone. My own stuff went great, even better than my original plans. Got some amazing material on the West Coast dock strike. But there were four Council members in the lab, waiting to pounce on me. One even had the nerve to ask why I didn't stay longer!"

"Of course. You have nothing better to do with your life than live it in another century," Isis said.

"Right." Nate took a long pull of his beer and smacked his lips. "Oh, that's good. Anyway, I never found David. Never even had any decent leads. One nut in the Village seemed to know him, but started calling him crazy names and said he went to Mexico. That's when I threw in the towel.

"No funds for another trip right now. They're briefing all Rippers going to the 1930s—there are three coming up—in case any of them wants to visit the Splinterverse instead of the main line. I'm not exactly sure what they expect them to do. Get his ID, his location, and come back with cops? And again, who would pay for everything?"

Rose smothered a giggle in her hand.

"What's the joke?" Isis asked. "We could all use a laugh."

"Weird legal issues: if Uncle David went to Mexico, what kind of extradition laws apply? Those between the U.S. and Mexico today... or in 1934?"

Nate rubbed his temples. "I've already got a headache. Don't make it worse."

"So when do you go back, Dad?" asked Hannah.

He shrugged. "Who knows? The whole program's in an uproar. What's been happening here?"

Isis ticked off her fingers. "The cops have sealed off David's place. They've taken copies of all our devices. Insulting, but understandable. They're keeping Rose's Ally, since it was left in the apartment, but she's coping."

Rose gave her dad what she hoped was an encouraging, I-shall-survive look.

"Finally, we're meeting the lead detective next Sunday, after Bertie's basketball game."

That seemed to trigger something in Nate. "My briefcase! I got goodies." Hannah dashed to the front hall and brought Nate his thirties-era case. He clicked the brass catches, rummaged around, then tossed two minis to Rose and Bertie. "Danny didn't have time to mark these, but one is the 1934 NFL championship game and the other's Ethel Merman in *Anything Goes*. You figure out which is which. Ethel's not wearing a leather helmet."

Rose was speechless with delight, but Bertie began whooping about sneakers.

"Not your originals?" Isis asked.

"Of course not. Those belong to Yale. But before the Council started grilling me, I told Danny to copy these. Highly unethical, but tough shit. Enjoy them, but in private. And this is for the future Dr. Greenbaum." He tossed a reflex hammer to his youngest child, who'd started collecting vintage medical equipment.

Hannah studied it carefully, fingering the hard rubber mallet. "Thanks, Dad Can I try it out on Bertie's head?"

Nathan Greenbaum laughed. "Now I know I'm home."

#

From the diary of J.D. Taylor, July 30, 1935

Cole Porter remembered his promise. I'm the rehearsal pianist for *Jubilee,* set for Boston tryouts in September. Apparently, he insisted on me; this show has a different crew from *Anything Goes,* and the musical director wanted his own guy. The producers sided with Cole. I hope the m.d. won't hold a grudge.

Which leads to the interesting question of how I'm affecting this timeline. I'm like a rock dropped in a pond, with outgoing ripples. There's the fellow who should be living in my apartment. Will his life change because he's on, say, Jones Street, not Cornelia Street? Who knows?

Will that other pianist starve because I got his job? I doubt it, since this is a limited gig, not a career-changing opportunity.

I once tried asking Nate about how Rippers might change history and the fallout from such actions, but he closed up like a clam. Well, I'm here with my plan and I'm going ahead, no matter how many lives take different paths. Call me a cockeyed optimist, as Oscar will phrase it in another few years, but I think any world with more great music in it is a better place.

Off to dig out my Ally, to study *Jubilee.* I use it so seldom, it's starting to seem weird, not like an electronic extension of myself any more. Just getting it out is a production, too, since I keep the modified extension cords and the units in separate hideyholes, in case any natives find them. I mean, I might get hit by a taxi. Then somebody else will rent this place. What will they make of this weird "bakelite," metal and glass thingy? Well, good luck getting past my super-encrypted password.

The other news is that I've disproved the family legend of Mort Greenbaum, the deli man who lost a finger and ruined his career as a jazz pianist. I went to Katz's Deli last week, watched him behind the counter, and asked some questions. He's a drummer, still capable of handling the sticks with nine digits. Last night, I went to hear his band at this dive in Queens. Mort never had a career in jazz because *he sucks.* Funny how stories change over time.

\#

From the diary of J.D. Taylor, August 16, 1935
Rehearsals have been mixed. Porter seemed pleased to see me again, marveled at how fast I learned his songs, and

hovered by my piano for about a week. Then he started bringing crowds of friends to rehearsal. They'd sit in the front row of the Imperial, making lunch plans and drinking cocktails expertly mixed by Porter's valet. Cole offered me a martini. I told him I stick to coffee for rehearsals. "Wise boy," he said, and patted my head. Could I make that up?

Porter's cavalier attitude is driving librettist Moss Hart bonkers. That's not a long drive—more like a putt—since Moss is highly strung to start with. He and Cole wrote this show on a world cruise with Monty Woolley, *Jubilee*'s dialogue director. At sea, they followed a strict work schedule; maybe Moss expected that to stay the same on dry land. To be fair, the score is nearly done, unlike that of *Anything Goes.* Porter can be disciplined, when he needs to be. Right now, he doesn't.

I did my part, playing terrific songs for the enormous cast. Other perks included watching legendary designer Jo Mielziner create amazing sets and Monty Woolley and co-director Hassard Short argue over everything. If vaudeville weren't already dying, they could have taken their bickering act to the Palace.

On the home front, Adam Finkelstein got a job in an Earl Carroll revue, one I know will run through November. I'm hoping he can land a spot in Rodgers and Hart's spring show, *On Your Toes,* which is dance-heavy and has a long run. Leo turned thirteen. We celebrated at the Bamboo Forest. While we were eating, I had a second-hand piano delivered to the Spinelli place. The look on Leo's face when we came back to the Seville Studios was priceless. Frannie complained I was spoiling him, but I told her I was making up for not having any kids of my own. Besides, he's really serious. He practices all the time (no a.c., so his music comes through open windows), even telling his buddies he'll play baseball later. That's dedication! He's also built a small wooden theatre where he stages the shows we've seen, using old tin soldiers as actors. I did the same thing at his age, only I used our 3-D printer.

#

From the diary of J.D. Taylor, October 20, 1935
Jubilee has a great score and an amusing plot about a fictional royal family cavorting with thinly disguised versions of Noël Coward, Johnny "Tarzan" Weissmuller, and society hostess Elsa Maxwell. It did great business in Boston last month. But we're not a happy company. Little things haven't gelled; film star Mary Boland was having trouble with the pace of stage rehearsals; Short and Woolley's quarrel ended with Monty's firing; costumes and props keep tearing and breaking. Worst of all, half a dozen people had family members die. Folks say the show is cursed.

Oh, yeah, and threatening letters and arson fires.

Someone—no one ever figured out who—sent death threats to Porter, the producers, and Boland, and set fires backstage in both Boston and New York. Everyone was understandably on edge. Boland sought comfort in the bottle in Boston, but fortunately sobered up for the opening at the Imperial, which was nowhere near as joyful as *Anything Goes'*.

I considered becoming a hero by catching the firebug in the act. I played Rutledge in *1776* at this theatre, and, though it's been remodeled between 1935 and 2076, its basic layout was familiar. For the first week of performances, I wandered through the wings, across catwalks, in and out of dressing rooms, and up and down rickety stairwells that smelt of mildew and greasepaint. My thighs were killing me and I developed a new appreciation for the fire-prevention methods of the future. Why this place hasn't burned down

139

is beyond me, with piles of oily rags in odd corners and exposed wood everywhere. There's one chemical fire extinguisher—a clunky steel thing—on each floor of this huge building, and buckets of sand everywhere else.

And have I mentioned the rats? There are rats in the Broadway theatres of the future, but their ancestors are bigger, nastier, and come in hordes. Yuck.

Then halfway to the boys' dressing room on the fourth floor, it occurred to me that capturing the nutcase might alter musical theatre history in a way I didn't intend. In real history, *Jubilee* didn't run long, marred by running costs, Boland's early return to L.A., and the death in January of King George V, which put a damper on royal hijinks. A shame, since it has such a marvelous score. If I caught the guy (or gal—some think it was a stage mother whose kid didn't get cast, or maybe a relative of Moss'), would Boland stay with the show longer, perhaps leading to a more successful run? Maybe.

What happened to my carefree, *laissez faire* attitude to changes in this timeline? Why wouldn't a devoted Porterphile want *Jubilee* to have a longer run?

Because Broadway, like so many things, depends on supply and demand. When *Jubilee* vacates the Imperial in March, Rodgers and Hart's *On Your Toes* will move in for its smash stretch. If it has to take a lesser house, *its* success might suffer. Of course, my Project will inevitably cause problems like that; new Youmans and Gershwin shows will dislodge shows from their places in original timeline, for good and for ill. As a kind of musical theatre Darwin, I expect the best will survive.

But my plans are still in their early stages. I haven't even had the chance to meet Lorenz Hart yet. So, while I continue to affect the timeline by taking other folks' homes and jobs, it's probably best if I let major events unfold as they did…at least, for a while longer. It will be easier to plan my actions if I know what Hart and Porter and Kern are doing, and where.

Besides, while I've been haunting the dim corridors of the Imperial Theatre, I've been missing out on history at the Alvin, just a few blocks away.

The hell with the firebug. I can't wait any longer to see *Porgy and Bess.*

#

From the diary of J.D. Taylor, October 21, 1935
The Alvin's manager, Mr. Jenkins, was surprised to see me when I turned up well before *Porgy's* curtain. "Mr. Taylor! If I'd known you were coming—"

"I've been busy at *Jubilee,* but I'm done now. I'll take whatever you've got."

Jenkins let me in, though the house wasn't open yet, and I made my way up to the balcony, where I sat watching the normal chaos unfold…and listening to the orchestra ready itself to tackle Gershwin's score.

Words can't do justice to that experience: the enormous set of Catfish Row, those gorgeous voices singing those immortal songs, Mamoulian's artful direction. I won't even try. I'm just thankful nobody was sitting near me, since I cried like a baby.

Mr. Jenkins noticed my red eyes as I was leaving. "This show gets to people."

I honked my nose in my handkerchief. "No kidding. Give me tickets for the next four nights, the best you've got."

#

Tonight I took Leo and Frannie to _Porgy and Bess._ As luck would have it, it was a night Gershwin attended. As we were leaving, I saw him in the lobby, surrounded by well-wishers. I wasn't going to intrude, but he spotted me, too, and waved us over.

"David! Did you like it?"

"My ninth time. It's so wonderful I hardly know where to start."

He grinned. "I keep listening and I can hardly believe I've written it myself! But who's this with you?" He stuck out his hand to Leo, who gravely shook it.

"Mr. Gershwin, these are my neighbors, Mrs. Francesca Spinelli, and her son, Leo. Leo's my student."

Ignoring the elegantly dressed swells standing by him, Gershwin took the hand of the immigrant seamstress in the russet wool coat. "I'm so pleased to meet David's friends." He winked at Leo. "Student, huh? Is Mr. Taylor a good teacher?"

"You bet!" said Leo. "He gave me a piano for my very own, on my birthday."

"Well, a pianist needs a piano. My parents bought our first one for my big brother, but I ended up playing it more than he did. What did you think of the show?"

"I loved it!" Leo said, bouncing up and down in his best shoes. "Especially the funeral, the way the actors moved and made shadows. Oh, and when Porgy killed Crown—yeah! But you know what else I liked, Mr. Gershwin? The way the orchestra played the same bits of music for different characters, a kind of sad one for Bess and a sly one for Sportin' Life. I liked Porgy's music best, the part when he comes in with his goat cart."

Gershwin threw back his head and laughed. "That's my favorite passage, too. I'm so glad you liked those themes. It took a long time to get them right."

"They're called motifs," I said, proud of my young pupil.

"You have a good ear, Leo," said Gershwin. "Keep practicing on that piano. Maybe you'll grow up to be a composer like me and Mr. Taylor."

Leo's eyes took in George's gold cufflinks, his fur-trimmed coat, his gleaming shoes, unaware that his background and Gershwin's were very similar. "Really?" he squeaked.

"Sure, but it takes plenty of work!"

Leo puffed out his chest, not so scrawny as it had been eighteen months ago. "I can work!"

"I'm sure you can." The toffs began shuffling impatiently, so Gershwin made his farewells. "A pleasure meeting you both. Call me this week, David, about Mexico. We were thinking of leaving at the end of the month."

"That's fine with me, George."

We ducked out into the blustery night to find a taxi. On the ride home, Frannie kept exclaiming over meeting Gershwin, but Leo was oddly quiet.

"You okay, pal?" I asked as the cabbie pulled up in front of the Seville Studios.

He started. "Huh? Yeah. Just thinking about the show. It was solid."

"Couldn't agree more," I said.

Chapter 6

"There's No Cure Like Travel" —Cole Porter

From the diary of J.D. Taylor, November 28, 1935

A curious quintet set sail for Veracruz on the *S.S. Siboney* three days ago: George Gershwin, noted composer; Edward Warburg, founder of the American Ballet; Marshall Field III, heir to the department store; Dr. Gregory Zilboorg, psychoanalyst to those three men; and David Greenbaum, time traveler. I'd met the others several times, usually at Gershwin gatherings. Field and Warburg were pleasant fellows, but I loathed Zilboorg even before we crossed paths. I knew him as a Svengali of guilty of ethical transgressions ranging from blackmail to sex with his patients. His European credentials were highly embroidered. He used his magnetism, keen mind, and improv skills to become the shrink of the stars, though there's no record he ever received a license to practice. He had been treating Gershwin for over a year, and would later have Lillian Hellman and Moss Hart on his couch, among others. He wasn't just their analyst; he moved in their social circles, including sporting events and country weekends. It was clear why many liked him; he could be charming, with interests ranging from linguistics and theatre to gourmet cooking. The evening I'd met him, he was knowledgeably discussing photography with George. Now he was on this Mexican jaunt, courtesy of his patients' wallets.

He'd ignored me, a mere eighty-eighter, at that party, but he was stuck with me now. I wasn't his patient, so he had no hold over me. What's more, he had counted on being Chief Indispensable Translator on this trip, and was annoyed that my Spanish was better than his. His Russian, German, and French could beat mine, but they're less handy south of the border.

I've got another reason to dislike him. There's a twenty-first century study that concluded, based on what was known about brain tumors in the thirties, Zilboorg should have recognized Gershwin's symptoms, possibly saving him before the tumor herniated. It's basic medicine, and even if Zilboorg exaggerated his psychiatric training in Berlin, he did get medical degrees in Russia and at Columbia. He just missed it, as did George's other doctors.

Zilboorg's treatment methods pissed me off, too. Every morning on this cruise, he has sessions with the trio, then everyone rehashs the details at breakfast. The patients can comment on each other's cases, but mostly Dr. Z runs them into the ground. The Ward Line has elegant china, with the cruise line's crest emblazoned on every piece. The more Zilboorg talked, the more I wanted to smash that pretty tea pot on his head.

"George still complains of his stomach and his headaches," Zilboorg said. He crammed a piece of pancake into his mouth, then continued. "I have told him many times that this is a common complaint of composers, whose emotional wellbeing is constantly in conflict with their need to create."

"Huh," I said, unimpressed. "I'm a composer and my gut's just dandy. In fact, the only composer I know with a bad tummy is Oscar Levant and he's a clo—he's like a copy of George. Maybe his stomach is trying to imitate Gershwin, too." I almost said *clone,* but that word wouldn't be around for decades.

The others chuckled at my joke. Zilboorg didn't. He poked a pancake, no doubt wishing he could jab me. "We are speaking of deep-set neuroses here—"

"We are?" I said. "I think George is a little down, but hell, who wouldn't be? He's just created a masterpiece, but the critics were too thick-headed to realize it."

Zilboorg muttered something obscene in Russian, then turned his attention to young Eddie Warburg, cousin to Jimmy Warburg (Kay Swift's soon-to-be ex). He peeled that poor kid like an onion. He'd done the same thing for the last two mornings—a litany of failure. You'd think Eddie was the world's biggest loser. I held my tongue until I saw tears in Eddie's eyes. How was this "therapy" helping? Eddie looked like he wanted to throw himself in the Atlantic.

"Really, Dr. Zilboorg," I said, gently setting my cup down. "Mr. Warburg is a talented young man from an accomplished family. He's founded a ballet company and helped it through some tough times, and he's on the board of the Museum of Modern Art. How many men in their twenties have similar resumes? You make him sound like a useless blob!"

Eddie rewarded me with a grateful look; George ducked his dark head, hiding a smile.

"Mr. Taylor, *you* are not a psychiatrist," said Zilboorg.

"That's true. I don't have a medical license." *Neither do you.* "But I'm well-read and I know people who've had treatment. I've never heard of therapy based on humiliation."

His impressive black mustache quivered. "Nonsense! I offer constructive comments. Your ignorance is staggering."

He addressed his patients. 'Gentlemen, I am not comfortable with Mr. Taylor hearing the details of our sessions."

"That's rich!" I said, and pointed to a plump matron several tables away. "You met that woman just yesterday morning, yet by cocktails you were telling her about George's anxieties. I've heard you discuss Kay Swift's treatments with Lee Gershwin at Ira's birthday party and describe George's enemas to damn near anyone. But *I* make *you* uncomfortable?"

Before Zilboorg could counter, I pressed my advantage: "Maybe we should put it to a vote. Do you fellas mind if I'm here?"

Sensing he was losing control, Zilboorg pounded the table, making the china rattle. "This is a psychoanalytical session, not a democratic caucus. Either Mr. Taylor goes, or my treatment ends."

The trio looked at one another, clearly uncomfortable. They might not be happy with Dr. Z.'s abuse, but they'd bought into the idea it was for their own good. I didn't want to force them into taking sides. Enough mischief for one day.

"Goodness, I wouldn't dream of standing in the way of science," I said. Rising, I neatly folded my linen napkin. Maybe it could sop up my dripping sarcasm. "If anyone wants me, I'll be on the sports deck."

#

From the diary of J.D. Taylor, November 30, 1935
That little tiff apparently changed the tone of the morning sessions. Eddie told me Zilboorg hasn't been so critical the last two mornings. Marshall came to my stateroom and said he wished he had the guts to stand up to Zilboorg. Gershwin, though, begged me not to fight with his doctor,

since "he's a decent sort." I said I didn't mean to quarrel, but I didn't like bullies. George denied that Zilboorg was a bully, but he hasn't missed the cutting remarks the good doctor makes about me.

We dock this afternoon. It may be hard to keep up this diary while we're ashore, but I'll try.

#

February 5, 2079
A week of school and rehearsals restored some order to Rose's world, though thoughts like _Uncle David would hate this blocking_ made the ache return. Zanzi faithfully stuck by her as she careered on an emotional roller coaster. Best of all, Zanzi refused to speak of David Greenbaum in the past tense, which even Mom and Dad were starting to do.

As they drove home from Sunday rehearsal, Zanzi asked, "So what's he doing in 1934? Hanging out with his Broadway buddies, like Sondheim and Rodgers and Hammerstein?"

Rose laughed, something she hadn't done much all week. "Sondheim's a little boy. And while Rodgers and _Hart_ are around, Rodgers and Hammerstein didn't team up until 1943's _Oklahoma!_"

"Ah, whatever. Your uncle's talented. David Greenbaum will survive!"

"I believe that, but I doubt he's using his real name."

"Oh, yeah. He's hiding from the Rippers. Though there are probably Greenbaums galore back then, like the guy at Katz's who cut his finger. Maybe he's staying with him, like a long lost cuz."

Rose shook her head. "That's not what I meant. If he is in theatre, he might change his name to something less Jewish. Weren't you paying attention in Ms. Hershey's tolerance class last semester? Anti-semitism in America?"

"Ms. Hershey is the world's biggest bore. I'm tolerant already; I put up with *you*, don't I? God, I deserve a medal for tolerance."

"No shit. You're a certified saint."

Zanzi's car rounded the corner into the Greenbaums' cul-de-sac and pulled up behind a red F/C Horizon, one of the earliest models from the merger of Ford and Chevy.

"Visitors?" Zanzi asked.

"The detective who interviewed us last week." Rose grabbed her backpack and hopped out into the icy Connecticut evening. "I'll let you know what happens. Thanks for the lift, Saint Zanzi."

"Blessings on you, my child," Zanzi waved her hand in benediction and drove off.

Rose shouldered her bag and tramped up the freshly shoveled walkway. Her dad groused that there was more snow every year. She took a deep breath and exhaled. *Always make a good entrance, Uncle David says.*

Any hope of staying dignified vanished when she saw her Ally—its cover custom-designed to look like a yellow-titled Playbill—on the table between her parents and Lt. Micheala "Mickey" Mertz. Rose barely suppressed a cry of glee.

"Come join us, dear," her mother said. "The lieutenant got here a few minutes ago."

"Just a sec," Rose said. As she hurried into the kitchen for some water, she caught Bertie's eye and mouthed, "How was your game?"

He grinned, indicating a win, and held up six fingers—his point total. She smiled back, filled her glass, and sat by him on the love seat.

"Good to see you, Rose," the officer said. Mertz was a heavy-set woman in her late fifties, with thick black hair, floral tats on her neck, and a prosthetic leg. Rose suspected little got past her.

"I was saying this is the weirdest case I've seen in thirty years of law enforcement. We know the perpetrator. We know he kidnapped his niece, made threats of deadly force, and misappropriated use of a device owned by a multi-national consortium. We know where he is—1934. Dr. Greenbaum says he spent nine months searching for him, and he's a veteran time traveler who knows the suspect better than anyone." She sipped her coffee. "In view of everything, we've determined to shut down this investigation."

"What?" Bertie squeaked. "Really?"

Mertz shrugged her broad shoulders. "How can we go on? We can't go after him. Even if we could, would we have more success than the professor? But the real reason is money. The city's budget has been slashed to the bone; there's not a dollar to spare anywhere. My superiors concluded that since David Greenbaum can't return to our timeline, he's no longer a threat to society."

"As if he ever was," Hannah said under her breath.

"They don't want to waste the taxpayers' money on an investigation with no possible resolution. Maybe the Ripper Council can do something on their own...You okay, Dr. Greenbaum?"

Nate coughed violently for a minute. "Swallowed wrong."

"Um-hum." Lt. Mertz pulled an EW-6000 Spark from her battered leather briefcase, a clear sign her department had no money. Bertie's lip curled with disdain at the outdated clunker.

"As I said, we know the who, what, where, when—huh! too many whens!—but the detective in me still wants to know *why*. So I'll tell you what our tech guys uncovered this week, and maybe you can help."

"We can try," said Isis. "But this took us completely by surprise."

"Understood. Your brother hid things, that's for sure. We've noted significant withdrawals from his bank that don't match any purchases, found four rogue Net accounts.

"Yet he didn't keep it all under wraps—he used his own account to buy books and downloads on history and 1930s cash, both dollars and pesos."

Nate jumped on that. "Pesos? That reminds me of this run-in I had in 1935 Greenwich Village." He described meeting Joe Gould, whose musical friend had gone to Mexico. "So drunk he didn't know Jack from jump rope, as they said back then, but he *might* have meant David."

"Mexico in 1935?" asked Rose. "Didn't they just have a revolution? Wasn't it messed up? Why go there, Dad?"

"Maybe it's connected to his visit there last fall," said Hannah. "He visited Ramon's relatives, but maybe he did more."

Mertz' fingers flew over the screen. "He *did* see the Abarcas...hmm...hotel records, meal charges. But I doubt the Mexican authorities could help us, not with that damn volcano blowing its top. Tracing Greenbaum's movements in Hong Kong is even harder; the Chinese are not cooperative these days."

As if rehearsed, the family said, "Hong Kong?"

The lieutenant seemed amused by their expressions. "Told you he had secrets. Yes, Hong Kong, then L.A., with a side jaunt to San Bernardino. You never knew? He put his hotels and air fare on his AmEx, but nothing else except theatre tickets in North Hollywood. Any idea what he was doing?"

Nate rubbed his chin, pondering. "He visited some friends in L.A. on his way back from Mexico; I could find their names. I can't imagine why he went to Hong Kong, but it doesn't seem good."

"Nope," said Mertz. "Finally, we did a limited facial recog search of the New York area CCTV. Not much beyond the usual shopping and stuff, except one visit to the English department at Columbia University. More research?"

"Professor Shanta Gholkar," Isis said with venom. "A friend of Ramon's, the one who got him into T3. Not a family favorite."

"Think Greenbaum wanted drugs?"

"Not a chance," Nate said. "David's drug was music. He battled for years to keep Ramon off that shit. Maybe Ramon left her something in his will."

The detective muttered "Shanta Gholkar" into her link, then closed the Spark. "If I could, I'd investigate everything: this woman, the rogue accounts, where his money went, those trips abroad, full tech searches. But my hands are tied. Three things in particular bug me. First, can anybody else try this? Because it looks like the perfect crime. I've had perps flee the country, but not the century."

"Well, I doubt other Rippers have actor-siblings who can impersonate them," Nate said, a faint flush reddening his face. "The Council is 'reviewing security protocol.' Locking the barn door. What else?"

"Time travel stories always have people going back to kill their grandparents or squash butterflies. Any chance of that? I mean, he's in 1934. You know him. Is this some elaborate suicide—is he gonna take out himself and this world, too?"

Nate flinched at the harsh words. "I can't go into details, but we're sure nothing's going to happen to our 2079. David's not going to change this world."

Dad's not mentioning the Splinterverses, thought Rose. *But how long the Council can keep that quiet? They're lucky Uncle David picked a busy news day for his trip: with Popocatepetl erupting, the assassination attempt on old*

King George, and the blizzards in the Midwest, the hijacked time machine hasn't got the attention it might have.

Mertz wiped her brow in mock relief. "Good. My first grandson arrives this summer. Which brings us to Number Three. He left a farewell letter—a handwritten note to you. You'll get it with the other stuff from his place, maybe next week. Got to say, it sounds like a typical suicide note. He's depressed, misses his husband, all that. But then he says, 'I can make a difference.' What does he mean?"

The Greenbaums looked at each other, confused. Finally, Rose spoke up. "He said that to me: that he could make a difference and he was doing it for Ramon. And in the car, he said, 'I need to disappear and I'm disappearing into the thirties.'"

Mertz subvocalized into her link again, looking unhappy. "That sounds like he was involved in something here."

She's like Javert after Valjean, thought Rose. *But I'm positive Uncle David wasn't doing anything criminal. Besides stealing the SlingShot, that is.*

"I know!" said Bertie. "What's that show Ramon loved so much, *The Follies?* Maybe Uncle David wants to see it for Ramon."

Rose made a disgusted noise. "You dope, it's *Follies* without any 'the.' 1971. Let's see, Uncle David would be..."

"Almost seventy! Whoa!" said her brother, the math whiz.

"Ramon died from his addiction," Hannah said slowly. "What if Uncle David wants to prevent the invention of the Tantalus drugs?"

"Then he'd want to go to the 2030s, not the 1930s," said Nate. "Besides, Dave barely got through high school chemistry. Designer drugs are out of his league."

Lt. Mertz got to her feet, shaking her head. "You folks have the oddest conversations. Guess that happens when time travel is part of your daily routine. I'll keep in touch, see what I can uncover without costing New Haven a fortune. Thanks for your help. Oh, and here are the keys to his apartment."

She tossed them on the coffee table, where they clinked softly. David had two key fobs: a brass oval engraved with the masks of comedy and tragedy and a small photo of Ramon encased in lucite. His handsome, dark face smiled up at the Greenbaums.

Rose felt a catch in her throat. *Oh, Ramon, do you have any idea what you've done? Of course not. That was always the trouble. You were the impulsive one, Uncle David was the thoughtful one. So he must have had a plan.*

#

From the diary of J.D. Taylor, December 1, 1935
Last night, we stayed in the Hotel Imperial, parts of which date back to the eighteenth century—not that we spent much time there. Sightseeing all afternoon, an excellent fish dinner at a restaurant Juan Guzmán had recommended, and then we went dancing. Dancing in Veracruz means the *danzón,* which came from Cuba. Eddie and George learned its sinuous moves quickly; George is a fine dancer. I've seen him do tap steps waiting for elevators, using moves Fred Astaire taught him. Now, a graceful older Mexican woman in his arms, he weaved his way between the arches on the *zócalo,* the main plaza. Marshall and Zilboorg drank rum punches and cheered us from the sidewalk cafe. The doc's Spanish is decent but Ramon's family came from Veracruz, so I'm used to the lisping, clipped dialect.

This morning, Juan drove us to Santa Elena, as Conrad Küster had generously offered the use of the house again. Zilboorg, the eldest among us at forty-five, claimed the cab, so the rest of us piled into the back, with the luggage and the big box of goodies I'd shipped earlier. While we rattled through the Orizaba Valley, I taught the guys some of Ramon's favorite *sones jarochos,* including "La Iguana," with its catchy call and response verses.

The Mexicanitos greeted me with great warmth: *"Profesor* Taylor!" ("A courtesy title," I quickly explained; no false academic credentials for me, even if my other papers are bogus!) Juan helped me unload my box, which contained a Singer sewing machine for Dolores, and many bottles of aspirins and Wenger pocket knives. Tomorrow we start exploring the back country, the *tierra caliente.* Victor says Pegaso can't wait to see me again. The feeling is not mutual.

#

From the diary of J.D. Taylor, December 28, 1935
We had a grand time in Santa Elena. Gershwin quickly made friends with everyone, playing music every night and even taking part in the boys' daily scorpion battles. He'd wager a single peso, but you'd think it was a grand on the Braddock-Baer match, the way he shouted with the kids around the limestone slab where the creatures went at each other. I'm not fond of scorpions, but I like those *chavos.* They're good with peashooters, as Dr. Zilboorg has discovered, to his dismay. Let's just say a couple of my pocket knives have good homes now.

Our ethnomusical travels started with day trips to nearby villages, then got longer and harder. One hamlet boasted a bass viol (its owner called it his *"cerdo grande"*—that's "big pig."); George took notes on its use in several long ballads. Another village in a narrow side valley featured a trio of different-sized guitars, a drum, and an ancient blind man on a flute. I had heard him before and marveled he was still breathing, living as he did in the crumbling remains of a colonial monastery. Everything seemed more withered than last year: barren hills, dead fruit and almond trees, patches of wasteland that once were tilled fields. Many of the young men had taken jobs in cotton or jute mills in bigger towns; the remaining folks survived by finding onyx bits on the hillsides and turning them into polished eggs, Olmec heads, and Aztec-style ashtrays for tourists. Gershwin fell upon one head with a glad cry—"It looks like Ira!"— and promptly bought it.

The longer trips proved too much for Zilboorg, who groused about sleeping on *petates* in thatch-roofed huts, with snakes and spiders. "I'll await you in Mexico," he said, meaning the capital. I didn't miss him a bit, and I think the others felt more comfortable, too, though no one said so.

Victor quickly discovered a friend in Marshall Field; the Mexican country kid and the millionaire both knew and loved horses. Marshall helped Victor with the dirty work, too, and I remembered he and his wife rescued broken-down racehorses and turned them into show jumpers. As for the rest of us, Pegaso and I resumed our wary relationship, Eddie Warburg had a natural seat, while George kept his by constantly muttering, "Tummy in, tummy out."

The best memory was our trip to Santa Lucia—three days' travel, including crossing a swift river in a *pango* jammed with peasants, three goats, a pig, and a crate of squawking hens. Gershwin, a speed junkie, whooped, "This is swell!" as he thumped the gunwale. All of us, including the livestock, got there on December 13 for their big fiesta.

The headman, Miguel Garcia, greeted me. *"Profesor* Taylor! You have come for our saint's feastday?"

"Yes, with my friends, and this is for the celebration." I passed him a box I'd bought in Veracruz.

"What is it, David?" asked Eddie.

"You'll see tonight."

We headed for the plaza, already packed with people from the neighboring villages ready to honor St. Lucia and enjoy plenty of beer and good food. Besides the familiar tortillas and frijoles, we munched on grilled chicken with peppers and lime, fresh salsa, and a terrific goat mole with plantains. Because of his stomach, George was wary of anything too spicy, but the goat stew was more smoky than hot. "What is this wonderful flavor?" he asked, mopping sauce up with a tortilla.

"Chocolate," I said.

He nearly dropped his bowl in surprise. "No! Really?"

As good as the food was, the music was better. Six separate ensembles played, providing plenty of variety. There was the usual array of different sized guitars, a trumpet, and a wheezy accordion. George tried it, much to the crowd's approval. He also hopped up on the small raised dance platform, the *tarima,* stomping out the beat with enthusiasm under the flickering lantern lights. His sense of rhythm never fails to astonish me.

Then came the *Danza del Tigre,* a masked dance possibly going back to Olmec times, depicting a jaguar hunt. A single musician alternated on flute and drum as the hunters darted in and around the plaza, chasing their prey. The lithe young man playing the jaguar plunged into the crowd, goosing girls and pretending to bite men in the crotch. Yours truly got singled out for such attention, which caused my American buddies to howl with laughter.

"It's a great honor," I spluttered, grateful for the dim light. I appreciate earthy humor as much as anyone, but I'd noticed that dancer earlier—great moves, tight tush, and yes, he looked eerily like Ramon, especially the eyes. The snarling yellow and black mask covered his handsome Latin face, but I had recognized a carefully mended tear in his white pants—and that ass. It's possible he's a relative; the Abarcas came from this area. I'd like to think so.

The fiesta ended with my mystery box: a glorious display of fireworks. I felt like Gandalf with the hobbits when all Santa Lucia came to thank me. Slightly buzzed and thoroughly sated, we bedded down on mats in Garcia's house. It wasn't a quiet night. Revelers continued carousing in the street outside. The baby fussed at his midnight feeding. Marshall Field snored horribly. And George got up to use the outhouse twice, tripping over me both times. I didn't mind—he'd given me the opening I wanted. After his return, I shifted on my mat and glanced his way. A shaft of moonlight illuminated Gershwin's sleek head, nestled on his folded sweater. I could make out the small scar by his right eye, a souvenir of a childhood brawl. *Somewhere inside that skull is a tumor. But not for long.*

A chorus of noisy green parrots woke us at dawn, but no one minded, as we wanted to hit the road early. Señora Garcia fixed us eggs and frijoles, but George didn't eat much and soon made another dash outside. I grabbed my coffee—kickass java!—and followed him. When he came out of the jakes, I was waiting on a low adobe wall outside the house. The Garcia kids romped past us, pushing a squealing toddler in a wheelbarrow. "Insides upset, George?" I asked.

His smile vanished. "I don't know if it's Montezuma's revenge or my usual stomach issues. I'm sorry I kicked you in the night, David."

"No, I was awake already. But I wondered if I might offer you something. I've got some supplements that are good for this kind of problem. They also help headaches."

"Well, I certainly get those! Is this what you gave Vince Youmans? Never seen him with so much color."

"Uh, these are a little different." I rummaged in my rucksack and pulled out two bottles. The bigger one held the immunotherapy treatment, the combination of antibodies and vaccines to target the tumor. The smaller one held the Boost, designed to combat the drug's side effects: nausea, diarrhea, and mouth sores. The only thing the docs hadn't been able to improve on was fatigue. George was young and fit—I hoped he'd blame feeling tired on our rigorous travels, not on his new meds.

"Take one of each kind at dinner for the next two weeks," I said, handing him the bottles. It all boiled down to this moment: the noise of the children and parrots receded; the watery December sunlight made everything look hazy. I felt strangely light-headed and could only focus on George's talented hands, taking the bottles from mine. *Was this really happening?*

He opened one and shook out some capsules. "These are the funniest looking pills I've ever seen! What are they made of?"

"Some kind of gelatin, so they dissolve slowly," I said. "So don't cut them in half."

"Okay, I'll give 'em a shot. I've tried different diets, but nothing seems to help."

I swallowed hard. "I've got faith in these, George. They'll do for you."

"Thanks, David, You're a *mensch.* Where are we headed today?"

I hopped off the wall. "A three-hour burro ride, but we get to see the *voladores* at the end. Not much musically, but these guys do crazy flying dances, dangling from ropes."

Gershwin does this little gesture when he's excited or interested. He thrusts his head forward, like a turtle stretching out of his shell to see more of the world. He did it now. "Let's go!"

We roamed the back country for another five days, then caught the train to Mexico City. The drugs were definitely affecting Gershwin; he was tired all the time, but after the first few days, his bowels settled down, which pleased him no end. I pretended to be more exhausted than I really was, complaining about the pace Victor set, so George's fatigue was less noticeable.

Returning to the comforts of the capital made a difference. The San Angel Inn, a converted Carmelite monastery, was posh next to dirt floors and mats in Indian villages. Reunited with Zilboorg, we did typical sightseeing in Taxco and Cuernavaca and the capital during the day, then sought out music in the evenings. George wasn't impressed.

"This stuff's monotonous," he complained while listening to another lengthy *corrido,* a story ballad. "I'm glad I heard more indigenous songs and instruments in the Indian lands."

Marshall Field grinned over a frothy glass of *cerveza.* "Wait until you declare that donkey jaw rattle and the lute made from an armadillo shell to the customs agent! He'll probably quarantine you."

"My concern's orchestrating those keen instruments," said Gershwin. "But I'm working on it already, up here." He tapped his temple.

I felt like shouting, "Aw, ya-whoo," Bertie's cheer when the Pats score. George Gershwin's original Mexican trip didn't produce any new work, but this one clearly would.

March 4, 2079

The two weekends of the Obama High School Players' production of *The Serene Ones* kept Rose from helping her parents clean out Uncle David's apartment. She was glad. Concentrating on Meredith Fullerton's mid-century neo-absurdist dialogue was tough enough without that kind of distraction.

But she was stuck now, taking the train to New York with her dad, walking the streets of Greenwich Village to that dingy building on 12th Street.

"I know I'm going to cry, Dad," she said as they headed for the foyer. "Buckets."

"So? There are Kleenexes. But you need to do your share, especially since you have the most interest in David's things."

The place looked different already, which helped. Her parents had straightened up the mess the cops left, but furniture was out of place. Plastic tubs with labels in Isis' impeccable writing lined one wall. The closets were empty, with the clothes donated to a T3 charity.

Rose steeled herself. "Okay, where do I start? The theatre books and playbills and music, of course. What are you going to do?"

"Papers. We got all the important 'loads and links; David left us a mini with those, but I'm looking for other things, like the physical copies of his birth certificate, their marriage license. And anything odd, of course. But Mertz is right about his keeping secrets. I haven't found anything connected to China or San Bernardino."

Rose squatted in front of a bookcase. Uncle David had already shared his digital libraries with her, but he had some amazing printed treasures, including autographed works by Stoppard, Sondheim, Estévez, Moss Hart, and Moonrise Johnson. She felt a thrill just holding them. And those playbills! Only the paper ones for her uncle, not digital downloads.

She was searching for her uncle's name in the ensemble of Pappadakis' *Owl in the Moonlight* when her father made a noise. "What's up, Dad?"

"Probably nothing. Your mom found a business card for this piano moving firm in Trenton in one of Dave's jackets and here's an ad for them, with 'August 8th, 2078' written on it. Piano movers? His piano's where it always has been."

That jogged something in Rose's memory. "When I stayed over with him last summer, he got really grouchy about some papers. I remember that ad was one of them. Maybe we should check it out!"

"What does piano moving have to do with 1930s research? It's crazy. Well, back to work."

Two hours later, Nate called for a lunch break at Katz's. "How are you doing?" he asked over the traditional pastrami sandwich. "Find any keepers?"

"Are you kidding? I want it all! I don't know where I'll put it, but I want it."

Her dad got a funny look on his face. "Your mom and I thought you'd say that. How about leaving it where it is?"

"Huh?"

Nathan Greenbaum studied his eldest over his cherry Coke. "Last December, David had us put our names on his lease. He said he was worried that something might happen to him, and he wanted to have the place available to you. He was sure you'd get into Juilliard. He even paid the rent through July. He's also made you and Hannah and Bertie his heirs, though God knows how long it will take the lawyers to sort that out."

162

She'd managed not to break down in the apartment, but knowing her uncle was still thinking of her and her future—not from the grave, but from his place in the distant past—made her start sobbing. No Kleenex in sight, and deli napkins were really lousy for blowing one's nose.

#

From the diary of J.D. Taylor, December 22, 1935
Tonight was the major social outing of our trip—and very nearly a disaster for my Broadway Revival Project. Estrella Elizaga, a wealthy composer and arts patron, invited us to a bash at her home. Vernon Duke had set up the meeting. He was her friend, and Gershwin's, too. Knowing Gershwin's keen interest in art, she assembled a glittering array of her country's best, including boisterous Diego Rivera, whose raucous laughter punctuated the evening; Miguel Covarrubios, a lantern-jawed young painter and caricaturist; his wife, Rose, a noted choreographer; Japanese-American Isamu Noguchi, then creating a relief mural in the Mexico City marketplace—and having an affair with Frieda Kahlo; David Alfaro Siqueiros, acclaimed muralist; and composer Carlos Chávez.

Elizaga's place was spacious and decorated with Mexican art, old and new. Rounded pre-Columbian heads sat cheek by jowl with modern, angular busts, yet it worked. Our hostess was a tiny thing, with bright, black eyes and an engaging smile. Her Spanish-accented broken English reminded me of Ramon's Aunt Josefina. *"Bienvendios.* It is the honor to having the fine gentlemen in Mexico. Eat, drink, enjoy."

"Muchas gracias," the guys said, about the limits of their Spanish. But Dr. Zilboorg somehow knew Elizaga spoke

French, so he reeled off something Gallic that had her giggling.

According to Eddie Warburg's description of this bash, George hung off to one side, isolated as Zilboorg abandoned his translating duties—the very thing George had said he feared during their analytical sessions. Gershwin didn't even play the gleaming white piano, since no one invited him. But I'm here tonight, so things will be different.

"Come on, George, let's mingle," I said. "I've always wanted to meet Diego Rivera." George seemed a little hesitant, definitely out of character, but I steered one master over to the other. I bowed to the artist, whose bulky frame was wedged into a leather chair. *"Señor Rivera, I am J.D. Taylor, and this is the famous American composer, George Gershwin."*

Rivera rose from his seat, setting his tequila on a small table. He was wearing a rumpled, stained black satin shirt, but nonetheless gave off an air of power. We shook hands. Rivera's were filthy.

"I admire your work," Gershwin said, as I translated. "Any chance I could commission a portrait?"

"Alas, no. I'm completely booked for months, and behind schedule, too," said Rivera.

"Well, do you mind if I sketch *you?*" George asked, pulling his little sketchbook from his coat pocket. He didn't even wait for my translation, but mimed drawing and pointed at Rivera, who barked a laugh.

"Go ahead, my fine fellow! Perhaps I shall write a song about you, in return!" He plopped his bulk back into the chair. "If you are free tomorrow, I would be pleased to show you my work at the National Palace."

"Splendid!" said Gershwin. He sat on the ottoman near Rivera, got out his colored pencils, and set to work.

Rivera began talking politics; no surprise, there. "We are doing great things here in Mexico, great things! The efforts of the people cannot be stopped. Progress, at last!" Siqueiros joined in. "We shall free humanity—and art—from oppression!"

I kept up with the translating, though it was obvious from our travels that the revolution had not brought about the improvements the country desperately needed. What's more, from my perspective of one hundred and forty years, I knew the "great things" Rivera promised wouldn't amount to *frijoles.*

Gershwin asked intelligent questions about these proposed wondrous social transformations, but he wasn't political. Dr. Zilboorg was, but of the opposite flavor from Rivera. In his twenties, he had served in the Kerensky government, fleeing Russia at the rise of the Bolsheviks in 1917. Now he stood in a room in Mexico City, wine glass in hand, scowling as Rivera, Siqueiros, and Covarubbios praised *los populos.* Zilboorg was so wary of these Mexican communists, he'd come to the party with a revolver in his waistband. He thought they were out to get him. I'm not denying that they were tough bastards—Siqueiros would later be involved in an assassination attempt on Trotsky—but Trotsky was a big fish. Zilboorg was just a secretary to the Minister of Labor.

For the rest of us, the evening was, as George would later write to Ira, "perfectly swell." The Mexican art scene naturally dominated conversations; the Americans especially admired Siqueiros' work, and George invited him to New York. Miguel jokingly critiqued George's sketch ("No, no, Rivera's nose is bigger!"), while Eddie Warburg, Rosa Covarrubios, and Estrella talked of ballet in mix of languages and gestures. Chávez discussed Mexican aboriginal folk music, with George jotting notes as I translated. That made me even more irked at Zilboorg, for not helping George at the original version of this party.

Best of all, George got to play. It was simple to arrange. I approached Estrella and said, *"Would you like Señor Gershwin to play? Yes?"*

Gershwin couldn't speak Spanish, but now he could contribute to the party in the way he knew best. He took his seat and looked at me. "What do you think they'd like, David?"

"Play 'I Got Rhythm,'" I said. He launched into the song, his eyes lighting up when I began singing: *"Tengo ritmo, Tengo música, Tengo mi mujer, Quien puede pedi algo más?"* Ramon taught me that one, of course.

We got a huge hand and followed up with "Swanee" and "Fascinating Rhythm." Then George played part of the "Rhapsody," stopping when he noticed Carlos Chávez practically salivating for a chance to play. Gershwin scooted over on the bench, and the two of them improvised a kind of whacked-out hybrid of *Porgy and Bess* and Mexican folk melodies. I wish I could have recorded it. Ramon would have loved it.

Don't snivel, Greenbaum. Get another drink and just enjoy it. I wandered over to the bar, grabbed another beer, and reveled in the music. About ten feet from me, Zilboorg, his back ostentatiously to the piano, was asking Noguchi about Japanese art. All I could think was, *How can you ignore that music?* In retrospect, I wish Zilboorg *had* kept ignoring George a little longer, because things got bad, very quickly.

When George came back from a bathroom break, he took off his suit coat. With the fireplace going full blast against the December chill, the room had got pleasantly warm. As he draped the coat on a chair, something rattled to the tile floor. "Oops, my pill fob!" George said. "Where did that darn thing go?"

We were on the other side of the room, but George's voice carried. Like a bloodhound catching a scent, Zilboorg's head whipped around. He turned to Marshall Field. "Pill fob? I did not know George was taking any medications." Marshall just shrugged, so Zilboorg drained his glass and got to his feet He began making his way to the piano, intent on finding out what George was taking.

Gershwin only had a few more days of the drugs, but I didn't want Zilboorg interrupting the treatment or examining the weird pills. Not that any thirties chemist could figure out what went into them. Hell, they were only just developing penicillin. But how to divert him?

To my right, Rivera and Siqueiros were chatting about *el socialismo* and *los compadres,* which gave me an idea. I interrupted their talk—rude, but necessary.

"Gentlemen, I don't wish to cause trouble for my fellow American, especially since we must travel together, but I believe Dr. Zilboorg has had the nerve to bring a pistol with him tonight. Political differences are one thing, but I find this insulting to our hostess." I glanced over at Zilboorg, who was saying something—*oh, God, what?*—to Gershwin. George seemed undisturbed; "Strike Up the Band" went on without a hitch. I feel funny about hearing that song now, like it's got evil associations.

The Mexicans weren't happy about my news. They glowered at the psychoanalyst. If you knew to look for it, the gun's shape was obvious where his coat pulled against his pot belly.

Rivera's eyes narrowed. "Reactionary pigdog!" he growled. He began stomping across the room, bellowing as he went. "Dr. Zilboorg, what is this? Have you come armed to Señora Elizaga's lovely party? You have no honor, señor!"

His voice was piercing. Conversations broke off. George stopped playing, completely bewildered.

Zilboorg flushed red. "It is for my protection, in case you Bolsheviks wish me harm."

"Even if we were enemies—and I believe we are, now—would we ruin Estrella's hospitality with bloodshed?" said Rivera, planting himself in front of the Russian. "Unthinkable!"

Realizing he was coming off badly, Zilboorg bowed to our hostess. "I intend no insult, Señora Elizaga, but you see—"

She no longer appreciated his cosmopolitan flair and interrupted him. "Dr. Zilboorg, please leave my home. My driver will take you to your hotel."

"But first," said Rivera. He held out his broad, stained hand, waiting for Zilboorg to hand over his weapon.

"Never!" Zilboorg spat out the word, but David Siqueiros was behind him and grabbed his arms. He had been an officer in the Mexican revolutionary army—not a force famed for training, but he had no trouble subduing a chubby middle-aged shrink.

Rivera nodded his thanks, plucked out the gun from Zilboorg's pants, and deftly removed its bullets while Zilboorg cursed him in a variety of languages. One thing I've noticed about this era is that guns are *everywhere.* The Spinellis even had one, until Sergio pawned it last month. One of my earliest memories is the Father's Day massacre of 2052, so all these firearms freak me out. There are still too many guns in the 2070s, but at least we're working on gun control.

Rivera handed the empty gun back to Dr. Z., who looked pissed enough to contemplate using it as a club, except Captain Siqueiros was watching his every move. Without another word, Zilboorg disappeared into the

168

foyer, where he snapped orders at the housekeeper for his hat and coat.

Eddie Warburg hurried up to me. "What was *that* all about? Why did he have a gun? That's just crazy!"

Yes, and he's your shrink. "Politics," I said.

Señora Elizaga heard me. "No more politics tonight," she said. "Only music and laughter."

Fat chance, with this crowd! But George sat down at the piano, and though the room still buzzed with talk about *el ruso loco,* the party went late into the night.

On the drive back in Estrella's limo, I casually asked George, "What was Dr. Z. asking you, there before all the fuss started?"

"Oh, he wanted to know what was in my pill fob. I told him you had given me something for my stomach, but then Rivera started yelling."

I didn't like that. Zilboorg still had his unpleasant sessions with his patients before breakfast. Maybe the Mexican Commie standoff drove those pills out of his head, but I couldn't count on it.

"Uh, George," I said, "maybe don't tell him too much about those pills tomorrow. Say you've finished them or something. He'll object to them since they're from me."

Gershwin looked dubious. "You mean I should lie to my analyst? I don't know, David. But I'll tell you this: I'm a big boy. I can take care of myself."

#

From the diary of J.D. Taylor, December 23, 1935
Luckily, Zilboorg left word canceling the morning session. We were having a late breakfast when he joined our table at the cafe across from the hotel. "Just coffee," he told the waiter. "I dined hours ago. Gentlemen, Mr. Field tells

169

me you plan to meet Rivera at the National Palace, then visit Siqueiros' gallery. I shall not be joining you. These Bolsheviks are out for my blood, but if you want to consort with them, that is your right."

The boys started to protest this guilt-trip, but he held up his hands. "No, no. Go, enjoy yourselves." With a patently phony smile, he sipped his coffee as we finished eating.

When we returned to the hotel lobby, he motioned to me. "Mr. Taylor. A word, if I may."

Uh-oh.

As soon as the others were out of earshot, he turned on me. "You have admitted you are no analyst, but are you now a doctor, that you prescribe drugs for Gershwin?"

"I didn't prescribe anything." *True! I got them through blackmail.* "Are you familiar with the placebo effect, Dr. Zilboorg?"

"Of course. I am a medical professional." Zilboorg looked more indignant than usual, if possible.

"Well, I gave George some pills and told him they'd help his stomach, and they have. I guess his brain did the real work. Haven't you said all along that his gastric woes are related to his mind?" *Way to obfuscate, Greenbaum!*

He rubbed his mustache, thinking. "Interesting. And can you explain what happened last night? You were standing near those daubers before they assaulted me."

"What's to explain? Rivera noticed the gun in your pants and took offense, as well he might." I resisted the impulse to say Mae West's famous line, as she wouldn't utter it until next year. "Pistols at a party, Doctor? That's *nekul'turno.*"

When I was at Juilliard, I knew this Russian gal who could have been a great director, but chose to raise horses for a living. "Easier than actors," she said. She taught me that *nekulturny* means boorish, uncivilized, uncouth; it's about the worst Russian insult ever.

Whatever he was about to say next popped right out of his head. He went white and threw a haymaker at my head. I blocked it easily and pinned his arm; Nate and I had far bloodier battles over the years. The hotel manager started yelling, and guests and staff stared.

"Look, doc," I hissed into his ear, "we don't like each other. Fine. But we head home in three days. I'll stay polite if you do, too. Deal?"

I released him. Zilboorg stepped back, adjusted his clothes, and shook his arm, giving the impression that I'd maimed him for life. The hotel guests looked shocked, but I suspect the staff was on my side; I'm a good tipper.

"You are beneath my contempt," Zilboorg said finally. "I cannot wait to see the last of you."

I watched him walk up the stairs to his room. I couldn't help wishing Rivera had pocketed that gun along with the bullets.

Chapter 7

"Getting to Know You" —Oscar Hammerstein II

From the diary of J.D. Taylor, January 18, 1936

Well, the not-so-good doctor didn't shoot me, but he's badmouthing me all over Manhattan. I haven't seen George since we got back from Mexico, but Eddie Warburg called me with some news.

"George has ended his sessions with Zilboorg. He said hadn't got enough out of it, even though he'd been at it a year. Maybe I should stop, too, but I'm such a creature of habit..."

"Eddie, do what you think is right for you. But it seems to me all he does is flay you with your own guilt."

"Yeah... I guess. But I thought you should know about George... and that the doc's saying some nasty things about you. He *really* doesn't like you."

"Sticks and stones," I said. "I don't like him either, but I'm a gentleman. You can tell him so."

"I haven't got the nerve," Warburg said gloomily. "See you around, Dave."

My presence in Mexico hadn't influenced Gershwin's decision; in real history, he ended the treatments after the trip, while Warburg continued for years. Could Zilboorg make trouble for me? Maybe. But I think my connections and my growing bank account can counter his dirt.

#

From the diary of J.D. Taylor, February 20-21, 1936
This year seems to be flying by. I'm putting in my hours at the Golden Eagle, giving Leo his weekly lessons, plugging away at a new song about a lovely señorita. George isn't the only one drawing inspiration from our trip. Tonight, I took Adam and Mabel out to see *The Ziegfeld Follies of 1936* for Adam's birthday. Great fun, with a score by Vernon Duke and Ira Gershwin, sultry dances by Balanchine, and starring Fanny Brice, Bob Hope, and Josephine Baker. After the show, we went to Dinty Moore's for a late dinner. Like good Jews, Mabel had the Irish stew; Adam, the corned beef and cabbage; and I ordered the lamb chop with a baked potato the size of a boulder. Expensive in thirties money, but tasty.

We were in terrific moods, drinking South Americans—a devastating blend of gin, curaçao, bitters, and lime juice. As I'd hoped, Adam got a part in the chorus of *On Your Toes,* which had just started rehearsals. The Finkelsteins would have steady income for months, as it would prove a smash hit. I'd invested heavily in it myself.

"This has been the best birthday," Adam announced. "It was great seeing some of Balanchine's completed choreography, now that I've started working with him. That '5:00 A.M.' number—hoo, boy!"

"So slinky, so smooth," Mabel said, a dreamy look in her brown eyes. She reached over and took Adam's hand. I suspected they'd go to bed once we got back to the Village, but not to sleep.

I smiled, but felt a little pang inside. Like Adam, Ramon was first and foremost a dancer, and there were many times when our discussions of dance led to choreography of a different sort. One Fred and Ginger marathon in particular…

The waiter—always glacially slow at DM's—lumbered up with our desserts, snapping me back to the present. Er, the past. February 1936. Lemon meringue pie is delicious any time.

"We should be heading home," Mabel said, peering at a tiny sweetheart watch, her Valentine's present. "Adam has rehearsal at ten."

"Aw, I thought we could go dancing at Barney Gallant's," I said. "The night is young and—" I stopped myself before commenting on her beauty. A cliché to me, but that song wouldn't become a hit until this summer. "—it's only a few blocks from home."

A small man suddenly lurched into our table, rattling the glassware and cutting off Mabel's reply. I had the outermost seat, so I caught him by the arm, and found myself looking into the dark, haunted eyes of Lorenz Hart.

"Thanks! Missed my footing on the linoleum," he said. "Let's see if I can make it to the gents' without killing myself."

Our booth was in the back, close by the restrooms; at the Ritz, it would be considered Siberia, but a chorus boy, a CPA, and a pianist didn't rate the likes of Eddie Cantor and Jimmy Walker. Or Larry Hart. "No harm done, Mr. Hart," I said.

Hart nodded at us, a tad blearily, then vanished into the john. He didn't emerge for some time. We'd finished our pie and drinks, I'd paid the bill, and Adam was fetching our coats when a pale, but more composed, Hart approached our table again. Bills fluttered in his stubby fingers.

"Here, folks, my apologies for disrupting your evening. Let me get this."

"It's settled, Mr. Hart," I said. "We were just leaving." Typical Hart behavior: reckless with his money, he often picked up the tab for total strangers.

"Do I know you?" Without asking, he plopped down on the seat opposite me. "You look familiar. You, too," he said to Adam. Then he turned to Mabel. "But I don't think I've seen you, my dear, because I'd remember that *punim.*"

We introduced ourselves. Hart apologized again for not realizing Adam was a member of his new show. "You're part of my family now! You must join me and my friends," he said, waving at the front of the restaurant.

Mabel picked up her handbag. "Thanks, Mr. Hart," she said with wifely resolve, "but we're going home. Adam has rehearsal tomorrow."

"So do I, but that's not stopping me." Hart laughed.

"David's game for more fun," Adam said. "He was just trying to talk us into staying up past our bedtimes."

Hart rubbed his hands together—a habitual gesture, I would soon learn. "Wonderful! Come along, Dave." He bounded off the seat and jerked his thumb at me. I stood up. Hart, barely five feet tall in his elevator shoes, did a double take. "Oy! Talk about altitude! You get enough oxygen up there?"

I shrugged; I couldn't do anything about my size, but I knew Hart was horribly self-conscious about his own height. *Don't dislike me because I'm tall, Larry.*

The Finkelsteins waved good-bye as I followed Hart to a huge booth at the front. Three blond youths, all with the same polished, brittle exteriors, looked up at us. They could have auditioned for the "Triplets" number in *The Band Wagon.* One actually curled his full, pouty lip at me. I mentally christened them Zeke, Deke, and Peke, after one of my favorite kids' shows in the early 2050s.

The fourth occupant of the booth was as gay as the Triplets, but far from flashy. Milton "Doc" Bender was a lousy dentist who'd recently begun a new career as a theatrical agent...and a parasite. I've mentioned Hart was terrible with his money. Well, Bender siphoned off a good bit of it as Hart's every-ready drinking and gambling partner, with an uncanny ability to find boys like the Triplets. They were pretty, but Bender was plain and balding, with thick glasses over his buggy eyes. The light from the candle on the table glinted off his spectacles, making it hard to read his expression. "Hey, Larry, we thought you'd slipped in the toilet and got flushed out to sea. Who's this?"

"David Taylor," Larry said. "Move over, Doc, and let's have another round. What are you drinking, Dave?"

"Just coffee."

Hart shook his head. His beard was thicker even than Gershwin's; he shaved twice a day to keep it down. The dark shadows on his chin made half his face vanish in the dim light. "Nonsense. We're drinking and *so are you.*"

Another South American would flatten me, so I ordered Irish coffee, which confused the waiter. I guess that drink hadn't caught on yet, so I described the ingredients. If Dinty Moore's suddenly starts serving them, I guess I've changed history in a way I never expected.

The conversation, as you might expect, centered on the theatre. When I said I'd just seen the *Follies,* Hart enthused over Ira's lyrics. "So intelligent, yet still with that popular touch. He's a gem."

"Josephine Baker was sublime," offered Zeke. Or maybe Deke.

"I had Fanny and Josephine over for a party last week," said Hart, lighting a fat cigar. "Miss Baker sashays into the kitchen and asks Big Mary Campbell, my housekeeper, for 'une tasse de café, s'il vous plaît.' Now Big Mary comes by her name honestly. She's from Jamaica and could break me in two. She puts her hands on her hips, looks La Baker in the eye and says, 'Honey, you're full of shit. Talk with the mouth you were born with!' Mary won't take guff from anyone."

One story followed another, delivered in Hart's hoarse, staccato voice. He knew everyone on both coasts and told tales with natural ease and grace. I laughed at his jokes; Bender did, too, perhaps too heartily, and made some awful puns on his own that Hart found hilarious. The Triplets smiled drunkenly, though I doubted they followed the wordplay.

Others joined our table, as Hart roped them in while they passed by, like a shepherd with a crook. Four chorus girls—one of whom had been in Hart's *Simple Simon*; two shady characters straight out of a Runyon tale; and writer Marc Connelly, late of the Algonquin Club. When the waiters finally announced it was closing time, Larry tossed a wad of cash on the table and shouted, "Back to my place!"

Even if I'd wanted to leave, I couldn't. Hart latched onto my arm like a leech and propelled me into a taxi, one with an extended wheelbase. Bender, Connelly, two chorines, and the boys tumbled in with us. I've been here almost two years, and I still croggle at the size of these vehicles. I'm used to SmartCars, GreenWheels, UniVeeks, but these are bloody battleships! They're *obscene,* even if gas is under twenty cents a gallon.

The taxi zoomed uptown through the quiet streets to the triple-domed cupola towers of the Beresford Apartments, where Hart lived with his aging mother and his actor brother, Teddy. Bender and the trio charged into the kitchen with familiar ease, emerging with platters of cold cuts, cheese, and olives. Larry scurried about, his elevator shoes clumping, pressing drinks on everyone, turning on the phonograph, and singing along in his husky, high voice. Card games—poker and pinochle—began, and Deke danced with one of the girls.

I don't play cards; while I would have enjoyed dancing with the Finkelsteins, I didn't feel like cutting the rug with this crowd. The nearby brick-lined den with its warm walnut bookshelves enticed me. I wandered in and started studying Larry Hart's eclectic collection. What words did the man F. Scott Fitzgerald called "America's poet laureate" favor?

Shakespeare, first and foremost, Twain, Proust, Chaucer, Heine (his ancestor), Boccacio, and, on a small table, a well-worn leather-bound volume of Shelley. Larry Hart spent only a year or two at Columbia, but he was exceptionally well-read, much like Ira Gershwin.

I settled into an overstuffed chair with a volume of Keats and promptly fell asleep, despite that Irish coffee.

I woke up when someone opened the door. A beefy black woman in a crisp starched apron stood framed in the doorway, back-lit by the lights in the living room. She gave me a hateful look, her arms folded across her ample chest. "They've gone home, sir, every last one," Big Mary Campbell said in tones of icy disapproval. *Except you.*

I jumped to my feet, and the Keats fell to the ground. "I'm so sorry. I was reading and I must have drifted off." I picked up the book and ran my fingers along the tooled leather, trying to gather my thoughts. My head pounded. I would have killed for a cup of the coffee I smelled brewing, but Mary wasn't offering any to the likes of me. I replaced the book on its shelf and edged past her.

She followed me to the door, muttering and picking up dirty plates along the way. "Damn Mr. Lorry's riff raff.

178

Eating us outta house and home. I swear, I'm gonna start hiding food in my room."

I grabbed my hat and coat from the rack where they were hanging next to Hart's small, tailored ones and hustled to the elevator before Big Mary clobbered me. In the lobby, the Beresford's uniformed doorman gave me a bored look. I wondered how many hungover men he'd seen leaving Hart's.

The chilly February air hit me like a slap in the face. *Coffee!* I hadn't spent any time exploring the thirties version of the Upper West Side, but I knew where I could find some. Cutting through Theodore Roosevelt Park, past the newly opened Planetarium, I headed for the Daitch Market on 80th Street. Like many stores of this era, it was poorly lit. I groped my way to the back where Louis Zabar rented an "appetizing counter."

I cleared my throat, not quite as noisily as Larry Hart. "Bagel, lox, and coffee."

The woman behind the counter served me in record time, slicing the bagel and giving it a generous *schmear* of cream cheese. A few spindly wooden chairs and tables stood near the counter, hard by the pickle barrels. My order in hand, I gratefully sank into one and inhaled my coffee in its cardboard cup. A decent brew. I'd had plenty worse here.

But then I tasted the lox. Epiphany. Glory. Angels singing. The woman noticed my beatific expression. *"Nu?"*

"Give me three pounds to go, and another coffee," I said with my mouth full.

"You got it." She wrapped the treasure in wax paper and brought to the table. "My husband smokes them himself. It's been so popular, maybe we'll expand the counter soon."

"You'll do well. I guarantee it." Zabar's would take over the Daitch market, then the entire block, filling thousands of orange and white bags with delicious goodies for decades.

But *nothing* I ever tasted in the twenty-first century came close to what I was eating here in 1936.

The heavenly meal revived me enough to consider the evening's adventures. I'd gone partying with Lorenz Hart. He and Richard Rodgers were moving into the final years of their long collaboration, when they'd create some of their finest shows: *On Your Toes, Babes in Arms, The Boys From Syracuse, Pal Joey.* At the same time, Hart's drinking and carousing would spiral out of control, propelled by his self-loathing and depression.

Could I do anything about that? No easy solution here, no miracle dose of Minarcin. I was confident I could keep him from dying of pneumonia in 1943 at forty-eight. But could I save him from himself?

I didn't know. But I'd finally met him, and I'd make sure that our paths would cross again.

Gathering my lox, I took a cab home. Leo, on his way to school, met me coming up the walk.

"You look something awful, Mr. Taylor." He shook his head in disapproval.

"A long night, Leo, but a useful one. I met a very great songwriter." Inside my apartment, I turned up the heat and sat down to write a thank-you note to Hart. In the 2070s, nobody writes letters, but in the 1930s people did all the time. I'm no party animal; I couldn't stomach hanging around Hart with Bender. But Hart's a literate man, and I'm not bad with words myself. I'll try connecting with him that way and see where it gets me. I stuck a three-cent stamp with Susan B. Anthony on it—three cents to mail a letter!—so I could pop it in the box on my way to the Eagle.

#

Rose and her father drove into the wilds of New Jersey, searching for Trenton Piano Movers. After some swearing at the GPS, they finally found a dingy office and a large garage for a fleet of vans. When they poked their heads inside, the place seemed deserted. "Hello?" Nate called.

A burly African-American man emerged from the back rooms. He looked like he could bench-press a piano before moving it and seemed startled to see someone walk in from the street, especially a man with a teenage girl. "Can I help you?" he asked in tones that expected the answer was "No."

"We did phone," Nate said. "About an hour ago. We talked to your receptionist, Camille."

The man glared at an empty desk, cluttered with papers and tiny pink penguins. "Girl's useless," he growled. "Well, you're here. My name's LaDainian Adams. I'm the manager."

Nate introduced himself and his daughter. "My brother, David Greenbaum, recently died in unusual circumstances. We're tracing his last movements and found papers about your company in his things."

"That name's not familiar, but let me check the records." Adams had an Ally with a Dura-coat cover clipped to his waist. He subvocalized into it, then shook his head. "We moved a piano for Cyndi Greenbaum in Cranbury in 2073, but not your brother."

"He might have given another name," Nate said. "Here's his picture."

That got a reaction from the manager. "Oh, *him!* Not likely to forget him. He wanted to know how to move pianos for a film project. Told him that would be one boring movie. But the name he gave was Gerald Something. Last

August, maybe. Let me look it up. Yeah ... here we go. Jerry Davidson. Three e-mails."

"That's probably a long-dead account—we know he had several—but would you mind forwarding those to me?" He rattled off his address.

Adams frowned, giving Nate a close look. "I wouldn't do it, but with that face, you just got to be related to the guy."

Nate groaned. "Listen, my life would be less complicated now if we had taken after different parents, instead of looking like clones of our Dad."

"Excuse me?"

Rose, who had been standing quietly behind her father, now spoke up. "Never mind, Mr. Adams. My dad's being difficult. Can you tell us anything else about my uncle and your company?"

"So the film story was bullshit? Huh." Adams shrugged his massive shoulders. "Well, I told him our insurance wouldn't let him even touch a piano we were moving. He didn't care. He just wanted to watch us load and unload pianos; see how we secured freight, installed padding, used clips and dolleys. He *paid* us so he could ride along, you know, like reporters and cops? He filmed us and asked tons of questions, like there's some history to what we do. Shit. We move pianos."

"You said it was August," said Rose, "but that he never moved any pianos himself? Because I saw him then, and he looked like he'd been doing heavy work. He was sweaty and sore."

Adams grimaced. "This had better stay between us. He did help out, for a little bit, there at the end. He'd been watching us for over two weeks when one of my guys had a death in his family. I was short-handed and Davidson offered to help for a week. I'd have been fucked if anything happened, but he was good. Damn good. Piano moving isn't brute strength. You got to dance with the weight, know the moves, the steps, the obstacles. Right, left, up, down, around. That guy was a natural. Sorry he's gone, because I would have hired him. What happened to him?"

Now it was Nate's turn to look uncomfortable. "We can't say, but thanks for your help."

The Greenbaums walked back to the car, more perplexed than when they had arrived. "I don't get it," Rose said. "All the things Uncle David could do in the thirties—singing, acting, playing music—and he's going to move pianos? That doesn't make sense!"

Her father rubbed the little scar on his chin. "But it sounds so damned specific, like he really needed to do this. Are there any famous piano movers you can think of?"

"That old movie with Abbott and Costello. No, the other comics. Laurel and Hardy. Maybe Uncle David thinks he can meet fellow musicians by moving their pianos, but you'd think there was an easier way."

"You said it—it doesn't make sense."

#

From the diary of J.D. Taylor, February 24, 1936
A return letter from Hart!

Dear David,

Here I was, moping and miserable, because I'd thought I'd offended you, so you left in a huff. But Mary tells me she found you in my library, sound asleep with a book of poetry! In this business, that's worthy of note. Too many theatrical folks don't read anything besides their own reviews. I won't lose track of a fellow verse-lover!

This show of ours has us jumping, as your friend Adam will no doubt tell you, but if you're free for lunch

this week, come to Ralph's on West 45th. It's our usual
haunt, hard by the Imperial, so Dick can drag me back
to work after.
  Who's your favorite poet? Mine's Shelley.

Larry Hart

#

From the diary of J.D. Taylor, March 2, 1936
My shifts at the Golden Eagle meant I couldn't take Larry up
on his lunch offer until now. I pulled my coat tight against
the late winter chill as I hustled along West 45th from
the subway. Ralph's was an Italian joint, popular with the
theatre crowd. I'd been there during *Jubilee*'s rehearsals.
Unlike places that resemble dungeons, it's brightly lit, with
the traditional red-checked tablecloths and wax-covered
wine bottles.

The maitre'd hooted when I asked if Mr. Hart was there.
"When *isn't* he here? This way, sir."

Hart shared the booth with Bender—who seemed
attached to his side like a sucker fish to a shark—Richard
Rodgers, Ray Bolger, George Balanchine, and Hans Spialek.
The composer, star, choreographer, and orchestrator of *On
Your Toes,* respectively, and some of the greatest names in
the history of the American musical. I felt like turning tail
and running.

Hart's dark eyes lit up as I approached. "Davey boy! You
made it! Have a seat."

Balanchine was scribbling Cyrillic in a notebook, but
Rodgers pursed his lips. His thoughts were easy to read:
Another of Larry's faggy friends.

But I had unexpected backup in Spialek, the "Bouncing
Czech." Hans hoisted his beer at me. "How's life? You
verking anyvhere, David?" Turning to Rodgers, he said,

"David vas rehearsal pianist for *Anything Goes,* und a gut von, too. Coley called him 'the Vizard.'"

Rodgers' brow relaxed. Maybe I was "musical," a code word for gays, but if I was also "musical" in the traditional sense, I might pass muster in his books.

"Thanks, Hans," I said, " I'm back at the Golden Eagle, but I'm working on some songs."

"You're in this racket?" Hart exclaimed. "I had no idea."

Bender gave me a predatory look that made my skin crawl. "Do you have representation, Mr., uh, David?"

"Professionally, I'm J.D. Taylor, but David to friends. I represent myself, Mr. Bender. I don't mean to intrude; I can see this is a working lunch."

Rodgers held up a large, well-manicured hand. "Correct me if I'm wrong, David, but you have money in our show. Four grand, yes?" *Trust Rodgers to know how much, down to the last penny.* When I nodded, he continued, "Then you're certainly entitled to join us. The veal marsala is excellent."

Hart rubbed his hands together, flashing his gold cufflinks. "You didn't tell me that, either, David. Just that you were neighbors with Adam Flint, one of our dancers."

That word got through to Balanchine. "Flint. *Da.* Flint moves well, especially the upper body."

I must pass that on to Adam; Balanchine's approval means a lot to him.

Ray Bolger's soft smile looked exactly like the one the Scarecrow would give Dorothy three years from now. He nudged Hart. "So, Larry, you didn't know what this fellow did for a living or that he was a backer. What *do* you know about him?"

Bender smirked, but there was nothing to smirk about. I'd been careful.

Hart took a long drink from a glass that definitely didn't have water in it. "David can talk intelligently about theatre and he's well-read." He cleared his throat, making a horrible noise; like the hand-rubbing, it was habitual. "Kkkkkkhhhh. That's plenty for me."

And talk of theatre we did, for a solid hour. Everything from the New Deal's Federal Theatre Project ("Marvelous!" Bolger declared. "All those jobs! I know folks who would starve without it.") to the recent closure of *Porgy and Bess* ("Damn shame," said Hart) to Kurt Weill's prospects ("Too European," Rodgers sniffed, while Spialek said, "No, Kurt's a gut fellow.").

I don't know if I was especially witty, but I held my own with these giants. I'd been in the past for nearly two years; while I'd stumbled a few times, I hadn't really screwed up.

And now I'd met Rodgers and Hart. They'd be busy for the next five years...and so would I.

#

From the diary of J.D. Taylor, April 18, 1936
On Your Toes opened last week to glowing reviews, as I knew it would. The opening night bash was a humdinger, too. I sat with Adam and Mabel and the chorus in the ballroom of the Ritz, but Larry Hart's whoops when the reviews came in were audible even at a distance, with the orchestra blaring Rodgers' music.

That was fun, but I enjoyed myself more taking the Spinellis to see it. Leo's dad Sergio even joined us. He's a short, taciturn Sicilian who was rarely home because of his job on the Caribbean liners, and I think his family preferred it that way. He definitely doesn't like me, or maybe he just doesn't like that Leo and Frannie like me.

The Spinellis loved the show. *On Your Toes* features Junior Dolan, a vaudeville hoofer (Bolger), encountering the world of classical ballet. "Slaughter on 10th Avenue," in which Junior has to keep dancing so mobsters can't shoot him, had the house ringing with laughter.

Afterwards, we ate dinner at the Village Barn on West 8th Street, not far from our apartments. The Barn has good, homey fare in a good, homey atmosphere, with horse collars and milk cans hanging from the rafters. I'm partial to their corn fritters and ham. They also have nightly turtle races, but unfortunately past Leo's bedtime.

Leo kept chuckling over "Slaughter." "Did you notice, when the three cops entered, the orchestra started playing 'Three Blind Mice'? Thought I'd split my sides."

"Composers like to play musical jokes, the way you use words to make puns," I said. "Rodgers is good at that, and so is his orchestrator, Hans Spialek." I explained how Hans slipped in Siegfried's hunting call to match Hart's lyric about decorative moose heads in "There's A Small Hotel."

"I get it!" Leo said. "Because they got the moose while hunting. That's so *sneaky.* I like it."

Frannie sighed. "That's our boy. He admires sneaky."

Sergio just grunted while digging into his pot roast.

"It's not 'sneaky,'" I said. "It's specialized knowledge. Anyone can appreciate that song—its music, lyrics, the way it worked in the show—but knowing Wagner's hunting call gives you another reason to smile. Or take the 'Princess Zenobia Ballet.' You liked it, right?"

"Sure!" Leo said through a mouthful of beef stew and biscuits. "When Junior was pretending to be an African slave in the chorus, he forgot to put the black make-up on his skinny white chest. A riot!"

"Well, that ballet is a spoof of a classical ballet called *Scheherazade*. The more you know about that, the funnier *Zenobia* is."

Leo thumped his fork on the table. "How can I learn about that? I wanna know all that stuff. How do I do that?"

"You can't," Sergio said, squashing the happy mood with two blunt words. "You're a little wop whose papa came over from Sicily to change the bed linens for the Broadway big shots when they sail to Bermuda. You can't be like those men."

Leo deflated like a popped balloon. I jumped to his defense.

"I disagree, Mr. Spinelli. Most of those men are immigrants or the sons of immigrants, many worse off than you. Irving Berlin's first memory was seeing his Russian home burned in a pogrom.

"But that's not the point. It's about learning. And anyone can learn nearly anything if he want to enough. Leo's already shown he's dedicated about his playing. If he wants to study more music and theatre history, that's great. He'll become a better musician."

Sergio huffed air through his bushy mustache. "You're talking through your hat. As if he could get anywhere tinkling on a piano. Bah."

Leave it to Sergio to spoil a pleasant Saturday. When does the Monarch of Bermuda sail next?

"Maybe Leo won't write for shows or films, but he can make a living with music," I said. *At least, it's easier to do in the 1930s than in another 140 years.* "Hotels, restaurants, night clubs, radio stations, churches, community centers all need pianists." I pointed to the Barn's band, Larry Funk's, playing schottisches and reels for the couples on the dance floor. "Music's all around us, and somebody's got to play it. Why not Leo, in a few years? Or he could teach. All schools have music classes." *Unlike my timeline, with arts programs cut!* "Hey, Leo, how'd you like to assign demerits instead of collecting them?"

"Sure thing! See, Papa, I can do it. Stop sounding like you're from Missouri, 'stead of Sicily!"

"Humpf," said Sergio, with a face like a bowl of cold oatmeal.

Frannie had considerable experience defusing her volatile spouse's moods. She said, "Some dessert, *caro?*" Not waiting for his answer, she cut a thick slab of cherry pie and slid it in front of him.

"Me, too," said Leo.

"Me, three," I chimed in. If the Barn's baked goods couldn't put Sergio Spinelli in a better mood, nothing could.

#

From the diary of J.D. Taylor, July 11, 1936
In the weeks after our outing, I stepped up Leo's classical education, starting with "The Three B's," as Junior Dolan explains in *On Your Toes.* That's Bach, Beethoven, and Brahms, of course. We do fifteen minutes of music appreciation before each lesson, which is good practice for me, too, and Leo's tackling the "Moonlight Sonata" with enthusiasm. He's also seen his first ballet (a lackluster *Swan Lake*), and Shakespeare—Orson Welles' famous voodoo *Macbeth,* which he adored, especially the drums and the witch with the bullwhip. This fall, we'll see Leslie Howard and John Gielgud's dueling *Hamlets.* To prepare for that, we've been reading one act of the play after each lesson; he may not realize it, but his vocabulary and comprehension are improving, especially since he insists on playing Hamlet. I managed not to giggle when he said "what a *rouge* and

peasant slave am I." Unfortunately, the extra time with me has resulted in some loud arguments next door that included my name and the words "fairy" and *"un finocchio,"* among others. No, Sergio hasn't warmed to me.

But the weather has, for everyone. The nation's sweltering through a horrendous heat wave. A hundred and six yesterday—I've never missed air conditioning so much. When I saw Mabel Finkelstein early this morning, her curls were already drooping. She gave me a feeble smile as I lugged my groceries into the lobby. "Oy, have you ever been in anything like this out West, David? I'm dreading the uptown bus," she said, fanning herself.

Actually, I have. I could tell you about global warming…
"It gets hot in L.A., but not so humid. Stay cool, Mabel." I went in to stow my purchases before they spoiled.

I'd also bought the *New York Times,* just a daily, but stuffed full of news and ads, a stark contrast to the slimmed down "Gray Lady" of 2079, with barely enough pages to line a bird cage. And the *Times* was just the biggest and best paper. The newsstand on Sixth Avenue near the courthouse sold a dozen others, plus scores of magazines. I enjoyed reading it cover to cover; not a patch on the Internet, but it's what's here.

I brewed a pot of coffee, fixed a tray with cornflakes and a toasted pumpernickel bagel from Gertel's, and took it to the Studios' rear garden. Only eight, and my apartment was stifling, so breakfast by the fountain seemed a better choice.

The headlines trumpeted stories about the heat wave: over seventy dead from heat stroke or drowning, twenty-six straight days of temperatures over ninety. It wasn't cooling down at night, either. When I'd finished the paper, I began my weekly letter to Larry Hart. His last one described his enthusiasm for his latest project with Rodgers, *Babes In Arms,* which would debut next spring: "We're only casting youngsters—fresh, funny, fast kids! Dick and I are writing the book ourselves, which is a challenge. Theatregoers are more intelligent than the average man, so we're trying to respect that in our material. In other words, more than just a simple Boy Meets Girl story."

I hadn't got beyond "Dear Larry" when Leo bounded into the garden. "Hey, Mr. Taylor, can I have my lesson early? Harold and Buddy and I are going to Coney."

"Sure, I don't mind." I plopped my papers on the tray to carry inside. The grim headlines stared up at me. "Say, Leo, you *do* know how to swim, right?"

"Naw, but we'll be okay," he said, with the supreme confidence of a teenager.

I stopped at the lobby door. "Yesterday, twenty-one people thought they could cool off in the river or the sea, even though they couldn't swim, and now they're dead. I'll give you extra money for ices and Cokes galore, but only if you swear you won't go in the water, not until you learn to swim."

"How'm I gonna learn to swim?" He scowled, looking like Sergio, minus the mustache.

"The WPA's opening another new pool next month, specially filtered against typhoid and polio. I promise I'll teach you how to swim. Deal?" *Sergio won't like it, but tough. Everyone should learn to swim.*

"Deal." Leo knew I kept my word, unlike his unreliable father. We headed inside, where he plunged into his lesson (*"Für Elise"*) with even more vigor that usual. When he finished, I praised his improving accuracy and sent him to Coney, his pocket jingling with change.

After a shower that wouldn't last long in this heat, I was dressing for work when the phone rang.

"Hello, David. Frank Tours here. I'm m.d. for the show Cole Porter's doing this fall. It's called *Red, Hot and Blue,* starring Ethel Merman. Cole asked me if he could get his Wizard again for rehearsals."

I'd been wondering if I'd get this call—and dreading that I'd have to refuse it. "Thanks for thinking of me, but I'm already engaged. But you know who would be a good fit? Lewis Kessler."

"The red-haired madman? I can see where Cole would like him; he's, um, pretty flamboyant. But Ethel?"

"I think he can handle her." In fact, Kessler and Merman and Porter would work closely together for the next fifteen years. As I'd seen at *Anything Goes,* Porter couldn't sight-transfer music, but it was second nature for Kessler. Porter would come to rely on him for auditions as well as rehearsals—and for some notorious drag parties—while Merman hired him as her personal pianist. That's why I didn't leap at Tours' offer. I'd miss playing some great Porter tunes and working with Jimmy Durante and Bob Hope … but, no. The Project meant I had to keep my head down for the next year.

#

From the diary of J.D. Taylor, December 7, 1936
I'm in a rotten mood. First, Bill Daly, Gershwin's good friend and a great musical mind, died of a heart attack this week. If I'd overloaded my suitcase with statins, I could have saved him, too. Damn. He still had so much to offer the world.

Then I realized that yesterday, the 6th, was David Warren Greenbaum's thirty-fifth birthday. In honor of the event, I got out my Ally and played the original 1970 cast album of *Company*—on my earbuds, of course. I could just picture Leo overhearing Sondheim and wanting to know about those ladies who lunch.

Playing *Company* was a mistake in a whole bunch of ways. Instead of smiling at the songs and the dialogue as bachelor Bobby's married friends wish him a happy thirty-fifth, I cried my eyes out. Not that I didn't have friends here to wish me a happy birthday. As Joseph David Cohen-Taylor, I had a great thirty-first party on March 22nd with the neighbors, coworkers at the Eagle, some folks from the Porter shows, even Vincent Youmans and Boots. No other celebrities, though. The Gershwins were in Hollywood; my relationship with Hart remains primarily epistolary; and Porter thinks I'm lower class.

It was the pain in Dean Jones' voice as he realizes how much he needs someone in his life, someone to make him aware of "Being Alive"; that's what had me sobbing.

I had friends, but I didn't have that kind of someone in the 1930s. I doubted I ever would, not with the demands of the Project. I *did* have it, for about seven years. Seven more than many get, even if the last few were a battlefield. *Damn you, Ramon.*

The album led to my next bad move: while I had the Ally out, I started watching vids and 'loads and photos of Ramon. There's a reason I don't watch these very often. I content myself with the photos on my walls and tables, especially the doughboy Ramon from *Versailles* and the one of Señorita Rose. Now, though, I couldn't help myself. I kept downing Cuba Libres and clicking away, though each one hurt more. Holiday trips to Veracruz; shots in dressing rooms in theatres that wouldn't be built for decades; homemade porn, of course. Our creativity knew no bounds and our stamina nearly matched it. But it was the "Why Do I Love You?" birthday message he sent me in 2073 that was the kicker. We were apart that December; I had a role on off Broadway in Fullerton's *Without a Compass,* while Ramon was in L.A., helping his mom after her knee surgery.

I didn't quite equal the Tennessee Valley floods in tears, but it was close. I stabbed the Ally, cutting off Ramon in the midst of Reason #19, "the way you sniffle when you chop onions. Really, David, you've got the sexiest sniffle in town." I blew my nose.

Fuck it. If I'm going to do dumb-ass things, I'll do it big-time. Why else get wasted on your birthday?

After stowing the Ally in its niche, I threw on my coat and my scarf from Frannie and charged into the chill night air. I grabbed a taxi on Sixth Avenue and told the driver, "28 West 28th Street."

The cabbie, a *Landsman* from his looks, didn't smirk as some did when I gave a bathhouse address. He drove along the icy streets in silence, pulling up in front of the Everard, a distinguished Victorian era building with an arched entry flanked with two green lamps. They gave the place the appearance of a police precinct. Rumor had it the Police Athletic League ran the Everard. Rumor lied. Plenty of gay history happened here, much of it tragic. In the thirties, however, it was one of the classier joints, reasonably clean and rarely troubled by the authorities. Maybe that's how the PAL rumor got started.

I hopped out and handed the cabbie an extra buck—smirkers got shitty tips. Rum-fogged and miserable, I stumbled up the stairs and through the doorway.

A ferret-faced clerk at the counter gave me a key, a bracelet, a towel (raggedy, but not stained), and a robe. I changed, stowed my gear in the locker, and walked into the big common steamroom. Two outrageous queens stationed near the entrance marked my arrival. They seemed to be providing running commentary.

"How about him, Timothy?"

"Heavens, no, I don't like beards!"

The first one slapped Timothy's thigh. "You liar! I once saw you *leap* into Monty Woolley's Caddie, up on 135th Street. You positively leaped."

"Well, he's *the* Beard, so that's different." Timothy giggled. "I was just lucky he saw me before the big buck further up the block!"

I ignored them and made my way through the haze of steam and cigarette smoke to a bench. There I sat, listening to the murmur of male voices, punctuated by rhythmic thumps, grunts and moans from the nearby private rooms.

It didn't take long. A slightly chubby redhead about my own age passed by and ran his hand over my shoulder. *A redhead. Good. No Latin Lotharios, please.* I followed him into one of the small rooms, dimly lit and smelling of musk, urine and mold. For a while, anyway, I didn't think of anything except the needs of my body and Mickey's body.

Afterwards, Mickey wanted to talk. "Ah, that was grand. My wife won't do *that*. She thinks I'm working late. Ha! I'm an architect, designing a new post office in Queens. What do you do, David? You hitched?"

"I'm a composer, and no, I'm not married. Not now." My physical aches soothed, I was regretting being there. The social aspect of the baths was fine in itself, but I wasn't in the mood tonight. I saw Mickey's toothy grin, his broad chest covered with appealing ginger fuzz, and Sondheim lyrics thudded in my brain. *He could never be that kind of someone I need, who needs me.*

"I got to go," I said, trying to figure out which was my towel. *As if it mattered.*

Mickey's smile vanished. "Of course. Some take it like that, and leave right away. But shootin' the breeze is nice, too."

I threw on the robe. It scratched. "You're right, Mickey. It's just ... not a good day."

"Sure. Here's hoping I meet you when it's a better one. I'm a regular here at the 'Everhard.'" He waved at his now flaccid member. "Well, I suppose I'm not living up to that nickname right now. And whose fault is that?"

I kissed him. "Thanks, Mickey. For making me smile."

"Any time, boyo."

As I made my way to the front, I noticed the two fairies hadn't gone to the bottom of the garden. They were puffing on cigars and didn't say anything as I went past. Maybe the stogies prevented further comments; maybe they just noted entrances, not exits.

By the time I'd cleaned up and dressed, I figured it was quite late, but when I put my watch back on, I was surprised to see it wasn't even one. *Some birthday, Greenbaum.* I walked to the corner, 28th and Broadway, the heart of old Tin Pan Alley, and pondered my choices. I could go back to my place, where Ramon's smiling picture would stare back at me. I could get drunk in a Village bar, like Joe Gould. Getting drunk wasn't a bad plan, as the rum was wearing off, but I definitely didn't want to see the little Professor. Joe Gould weirds me out, even on good days.

I opted for uptown, the heart of the theatre district, and ended up at Louie Bergen's place, always friendly to gypsies. It was also cheap. I'd recently invested a ton in *You Can't Take It With You* and had other hits lined up, so I wasn't hurting, but I was being careful. I walked in, a trifle unsteady, and a gang of familiar faces waved me over: chorus boys and girls and a few musicians, now all working on *Red, Hot and Blue.*

"We miss you, David," said Vivian Vance, her pixie face beaming. "We miss our Wizard."

"Nice to be wanted," I said. "Beer, please." My own era's beers are tastier, with microbrews and artisanal ales and offering from every hoppy nation on earth. The best I've found here are some decent darks in German-dominated Yorkville.

I sat with the gang, listening to stage gossip, including tales of Lew Kessler's latest drag party. The aimless chatter and the booze were doing a good job numbing my feelings. I was on my third mug when Larry Hart, Doc Bender, Vernon Duke, and George Balanchine tromped past our table. Hart was three sheets to the wind, as usual, and Duke and Balanchine were singing Russian songs.

"David!" Hart leaned over Vivian and punched my shoulder. "How's tricks?"

"Lousy," I said, raising my mug. "To Bill Daly." I couldn't speak of my personal woes, but all Broadway shared that loss.

Hart's face sobered, if not the rest of him. "Damn shame. Daly was a prince."

Duke stopped singing at the mention of Daly's name. "Oh, David, wasn't that just the worst news ever? George must be devastated. They were friends for twenty years."

Hart looked from me to Duke. "You know David?"

"From George's, where else?"

Hart wobbled and clutched at the table. None of the gypsies said a word; who knew when they might need his good will for a job? He wagged a finger at Duke. "David's my pen pal, a great theatre mind. The things he writes—they make me *think.*" That large head on the too small frame swung around to me. "David Taylor, every day I find one of your letters in the post, that's a gala day, a red letter day. It's like sunlight through the gloom."

"C'mon, Larry, let's get Bally his whatchamacallit," Bender said. *No, he doesn't like Larry liking me, not one little bit.*

"*Smetannik!*" Balanchine said, slurring the word.

Duke translated: "Sour cream cake. The chef at the Hotel Bossert makes it just like in the Old Country."

"Want join us in the wilderness they call Brooklyn?" Larry asked, not noticing Bender's displeasure.

"I'll pass, Larry. I've got work tomorrow morning. But thanks."

It was still a shitty day. The grief that weighed me down earlier hadn't left. In so many ways, I was "alone, all alone," as in that stupid song from that stupid flop Ramon and I loved.

But my letters were getting through to Lorenz Hart. That was something to cheer, anyway.

Chapter 8

"The Cradle Will Rock" —Marc Blitzstein

From the diary of J.D. Taylor, February 22, 1937

It's been an eventful month at the Seville Studios. Adam and Mabel announced they're expecting a baby in September. Frannie and Sergio had a huge fight, but about his gambling, not me. Yours truly sold another song to Dreyfus at Harms, a rueful love song that grew out of my gloomy birthday in December.

I've also sunk $1800 into a new Vincent Youmans show about barnstorming aviators who (naturally) fall in love. Given the way Youmans pisses off everyone and keeps saying he'd rather be doing "serious" work, this is a gamble for the Shuberts. Gossip says Boots threatened to leave him if he didn't buckle down to this job.

Will it be any good? Who knows? Even if it takes off, no pun intended, there may be trouble with headlines. Amelia Earhart will vanish this summer, but only I know that. I can't tell Vince or the Shuberts. Whatever happens, I'm hoping Youmans will create some songs that live beyond the show's run.

I'm not getting many letters from Larry Hart, who's readying *Babes in Arms* for its spring opening. Still, we had an interesting exchange not long ago where I told him about Leo's youthful perspective on theatre. Leo preferred Gielgud's *Hamlet* to Howard's ("Not so phony, and Ophelia was better."); Coward's *Tonight at 8:30* bored him, and Porter's *Red, Hot and Blue* was too corny, though he liked Merman's torch number, "Down in the Depths." The show that most intrigued him this fall, both musically and in subject matter, was Kurt Weill's satire on war, *Johnny Johnson,* which bombed. Leo deemed it "keen." I suspect my tastes are rubbing off on him, because I'm crazy about Weill's music.

Hart wrote back:

Dear David,

Your young friend is on the money! I think he won't find our new show drippy. I'm proud to say that a key plot point centers on racial injustice. We're trying to Sign the Nicholas brothers, headliners at the Cotton Club. Can those young men dance! A good notice from Leo would mean more to me than any critic's praise. Intelligent theatre patrons—and he clearly is, despite his age—can appreciate innovative, daring productions and plots that are weightier than marshmallows! But try telling that to producers.

Larry

#

From the diary of J.D. Taylor, June 16, 1937
Years ago, while I was researching *Second Chances,* I read an interview with some early twenty-first century drama critics about time travel, long before the Rippers. Most of them agreed that if they had a time machine, they'd go back to Elizabethan England to see the very

first *Hamlet,* with Richard Burbage as the Dane and Will as the Ghost.

Except for one guy, who picked June 16, 1937, so he could watch the opening night of Marc Blitzstein's *The Cradle Will Rock.* As far as plays went, there's no contest: *Hamlet,* a masterpiece! *Cradle,* a heavy-handed allegory with broadly drawn characters and pointed, stirring songs. It's not quite 100% agitprop—Blitzstein saw it as a morality play showing how oppression forces people to sell out in all walks of life, whether they're artists, factory workers, doctors, teachers, or prostitutes. But it's close.

Had history taken another turn, *The Cradle Will Rock* would have opened as just another production of the Federal Theatre Project, caused a slight stir, then vanished. Only fans of Blitzstein's flops—and he wrote his share— would know its score.

But when bloody strikes were weekly news, Blitzstein's pro-union stance alarmed conservative politicians, who tried to shut down the show as it prepared for previews. Congress ordered huge cuts in the New York staff of the FTP, then issued a moratorium on all new plays. That was aimed at *Cradle,* since two other shows opened despite the ban.

Director Orson Welles and producer John Houseman, however, wouldn't back down, resulting in one of the most exciting nights in theatre history. They vowed to find a theatre and stage the show. Unlike that long-ago critic, I was here, my ticket bought weeks ago. Along with the precious bit of pasteboard, I had my pockets filled with cash. Though I'd been part of the theatre scene for three years, I didn't know a soul in this company, but I had a plan to get an insider's view. Mr. Terracino gave me the day off, and at eleven I headed uptown for Maxine Elliott's Theatre on West 39th Street.

The Maxine Elliott is an elegant house, very French, with white Corinthian columns. Its handsome gold-trimmed doors were closed, with a shiny new chain and padlock on them and uniformed, armed guards on the street. The guards let company members inside, but had orders to keep them from taking anything out that could be considered government property.

In Houseman's memoirs, he wrote that while the company huddled inside and they struggled to find a new theatre, "well-wishers" brought them food and drink. A song in *A Chorus Line* came to mind: "I Can Do That!" I'd bring them lunch!

The Elliott was in the Garment District, where Frannie worked. She recommended a deli at Broadway and 39th. I found it easily, though the corner looked weird without the bust of Golda Meir. The deli owner beamed when I ordered seventy-five sandwiches (chicken, tuna, egg salad, roast beef, pastrami), several cases of Cokes, Rheingold, Dr. Brown's cream soda and Cel-Ray, apples, and candy bars. He and his four daughters built the sandwiches in an assembly line, then helped me deliver everything down the street to the Elliott.

This time, I went to the stage door in the side alley, which had its own cluster of bored guards.

"Izzat my lunch?" a cheeky one asked, pointing to our bags.

"These are for the starving artists inside," I answered. "Can we please go in?"

The oldest guard sighed and pulled out his keys. "Damn fuss for a buncha Reds," he muttered.

The backstage area impressed me; it was as handsome as the exterior. The dressing rooms had windows and full-length mirrors. My young assistants from the deli, however, gasped when we pushed our way into the Louis Quatorze auditorium, with gold silk and ivory everywhere.

"Jeepers," said the smallest one, gazing up at the chandelier. "Pretty posh."

Dozens of actors and musicians were seated on the brown velvet seats or sprawled on the edge of the stage. They looked up in surprise at our entrance.

"What's this?" one woman asked. "The kiddie matinee?"

"My name's David Taylor," I began, then realized I better project if I wanted everyone to hear. "I'm a composer, and I've acted a bit, too. I had a windfall lately and decided to spend it helping *The Cradle Will Rock,* especially after I saw your amazing dress rehearsal last night. So I brought you lunch." I hadn't been at the dress, but that gave me an excuse for being familiar with the work, which I was. I played the druggist's son in a dreadful production in Jersey City, just after I graduated.

"Well, thanks!" The woman was petite, barely older than Rose. I guessed she was Jean Rosenthal, production assistant, especially when she filled a box with sandwiches, apples and drinks. "I'm taking these downstairs for Orson and John. Save me an egg salad and a Coke. And don't spill anything."

"Why? Will the Federal Theatre spank us?" a thin actor asked.

"No, but the Shuberts might. This is their house."

"Ha! Now I'm tempted to smear mustard everywhere!"

The cast and crew fell to, unwrapping wax paper and chowing down. They graciously divided the bounty, as I'd underestimated the numbers. The black chorus members held back, not taking their share until Will Geer urged them. Geer was one of the few cast members to have a notable career, despite being blacklisted in the fifties. In the years when he couldn't get work, he built an outdoor stage on his property in Topanga Canyon, where his family and friends put on shows. The Theatricum Botanicum eventually became a center for classical theatre in southern California. Lovely place, though I haven't seen it since they rebuilt it after the brushfires of 2074.

I kept a low profile, sitting on an aisle seat and chatting. Mine wasn't the only delivery—during the afternoon, a platter of turkey sandwiches, boxes of cookies, a crate of Florida oranges, and a tray of steaming meatballs on toothpicks arrived.

The atmosphere was charged, but with an undercurrent of fear. This was one of the worst years in the Great Depression, the so-called Roosevelt Recession. Actors rarely enjoy steady work, but *Cradle*'s uncertain future was especially nerve-wracking. "Think you'll have a show tonight?" I asked Howard Da Silva, knowing the answer better than he did.

The actor shrugged. Like Geer, he was an established pro and activist, with a distinguished career ahead of him despite the blacklist. Six years from now, he'd appear in the original cast of *Oklahoma!* "Beats me. John's working with a broker downstairs where there's a phone. If we find a house, we'll have to perform without props or costumes or scenery. And for me, no hair!" He ran his hand over his balding scalp. "I *really* want my blond toupée, but it's 'government property.' What does Uncle Sam want with my rug?"

"Maybe he likes you as a brunette," said a girl whose own red hair came from a bottle.

"You know, the show might be better without the set and those cursed glass wagons," said Geer. He waved his crusts at the stage. "The design's too fancy for such a straightforward story. David, what'd you think of the wagons at the dress? Darn things took forever to move on and off."

"The glitches didn't bother me," I said, ad libbing. "I was caught up in the story."

"But Thoreau says, 'Simplify, simplify, simplify.'" Geer brushed crumbs from his vest. "Any more candy bars in that bag?"

"Sure." I passed it to him. He chose a Chunky, unfamiliar to me, as were the Seven-Ups. I took a Three Musketeers, only to find the interior was a weird Neapolitan nougat, not the filling I knew. Yuck.

Later in the day, the creative staff emerged from their lair. John Houseman was a Romanian-Brit in his late thirties with the stately bearing he'd keep all his life. Orson Welles, instantly recognizable to any film buff, followed. The twenty-two-year old *Wunderkind* had his pipe clenched in his teeth and his hands behind his back. Trailing them came composer Marc Blitzstein. He looked green with worry.

Houseman beckoned to Jean Rosenthal, who rushed over. He pressed money into her hand. I could barely make out their conversation: "Here's ten dollars. Find a piano and a truck, then ring back here every fifteen minutes for further instructions. If—no, *when*—we get a theatre, it won't do us any good if Marc doesn't have a piano."

Rosenthal practically saluted. She grabbed her purse and rushed out. It was nearing five o'clock; curtain was scheduled for eight-forty.

The company quieted as Houseman, Welles, and Blitzstein mounted the stage. "Ladies and gentlemen," Houseman said, "thank you for your patience and your loyalty." His normally sonorous voice sounded ragged after hours on the phone.

"We make progress, if in increments. The play *will* go on tonight, in the face of artistic suppression. Somewhere, somehow, we will find a theatre. Marc will play his brilliant score. That much is certain." He gestured behind him at the glass and metal platforms Geer had complained about. "Thanks to the government and their Cossacks, we are without our sets, our costumes, our props. But we still have our voices and our determination."

Welles stepped forward. "Unfortunately, we also lack an orchestra. The Musicians Union, Local 802, says that if any of our boys plays in the pit of a theatre other than this one, we have to pay full Broadway scale. We'd also have to hire more to meet union standards. Since we've barely got two nickels, that's out."

"Marc, however, is not a union member," said Houseman, "so he will play his score himself."

"The musicians' union isn't the only one giving us grief," Welles continued. "Actors Equity says since the FTP hired you, you can't perform *Cradle* for us on a commercial stage without new contracts." He spread his hands in a "What can you do?" gesture. "How's that for irony? Our show's pro-union, but the unions are blocking us."

Blitzstein, standing behind the pair, his cigarette drooping out of the corner of his mouth, winced at Welles' words. They had to hurt.

"Fortunately," Houseman continued, "Orson had a brainstorm. While Equity won't let you play your roles *on a commercial stage,* there's nothing to stop you, as American citizens, from sitting with the audience and saying your lines, singing your songs from there. A tricky legal point, I grant you, but perfectly correct. That applies to our musicians, too."

This stunning statement produced a variety of responses. Some looked pleased at the prospect of defying the shutdown; Will Geer laughed long and loud. Others murmured, "Crazy… *meshugge* … nuts … "— understandable reactions.

But most simply looked scared. Ninety per cent were relief workers, utterly dependent on their weekly FTP twenty-eight dollar checks. If they followed Welles' suggestion, would they lose their jobs? I wanted to reassure them that it would be fine, even historic, but Da Silva more or less said it for me: "If we pull this off, folks'll be talking about it for years."

Decades, Howard. Going on a century and a half.

"This is voluntary," Houseman said. "Unlike those boors who are trying to silence us, we won't force anyone to join us. It has been an honor having you in our company. We will not think any less of you if you choose not to partake in tonight's production." He coughed. "You must do what seems right to you."

The trio exited to applause, cheers, and tears. Blitzstein grabbed a Snickers bar from my bag and smiled at Welles as they went back downstairs. The dapper composer was part of my Project, though I wouldn't need to intervene in his life for nearly thirty years.

I made a second deli run around six, accompanied by two African-American men from the chorus. They hesitantly asked me if they could bring the bottles back for the deposit. Pennies truly mattered to people here. On the way back, one of my helpers suddenly exclaimed, "Look at that! She found a piano! Hey, Jeannie!"

A rust-stained white truck with Jersey plates idled at the light at 39th and Broadway. A battered upright was strapped in its bed, Jean Rosenthal riding beside it. Hearing the shout, she leaned over the side. "Tell them to find that darn theatre, and fast! This driver's getting tired of driving around the block!"

"Will do!"

The alley by the stage door was getting crowded: mostly reporters, but some early-arriving patrons and gawkers. I knew more people were gathering by the box office, where Da Silva and Geer would soon go out to entertain them while they waited. We went inside with our boxes, fed the ravenous cast...and watched the clock.

It was well after seven when footsteps thudded and war whoops echoed from backstage. Houseman and Welles burst into the dim house.

"A miracle!" Houseman crowed. "We have booked the Venice."

"Where the hell's that?" someone called.

"Used to be Jolson's 59th; it's an Eye-tie opera house now, but beggars can't be choosers," another said.

A mass exodus began under the disapproving scrutiny of the guards, who seemed pissed that *Cradle* had found a home. The company members who decided to perform in the mad scheme scurried for taxis, buses, subways and cars, like rats fleeing a sinking ship.

I set out, too, ready to join the hundreds of patrons for the thrilling march twenty-one blocks to the Venice. The weather was lovely, a balmy spring day, and, since it was nearly the solstice, there was still a bit of daylight in the sky.

As I squeezed through the jammed alley, several actors shook my hand, thumped my back, and thanked me for the food. "Break a leg," I told each one. "Can't wait to see what happens."

I'll never know if that little delay saved my ass or not. I was part of a knot, maybe a dozen people, that squeezed onto West 39th Street. The crowd by the box office was enormous—easily over five hundred—with a battalion of reporters, scribbling in notebooks. I couldn't see Houseman addressing the mob from the main door, but the words "Venice Theatre" were repeated like a mantra.

I started to press forward for a better view, when I saw him. I hadn't laid eyes on him in over three years, but his profile was unmistakable.

My brother, Nathan.

#

October 15, 2079

It had been more than nine months since Uncle David hijacked the SlingShot and went back to 1934, and Rose had the feeling that everyone, including her parents, wanted to sweep the whole thing under the rug. She and Dad and Lt. Mertz (working off the clock) spent the summer searching David's records, but found no further clues to his intentions. Then fall came. Mertz had a grisly murder to solve, Dad was teaching and writing a major study of the 1934 dock strike, and Rose began classes as a freshman at Juilliard.

The others might have shoved his memory aside, but Rose was living in David's apartment and taking classes at his alma mater. She couldn't help but think of him every day. _Why did he cut holes in the walls? What would he think of Dr. Paloma's interpretation of_ Travesties? It irked her that no one mentioned David at all when she came home for Hannah's birthday.

She complained about it to her siblings.

"I do so think about Uncle David," Hannah said. "I'm just not a drama queen. I keep my thoughts to myself."

Rose swallowed the retort she might have made when she was younger. "Okay. What do you think?"

"I think he's having a great time, surrounded by the music he loved. Maybe he's met Gershwin. Sure, I miss him, but if anybody was meant to live in the 1930s, it's Uncle David. Even his bedroom is Art Deco!"

Bertie sprawled on the floor with his Ally. He paused his game long enough to look up at his sisters. "Something bothers me. Will Uncle David be able to find somebody back then? You know, somebody new." He blushed. "I mean, it wasn't so easy for gays then, right?"

"Good point," Rose said. "Another reason for him to stay in theatre. But it's going to take time to get over Ramon."

"I miss Ramon, too," Hannah said. "Let's watch them in *Versailles.*"

The recording was nearly done when their parents came home. Both of them instantly recognized what the kids were watching; Isis' cheery greeting broke off in mid-sentence, and Nathan visibly winced, then gathered himself.

"Say, gang, could you turn that off? Just for a minute," he quickly added, as all three of them began to protest. "I've got news. Big news. Next March, I'm going to 1937, in the Splinterverse."

"You got funding?" Rose asked. *I'm glad Dad let my sibs in on the Splinterverse stuff. It makes it easier to talk about it.*

"Yes. The usual pittance from my department to cover some of the major sit-down strikes. There were so many that year, one newspaper said they'd replaced baseball as the national pastime. The Dust Bowl researchers want more data from black blizzards in Kansas and Colorado. The damn media's providing the most money, of course, but for a pretty horrible reason. I have to film the destruction of the *Hindenburg.*"

"What's that?" Hannah asked.

"It's this blimp that blew up and killed people," said Bertie. "But there's film of that already! I've seen it."

"They want more," said Nate. "Ghouls. At least Jaelen Barrett, our Romanist, got data from Pompeii to compare with the recent eruption, even if most of his footage was for that stupid reality series. I doubt we'll learn much more watching the poor *Hindenburg* burn. But my bosses decide things, not me. I'm just grateful they haven't totally sold Ripper technology to the media, that each trip has to have academic and scientific purpose. Otherwise, I'd just be a cameraman for historical horrors." He sank down onto the couch and poked Bertie. "Feet on the floor, not the coffee table."

"Will you look for Uncle David?" Rose asked. *Quit tip-toeing around, Dad.*

"Yes. I think I'll find him, too," said Nate. "Come on, Rosie. Nineteen-thirty-seven. The weirdest opening night ever? Yale Drama wants me to film the whole thing."

Rose felt like an idiot. "God. *The Cradle Will Rock.* I should have thought of that."

"The what?" asked Bertie.

Nate explained the background of the musical, the conflict with the government, and the memorable opening night. "I just remembered something. David performed in this musical when he was twenty-two, when I was starting with the Ripper program. I already knew *Cradle*'s history— after all, it's a show that combines our interests, labor and drama. He said he wished he could use the SlingShot to see that opening night."

Isis put her hand on her husband's shoulder. "So you solved it. He went back for this show."

Nate frowned. "No, there's got to be more to it than that. But if he's in New York in June 1937, he'll be there."

#

From the diary of J.D. Taylor, June 16, 1937
Nate was wearing a gray striped suit, a blue-gray fedora and his Ripperglasses. He was facing the main door, but he'd spot me if he turned his head. We're both tall for this era.

I pivoted with a smoothness Ramon might have envied and hustled in the opposite direction, towards Sixth Avenue. Many of the cast were doing the same, rather than fighting the horde on 39th.

Damn, damn, damn, damn. Nana always said the Greenbaums don't raise dummies. The opening night of *The Cradle Will Rock* is one of those singular nights in theatre history, like the record-breaking 3389th performance of *A Chorus Line*; the closing night of *The Phantom of the Opera* in 2033; the "gypsy" (stage pros only) run-through of *Gypsy,* reportedly Merman's finest performance; Chris Pine dying on stage as Lear in 2067 at eighty-seven, but still carrying his Cordelia and hanging on through the last "O-groan."

Of course I'd be at *Cradle.* Of course he'd realize that.

When I reached the corner, I ducked out of sight around a furrier's warehouse and leaned against the wall. *Now what? Dash home in a panic? Miss this magical night? Hell, no!* I'd spent a pile (in 1937 dollars) feeding the *Cradle* company. Nate might keep me from the audience, but they could find me a place backstage.

I crossed Sixth and flagged a cab. "Venice Theatre, and there's an extra fin if you step on it!" *Wow, I just told a cabbie to "Step on it!"*

"Sure thing, mister!"

When the light changed, the cabbie floored it. I dug my fingernails into the ripped leather upholstery as he wove through the traffic like a NASCAR pro. He earned his tip; when I leaped out, only a few had got there ahead of me, including Jean Rosenthal and her hired truck. Its grumpy driver was still kvetching as I approached. "—too damn long. I wanna go home."

Rosenthal nervously watched as four firemen from Station 23, next door to the theatre, studied the best way to unload the piano.

I'd researched piano moving for another part of my Project, skills I'd need later this month. Maybe Fate was on my side, after all.

I ran up to them. "Can I help with that? I used to work for a piano-moving firm."

Rosenthal gave me a blank look, then smiled. "Oh! David-with-the-sandwiches! How versatile you are! Want another pair of hands, Captain McMahon?"

"Many hands, light work, Ma says."

They'd done the prep—a ramp positioned, the keyboard lid secured, and the route cleared of obstacles. No dolley, unfortunately. Well, we'd take it in stages. I tried to remember everything LaDainian Adams had taught me as I positioned my crew.

"Uprights are like zaftig women," I said. "The weight's in the top half, which is nice, but it can make them hard to handle." That earned a chuckle from the firemen. "And while the legs look like a handy place to grab, they're too fragile."

"Can't we just tip it on its side?" asked McMahon.

I scratched my beard. "We could, but Mr. Blitzstein plans to play it tonight, and that would make it sound worse. Ready? One, two, three, go!"

The firemen were shorter than me, but they were strong. While Jean cheered, we maneuvered the piano to the enormous eighty-foot stage. Capt. McMahon gallantly touched his finger to his head. "Hope your show's a corker!"

He and his men went back to their station. I stood by the piano, looking around the theatre for a hiding place. The Venice used to be another Shubert property, named for Al Jolson. Where the Elliott showed signs of early twentieth century luxury, the Jolson showed how the Shuberts squeezed nickels until the buffaloes shit in their hands. The brothers converted the old Central Park Riding Academy into a legitimate house, keeping its long, narrow structure and spending little on decor. Sold in the early thirties, now it staged events for the Italian immigrant community. The faded backdrop featured the Bay of Naples with a smoking Mount Vesuvius, the Italian fascist party flag draped over one box. Altogether, a weird place for staging Blitzstein's fable of corruption and greed.

As I looked around the auditorium, I found the answer. High in the balcony, lighting designer Abe Feder was wrestling his follow spot in position. I ran for the stairs.

"Goddamn rotten piece of shit!" Feder, a small, dark Jew in his late twenties, was cursing loudly as I approached. He hopped up and down, holding one hand with the other. He looked up, growling, "Cut my hand on the damn shutter."

I pulled out two hankies. "Hay fever. I always carry extras." I knotted them around his bleeding hand, then fastened it with my tie pin.

"You're a regular Boy Scout, you are," Feder said. "Thanks."

"Need any more help with that light?" I asked. I'd taken classes in lighting design—classes where we studied Feder's and Jean Rosenthal's work!—and I knew the principles.

"Just move the *verkakte* thing a foot to the left and make sure it's secure." He adjusted the makeshift bandage while I shifted the follow spot. "I am a worker in light," he complained, "and *this* is all I get to use tonight. Only working light in the place. Disgraceful."

"The dress was impressive," I lied.

"Impressive disaster," Feder said. "But we would have got it right, in time. Wonder if we'll ever have the chance. Ah, well. Push back the darkness!" He flipped the switch and a thousand watts blazed through the dim house. The handful of people below gave rowdy cheers. Feder swiveled the spot, illuminating the orchestra, the boxes, before finally settling on the piano onstage. With a master's keen eye, he adjusted the focus until it suited him.

Blitzstein waved a hand to Abe and walked into that circle of light, sitting down at the piano. What he heard didn't please him; he shook his head, ran off stage, and quickly returned with tools. *He's taking the front off to improve the sound. This place is twice the size of the Elliott, and there are no mics. God! They'll be opening the house soon! And Nate will be down there.*

"Say," I said to Feder, "do you mind if I stay up here with you?"

"Machts nichts," he said. "Go ahead."

I brushed the smooth metal of the spot. What better place to hide than in the shadows behind that dazzling light? If Nate looks up here, the Kliegl Brothers will blind him to me.

And the cradle will rock!

#

June 16, 1937
Nate thought he was getting there early, but hundreds of people were at the Maxine Elliott by six-thirty: patrons, theatre folk, reporters, activists with leaflets protesting the Federal Theatre cuts, looky-loos, but no David. He pocketed the protesters' handbills. *Research, if nothing else.*

Several times, he saw the show's p.a. with her hired piano, driving around the block in a noisy pick-up. *I remember David telling Rose the story of* Cradle *'s opening night when she was around ten. We were at Mom's house, with David on the old recliner and Rose sprawled on the Persian rug, her finger playing with the tassels. She loved the part about the girl and the piano. He must be here!*

215

Around seven, two of the actors elbowed their way to the top steps. "Folks," said one, "we're close to finding a house, but while you wait, we'll give you a taste of what's to come." He launched into one of Mr. Mister's nasty speeches and the other man sang the title song while the crowd continued to swell. Nate dithered over keeping his Ripperglasses on the performers and scanning for David. Given that Yale's drama department had provided some of his funding, he watched the actors until Houseman announced that the Venice Theatre would host the opening, with curtain at nine.

Wild cheers erupted. The mob, over five hundred strong, surged towards Broadway. Nate leaned against a delivery van, forcing the excited throng to maneuver around him. Even with his height, he still couldn't see everyone.

Irritated, he elbowed his way onto 39th and stole a taxi from three women who didn't want to make the long walk. "Drive north on Broadway, but not too fast," he told the driver, but all the time he was thinking about those women. *Maybe David's in a taxi. But how could he miss this march? I'm sorry I'm missing it!*

The cabbie clicked his meter. "What's with this crowd, anyway?"

"Crazy theatre people."

Once the cab moved ahead of the marchers, Nate peered out the window, trying to spot a good vantage point in the twilight. "There! Pull over!" He shoved bills at the puzzled driver and jumped out at West 53rd Street. In his own time, he knew this area well. His late father's attorney had offices in the modern granite skyscraper built above the Broadway Theatre, where David and Ramon played in *Versailles*. In 1937, the Broadway was a brick and terra cotta Italian movie house called the Cine Roma, and those offices didn't exist.

Nate's attention was drawn to the shops opposite the cinema: an army-navy supply store and a shoemaker, with modest offices above them ... and a lovely fire escape.

A young lawyer just leaving the building was happy to let Nate onto the escape to look for David as the crowd passed, even though it took what seemed like forever. "Easiest fiver I ever made," he said, pocketing Nate's money. "The landlord here just raised the rent."

Nate glanced around. *His whole office could fit in the lobby at Dad's lawyer's place.*

"Did you see your brother pass?" the lawyer asked.

"Nope. Maybe I'll find him at the theatre. Thanks for the help."

He took another taxi to the Venice and kept filming the arrival of the marchers, but still didn't see David. The scene was one of merry confusion. When the house opened, no one took tickets or even sold them. No programs, no assigned seats The only reserved section was in the front rows, where the young conductor gathered his chorus.

Nate shoved his way in. He draped his coat on a fourth-row aisle seat and gazed around. He lacked David's expertise at estimating a house, but it had to be over fifteen hundred people. The long, narrow auditorium seemed to stretch forever. *Cradle* was officially standing room only, with people jamming the rear of the house and the aisles.

No David anywhere, Nate thought. *Maybe the facial recognition program can spot him.* He looked all over, wandering in the lobby and into the restroom, recording all the while, until a kid began ringing a tinny bell.

"Five minutes to curtain!"

Nate got back to his seat just as a young man climbed up to a box and ripped down the fascist party flag hanging there. The crowd whooped. John Houseman and Orson Welles came out, lit by a single spotlight. They spoke briefly, thanking the audience for their patience. Then Houseman announced, "Ladies and gentlemen, *The Cradle Will Rock!*"

The faded curtain slowly rose, revealing Marc Blitzstein in his shirtsleeves and red suspenders at a frontless piano with a bowl of nuts on top. The composer was pale and sweating, but he turned to the audience and said, "Scene One." He read his own scene description aloud, telling the audience they were in Steeltown, U.S.A., on the night of a fateful union meeting.

Blitzstein took a deep breath, steadying himself as he began to play and sing the first song, "Moll's Lament." A few lines in, a woman's voice joined his.

A few seconds later, the guy with the follow spot swung the light towards a slim red-headed girl in a green dress, standing resolutely in a loge box. As she sang, the confidence in her voice grew with each line.

Blitzstein said, "Enter Gent," introducing the next character. Again, the actor playing that role rose and took over. He was in the middle of the house, below the Moll; as their duet progressed, the follow spot shifted back and forth. When they finished the song, the house buzzed with excitement; flashbulbs popped like shotguns. If people hadn't realized it before, they knew they were at an event now.

The whole show went like the first number. An accordion, somewhere in the balcony, joined Blitzstein on some songs, and Nate thought he heard a piccolo—the only musicians who dared skirt their union's rules.

Like the lighting man, Nate kept shifting in his seat to track the actors. Not all of them were there; one man, standing in the aisle behind Nate, played several roles while Blitzstein did more.

At least I'm getting good footage, especially that guy behind me. It's like a musical tennis match, watching him play the slimy Reverend Salvation opposite the despicable Mrs. Mister, way up in that balcony box. Where is David?

#

From the diary of J.D. Taylor, June 16, 1937
As more folks poured into the Venice, I wondered if Capt. McMahon would squawk. *Cradle* filled the place way past capacity. And somewhere down there was my brother. Peeking over the brass rail, I spotted dozens of guys in gray suits, so I slouched down into the safety of the shadows. I covered my face with a discarded program from *Don Giovanni.* Before I knew it, the house lights started blinking.

"Nice nap?" Feder grinned. "It's showtime." Despite his hurt hand, he trained the spot on Welles and Houseman as they walked out to address the audience. Then the curtain rose on Blitzstein and that piano, alone on the gigantic stage.

I quit worrying about Nate and reveled in the experience, from Olive Stanton's first hesitant lines as the Moll to Feder's choreography, making that single spot dance from actor to actor to composer.

Here's where I have to confess I don't like *Cradle*'s score. I love the whole improbable adventure of the opening night that nearly didn't happen. I admire Blitzstein's near-cinematic flashbacks, as well as his range of styles, from Tin Pan Alley pop pastiche to Yiddish love songs to arias and tangos. Bu it just doesn't jell. I can't get past the didacticism and the deliberately two-dimensional characters. I prefer Kurt Weill, whose work was a major influence on Blitzstein.

Yet I wouldn't have missed this night for anything, defying Nate as Welles and Houseman defied Congress. In a way, I was a small part of the *Cradle* family. I fed them while they were barricaded in the Elliott; I moved the piano and helped with the spotlight.

Maybe that's why, with the audience's excitement at fever pitch, I joined the chorus when Da Silva's Larry Foreman started the final reprise of the title song. I couldn't help myself.

Feder, ping-ponging his light between Da Silva, Blitzstein, and the chorus in the front rows with conductor Lehman Engel, gave me a curious look. I didn't care. I kept on singing to the last defiant verse.

On the last line, Da Silva raised his clenched right fist, framed in the circle of light. Blitzstein played the last chord. Feder plunged the Venice into darkness.

Silence... for several seconds. Then utter pandemonium as the place exploded and the house lights came up.

\#

June 16, 1937

As a professor of labor history, Nate knew more about unions and strikes than any of the cheering patrons in the Venice. He had the benefit of nearly a century and a half in which Marc Blitzstein's communist utopia never happened and the Soviet Union itself collapsed. As a Ripper, he'd been wounded in the Battle of Toledo and filmed many other conflicts.

He prided himself on his scholarly detachment, yet all he could think through the din was *Damn! No wonder they wanted to pull the plug on this show! It's incendiary!*

He filmed through Welles' and Archibald MacLeish's closing remarks, wondering where his brother could be. He'd been sure he'd find David here. Well past midnight, the crowd slowly began to file out. Nate took one last sweeping shot of the Venice: the stupid backdrop of Mount

Vesuvius; the battered piano, where Blitzstein munched peanuts and accepted congratulations; the lighting guy in the balcony, still fiddling with his spot; the chorus members hugging each other.

Maybe that crazy Village drunk was right. Maybe David is relaxing in Mexico. Americans could live lives of luxury there in the thirties. Damn.

He trudged up the aisle and pushed his way through the tawdry lobby, filming all the while. People on the street were still chattering over what they'd just seen, but few were over six feet tall and none was his missing brother.

He sighed and flagged a cab. When he slid into the warm leather interior, he reached up to the temple of his hornrims to switch off the camera. He'd screen it in his hotel room and run the recognition software, but he wasn't hopeful.

He'd failed. Tomorrow, he'd leave for Ohio, for the Youngstown steel strike—a scene more horrific than anything Blitzstein created.

Oh, well. Rose will enjoy the recording.

#

From the diary of J.D. Taylor, June 16, 1937
I slouched down behind the spotlight while the crowd exited, then helped Feder lug it downstairs.

"I noticed you joined in there, on the last number," he said.

"You going to squeal on me for that?"

"No, no. Just surprised me. Then I remembered you saw the dress. You got a good memory."

"Only for song lyrics."

Backstage after curtain is usually happy chaos. But since *Cradle's* actors, seated in the house, left through

221

the front with the patrons, it was eerily quiet. Welles was there, bouncing up and down on the balls of his feet. He motioned for us to hurry.

"Great job, Abe, but we've got to clear out. Jack's already had to fork over another twenty to the shysters who own this firetrap, since we ran past midnight. Let's not give them a nickel more."

Feder shoved the light into a large, rickety cabinet and began coiling cables with a speed I couldn't match. He glanced at me. "Say, could you turn on the ghost light? It's in the wings, stage left. I got to clean up this mess."

"Of course." I sprinted for the light, placed it center stage, and clicked it on. The bulb in a wire cage glowed just enough to appease any resident ghosts. A weird theatrical superstition, but one that's still around in the 2070s.

"Abe! Hurry up!" Welles roared.

I hustled through the unfamiliar corridors, reaching Abe as he slammed the cabinet shut. We headed for the stage door, where Welles waited to lock up. I held my breath, afraid Nate lay in wait for me, but the alley was nearly empty. A few cast members greeted Welles with cheers.

I touched my hand to my hat in farewell. When I reached the glow of 58th Street, I hunched over to look shorter. Minutes later, I was heading home.

I'd not only witnessed the amazing opening night of *The Cradle Will Rock,* I'd helped make it happen. Hell, I'd even sung in it.

In spite of my brother.

Chapter 9

"I Love a Piano"—Irving Berlin

From the diary of J.D. Taylor, June 30, 1937

This is an important year for my Broadway Revival Project, so I'm not going to let a little thing like Nate stop me. I'm in Bronxville, just outside Manhattan, playing a role. I've even shaved. Daring, given Nate's reappearance, but necessary. Theatre folk picture J.D. Taylor with the beard and glasses, but I'm not J.D. Taylor today. Frannie and Mabel approve. As soon as this gig is done though, I'll grow it back. Protective coloration, if nothing else.

I'm decked out in a dapper blue suit, brighter than I usually wear, a pince-nez, a gold-topped cane, and a curly light brown wig. I haven't been cast in anything—this is a role I've invented. *Ich heisse Heinrich Freitag,* professor of musicology, with papers to prove it.

Back when I was in high school, the Brits resurrected this old series called *Doctor Who* for its hundredth anniversary. A clever show; it ran another decade, into the early days of the SlingShot, which let them write funny episodes with the Doctor and Rippers. I remember the time-traveling alien used "psychic paper"—anyone who looked at it would read whatever the Doctor wanted him to read: a passport, a party invitation, a letter from Queen Victoria. No psychic paper, but before I left 2079 I forged identity papers and a letter from Jerome Kern in Beverly Hills, asking that Professor Freitag supervise the Steinway Company's packing and loading of Kern's treasured pianos.

I took an early train to Bronxville and a taxi to "The Nuts," Kern's lovely three-story colonial-revival home on Dellwood Road. The regular movers, Morgan Manhattan, were already carrying boxes into two big red trucks. I suspected Kern's antiquarian book collection would fill one on its own.

I dodged two movers and rang the bell, though the door stood wide open. A middle-aged woman, auburn hair covered in a blue kerchief, snapped at me: "We're not buying anything. Can't you see we're moving?"

I gave her a smart bow, but figured clicking my heels would be overkill. "Madam, I assure you, I am not here to sell anything. *Mein guter Freund,* Jerry Kern, has requested that I supervise the shipment of his pianos. My papers." I presented them with a Continental flourish.

"I don't know." The exasperation in her voice was plain. "Mr. Kern didn't mention you." She looked at the papers again. "Professor Heinrich Freitag, University of Tub—, Tubing?"

"Tübingen, dear lady. Professor of Musicology. I understand the Steinway Company is coming today, to pack both their instrument and Jerry's most beloved, the Blüthner, *ja?* I will make sure they do a proper job of it."

"Well, that's Mr. Kern's signature, all right. Nobody tells me anything. His library's this way."

The Kerns had built The Nuts in 1916—a big, rambling place where they kept many dogs and cats and raised their daughter, Betty. No critters now, just movers. They hadn't started on the library yet, so it looked as it did when Kern composed the scores for *Sally* and *Show Boat*... on that very piano.

"*Ach, ja,* a thing of beauty," I murmured. I wasn't acting. It was gorgeous.

"He loves that piano like one of the family," said the housekeeper.

"*Aber natürlich.* It is the finest in the world." I noticed a small bust of Wagner on a shelf, overlooking the piano. "Herr Wagner! Tell me, when he has trouble composing, does Jerry still turn the bust to the wall, declaring, 'Mr. Wagner is not pleased'?"

Her stern face cracked into a smile. "Now I know you're the goods. Yeah, he does that. I stay away when that bust is facing the wall. Got a temper, Mr. Kern does." She sighed. "I don't know when those piano movers are due, but why don't you wait here? I got work to do."

Without another word, she left me, surrounded by Kern's rare books and stamp collection. But I had eyes only for that piano. I slid onto the bench and ran my hands over the smooth wood. It resonated with age, style, craftsmanship, and I hadn't even played a note. I tried a tentative chord. *Ooh. Nice.*

I launched into a Kern medley: "Ol' Man River," "I've Told Ev'ry Little Star," "A Fine Romance," and "I Won't Dance." The Blüthner was easily the finest piano I'd ever played, and I've played Bechsteins and Fazolis. Warm, rich, dark tones; no wonder Kern felt a mystical connection to it. You couldn't compose junk on this instrument. It wouldn't let you.

When I finished "The Way You Look Tonight," a round of applause startled me.

"Sorry to interrupt your recital, but we're supposed to move that piano," said a broad-shouldered man in the doorway. His ruddy face was bemused. His crew stood behind him.

"Indeed," I said. "Mr. Kern has asked me to supervise your work." I held out the papers.

The foreman's pleasant expression vanished. "Kern thinks the Steinway Company doesn't know how to move pianos without somebody holding our hands? That's baloney. All we do is move pianos!" He glared at me, then stabbed a thick finger at the letter. "I've got a good mind to call this joker... "

"That is true, you could call this joker, who is one of America's greatest composers," I said with an air of calm. "But please note that Mr. Kern lives in California, where it is not yet six. His housekeeper will testify to his formidable temper." *Of course, she could also say that Kern's an early riser, unless he's been out playing cards.* "I shall not interfere, gentlemen, merely observe to see that all goes well. I have full confidence in your skill." I caressed the Blüthner. "One hears horror stories of shoddy moving companies, those that damage fine instruments through carelessness. Why, I know one poor man whose nineteenth-century Bösendorfer was destroyed by movers. *They drove a packing screw through its soundboard!* Can you imagine?"

The Steinway foreman drew himself up. "We'd never do such a thing. Disgraceful. You go right ahead and 'supervise' us, chum. We're professionals." He glanced over his shoulder to make sure the housekeeper was out of earshot. "We don't do shitty work."

I was pleased. Now that I'd challenged their honor, they'd take extra care. Or I hoped so. In my original timeline, these men ruined Kern's Blüthner just the way I described. When it was unpacked in Beverly Hills and Kern saw the damage, he nearly collapsed.

He'd had his first heart attack only three months before; six days after the ruined piano arrived, he had either a stroke or another heart attack. I couldn't do anything about Kern's earlier attack; he's been in California since I came to this era. *But maybe he'll live past 1945, without the stress over his Blüthner. At least I've saved an amazing instrument from harm.*

The crew expertly carried the Blüthner and the Steinway out to the street, where they began making custom crates. Trying to be useful, I carried out the bench, which weighed a ton. The foreman paused in his measurements to laugh at me.

"Hey, Professor, when's the last time you actually moved a piano, or are you just big talk?"

I eased the bench down, grunting with the effort. "Two weeks ago," I said, "I helped install a piano for a show at the Venice Theatre—not nearly so nice as this." *I'll say!* The packing went smoothly. The foreman took extra care with the screws on both crates. When the job was done, I gave the crew a fat tip, which improved their view of me. "Excellent, gentlemen! A most professional job," I said.

"That's us. Real pros!" The Steinway truck roared to life and rumbled away through quiet Cedar Knolls. I didn't want to bother the housekeeper, so instead of calling for a taxi I walked back to the train station, not quite two miles.

The day was sunny, the streets were winding. I kept thinking of "There's a Hill Beyond a Hill," a song Kern and Hammerstein wrote for *Music in the Air,* which had a lyric about how singing can make long journey seem short. Kern was well liked here, so I doubt his neighbors minded my singing his songs on this warm June day.

#

Another heat wave, though not a patch on last July's. When Leo finished his lesson, he was drenched in sweat, so I proposed going to Washington Square for something cool. Besides, I needed the Sunday *Times*.

"I can't decide if I want watermelon or coconut," Leo said as we walked through the Village.

"Coconut?"

"Yeah. Sliced coconut in ice water so cold it makes your head hurt." Leo smacked his lips. "Only I bet the peddler's sold out by now. Look at that crowd."

The square was jammed with sunbathers, picnickers, kids running and screaming and splashing in the fountain, mothers pushing baby carriages, a guy on a box playing a violin, and dozens of peddlers in white coats with pushcarts or shoulder boxes. Joe Gould, in a filthy yachting cap, was feeding his pigeons by Garibaldi's statue.

Leo shielded his eyes from the sun. "Aw, nerts! I don't see the coconut man. He always wears a straw hat with a big red feather."

"So? Watermelon?"

"Nope! Shaved ice!" Leo took off like a shot for a pushcart near the arch. I followed more slowly. It was too sticky to move fast.

When I got there, the shaved-ice guy, a pock-marked Greek, was scooping the ice into a paper cup. Leo was urging him to pile it higher. "What flavor are you getting?" I asked.

He gave me an incredulous look. "You kidding? Rainbow, of course." In an aside meant for my ears alone, he added, "You get more syrup that way."

"I'll stick with orange," I said. Ices in hand, we grabbed a piece of shady grass (more like dry, dirty stubble) just as an African-American family vacated it.

"Thanks for the treat," Leo said, digging in. "This hits the spot."

"Well, when you're done, pay me back by finding a newsboy. I need today's paper." I tossed him a quarter. "And keep the change."

We ate the ices in shared silence. There was noise enough around us. Leo finished well ahead of me, chucked his cup into an overflowing trash can ten feet away, applauded his own good aim, and ran off on his errand. He'd turn fifteen next month. In some ways, he was a typical American teenage boy from any era. His impulsiveness, his obsessions, and his enthusiasm all reminded me of myself, Nate, our high school pals, even Rose's male friends I'd come to know. Yet there were differences. Leo'd had part-time jobs—newspaper boy, sweeping out stores, dishwasher—the last two years. He was part of the work force. Frannie depended on him.

You'd think that would make him more mature than teens from more prosperous eras, but he still seems so much a kid. He does his work, he practices his music (always!), then he plays games in the streets. He howls at really stupid jokes, tells ghost stories in the courtyard with his pals. Rose's friends, with their eyes on college and the future, their minds tuned to the data-rich world of the late twenty-first century, have a maturity and sophistication I don't see in Leo. The only thing Leo is serious about is music. His attitude is like Bertie's, and Bertie wasn't quite twelve when I left our era. Leo's still a kid, even if his shoulders are getting broader.

I have no idea what any of this means. How do kids grow up? Who knows? I leave it to the experts. I'm just grateful I've got the Spinellis and the Finkelsteins as neighbors. Tutoring Leo fills a need in me, the urge to pass on my love for musical theatre to another generation, since I'll never

229

have kids of my own. I thought I'd lost that when I said good-bye to Rose in the lab, but I was wrong.

Leo came back with the paper and a bag of hot buttered popcorn, which he offered to me.

"No, thanks. I just want to check the headlines." I read the front page and couldn't help myself. I grinned like a damn fool.

"What's so funny?" Leo asked. I passed him the paper. I'd seen all I needed to see. He studied the front page. "Heat wave, Roosevelt's going on vacation, Japs running around in China, Seabiscuit won again, Giants over the Bums, still no trace of Earhart. I don't get it."

"Ah, Leo, sometimes it's what's *not* in the papers that's the best news of all."

He gave me that *Grown-ups are crazy* look that all kids know, whatever era.

I stood up and brushed the grass off my rear. "Hey, here's an idea. Let's stop at the market for a whole watermelon and I'll split it with you and your mom."

"Now you're talkin'!"

Leo had no way of knowing I'd already read the *Times* of July 11, 1937—but that copy had an article about George Gershwin's critical condition, and the next day's issue carried the report of his death.

The newspaper I tucked under my arm as we walked to the A and P mentioned George Gershwin not at all.

#

March 17, 2080
As Nate expected, the facial-recognition program didn't find David in the *Cradle* audience. The Yale Drama Department and University Library, however, were thrilled with the footage of the historic opening. It also helped

230

bring Rose out of a bad case of the blues. Nothing was going right. Her pants didn't fit—she'd been eating too much deli food. Some asshole stole her backpack. She missed her family. She'd signed up for an extracurricular project, a concert-style musical for a children's charity. It sounded great, but it ate into her regular classes and she loathed the material: the moronic *Brick Wall Brandy,* adapted from the equally idiotic (but popular) movie. She played endless Sondheim, Estévez and Pappadakis, and Johnson to wash the dreck out of her head. She had a fight with Zanzi ("Why aren't you happy? You're playing Brandy!" "I'd rather play a chorus member in something decent than the lead in garbage!").

So the *Cradle* recording made a good diversion. Rose had never seen the show in person, but she'd seen filmed versions of stage productions, including Patti LuPone in 1986, Santiago Alvarez and Jessica Mayehoff in 2037, and a very young David Greenbaum in a bootleg of a regional mounting. She also recalled a terrific evening with her uncle watching Tim Robbins' film based on *Cradle*'s improbable history. David kept pointing out where Robbins fudged for dramatic effect.

After Nate had got a few good nights' sleep to recover from his trip to the 1930s, the whole family enjoyed the recording. "Listen to that," Nate said after the first astonishing number. "That's the flashbulbs popping."

"What are flashbulbs?" Bertie asked. "Exploding tulips?"

Her mom and siblings judged the show weird, but interesting, but for Rose it was thrilling, miles away from *Brick Wall Brandy.*

She was watching it for the third time when Bertie came home from Little League practice. He tossed his gear in the closet and stopped, staring. "The *Cradle* thingy—again? You're obsessed, ace."

But Rose had noticed something odd, right near the end. She paused the recording. "Come here, Bertie. Listen to the part when the chorus joins in. Most of them are on that side of the house. See? Dad got a good shot of them and the m.d."

"*You* need an M.D., ace."

"Shut up. And stop calling me 'ace.' Listen to the singers as Dad pans to his right... " Rose hit the remote and the scene played again.

"What? You're rancid, ace." Bertie clattered into the kitchen for a sandwich as Rose played the segment over and over, now with headphones. Bertie made faces at her while he munched a pickle. She ignored him; she had practice. After running the clip a fifth time, she took off the headphones and walked over to the stairs.

"Dad?" she yelled.

"Rosie, I'm trying to work."

"Come down, please. It's important. Two minutes—literally."

Bertie bounced on the arm of the couch. "Ooh, literally. I'm gonna time you, ace. Literally. Mwah-hah-hah."

Nate bit off his grumbles when saw the unsettled look in his eldest child's eyes. "This is...weird," she said. "Listen to the reprise of the title song, right after your footage moves away from the chorus to the right. A phrase in the final verse.'"

She punched the remote again. Nate's hidden camera took in Howard Da Silva, then the chorus with Lehman Engel, and moved to the right. There was one actress standing in the rear orchestra. Hiram Sherman, playing multiple roles, stood in the aisle. Nate listened intently for the verse Rose had singled out. "No..." he breathed. "Play it again, Rose."

"'Play it, Sam,'" Bertie said. "Get the quote right, ace. And two minutes, thirty seconds is not *literally* two minutes!"

"Bertram, another peep out of you and you'll be sorry," Nathan said. His son hustled back into the kitchen, peeping softly.

Rose ran the segment again. Now that she'd pointed it out, it was unmistakable, but only distinct for about four words. The mic in his Ripperglasses picked it up just for that brief moment he was facing away from the main chorus. *The timbre, the tone. I've heard that voice sing show tunes my whole life. How did I miss it?* He felt stunned. "You're right. But where is he?"

She gestured with the remote at the paused scene, her hand shaking slightly. "The only performer in this section is that woman, yet it's clearly a man's voice. His voice. He's above her. He's with the guy with the follow spot."

"My God. You found him." Nate stared at the screen, then at Rose. "You found him!"

Realizing something was up, Bertie popped back out of kitchen. "What? What? Found what?"

Rose began scanning through the recording, searching for any shots of that balcony. There weren't many; Nate had concentrated on the performers. But then she found one where the spotlight was pointed far to the right, not directly at the camera. She zoomed in and enhanced the picture. A second shadowy figure, taller than Abe Feder, lurked behind the spot's glare. She pointed at it. "I found Uncle David, *ace.*"

#

From the diary of J.D. Taylor, July 14, 1937
I was nearing the end of my set at the Golden Eagle when Hank Ito whispered in my ear while I was playing one of my favorite Rodgers and Hart tunes: "Where or When?" from this spring's *Babes in Arms.* "Table Six—when you're done."

Cramped in my corner, I peered through the smoky gloom and made eye contact with Vincent Youmans, his wife Boots, composer-lyricist Ann Ronell, and writer Raymond Knight and his wife, Lee. Like me, Ronell was a young songwriter whose career had got a boost from Gershwin. I'd seen her at George's gatherings; they'd probably had an affair in the past, and were still good friends. Youmans, Ronell, and Knight were working on *High Flyers* for the fall. I suspected they weren't here for Mario's gnocchi.

I played Youmans' "Tea for Two" and Ronell's "Willow, Weep for Me," and told the crowd they were there. They got a nice hand, but they weren't the only ones. Several regulars insisted I sing my own "Second Chances" before I stood up. *I'm getting a fan club.*

As I edged my way to Table Six, I caught Jimmy's eye and saw him start mixing a Bronx cocktail for me. "What brings you down to the Village?" I asked, giving Boots a peck on the cheek.

"Bad news, what else?" Youmans said. "Lee Shubert's pulling the plug on *High Flyers.* He thinks nobody will want to see a show about aviators after Amelia vanished."

"Hogwash," I said. *"Babes in Arms* is going gangbusters and it's got an aviator."

Ann stabbed out her cigarette. "But not an *aviatrix.* Shubert's running scared."

"You're a major backer, David," Boots said. "Can you do anything?" Her voice lacked its usual confidence. Looking around at the Eagle—not the classiest joint in town—she must have wondered how I had any money to invest at all. I stayed because I loved the Village and the place let me keep performing.

But could I pick up the slack on this show, on my own? I wasn't sure. Thanks to knowing what I knew, I'd invested heavily in most of the long-running shows of the past three years. I had money in *You Can't Take It With You, Room Service,* and all of Rodgers and Hart's hits. I missed *Abie's Irish Rose* and *Tobacco Road,* but I've earmarked big fat checks for next year's *Life With Father* and *The Man Who Came To Dinner.* Those two will pay my bills for years.

But *High Flyers* was a gamble. Youmans hadn't had a Broadway success in ages and Shubert had a point: Amelia Earhart filled the news.

Oh, hell! Why else did I travel through time to dose this aggravating alcoholic with Minarcin? But it will have to be on my terms, even if my terms are a little strange.

Karl brought me my drink. I took a long pull at it before answering. "Here's my proposal. Instead of ignoring Earhart disappearing, deal with it straight on. Have the lead—what's her name? Marcy?—sing about what Earhart meant to her. She's inspired thousands of women trying to compete in a man's world. You can understand that, Ann." She nodded. I went on, "Show that admiration and love in a song. It's a tall order, but that's just the start. This show has to be more than a battle-of-the-sexes jokefest. Sure, keep the two comic songs; 'Barrelroll' is hilarious. And the ballad is beautiful. But instead of focusing on the guys-against-the-gals race, find another way to show the audience that Marcy's skills match Paul's. Maybe Ray can create a scene where they have to work together."

Knight's face suddenly lit up. "How's this? Like Balto, the pilots have to deliver a vaccine to the middle of nowhere. Several planes start out, but they don't all make it. Paul does, but only because Marcy refuels his plane in flight."

I had no idea who Balto was, but the others did, so I played along. The idea was dramatic and might work. (Later, I looked up Balto on my Ally. He was a sled dog that led a team to Nome in 1925 with medicine during a diphtheria outbreak.)

"That's good," I said, "but there's more. I don't have dough like Shuberts, so this can't be a Shuberty show. Think small. Scale down the 'Flying Circus' dance. And Marcy needs rewriting. Women characters these days are either are catty monsters, like in *The Women,* or they're namby-pamby ingenues. Sweet, but bland."

"Then there's Ethel Merman," Boots said. Her grin was evil.

I laughed. "She's one of a kind. Our Marcy should be real, somebody who can carry on Amelia Earhart's work."

Knight looked worried. "Huh. Maybe Rachel Crouthers should pen this, not a radio comic like me."

Crouthers had written influential plays in the twenties about sexism and women's issues, but she was busy with her own fall offering, *Susan and God,* which would be her biggest hit. I had five hundred in it and couldn't wait to meet Gertrude Lawrence, the star. Besides, Crouthers didn't do musicals.

Knight's wife, Lee, wagged a finger at him. "Balderdash! You can do it, and us gals can give you pointers on what's important to women. 'Spread your wings,' as Ann's lyrics say. I like David's ideas."

"What do you think, Vince?" I turned to the composer, who had been unnaturally quiet during the discussion. Youmans was a slow, painstaking worker. *Could he rewrite fast enough?*

"Hmm? Yeah, great. Boots, a pencil, please." He began scribbling on a Golden Eagle menu, a good sign. Something in our talk had got his juices flowing.

I finished my cocktail. "If you come up with a libretto along those lines and songs to match, including an Earhart anthem, I'll produce it."

"Then I guess we'd better get to work," said Youmans, putting the menu in his pocket. He waved at Karl. "Another Coca-Cola, please."

Another good sign! I figured those were Cuba Libres. Maybe High Flyers will take off after all.

\#

From the diary of J.D. Taylor, August 17, 1937
I'm not just a backer any more; I'm a real live producer with a real live show starting rehearsals tomorrow in a crummy hall on 54th Street! The gang is working like demons on my proposal. Knight's book is still schizo, veering between the biting wisecracks of the original and the more serious revised plot. Maybe audiences won't care much, especially since we've cast a new gal named Eve Arden as Marcy, and I know she'll land those zingers. I still want it tighter.

I'm happiest about the score, especially that Youmans wrote three new songs in a month. Well, two; he raided his trunk for one. That Ronell is a composer herself helped speed things along. "Challenge," the anthem, is marvelous. Youmans' melody pulls at the heart and Ann adapted some of the lyrics from Earhart's quotes. It's a classic. Eve's taking vocal lessons—she's not a great singer—to do it justice. I also love Vince's underscoring for the final dramatic plane ride and the big ballad, "You Make My Heart Soar." Some of those songs will last, even if the show doesn't.

We've cast Ray Middleton as Paul—solid, if unexciting— and Boots as Marcy's best gal pal. Not a big role, but it means she can keep an eye on Vince. A young man named Joshua Logan is our director. Somehow, I think he'll do okay.

I can't be a producer without an office, so Taylor Productions now holds court on the third floor of the

Music Box Theatre. The notion I had three years ago at the Bamboo Garden is coming true, bit by bit. Three tiny rooms: my office, an anteroom with a receptionist (Adam's cousin, Bertha), and an office that Mabel (accounts) and Nick Santino (lawyer) share with our press agent, Alan McDermott. With *Flyers* our only show, Mabel and Nick are on retainer. They shouldn't quit their day jobs until I can make it worth their while to be here, and Mabel, of course, is expecting next month.

McDermott, an eager kid of twenty-three, was recommended to me by Shep Henkin, the Golden Eagle's agent. He's a hunk, with sandy brown hair, freckles, a faint Scottish burr, and a boundless enthusiasm for theatre that reminds me of Moss Hart in *Act One*. He's got a girlfriend, too, but he makes tasty eye candy. Alan's here all the time, drumming up support for *High Flyers*. Whenever I come in, he's on the phone or typing press releases. I suspect he sleeps here.

Leo is our office boy, at least until school starts. I have the neatest, cleanest office in Manhattan. Frannie yells at him to take out the trash at home, but here he does it unasked, even if there's only one crumpled sheet in the can. He'll also be our gofer during rehearsals, but he's pissed he'll miss tryouts in Princeton. *God, tryouts in a month—terrifying.*

I've booked the 49th Street Theatre, an intimate house with only seven hundred fifty seats. It's next to the Ambassador. Vince is peeved. He claims he deserves better, but it's a good match for this property and fits my budget. Like the Venice, where *The Cradle Will Rock* debuted, the 49th Street was a Shubert house auctioned off in the early days of the Depression. In real history, the new owners turned it into a movie palace in 1938 and wrecked it two years later. *High Flyers* will displace a couple of Federal

Theatre shows, but, with so many struggling venues, I'm sure those productions will find other homes for their brief runs.

One more note: like J. Pierpont Finch in *How to Succeed in Business Without Really Trying*, I've had my name painted on the door in gold. All capitals, block letters.

#

From the diary of J.D. Taylor, September 18, 1937
Mabel and Adam have a baby girl, Sarah. She's adorable. I'd forgotten how tiny babies are. It makes me ache for Rose, Bertie, Hannah, and the family I never had with Ramon.

Everybody with *High Flyers* is in Princeton for the previews that start in two days. I'm joining them tomorrow, but I couldn't miss George Gershwin's farewell party before he sails for Europe. Marshall Field III is hosting it at his humongous estate on Long Island's Gold Coast—in my era, the mansion and grounds are a state park! I've got two reasons for to go. First is to see George, back from Hollywood. Second is to call in a favor from the trip to Mexico. Marshall is a member of the Piping Rock Club in Locust Valley. Though I'm no horseman (just ask Pegaso!), I need to be in the Club's stables on October 24. I'm counting on Marshall's help.

I arrived late, taking the train to Long Island after my shift at the Eagle, then a taxi to Marshall's place. Let's just say Jay Gatsby's digs got nothin' on this house. A footman took my overnight case ("You are in the Japanese room, Mr. Taylor. Second floor, fifth room on the right."); the butler led me into the massive salon.

I spotted George in the crowd right away, chatting with Kay Swift. George…laughing, tanned from the southern California sun, fit, *alive*. I couldn't help myself. Happy tears welled up in my eyes. I scuttled behind a potted palm, dabbing away with my hanky. Two people noticed me. One was Gregory Zilboorg, who gave me a withering glare before turning away. The other was Oscar Levant, not exactly my best bud.

I had just managed to quit sniffling when Levant peered through the palm fronds, like on safari. "J.D. Taylor, I presume? You okay?"

"Uh, yeah. Allergies. Ragweed or something."

"Bullshit. You turned on the faucets *after* you came in the room. What's the lowdown?' He lit a cigarette, waiting for my reply.

"Maybe I'm allergic to you," I said. "Allergies come from irritants. God knows you qualify."

He ignored the jibe. "It's George, isn't it? You know, Silly Zilly keeps telling everyone you're a fairy."

"Are those two statements supposed to go together?" I said, deflecting his challenge.

"You tell me." *Back in my court.*

I put my hanky back in my pocket, thinking. "If I were a fairy, what's it to you or Zilboorg or anyone else? As for George, of course I love George. You love George, Kay loves George, Ira loves George, the American public loves George. We all love George in our own ways. So, yeah, I guess I got a little choked up just now. I haven't seen him in over a year. Want to make something out of it?" *That looks like a Ming vase on that pedestal to my left. How big a crash it would make if I threw Oscar at it?*

But for once he wasn't belligerent. "Nope. But if you're pining for him, you're wasting your time. He may play around, but he won't end up in bed with you."

Now I had to laugh. History has wondered about Gershwin's sexuality, especially since he died single at thirty-eight. I'd seen him with several girls, never a man, but that didn't have to mean anything. I like the theory that George's music meant more to him than sex, whatever flavor. I wouldn't have minded, but I'd focused on curing that tumor, not sex. To say nothing of the awe factor. I mean, it's *Gershwin*. "Oscar, we camped together for weeks in the Mexican countryside. Nobody got in anyone else's bed, except an alligator lizard once. Ask Eddie or Marshall. Zilboorg's an ass and I don't care who knows I said so."

"I agree! What I always say about psychoanalysts is, fuck Dr. Freud." He stubbed out the butt in the defenseless palm's pot and changed the subject. "I hear your show opens soon. You're crazy to take on Youmans—"

"Thanks for the confidence!"

"—but the world needs more of his tunes and less of his grousing. Congratulations! Now—when will we see a score by J.D. Taylor?"

Say what? Oscar never showed any interest in my music; when we first met, he seethed whenever George played my tunes. My incredulity must have shown; Levant mimed being hurt. "What, you think I don't know your songs? I do. All of them, including that new torch song. They're different, intriguing. Give me more to hear." With that, he walked over to greet Jimmy McHugh, who was descending the main staircase.

His interest and the way he unknowingly paraphrased Sondheim rattled me more than his cracks about my sexuality. I couldn't do anything about people thinking I was gay. With Zilboorg trumpeting it for two years and with no girlfriend, it was kind of obvious. So far, it hasn't been a problem. I'm pleasant, a hard worker. I've got a large bank account. Most folks on the Great White Way will overlook all kinds of things to work with men like that. *Hell, everyone knows about Noël Coward, and they still fight to be in his shows.*

I've been too busy with the Project and now *High Flyers* to do much with my own stuff. The late, lamented Bill Daly taught me a lot; Dreyfus has published a handful of my tunes, and a couple have been recorded. *But a show of my own? What a crazy notion! I came here to rewrite history, not write shows.*

I wandered through the crowded room toward the bar. I needed a drink.

As George was guest of honor, I got only a moment with him. It was enough that he said he was "in the pink" when I asked about his health.

"No headaches?" I asked.

"Only when I have too many beers," he said.

He told me he was finishing the notations on the string quartet—never completed in my era—and had plans for a symphony after his vacation. Not entirely a pleasure trip, it included concerts in London, Paris, Rome. Not Madrid: the civil war is on.

"Ira's happy in California?" I asked.

"I miss him like the devil, but he and Lee adore the sunshine. Still, it will be handy the next time Hollywood comes calling. *If* they come calling again! Those people! Do you know, Goldwyn complained to me, 'Why can't you write hits like Irving Berlin? Songs that I can whistle!'"

"Ouch. But what about Broadway?" *"Tell Me More," as Ira wrote!*

"I'm considering some projects—with DuBose, with Lynn Riggs. Eddie's Aztec ballet, too. Maybe Broadway, maybe not. Everything in its own time, and a time for everything, as somebody said. You know, I'd need a hundred years to put on paper all the music I have in my head."

Maybe not a hundred, George, but you've got more than thirty-eight now.

"Maybe I'll produce a show. I heard you're backing Vince's latest—that's swell. Can't wait to see it when I get back." He thumped his fist in his palm. "Say, there's Moss. I have a message for him from Ira, then I'll play some numbers from the new film." He shook my hand and dashed away.

I watched him go, then went back to the bar. Oscar Levant's sardonic gaze met mine. He was leaning against a marble pillar, smoking, watching. I ignored him and got a stiff one from the square-jawed black bartender. I'd need it. If the sight of a healthy Gershwin, three months older than he ever was in my era, got me misty-eyed, who knew what hearing new Gershwin rhythms would do to me?

George gave us two songs from *A Damsel in Distress,* scheduled for release next month. Those I knew well: "A Foggy Day" and "Nice Work If You Can Get It." Then he played the first part of a ballet he'd written for Balanchine; they'd created the scenario in my era, but he died before writing a note. Gorgeous. As with *An American In Paris,* the whole story came through in George's melodies. I choked up a few times, but managed to hold myself together.

After all, I had work to do at this party. I needed to wangle that invitation out of Marshall Field.

#

From the diary of J.D. Taylor, October 5, 1937
High Flyers opened last night; I'm *so* hung over. I insisted on having the party at Sardi's, even though that wouldn't become *de rigueur* for a few more years. I might not have this chance again, and I wanted to do it right. Vincent Sardi himself brought me a Bronx cocktail. *Flyers* isn't a turkey, but it's no blockbuster. We're benefiting from one of Broadway's slowest seasons ever; nearly everything else that's opened has flopped. The season's big hits (Rodgers

243

and Hart's *I'd Rather Be Right* and Harold Rome's *Pins and Needles)* will open next month. With so little going on, our intimate show of rival aviators is getting noticed. The reviews are mixed. Half love the tightly focused story, the small scale, and Arden's tough but endearing Marcy. Half complain about the lack of production numbers (just one dance at a western picnic) and feel Arden is too brash. One sniffs that women shouldn't take jobs from men, even in musicals!

The triumph is Youmans' score; nearly all the reviewers agree on that. The composer sat at a table up front, knocking back gin rickeys, with Boots and Ann Ronell on either side. He basked in approval like a cat in a sunbeam. I hoped his good mood would last.

I got some kudos, too. Lee Shubert approached me, a little unsure who I was. "Taylor, right? You've got some *chutzpah*! I chickened out on this one and you didn't. Come see me when you want to do a show in a house that's bigger than that shoebox on 49th."

Rodgers and Hart greeted me after Shubert left. They looked frazzled. George M. Cohan was giving them fits during rehearsals for *I'd Rather Be Right*. Despite star trouble, it would be another smash, and I was backing it to the hilt.

"Good show," Rodgers said. He introduced his wife, Dorothy. She was wearing a full-length mink coat that must have cost a fortune.

"I love the number for Amelia Earhart," she said. "It made me cry. I just heard Kate Smith wants to record it."

Oh, yeah! That's what I want to hear!

"I'm tickled pink for you, David," said Hart, grabbing both my hands and shaking them. "May this be the first of many hits!"

"From your mouth to God's ear," I said. "I still can't believe I'm here."

"You kidding? You're *meant* to be here," Larry said. Rodgers' approval was polite, but the tiny lyricist seemed genuinely happy for me.

I looked around the crowded, noisy restaurant. Youmans, Kate Smith, Cole Porter, and Ethel Merman were standing by Renée Carroll's hat check stand. Youmans had clear lungs and ruddy cheeks, thanks to the Minarcin. Porter, dressed to the nines, stood straight and elegant. *And I mean to keep him that way.*

Chapter 10

"Ridin' High"—Cole Porter

From the diary of J.D. Taylor, October 24, 1937

At the party for George, I spun Marshall Field a tale about wanting to write a song—maybe an entire show!—set at a country club. I dropped not-so-subtle hints about fabulous Sunday luncheons and how the clip-clop rhythm of horses' hooves might work musically. Utterly shameless, but Marshall is a *mensch* and chalked my behavior up to artistic temperament. Besides, he knew I'd never get into the Piping Rock Club on my own. They don't accept Jews as members, but will turn a blind eye to members' Jewish guests. I guess they disinfect anything our grubby Semitic fingers touched.

I held my breath, hoping he'd be free for the right date —October 24th—and exhaled when he was.

His chauffeur, James Haslam, picked me up at the Locust Valley station. "Mr. Field's already at the club, sir. He brought one of his favorite mares to ride. Not that there's anything wrong with the Club's horses," he assured me.

"I wasn't worried," I said, feeling funny as he opened and closed the car door for me. The whole notion of servants strikes me as unnatural, yet Haslam seemed to like his work.

Fields' kids called him "Uncle Jimmy." But it's a way of life I didn't care for.

The big towncar quickly reached the Piping Rock grounds. We passed through two stone pillars and along a winding road lined with pines. When the main compound finally came into view, it didn't dazzle with pretension. The architect, Guy Lowell, created a homely, rustic air, centered on a crested Dutch Colonial farmhouse with white woodwork, porches, and pillars. On one side were clay and grass tennis courts and rolling golf greens. The other side featured the stables and a steeplechase field bordered by woods filled with bridle paths. This was where the "elegantsia" came to play—just thirty miles from Manhattan, but a whole different world.

Marshall was standing on the porch, looking casual but dapper—an effect only the best tailors can create. Yet I fondly remembered him borrowing one of Victor's ragged pink cotton blouses after ruining his own shirt chasing Pegaso into the Mexican brush. *"Hola, amigo!"* he called. "That's all the Spanish I remember. All the *clean* Spanish, that is. Why do swear words stick better than polite phrases? You ready to ride?"

"I guess," I said. "Thanks again for having me. With luck, this will give me some song ideas."

"Riding does have certain rhythms," Marshall said. "I think a country club setting for a romance could be cute, though maybe better for film than stage. Easier to clean up the dung in the films. I bet Fred Astaire would love it; he's got horses, too. Anyway, I'm happy to help. It's by way of paying you back for everything you did for us in Mexico."

He led me to the stables, which seemed to go on for miles. Stall after stall after stall, all smelling of hay and manure and, yes, horses. Marshall walked along the rows, patting heads and offering carrots and sugar cubes from his pockets. A zit-covered stable boy with floppy tawny hair stood waiting for orders.

"'Morning, Kevin," Marshall said. "Mr. Taylor needs a horse with training wheels."

"Oh, I'm not that bad, am I?"

Marshall just laughed as he kept walking through the stalls to his own horse. *Good. I'd rather he didn't hear this.*

Kevin sized me up, scratched a blackhead with a grimy finger, then moved to a nearby stall with a dappled-grey horse. She seemed bored with the world. "This is Blossom," Kevin said, "a real sweetie."

"If Blossom's nice and easy-going, which are the ornery horses?"

"Black Henry," Kevin said promptly. "Three stalls over. Handsome brute, but a devil. Nyetta—that roan—she's another tricksy ride. Believe me, sir, you don't want either of 'em." He led Blossom into the yard. I followed, thinking fast.

"A friend of mine, Mr. Cole Porter, will come riding here later today—and he'll likely want a feisty horse like Black Henry. He thinks he's a much better rider than he is. I'm truly afraid for him. I know I sound like a mother hen, but could you make *sure* he doesn't ride Henry or any other skittish horse? He's not a big man, but he's got a big ego. I'll make it worth your while. It's sort of insurance for me; I have money in his next show. If he gets hurt, it would be a disaster." I pulled twenty bucks out of my pocket. *Not carrots, but the right treat for the job.* It's an outrageous amount for 1937, but I didn't want anything going wrong here. Besides, this place drips money. Now it's dripping on Kevin.

His green eyes widened. "You got it, sir. No rowdy rides for Mr. Porter." He nodded solemnly. I half expected him to tug his forelock, but he jammed the bills in his back pocket and ran off to get a saddle for me.

Blossom and I were studying each other when Field approached, leading a black horse whose graying muzzle betrayed her age. "Kevin taking good care of you?" he asked.

The Irish youth, panting a bit, hurried back just then with my saddle. "Oh, yes," I said. "I'm sure we'll have a lovely ride. Won't we, Blossom?"

The mare whinnied something rude.

To my surprise, it *was* a lovely ride. Blossom gave me far less trouble than Pegaso. Marshall chatted about his favorite cause—rehabilitating old racehorses. I told him about a distant relative who did the same with greyhounds. I didn't say she was my great-grandmother, and she wasn't born yet. The October weather was crisp and cool, the bridle paths through the dogwood and pine trees were delightful. I'll never be a horseman, but, to my astonishment, I enjoyed myself.

When we got back to the stables, Kevin took charge of Blossom, while Marshall tended to Twilight. "Mr. Porter's party isn't here yet," Kevin said, "but I'm watching for them."

"Good man," I said, and tipped him again.

One of Piping Rock Club's key attractions was the Sunday luncheon. Field's wife, Ruth, met us in the dining room. She was a charming, lively lady. And she praised *High Flyers,* proving she had good taste, too.

We sat by the window; I had a partial view of the stable and kept watching the riders heading for the trails. Ruth noticed. "You looking for someone, David? You seem very intent."

"Maybe I'm starting to like horses. At least from a distance. This clam chowder is amazing—the freshest I've ever tasted."

We discussed the headlines, the theatre, Mexico. The Fields described other country clubs in great, glowing detail.

Yeah. The rich are different! The waiter had just brought us thick slabs of chocolate cake when another group of riders went by. I recognized the Countess Edith de Zoppola, a socialite who lived in nearby Oyster Bay, leading a group of swells: the Duke of Verdura, Diana Vreeland, Benjamin Moore. And Cole Porter trotted by on a handsome chestnut. *A nice, placid chestnut. I hoped.*

"David, you look pleased," said Marshall. "Got an idea for that song?"

"Not exactly. But I'm sure some good music will come out of this day's work."

#

From the diary of J.D. Taylor, December 28, 1937
With *High Flyers* up and running, I've finally had a chance to catch up on current shows, with Leo (and sometimes Frannie) accompanying me. Leo couldn't hide his tears at *Golden Boy, Juno and the Paycock,* and *Of Mice and Men,* though he feared I'd think he was a "sissy." He howled at George M. Cohan as FDR in *I'd Rather Be Right.* But of all the shows he saw on his break, he liked Welles' modern-dress *Julius Caesar* best. He wasn't the only one. I grew up in an era that takes special effects for granted, but young Jean Rosenthal's dramatic lighting scheme stunned me, with stark rays stabbing through the darkness like the senators' knives, and oppressive shadows to establish mood. Add a dynamic cast and Welles' creative direction and you had something truly memorable.

As usual, the shows led to lengthy discussions. We sat in the Jefferson Diner, at Sixth and Greenwich, having chocolate malteds at the long counter. I promised myself several long bouts with my punching bag, like Clifford

Odets' Joe, to burn those extra calories. *Maybe a run, if the weather stays clear.*

"Soooo," said Leo, drawing out the word, "could you turn a play like *Golden Boy* into a musical? The character of Joe is a violinist, so adding music seems natural to me. But maybe people only want happy musicals. *Porgy and Bess* was a pip, but it lost money."

I ducked my head, pretending to study the bottom of my glass, so Leo couldn't see me smiling. His comments were funny for two reasons: *Golden Boy* would become a musical in 1964, starring Sammy Davis, Jr.; and he sounded exactly like Little Sally in *Urinetown,* begging Officer Lockstock for a less gloomy musical next time.

But Leo wasn't joking, so I answered him in that vein: "There haven't been many serious musicals, but you know there have been serious operas. I think people need to get used to the idea. *Show Boat,* back in 1927, tackled some harsh topics, but Hammerstein still softened the novel's ending. As for *Golden Boy,* you make a good point about Joe being a musician." I briefly explained the difference between a diegetic song (in which the characters know they're singing) and a non-diegetic one (in which they don't). Leo caught on in a flash. Then I asked him, "How would *you* tackle a *Golden Boy* musical?"

His dark face flushed; teenagers hate being put on the spot. He rocked on his stool. I don't know why, but all the stools at the Jeff are wobbly. I think they're made that way. "Mr. T!" Leo squawked, "I can't write a musical! I'm still learning to play piano!"

"I'm not asking you to write the songs, just think about the show's dramaturgy."

"Drama turdy!" Leo cracked up. Despite his growing sophistication in theatrical matters, he was still fifteen.

I translated. Leo eventually stopped snickering and suggested some scenes worthy of song treatments. *Good thinking, Leo. Strouse and Adams picked those scenes, too.*

While we were analyzing the show, Joe Gould wandered into the diner, one of his regular haunts. He zoomed in on me like a heat-seeking missile.

"Hello, Joe," I said. "How about a bowl of soup and a cheese sandwich?"

The gnome-like man climbed on a stool, placing his ragged portfolio on his lap. "What're you having, Bronko?"

"Chocolate malted."

"I'll have one of those, too. *And* the soup and sandwich."

Incorrigible. I gave the order to the counterman. "You got a place tonight, Joe?" When he didn't answer, I passed him fifty cents.

He chuckled and wheezed, "Now I do." I tried not to flinch at his boozy breath. As it wasn't supposed to freeze, odds were he'd spend it on gin and ride the subway all night.

For once, Gould wasn't feeling chatty. He chowed down while Leo and I went on talking. I wondered what Edward Hopper would make of us. In another few years, he'd paint *Nighthawks at a Diner,* with three loners at a Village eatery much like the Jefferson. *Hmm. A gay time-traveling composer, a skinny Italian-American teen, and the self-proclaimed "Last of the Bohemians." More like* Gooney-birds at a Diner.

Leo tilted his head back to drain the last of his malted, then banged the glass on the counter. "That's interesting, thinking about a show like that. Maybe it could work, even with the sad ending, since the story's strong. Not like *The Star-Wagon.* Sheesh, what a load of hooey!"

Maxwell Anderson's *The Star-Wagon* concerns a man who goes back in time to marry a different woman, realizes his original timeline was better, and changes back. My young neighbor wasn't impressed when we saw it last month. I usually like Anderson, but the subject matter weirded me out. *Too close to home!*

"We're supposed to believe some sap who designs tires can build a time machine?" Leo's lip curled in a sneer.

"It's called suspending disbelief. You accept the premise for the story's sake."

"But that's just for starters. Instead of doing something keen, like maybe seeing dinosaurs, he goes back to when he's a young man."

"That was important to him. He and his wife needed to learn they were happier with the way things were."

Leo wasn't buying it. He leaned around me to address Gould, who was pouring extra sugar—lots of extra sugar—in his malted. "Hey, Professor Seagull! If you had a time machine, what would you do with it?"

Gould blinked twice and slid his glasses back up his nose. "March twenty-eighth, nineteen-nineteen, Boston. The date of my father's death. That is, his second death. His untrue death occurred in the previous summer." His bloodshot eyes took on a faraway look which left only when he shook himself like a wet dog. He picked up his long black cigarette holder and pointed it at me. "Ask Bronko. He knows about time machines, because he's a man out of time. Heh, heh, heh."

Luckily for me, Leo was familiar with Joe's drunken rambling, and took this for more of the same. It sent chills down my spine. *They say the mentally ill have different perceptions—was Joe picking up something about me that normal people couldn't see?*

"Okay. When and where would you go, Mr. Taylor?" Leo asked.

Been there, done that, as the old saying goes. "I think I'd use a time machine to see loved ones I've lost."

"Like the doughboy and the pretty girl in your living room?" I'd noticed Leo looking at my photos before. I nodded. He chewed on that. "I've got grandparents in Italy, but I don't care if I ever see them, in the past or in the future. My vote's for dinosaurs. I could be the first man to photograph a *Tyrannosaurus rex.*"

"If it doesn't eat you," I said. "Come on, let's head home." We left Joe giggling into his malted.

#

April 27, 2080
Nate took some recordings of David singing and the original of *The Cradle Will Rock* to Danny Pillich, the lab tech. "Rose and I think this is a match for David. Can you confirm it?"

With a flip of his hair, Danny said, "Oooh. Shitty Ripperglass audio files. You're lucky I love a challenge. I'll let ya know if I get anything."

Despite his grousing, he brought the results to Nate's home in just a few days. By luck, Rose had come up for the weekend to celebrate Hannah's making the finals of the state science fair. With the family assembled in the living room, Danny took off his leather-sleeved fifties bowling jacket, a black, red, and white monstrosity boasting the name "The King Pins." He pulled a mini from the inner pocket.

"Love the jacket, ace," said Bertie. "I want one for my birthday."

"Dr. Mesrobian gave me this after his last 'Shot; said he never wanted to see it again," said Danny, linking his Ally to the monitor in the family room. The screen lit up with several files labeled with cryptic letters. "Okay. Show and tell." He clicked on a file, and the *Cradle* chorus sang the final verse. Another click: the man's voice from the balcony, amazingly isolated, with an accompanying graph. A third click: a weird composite of David Greenbaum's voice and a second graph. "Drum roll, please," Danny said, clicking a final time. The two spectrographs merged, matching almost perfectly. An animated line of buxom Yale cheerleaders appeared, squeaking, "Go, Danny!"

"Uh, that part's not in the full report," he said. "But given what we've got, it's a match. Might not hold up in court, but I'd swear by it."

Rose stared at the merged graphs. She didn't need the voiceprints; she knew she was right. "Now what, Dad?"

"I'll present this to the regional Council. It's their call. Maybe another Ripper can look for him in June 1937."

Bertie was fingering the embroidered ninepins on Danny's jacket. "Why not you, Dad?"

"He's already there, recording the show and the strikes," said Isis. "In the early days of the Ripper program, they lost a man who tried to do more research in the same year he'd already visited."

"Cyril Keppleworth, July 1642," said Danny. "Nobody's gone to the English Civil War since then."

"Spooky," said Bertie. "Maybe there's two of him wandering around then."

"What do you think the Council will say?" asked Rose.

"God only knows."

#

From the diary of J.D. Taylor, January 17, 1938
The fall hits stole _High Flyers_'s thunder; we're on our last legs. With luck, we'll last another month. This little show called _Our Town_ will steal what's left of our audience. Still, it's not all bad news. We cut a movie deal with Warner

255

Brothers. Kate Smith's "Challenge" is a hit record. So are Benny Goodman's swing version of "Flight" and Tommy Dorsey's "You Make My Heart Soar." Youmans doesn't like swing—most Broadway composers don't—but he likes money, and the big bands are huge.

Overall, I'm happy. My production's better than the one the Shuberts would have mounted. It's less hokey, more structured, and "Challenge" is destined to be a classic. *High Flyers* didn't run long, but I bet it gets revived in later decades. That won't happen with *I'd Rather Be Right* or *Pins and Needles,* this season's big hits.

The social news is that Cole and Linda Porter are getting a divorce. I saved his legs and ended his marriage. In my world, they'd been going through a rocky time in 1937. Cole spent his time in Hollywood at work and play— lots of play with pretty boys. Fed up, Linda was on the verge of dumping him, but his accident brought them to patch things up. Here, as Walter Winchell puts it, she got a "Reno-vation."

#

From the diary of J.D. Taylor, March 23, 1938
High Flyers closed in the red, but not too badly. Taylor Productions is staying busy. I'm mounting a small production of Youmans' show from a decade ago, *Rainbow*—one of those "ahead of its time" shows, with a smart book by Lawrence Stallings and lyrics by Oscar Hammerstein. It deserves another chance.

I'm also trying to convince Vince to start another new show, with the Shuberts as my allies. Unfortunately, he's noticed the praise George has got for his string quartet, and how the critics and public are panting for him to finish his new symphony. The "Old Man" is in all the news, so

"Junior" won't be outdone. We're not getting anywhere with him.

I took Frannie and Leo to see *Our Town* last week. For me, the show seems painfully clichéd, but, in Leo's wide dark eyes it was revolutionary. I've studied a century and a half of metatheatrical plays and endured countless "bare bones" stagings, but here's where they started. Leo didn't even worry about being a sissy this time. He wept openly, as did Frannie. I learned afterwards she'd had another son, who died at three, and a stillborn daughter. Maybe that's another reason Wilder's play resonates with a thirties audience. In my era, barring accidents or stupidity *(Are you listening, Ramon?)*, folks live to ripe old ages. Not here. No wonder the Finkelsteins were so scared over Sadie's croup last month.

#

From the diary of J.D. Taylor, June 3, 1938
The revival of *Rainbow* is set to open at the 44th Street Theatre in two weeks. I'm hoping it will do well in a weak summer. Rodgers and Hart's *I Married An Angel* dominated the spring. The Shuberts' latest, Porter's *You Never Know*, opened last night—pleasant, but not likely to dethrone *Angel.*

It turns out I've affected *You Never Know* in more ways than I intended. This is the show Porter was writing when the horse crushed his legs, delaying its opening until fall 1938. Not surprisingly, it wasn't his best work, but it wasn't helped by the brothers' decision to "Shubertize" the show. They turned a charming drawing-room piece into an extravaganza with gigantic production numbers, throwing everything out of balance. Here, it's playing at the Lyric, not the cavernous Winter Garden. At Sardi's last night, Lee

Shubert told me it was *High Flyers'* intimacy that convinced him to take the same approach with *You Never Know.* "My brother J.J. wanted to stuff it full of girls, like usual, but I said it's not that kind of show. It's more like your *Flyers*—damn good show, that one. I guess sometimes size isn't everything!" He laughed coarsely.

You could have knocked me over with a feather.

I also saw Cole at the party. And he saw me. He air-kissed Gertrude Lawrence (who had starred in the play version of *You Never Know)* when he noticed me. He clasped Gertie's hands in farewell and buzzed across the room to me. I've seen bees go to flowers with less direct routes.

"So, Wizard," he said. "How's the air up there?"

"Fine. I enjoyed the show, especially the second act ballad." *The one you didn't write in my timeline.*

He dipped his sleek dark head. "Thanks. You know, I'm still having trouble believing my rehearsal pianist, the chappie in the ugly wool cap, grew up to become a big producer."

That cap kept my head warm in that freezing hall! "Let's be accurate, Mr. Porter," I said, "I'm a *tall* producer, not a big one."

Cole chuckled. "Got a light, Wizard?" Our eyes met. He might have wanted a light, but that wasn't all he wanted. *Yowza! Cole Porter's coming on to me!*

I smiled back at him; his smile grew larger and he moved a little closer. Then I spread my hands, miming helplessness. "Sorry, Mr. Porter. I don't smoke. But isn't that your lighter, there in your pocket?"

"Why, so it is." He lit his cigarette in its elegant holder, nodded curtly, and went to chat with Edna Ferber and Buddy DeSylva. Oscar Levant witnessed the entire scene and was cracking up. Cole's posture didn't reveal anything, but the tips of his ears were pink.

Cole, I love your songs like anything. I'm so damn glad you're walking on two good legs, not spending decades in pain. But you're a snob. And you're into rough stuff—not my style. Stay well, write more, and I'll see you at your next opening night.

#

From the diary of J.D. Taylor, June 17, 1938
Rainbow opened last week. Folks are calling me nuts for opening so late in the season, but business has been decent. Many people have no idea it's a revival and are surprised by the uncompromising plot involving a gambler who has to clear his name. That's why I wanted to give this little lost show some love. I'm pushing for a record deal, too, to keep the score alive, even though cast albums are in their infancy now. Getting a chance to work with Oscar Hammerstein wasn't shabby, either. Genuinely classy guy.

Taylor Productions is gearing up for an original revue next year—*Ladies First,* with material entirely written by women. No doubt about it: this is a sexist era. There are plenty of creative, intelligent, sophisticated professionals who deserve more chances, but don't get them because they're women. In particular, I've had my eye on Kay Swift. She'd divorced her husband while her lover Gershwin was in Hollywood. In my timeline, Kay always insisted George told her he was coming back to her after his film contract ended. Thanks to me, George is alive, but their relationship seems dead. They're still friends; Gershwin is so engaging, all his exes stay pals.

But Kay was clearly hoping for more. I've seen her since George came back from Europe. She's hurting. I doubt Dr. Zilboorg is making her feel any better. Maybe this show will distract her.

From the diary of J.D. Taylor, July 10, 1938
Leo's on summer vacation, so we're stepping up our lessons and seeing shows. He's also writing his first song. The same phrases keep coming from their apartment, over and over. It's driving Sergio bonkers, but Leo's working out the kinks. Speaking of Sergio, I don't like his yellowish color. His cheeks look more pinched then ever, but he won't go to the doctor. The *Monarch of Bermuda* sails next week, and he won't miss it.

Leo gave a big thumbs-up to *I Married An Angel,* but thought the plot device of *You Never Know* (baron and his manservant swap places; hilarity ensues) was "inane." He had a point, but I think part of it was rooting for the home team; our young director from *Flyers,* Josh Logan, directed *Angel.*

We got into a long discussion at Sardi's over *Angel's* second act ballet, "At the Roxy Music Hall." Leo liked it better than the "Princess Zenobia" ballet in *On Your Toes,* no doubt because he understood more of the satire.

"Top drawer," he declared. "Loved the dancing, especially the sea monster, and Hart used some great rhymes."

"True," I agreed, sipping my Bronx cocktail. "But the plot's set in Hungary. How come we suddenly get a huge production number about New York and the Rockettes?"

"Huh." Leo hadn't noticed the inconsistency. "It is a kind of a digression."

"Josh Logan also questioned Larry and Dick about adding 'Roxy.' But it worked so well, he decided that if you don't have a reason for putting something in a musical, you shouldn't bother to give one. Just do it. I know you admire Josh, but what do you think of that?"

Leo chewed on a french fry, considering. "No. A show is stronger if the parts come together. We did a lot of that in *Flyers*! But I think Rodgers and Hart did at least *try* to explain the New York bit—the actors had rhymed dialogue, and there was some swell underscoring leading into the ballet. That sort of eased the audience into the Roxy theme."

"Oh, you noticed?" I said. *Good for you!*

"'Course I did," said my pupil. "That dialogue was *relevant*. It made the number all right, even if it came out of left field."

Relevant. Inane. Digression. Sergio and Frannie don't talk like that. All this theatre really is building his vocabulary. He eats words like they're french fries. I looked at my plate. "Hey, where are my fries?"

"What fries?" Leo glanced heavenward, like a Raphael cherub.

#

From the diary of J.D. Taylor, September 23, 1938
Good news—we're lining up contributors for *Ladies First*: Kay Swift, though she's committed to be a musical director for the World's Fair; Dorothy Fields, once she's done with her current show; Ann Ronell, of course, doing her own music and lyrics; sketches by Edna Ferber, Dorothy Parker, and Claire Booth Luce; and I've asked a very young Betty Comden to do the lyrics for one comic tune. She, Adolph Green, and Judy Holliday are just starting to hit it as "The Revuers," and I don't want to screw up that future by asking any more of her than a single number.

Bad news—Sergio went to the hospital last week and never came out. Some kind of cancer; Frannie wasn't forthcoming and seemed embarrassed I asked, like it was his fault. That's a common attitude here. Disease is not a subject for discussion, but something shameful. Idiotic!

Yesterday, Nick Santino and I handled the funeral. Only a few people came. Maybe it was the aftermath of the Long Island hurricane two days ago, but I suspect Sergio didn't have many friends. Most of the ones who did show up were there for Frannie or Leo. Would his own wife and son miss the surly Sicilian? Possibly. But the events of this evening made it clear how much they'd miss his salary.

I had spent the day planning publicity with Alan McDermott, trying to squeeze another few weeks out of *Rainbow*. As soon as I got home, Leo knocked on my door and delivered an announcement in flat tones: "I've got to quit my lessons, Mr. Taylor. I need to take another job to help Ma." He began heading back next door, but I grabbed his arm.

"Hold it, pal," I said. "Does your mother know about this? My arrangement was with her: laundry in exchange for lessons."

"What good are lessons, with no time to practice? I should probably sell the piano, instead of letting it get dusty." His thick black hair was rumpled, his eyes red-rimmed.

Leo had talent and dedication and love for the arts. I didn't want him chucking all that because fate dealt him a bad hand at sixteen. "Go get your mother. Do it."

He looked sullen, but did as I asked. I left the door open, despite the cool drizzle, and fixed three stiff Bronxes. The Spinellis came in a moment later, Frannie pulling her flowered housecoat against the damp in the air. She started apologizing for Leo's bugging me.

"Basta!" I said. "Sit down, drink up. You too, Leo. It's medicinal. We've all had a big shock." Frannie kept silent, but clearly wasn't thrilled about my offering her teenager

a strong cocktail. Wine, yes, in an Italian household, but Sergio went on regular benders, and she didn't approve of spirits.

Leo did. I was treating him as an equal, not a kid. He drank, making an obvious effort to sit up straight and tall. *Sorry, son, but you'll never make it to five-eleven, even if your shoulders have filled out this summer.*

"I want to propose another deal," I said.

"No charity, David." Frannie set her glass down with a thump.

"I said 'deal.' I've invested four years teaching this young man about music and theatre, and I'm not having him quit without thinking it through. Do you want to give up music, Leo?"

"No, but we need the dough! I don't want to move to my cousins in Queens or Jersey. It's too far to Ma's job, and all my pals are here."

"Doing what? Washing dishes, delivering telegrams? That's peanuts. And once you're stuck doing it, you'll never escape. But if you keep up your lessons and go to college, you'll have fatter paychecks. I guarantee it." I held up a hand as he started to squawk. "So you need money now. Fine. I'll cover for you whenever you're short. Not charity, but an extended loan. Pay me back when you start earning regularly. I plan to produce a lot of shows in my life. I'll need rehearsal pianists, pit players, composers. You're not qualified yet, but you will be. For now, stay in school and keep sweeping my office."

"David, why should you do this? We're not your relatives, not your responsibility." Misery overwhelmed her normally warm, smiling face.

"I haven't got any relatives." I pointed at the photoshopped pictures by the piano. "The girl in the shawl had the makings of a fine actress. The doughboy could dance like Astaire. The boy loved sports, while his sister hoped to be a doctor."

"A girl with a colored ma?" That sounded impossible to Leo. For late-thirties America, it probably was.

"Well," I managed, "Hannah had big dreams. But I'll never know what any of them might have been." *True enough.* "Your skins are different, but I see similarities between you and my, uh, cousins. I can't spend all my money on myself. I don't need much. So why not?" I rummaged through my desk for a small notebook and some cash. I wrote "Twenty dollars, September 23, 1938" on the first page. "See? We'll keep track. If it gets complicated, we'll ask Mabel for bookkeeping advice."

As if on cue, little Sadie's irritated wail floated through the window. I slid the cash across the table to Frannie. "Take it. Don't argue."

Without a word, Frannie slipped the bills in the pocket of her housecoat. She stood up and hugged me. "I know Leo will pay you back soon."

"I don't doubt it," I said. *Of course, a few years from now, the whole world will be at war. Leo's bound to be in it; I just hope he lives.*

#

From the diary of J.D. Taylor, October 5, 1938
I was at a party at Sardi's tonight, but not an opening-night bash. The next one of those is two weeks away, Kurt Weill's *Knickerbocker Holiday.* Paul Whiteman, the "King of Jazz," hosted tonight's event in honor of the publication of Dorothy Baker's novel, *Young Man With a Horn.* Why is J.D. Taylor, Broadway producer, hanging out with jazz babies and swing dings?

Because I snapped up the stage rights to Baker's book. It's the tragic tale of a talented young cornet player whose life is cut short by alcoholism. Baker's inspiration came from the music of Bix Beiderbecke, who met a similar fate. Bix had been a player in Whiteman's band, which explains why Whiteman was hosting. I've sent George Gershwin a copy of the book, asking him to consider the project. It's a perfect match.

That's all in the future, though. Tonight I mingled, listening to wild rhythms with a Bronx in my hand and a smile on my face. People would pay fortunes to hear the guys jamming here: Bobby Hackett, one of Bix's closest followers, wailing away on his cornet to "I'm Coming, Virginia." Paul Douglas, host of the "Saturday Night Swing Club," one of the most popular show on radio, acting as informal emcee. Phil Cohen, the Swing Club's producer, taking a turn on his sax.

And, of course, Whiteman himself and his band. I nearly hyperventilated shaking his hand. He seemed so ordinary, a hefty fellow with piggy eyes and a thin mustache. But, aside from his own formidable achievements, this man commissioned the "Rhapsody in Blue." I felt like kissing his shoes.

He did a lot to put me at my ease—the mark of a truly great band leader is his skill at knowing his audience. "You bought the rights, I hear. Swell. Dorothy's a blip, I tell you."

"I've only corresponded with her this far," I said. "Could you introduce me?"

He waggled his fingers. "Piece of cake. Follow me." People parted like the Red Sea as "Pops" made his way across the restaurant. He stopped at a booth where a slender, prematurely gray-haired woman in a navy blue dress sat next to a balding academic type. "Dorothy, this is the fella that wants to turn your book into a show."

We exchanged introductions. The professor-type was her husband, Howard, who taught English at Harvard. "Mr. Taylor," Dorothy said, "my publisher said you were asking for the rights before my book even came out. Are you a gambler, to take such a chance on a first novel?"

"Anyone involved in Broadway is a gambler," I said. "But this is a winner."

"Have you given thought to a composer?"

Have I! "I've sent it to George Gershwin, but—assuming he's game—we may have to wait on his schedule. That's happened before. George wanted to do *Porgy* in 1925, soon after the novel was published, but the world didn't get *Porgy and Bess* for ten years. This is so right for him, I'm willing to wait."

Whiteman hooked his thumbs in his belt, tossed his head and laughed. "Gershwin! That'd be killer-diller, Jack!"

The Bakers looked shellshocked. Whiteman clapped me on the back. "Sit down. You three have stuff to talk about."

I spent about half an hour with the Bakers, often interrupted by well-wishers. We kicked around the notion of doing a straight play first, as the Heywards did with *Porgy.* "Do you think we could take a whack at that?" asked Howard. "We're not entirely hopeless with a pen."

I knew the pair would try Broadway in 1944 with an adaptation of Dorothy's controversial novel about lesbianism, *Trios,* but I was hesitant. They were novices; the Heywards would be a better fit (and appeal to George, too). "I'll consider it," I said, not committing to anything.

The terrific music went on while we talked. I wasn't paying much attention when Paul Douglas, by the bandstand, announced, "Here's a man who needs no introduction—so he won't get one!" Dorothy was asking about casting issues when my ears pricked. I gestured for her to stop—I hope not too rudely—and slowly rose to my feet. Others in Sardi's had noticed as well. Conversations petered out, one by one.

It was the "Rhapsody in Blue," and only one man could be playing it like that. Well, maybe Oscar could, but he was home nursing a sprained wrist from a ping-pong match with Vernon Duke.

I don't know what it is about the "Rhapsody," but it has this physical effect on me. My skin tingles, my pulse quickens, I seem to get more oxygen from every breath. I couldn't see the pianist, but I could see Whiteman, his arm around Vincent Sardi, beaming like a proud papa. This was shaping up to be an interesting evening.

# #

From the diary of J.D. Taylor, December 4, 1938

I've kept up my correspondence with Larry Hart, but haven't got more than scrawled postcards from him most of this year. Partly that's because he's been insanely busy, with *I Married An Angel* this spring and last month's *The Boys From Syracuse.* Unfortunately, his carousing has escalated to match—or counter!—his workload. I've seen him at his regular 45th Street watering holes, knocking them back with Doc Bender. Rumor had it he'd driven Rodgers to distraction.

Still, I hoped for a good visit with him today. His boisterous ways have landed him in the hospital with pneumonia. I lugged some goodies from the Hester Street market into Mount Sinai Hospital, where the girl at the desk told me Mr. Hart was in Room 318. I rode the elevator to his floor, bribed his nurses with gumdrops from Julius the Candy King, and got in. "Go ahead, sir," the floor nurse said, "Mr. Hart had a quiet night and is happy to have visitors."

I stuck my head in the room. Larry had his nose in a book, while a small radio played softly. He looked like hell—his face pasty, his eyes two burning holes. He had on blue and white striped pjs and a navy bathrobe with a red fleur de lis pattern. A dose of Minarcin would put him right, but I knew he'd recover from this bout, despite his ghastly appearance. That wasn't true in 1943. *Well, this will be a different 1943.*

He beamed at me. "Davey boy! You fabulous sonofabitch! What's with the bags? Looks like enough to feed an army."

"I brought you brunch. Bagels, lox, cream cheese, pickles, whitefish, fruit, knishes, candy."

"Such a *mensch*! What kind of knishes?"

"Potato, cheese, blueberry—from Yonah Schimmel's." Yonah Schimmel's knishes, I'm happy to say, are just as tasty in 1938 as they are in 2079.

"Mmm. Cheese, please." He put the book on his bedside table and hitched himself up straighter. The big white bed dwarfed him, leaving me plenty of room at the foot to spread out the bounty. I handed him a knish in waxed paper, which he unwrapped and bit.

"Delicious," Larry said, crumbs falling on the starched sheets. "You'd better join me, or I'll have a relapse."

I fixed a bagel and lox for myself. "I saw *The Boys From Syracuse* last week. That's some of your best work."

"Thanks. I haven't even seen the finished piece yet—damn lungs have plagued me since October. I hear Abbott whipped things into shape. I'm mostly thrilled for Teddy." Teddy Hart, Larry's brother, played one of the comic servants in their adaptation of *The Comedy of Errors*.

"It's a smash, so you'll have plenty of chances. When will they let you out?"

"Another week or so, then Mama and I hightail it to Miami, away from the snow. What's new with you, David?"

Hart hadn't yet read *Young Man With a Horn*, but had heard of it. "The Heywards are writing it as a play and George will get to the score...whenever. He's expanding the 'Second Rhapsody' into a symphony first."

Hart was ill, but he was still sharp as a tack. We discussed the challenges in Baker's novel, not just the tragic arc of an alcoholic protagonist, but in presenting African-American characters. Though I admire the 1952 movie, it kept him alive at the end and changed one of his black mentors to a white one. Not my production!

"Casting Negroes is bold, David. I like your *chutzpah.*"

I bit into a crisp, bright green pickle and shrugged. "Too many shows today are trite romances. Even most satires have little bite. I'm trying to buck that."

"Good for you, but I hope you don't lose your shirt. After all, you got to eat. Pass the pickled herring, please?"

We talked about my growing list of contributors to *Ladies First:* Hart was duly impressed, though he warned me there was a show with the same name back in the teens. "Not that anyone except nuts like me would remember. Well, the Gershwins might; they had one of their first songs in it."

It had been a lovely visit for us both, talking theatre without interruption, without booze, without the odious Bender. Now it was time to go fishing.

"I love producing," I said, "but I miss playing at the Golden Eagle. I've had a piano installed in the office, just to stay fresh. I've even been playing with a melody, but the lyrics are giving me fits." *Cast the line...will he bite?*

Hart's head jerked up from the orange he was peeling. "Can I help? No piano here, but you've got nice pipes. Let me hear it." *Yes!*

I shut the door, not wanting to disturb other patients, and sang "Red Sky at Morning." It wasn't new—it was from a failed one-act musical I'd written about a vet from the conflict in Nigeria, coping with PTSD. I modeled him on a friend of my dad's who ended up killing himself. None of that obvious from the lyrics I sang, just a vaguely unsettling song about isolation and not fitting in, things Larry Hart knew well.

"Sing it again." Without taking his dark eyes off me, he dumped the knishes and began scribbling on the brown paper bag.

When I finished, he gave me a long, hard look and cleared his throat. "Kkkkhhhhh. That doesn't sound like anything I've ever heard, but I kind of like it. Is it for a show? It seems specific to a character."

"It's from a one-act that never went anywhere, about a man with, uh, shellshock, based on a family friend. I tried recreating his daily struggles in the song. The show belongs in my trunk, but I thought maybe I could salvage this song."

"Where is this man now?" Hart's pudgy fingers plucked at the edge of the sheets. When I shook my head, he visibly gulped, saddened by the death of a man who wouldn't be born for decades. "A damned shame. Do you want to hint at that bleak future or give a glimmer of hope? Let's do both!"

We wrangled for close to an hour. Lyrics poured out of Hart at light speed. They weren't always perfect; he could be sloppy with meter and syntax. I'd counter, tinkering with his suggestions. It was exhilarating.

The bedside phone rang. "Damn! Who's interrupting us? Hello? Oh, Mama! Yes, very fine night. Sure! Bring your appetite." He hung up, smiling. "My family's on their way."

I began gathering paper bags covered with Hart's scrawls. "I've pestered you too long, but I truly appreciate the help. If I can convince Dreyfus to buy a gloomy tune like this, you're getting credit."

He sucked on a peppermint stick. "Don't be an idiot. This was more fun than a barrel of monkeys."

Of course, because you were working on your own terms. "Well, if you ever get tired of that Rodgers fellow, give me a jingle."

Hart harumphed. The idea was preposterous. He and Rodgers had been together since 1919, the most successful team in American musical theatre. They'd just staged two of the biggest hits of 1938. They were at the top of their game.

But I knew that in five years, Rodgers, frustrated with Hart's wild ways and lack of interest in adapting a Lynn Riggs western play, would go with Oscar Hammerstein instead. *Oklahoma!* would usher in the golden age of musicals. Hart would die at forty-eight, a few months after its opening.

Did I imagine I was fishing earlier, trying to get Hart to help with my lyrics? No, I've planted a seed, one I hope will bloom years later.

I thanked Hart once more, and slipped out before Frieda came to see her son. She didn't like Larry's gay friends. While my relations with him have always been professional, she still gives me the fisheye whenever our paths cross.

Before going back to the Village, I stopped at the St. James box office to buy Leo's Christmas present: tickets to Maurice Evans' uncut *Hamlet,* with a dinner break at Sardi's for $1.25 per plate. Such a deal!

Chapter 11

"Make the Man Love Me" —Dorothy Fields

From the diary of J.D. Taylor, September 7, 1939

The world's at war. As a time traveler, I've changed musical theatre history, but I have no control over the global stage. The last few nights, I've huddled with the Spinellis and the Finkelsteins, listening to reports of the German invasion of Poland. Most of their families have long since come over, but Mabel still has cousins in Warsaw. She wept as she clutched Sadie and tiny Isaac, all of two weeks old. Adam clumsily patted her shoulder.

Frannie's eyes grew moist, too, when talk turned to when—or if—we should join the fracas. "Hell, yes!" her son answered. "Hitler's nothing but a bully. Didn't you teach me to stand up to bullies, Ma?"

Frannie bit her lip and hurried into the kitchen for more coffee.

I'm upset, too. I doubt I'll get called up; I'll be thirty-seven (actually forty!) the spring after Pearl Harbor. I wish I could do something to make sure Leo gets through okay, but I can't think of anything.

With blood spilling abroad and the Depression dragging on here, it's positively indecent that I'm doing so well. I played angel with three hits early in the year—*The Little*

Foxes, The Philadelphia Story (Hepburn!), *No Time for Comedy* (Cornell! Olivier!)—and have even bigger ones coming this fall *(The Man Who Came To Dinner,* the record-setting *Life With Father,* Rodgers and Hart's *Too Many Girls,* and Porter's *DuBarry Was a Lady* (with Merman and Lahr).

That dough is handy, since *Ladies First* sank in a sea of red ink. I should have found a theatre for it sooner, but I knew *Blackbirds of 1939* wouldn't last long at the Hudson—nice house of about a thousand seats—and the Shuberts would jump to get a new tenant. They gave me a great deal, and our little all-woman revue opened March 2nd to good reviews. *The New Yorker* even singled me out as "consistently producing intelligent, well-mounted, thoughtful entertainments."

Then the World's Fair opened in late April, stealing our audience. Still, *Ladies First* had several damn good songs, especially Kay Swift and Betty Comden's comic gem, "Will and Liz," about Shakespeare and his queen; and Swift and Dorothy Fields' "Go Far." That one will be popular with mothers who'll watch their sons go to war. Fields' lyrics have a nice combination of wit and warmth, less ironic than her usual.

At least I'm not shouldering the whole loss myself; Gershwin invested twenty grand out of fondness for Kay.

Speaking of George, I'm thrilled he adjusted his schedule for *Young Man with a Horn.* This summer had yours truly, assistant Leo Spinelli (just graduated), the Heywards, the Bakers, and the Gershwin brothers hanging out in California sunshine, planning the show. The only thing that kept it from being paradise on earth was missing Ramon. We spent most of the time in a mansion George rented near Ira's place in Beverly Hills, with a few weeks at the Bakers' ranch in the Central Valley. If I had doubts about too many cooks spoiling the broth—er, the libretto—they vanished as soon as the two couples got together on the veranda, surrounded by orange trees. Of course, it helps that DuBose is a total gentleman, Dorothy Heyward is a charmer, and all four of them are brilliant. The Heywards had the experience, the Bakers had the passion and the intimate knowledge of the twenties jazz scene. As a group, we hacked the novel to pieces, argued structure, spotted places for songs. After much wrangling, the quartet came up with a solid libretto. They've made some changes necessary for Broadway: consolidating characters, building up the girl's part, making Rick Martin older. I insisted they keep Rick's close ties to the African-American musicians and his hopeless spiral into death. Bold material for a musical, but we're standing behind it.

The best part has been watching George and Ira write songs—a weird, symbiotic process. I swear they're telepathically linked. Music flows out of George, either right at the piano or jotted into a red plaid binder. Ira scribbles in notebooks, walks back and forth a lot, mutters. Sometimes he warms up by sitting in a corner, doing crosswords. George yells, "No, no, try it this way!" and improvises a whole new melody on the spot. Then Ira matches it, suggests something else, and they're off again.

It's not all on Ira's shoulders, though. The lyricist credits are even more complicated than the ones for *Porgy and Bess*. DuBose and his Dorothy helped on four songs, including the "Leavin' L.A." number. (Ira joked, "Maybe I had trouble because I don't *want* to leave L.A.!") Howard Baker came up with a sexy nightclub number that his Harvard buddies will likely ban in Boston. The rest is pure Gershwin.

Leo freaked out over how many songs the brothers rejected. "But, Mr. Gershwin, this one was a corker of a tune! 'Big Apple Rhythms' was keen, too. Why did you chuck them?"

"The first didn't fit the scene. The other was junk. Leo, I often write twelve songs a day, just to get the garbage out of my system. Maybe one will be a keeper. Maybe not. Eventually, I'll write a 'Big Apple Rhythms' that's right."

That was worth any number of lessons from me. Always a fan, Leo has turned into a Gershwin acolyte. At first, he was terrified to speak in George's presence; a week later, he was chiming in with suggestions. Good ones, too. He was disappointed when we took the train back to the East Coast, leaving the boys to finish the score. Starting classes at Columbia distracted him...at least until Germany invaded Poland.

A few other things cooking: this spring, I cut a record of "Red Sky at Morning" on my own nickel. It's not getting much airplay (even though I used Larry's more upbeat final verse), but it's got some interesting comments. Oscar Levant wrote, "Now *that's* what I'm talking about!" Ira Gershwin and Richard Rodgers both wanted to know about the song's origins. Ira commented with professional interest, "There's more here than meets the ear, I believe." But Rodgers was barely civil, irked at Larry's co-lyricist credit.

I understood his reaction. They're readying *Too Many Girls* for its opening, and Larry's drinking has forced Rodgers to write some lyrics himself. The idea of Hart scribbling words for another guy's tune while ignoring his own show must have had Dick boiling. I told him we'd worked on the song back in December.

#

From the diary of J.D. Taylor, April 23, 1940
We're in Philadelphia with *Young Man With a Horn* in tryouts, me at the helm. Marc Connelly started as our

director, but I fired him when early rehearsals didn't go well. That raised a stink—Connelly's far more established; a member of the Algonquin Circle—but it was the right move. I have very specific ideas for this show, and the cast responded immediately.

Broadway's in the doldrums, so it's a good time to open. Flops abound; even Rodgers and Hart will lay an egg with *Higher and Higher.* (Dick was pissed when I didn't back it.) The sole hit from the fall is Porter's *DuBarry Was a Lady,* with six good songs *not* written in my original timeline! Our main competition will be Irving Berlin's *Louisiana Purchase* in late May. Generic musical comedy, very different from ours.

We're an out-of-town hit, anyway. Although the stodgy Wednesday-matinee ladies sat in icy silence, the rest of Philly likes *Young Man,* especially our lead, Burgess Meredith. A former boy soprano, his mature voice has warmth, though not a lot of verve. Plus, he can play the trumpet, which is valuable, even though he's only miming the action. Dorothy Baker suggested putting a trained "Gabriel" in the wings: Bobby Hackett. Signing him was a big feather in my cap; he's *perfect.* The other night, he told me, "I know this isn't really Bix's story, but I feel like I'm honoring him every performance. Damn, I'd almost do this for nothing!"

"I can arrange that," I said, to general laughter backstage.

The Irishman threw up his hands. "I said 'almost,' David!"

We've played six shows at the Forrest Theatre. Every night, the place goes crazy when Bobby emerges for his curtain call, horn in hand.

That's just for starters. We've cast Edward Matthews, who played Jake in *Porgy and Bess* and will later teach music at Howard University, as Rick's closest friend, Smoke Jordan.

Gladys Boucree, from the recent *Swing Mikado,* is Smoke's sister (Lena Horne wanted too much money and teenager Dorothy Dandridge's mother-manager turned me down). Avon Long, a Cotton Club veteran and songwriter himself, plays Jeff Williams, the leader of the band that introduces Rick to jazz. (I chuckled when Ira, watching Avon work on a tap number, mused, "He'd have made a good Sportin' Life." In my world, Long did play the role in 1942.) Gorgeous Kitty Carlisle shines as the pre-med student who marries, then divorces, Rick.

Speaking of Kitty—she and George are having an affair (not their first); no idea what will come of this, but he wrote two kickass songs for her character. I'm happy for them, but keep wondering if this stops her from marrying Moss Hart, as she did in 1946 in the world I left behind me. I didn't think about personal repercussions before I hijacked the SlingShot. Maybe I should have.

Finally, I signed Louis Armstrong as Art Hazard, who teaches Rick the trumpet. This isn't Satchmo's first Broadway venture. He played Bottom in last year's *Swingin' the Dream,* a swing version of *A Midsummer Night's Dream* that lasted all of two weeks. Lip troubles keep him from doing many numbers, but his presence is overwhelming. He appreciates the chance to play something more than jovial Satchmo.

It's a dream cast doing an incredible score, especially Burgess. If there were Tony (or even Donaldson) awards now, he'd get one. From Rick's early obsession with music to his relentless spiral to death, he's onstage nearly every minute. How he makes his eyes so bright at "Curtain up!" and so dull and lifeless at the end is beyond me. His performance is exhilarating and devastating at the same time. "Always leave 'em weeping," he said to me this evening after yet another audience dissolved into tears.

Of course, this is Philly. What will New York think of *Young Man With a Horn?*

#

From the diary of J.D. Taylor, May 10, 1940
Opening night at the Majestic, big bash at Sardi's. The audience loved it. But, since most were from the theatre and the jazz worlds, they're already on our side. Showers of praise for the whole cast, especially Burgess, Edward and Kitty, and for the amazing score. I overheard Burton Lane say to George, "I never imagined you could do something like this on the musical stage. You make me think anything is possible."

I wandered around, basking in the warm glow of a hit—and several Bronx cocktails. I'm not getting much attention as the show's director; that's a theatrical role whose importance will grow in the next few decades. But I've certainly made a mark as the producer. A "Taylor Production" is getting a reputation as a particular kind of show. Not for the lowest common denominator of theatregoers, but for those who want meat on their shows' bones. I'm very, very happy with the result.

The plaintive eleven o'clocker, "I Can't Be in A Band," rang out from the piano in the corner—played not by George or Edward, not even Oscar Levant (though he's completely gaga about the score), but Mr. Leonard Spinelli of Columbia University, my production assistant. "I'm gonna flunk my chem final tomorrow," he said, grinning like a loon. "But I don't care."

I leaned against the piano, idly wondering when George would evict Leo. Then a small, dark tornado attacked me. Larry Hart wrapped his arms around me, his dark head pressed against my ribcage. "Magnificent, just magnificent," he mumbled into my shirt. "I'm at a loss for words."

"You, Larry? Words are your business."

He pulled back and looked up at me. His eyes were red, but from crying, not from drink. "I could see what you were doing in every single scene. You put it all together. And I *know* it was you. It's everything you've said in your letters for years: complete integration of book and song. Dick and I tried it with *Chee-Chee,* but didn't come close to this. Fuck, I'm in awe. How is it possible this is the first show you've staged? It's brilliant. You make the rest of us look like pikers."

"Thanks, Larry—that means so much to me. But I'm no virgin. I worked in L.A. and in Mexico, remember."

He waved to a waiter for another drink. "So you've said. Must have been underground, because I've been to L.A., I've been to Mexico. I asked around. Nobody's ever heard of J.D. Taylor."

Uh-oh. Think fast. "I hadn't changed my name yet. I was Joseph D. Cohen back then." I nodded at Leo. "My young friend was there the night my neighbors suggested a less Jewish moniker."

Leo finished "Big Apple Rhythms" and segued into "No Answers There." "It's true, Mr. Hart. I remember Ma dragging me over to meet Mr. Taylor. I didn't want to come, but gosh, I'm glad I did now."

Hart wasn't interested in that. He shoved me into an empty booth, peppering me with questions about the show. Who determined the balance between hot jazz and traditional Broadway numbers? (My suggestion, George's execution.) Why did the decor in Rick and Amy's apartment subtly change in each scene? (To show their growing alienation, until the only thing left of Rick's is his record collection.) Was I concerned that popular singers would have to clean up the lyrics? (No, because the book songs— the non-diegetic ones—are so integrated, they're not likely to get air play. The jazz numbers for the nightclubs are naughty, but I don't care if they get turned into harmless swing numbers. That's the 1940 music scene for you.) The one thing Larry didn't mention was the alcoholic lead. *Too close to home?*

While we talked, the reviews came in. Everyone crowded around to hear Edward Matthews read them in his booming voice. The *Post* called it a "masterpiece," though it cautioned that *Young Man* contained "highly unusual subject matter for a musical." The *Herald Tribune* called the Gershwin score one of the best in years. The *Sun* compared Rick Martin's arc to Greek tragedy: "His fate is inexorable, like that of Oedipus. One hopes fervently that something will divert him from his destiny, but realizes with wrenching sadness that such a wish is futile." Man, they don't write reviews like that in 2079.

The all-important *Times* review came in last. It began well enough: Brooks Atkinson praised the actors, especially Burgess, and the score. But where his colleagues accepted doomed Rick Martin as the protagonist in a musical, Atkinson balked. "One cannot deny the professionalism in *Young Man With a Horn,* which is evident in every aspect from scenic design to Mr. Taylor's staging to the poignant songs by the Gershwins and their fellows. But these impressive talents are devoted to portraying the downfall of a drunkard. A talented man, yes, but one given over to inner demons and whose life, ultimately, is a failure. Regretfully, we question the reasons behind presenting this as a musical entertainment. Though it is expertly done, can one draw sweet water from a foul well?"

Matthews faltered while reading those final harsh words. A stunned hush fell over Sardi's. Larry Hart, standing on a chair, looked as though someone had hit him in the stomach. "What? What?" he cried. "How could he say that?"

He slid down into the booth, his head in his hands. "God, I thought better of Brooks. How could he misunderstand this show?"

I found myself consoling him, even though it was my production. I'm good at holding in my feelings, while others—like Ramon and Larry—put it all out there. While I patted Hart on the back, George called out, "I'm not letting one bastard get me down! This is a terrific show! Move over, Leo." He began playing the score's liveliest number, "Magic," and Kitty Carlisle, a vision in gold and red, began singing Ira's lyrics. The party went on, as the *Young Man* family and friends set aside Brooks Atkinson and his misguided opinion.

Except for me. Because I'd seen that Atkinson review before—or one eerily similar, down to the last line. It's what he wrote after seeing Rodgers and Hart's *Pal Joey* in December 1940. The show impressed him, but he couldn't get past the louse of a lead character. His comments crushed Hart, who felt—rightly—that he and Rodgers were taking musical comedy to new levels of sophistication. To Atkinson's credit, when *Pal Joey* was revived in 1952, he changed his tune. Not that it did Larry Hart any good then.

So I sat there in Sardi's, handing my spare hanky to Larry, proud as hell of my show, but puzzling all the while: having criticized a character like Rick Martin, what will Atkinson say about that charming, two-timing heel, Joey Evans, now?

#

From the diary of J.D. Taylor, September 30, 1940
Fall-out from *Young Man With a Horn*: after working hard on our show, Ira Gershwin declined Moss Hart's invitation to do the lyrics to Kurt Weill's music for *Lady in the Dark*.

In my original timeline, that was the show that got Ira out of his shell after George's death. Moss realized Ira's wit and whimsy would be perfect for a musical about a high-powered woman executive who's undergoing psychoanalysis to make sense of her life. The clever conceit is that all the musical numbers show her dreams.

But Moss and Kurt planned to start work right after *Young Man* opened, and Ira wanted to relax in California. Howard Dietz will do the lyrics. Howard's good, but I'm going to miss the lyrics I grew up singing. I've still invested in *Lady,* counting on Moss, Weill, and star Gertie Lawrence's skills, but not as much as I would have if Ira were involved.

Young Man continues to play well, despite the gloomy war news. Speaking of that, I've been helping Gertie Lawrence and Antoinette Perry with the American Theatre Wing's branch of the British War Relief Society. We're selling BWRS matches, compacts, and pins in the lobby at *Young Man*; I've also staged some sketches for their benefits—Leo contributed one song, his first professional credit. I've even knitted blankets for "Bundles for Britain" in the Theatre Wing's sewing room on Fifth Avenue, trying not to drop a stitch while sitting next to Vivian Leigh. Thanks to my Nana for indulging her grandson's early interest in clothes! I don't have Frannie's skill, but I'm good at the basics.

#

From the diary of J.D. Taylor, December 25, 1940
Pal Joey's opening night; how Ramon would have loved this! He was a huge Gene Kelly fan, and always wanted to play Joey himself. God knows I loved him, but his talents weren't up to this part.

I got invited to Larry Hart's party at his penthouse in the Ardsley on 92nd and Central Park West. It's a gay landmark; Barbra Streisand owned it later. He moved here last year after his brother married. I don't like it half as much as the Beresford. Oh, it's stylish, with decor by Dorothy Rodgers (Dick's wife), but it's sterile. Larry's mother and Big Mary have the upper floor; a soundproof door lets Larry throw raucous parties below. But it doesn't look lived in. Larry has a room, but mostly sleeps on a couch in the gigantic den. The den has a lovely terrace commanding a view of the city, but *no bookshelves.*

I wandered around, a Shaefer lager in my fist, seething quietly. Boxes of books were stacked on the landing, few of them opened. *This is the home of a guy who packed a complete Shakespeare when he went to summer camp. I've got to do something about this pretty soon.*

I drained my bottle, filled a plate with Barney Greengrass' potato salad and sturgeon, and people-watched. I didn't know many folks here; it was mostly cast, crew, Hart family members, and the ubiquitous Doc Bender. I chatted with two chorines who'd been in *Ladies First,* then sat at the piano, playing *Pal Joey*'s score. Nobody wondered how I had it memorized. Maybe Dick Rodgers would have noticed, but he was celebrating elsewhere.

Around midnight, the phone rang, and Big Mary called Larry over. He listened intently, puffing on a cigar. "Yeah? Yeah? Great! Thanks a heap!" He hung up, briskly rubbed his hands, and motioned for me to stop playing. "Atkinson is calling *Joey* 'a milestone;' says Dick and I have 'challenged frontiers,' even though he thinks Joey's 'a punk' and my lyrics are 'scabrous!'" He threw back his head and roared. "Well, he's absolutely fucking right! Joey's a son of a bitch, and my lyrics *are* filthy! Give me a fresh one, John; we've got a hit on our hands!"

John O'Hara, *Joey's* librettist and a hard drinker himself, filled another tumbler of whiskey and passed it to Hart.

Though Larry read only part of the review, Atkinson had softened the critical comments he wrote in my world, the ones that so hurt Larry Hart. I suspect the "odious story" of *Young Man with a Horn* made Atkinson see Joey differently. He was right: the show was a milestone, the height of the Rodgers and Hart collaboration. But it was also a turning point. Larry's disorderly ways had Dick Rodgers looking at life without his longtime partner; he'd already begun producing shows behind Hart's back.

At some point, I'd try to step in and pick up the pieces. For now, I kept playing, watching Larry, rumpled and glassy-eyed, dancing in his clunky elevator shoes.

This won't be easy.

#

From the diary of J.D. Taylor, January 16, 1941
At about one this afternoon, I stood in the mirrored, marbled Art Deco lobby of the Ardsley, talking on the phone with Big Mary Campbell. "Mr. Lorry jest got outta bed. He says come on up, Mr. Taylor." Mary didn't like me the first time we met, when I fell asleep in the library, but she's changed her mind. I'm better than the "riff raff."

When I came in, Larry was still at the kitchen table, in black pajamas with a Peter Pan collar and a baggy bathrobe that looked like a horse blanket. A portly African-American man was shaving his cheeks, tanned from his annual trip to Florida. Mary, clearing away dishes, smiled at me, but Frieda glared. She sniffed and went back to reading a German novel.

Larry looked hungover but happy to see me. "Davey boy! What can I do for you?"

"I'm here for you, Larry. We're going to unpack your library. At the party, I couldn't help noticing the boxes. For God's sake, why have a den with no bookcases?"

He shrugged, uncaring. *A bad sign.* But Frieda and Big Mary were pleased. Frieda actually clapped her hands and cried, *"Wunderbar!"*

"It's Dorothy's design," Larry said, as if that explained everything.

"Dorothy Rodgers doesn't live here; Lorenz Hart does. Get dressed. We're going to work. Those books need to come out." *Whoa, there's some subtext, Greenbaum! Though I'm not sure they used that phrase for anything but debutantes in this era.*

His brow furrowed, but only for a moment. A spark flared in his dark eyes. "Okay, you're on, you s.o.b.!" The barber slapped some eau de cologne on his cheeks, then applied powder. Hart pulled bills out of his bathrobe for the man. "Thanks, Sam. Plan on a brutal game of pinochle tomorrow." He scurried into his room, the robe flapping loosely against his short legs.

"You want some coffee, Mr. Taylor?" Big Mary asked.

I took a a cup and drank it in the den, looking out at the city from the terrace. Mrs. Hart appeared at my elbow, startling me. I prayed she wouldn't start a scene; she once told a handsome young actor friend of Larry's, "If you go out vith my son, I vill jump out the vindow."

But she just said, "This is gut. My boy needs his books. Alvays vith his nose in books, he vas."

I suddenly felt I needed to make things clear to this woman. She had to know by now that her fantasy of Larry marrying and having kids was just that. But I wasn't a bad guy. "Mrs. Hart, I will never hurt your son. Never."

A brief nod, a touch on my arm, and she went back to the front room. I started ripping open boxes, stacking books in piles. Jerome Kern undoubtedly had a more valuable collection; Larry had perhaps several dozen first editions and rarities. But did Kern *read* his books or just own them? These books were loved and cherished, with worn covers and little slips of paper tucked inside.

By the time Larry reappeared, I had a third of them opened. "I made some unofficial categories: classics, plays, literature, history, novels."

He sat on the floor beside me, so close I could smell his cologne. "That's swell, David, but what am I going to do with them?"

"Read them, you dope. Here's Chaucer. *'Whan that Aprill with his shoures soote...'* Damn, I forgot the rest."

Challenged, Larry rattled off the entire prologue in perfect Middle English. He leafed through the book. "I love this stuff. 'The Miller's Tale' proves low humor is eternal." He glanced around the room. "Maybe I *should* get some shelves in here..."

I put down a morocco-bound copy of the *Iliad* and pulled a business card from my pocket. "These guys did my office. They can have a man here for estimates at four."

He slapped my knee and took the card. "Hell, I'll do it."

"Thought you would. I already called them."

His face registered indignation, then disbelief. Then he tossed back his head and laughed. "You bastard! What *chutzpah!*"

"Larry, it's common sense. You've been here a year; make it your home, already. Look, here's Ibsen. Remember the letters we exchanged over *Hedda Gabler?*"

We spent the rest of the day unpacking books, discussing authors, quoting poetry and Shakespeare at each other, getting high on words. I knew he'd be back inside a fifth of Schenley's by dinner, but I'd reminded him of a world he'd ignored the past couple of years. A world where he was a giant.

From the diary of J.D. Taylor, February 8, 1941

I've hired a car. It does nothing but sit from roughly nine-thirty to three on Central Park West, not far from the Ardsley's entrance. I'm sure Ray, the driver, thinks I'm nuts. I told him I had second sight, that a pal of mine would be in trouble here. "It's your dough, sir," he said. "I'll drive to Albany or park it, long as I get paid."

As a time traveler, I can usually bank on my "premonitions," but I don't have an exact date for this one. So Ray and I have sat here, listening to the radio or reading by flashlight, for eight nights running.

I sent him home early twice, after spotting Larry (once with Bender, once alone) hailing taxis from the waiting stand. No trouble those nights; at least, not the kind I could do anything about.

But tonight was different. It was close to eleven when Larry and a stocky man with sandy hair moved out of the bright rectangle of the lobby windows and into the gloom at the building's side. Street lighting in this era sucks. Sure, Times Square is a blaze of bulbs, but it's an exception. In the shadows, the bigger guy's body language—aggressive, angry—was enough to set me off. He shoved Larry against the wall.

"This is it, Ray," I said. I tossed a fiver at him and opened the car door.

"Need some backup, Mr. Taylor?"

"Thanks, but I can take him." I slammed the door and ran like hell across the street, shouting, "Hey! Hey, asshole! Yeah, you, fuckface!"

The brute was about to clop Larry on the jaw—a wallop that Dick Rodgers said left his partner unable to eat anything but ice cream and scrambled eggs for a week. My yell distracted him. The blow caught Larry's ear instead, still hard enough to knock him down. He made a muffled, mewling sound, and drew himself into a ball. The jerk began kicking him, but I tackled him. Bertie's beloved Patriots would have been jealous.

I haven't been in a physical fight in years. Ramon and I fought, but always with words. (Well, once he threw a salad bowl at me, but he was stoned.) But Nate and I tussled, as brothers do, from tykes to teens. We made Mom frantic, but I learned plenty. Beside that, I've been boxing in my apartment for six years. My biceps might not match George's (whose do?), but they're solid.

Plus, that tiny whimper from the fallen lyricist spurred me to lay into the shithead. It hurt. Unlike punching bags, people have bones. He fought back, too, scratching my cheek and smacking my temple, but I was way ahead on points. The taxi drivers wandered over to watch; the Upper West Side wasn't usually so exciting. "A buck on the kike in the tweed coat," said one.

"I'm not takin' that," said another. "He's poundin' the snot outta the other joe."

The blond guy broke free and rolled to his feet. I scrambled to mine and took a step, putting myself in front of Larry. A quick glance told me he wasn't hurt, just scared. My opponent and I sized each other up. I had four inches on him, though he was younger. He had a knot over his left eye and a mouse under it, plus a split lip and a torn shirt. His breath stank of whiskey. In comparison, I looked spiffy, though my glasses were broken.

"Want some more?" I asked. "How does it feel being on the shorter side of things?"

"Fuck you."

"A card! Well, I dealt with you."

He tried to sneer, but it made his lip bleed. "Fucking pansies."

"Yeah? Some of us can fight back. Get lost. And don't come back."

He reached up, fingering his chin. *Want Round Two, asshole?* Then he flipped me the bird and walked down the street. *Good. He's limping.*

Larry had gotten upright and was staring at me. "David? What are you doing here? Besides saving my sorry ass, that is."

"I was in the neighborhood," I said. *True enough.* I waved to Ray, who waved back and drove off. "Are you all right?"

"Couple of bruises. Would have been worse if not for you, you goddamn *deus ex machina!* Shit, you're bleeding! *Gevalt!* Come upstairs with me; that needs a bandage. I hope Mama's gone to bed. She'll have hysterics."

Luckily, Frieda had retired. Larry waved at a kitchen chair. "Sit there, let Dr. Hart get to work. Apply this internally, then I'll find something for your outside." With shaking hands, he poured whiskey into two tumblers and downed his in an instant. Then he fumbled around in cabinets for first aid supplies. He scooped up an armful of bottles and boxes and dumped them on the table. Most of it, like bicarb and hair tonic, was utterly useless. When they passed out the practical gene, Larry stood in a different line. But he was trying, in an endearing way.

I started to rise. "Larry, it's okay. I'll just wash it off."

"No, no! Please! Let me!" He shoved me back in my seat, took a washcloth to the sink, then returned, dripping puddles all over the floor. *Big Mary's going to have fits.* He tenderly applied the cloth to my face, mopping away the blood and grit. "Is that too hot?"

"Depends on how you mean that." I reached up, putting my hand over his. It would have been more romantic if he hadn't been soaking me with the damn washcloth.

"Uh, right." He pulled away, looked at the washcloth in confusion, then pitched it in the sink. He started drying me with a delicate embroidered hand towel clearly not meant for tidying up fistfights. Given the amount of water and the size of the dainty towel, he wasn't getting anywhere.

He patted my soaked shirt for a moment, then stopped. "This isn't helping, is it?"

"Nope."

We both started laughing. "Hang that up to dry," he said. "Then we'll put something on that cut, or it will spoil your boyish good looks."

I hung my shirt near the radiator. The atmosphere had changed since I touched his hand. Now I was standing there, shirtless and eager. Larry sort of blinked, like he couldn't believe his eyes. He had to know what I was; Dr. Zilboorg spent years telling half Manhattan that David Taylor was a homosexual pervert. But I'd *never* let any personal feeling come out in his presence. Larry Hart always surrounded himself with a crowd, many of them gay, but I didn't like those folks.

But now it was just the two of us, in his quiet apartment.

I moved to hold him, but he stopped me. "I'm not kidding about that cut. Let me put some Mercurochrome on it."

I had no idea what Mercurochrome was, but I found out. It's a horrible topical antiseptic that stings like hell and tints your skin a weird orange-red. The lid of the bottle has a strange glass applicator, which Larry used to paint my scratches with the stuff.

"Ow! What is that, sulfuric acid?"

"Sissy," he said. "Hold still and let me play Picasso on your gorgeous *punim.* There! Now for a bandage."

The cut had stopped bleeding. I wasn't waiting any longer. I grabbed the roll of gauze out of his hand and pulled him close, trying to undo that damn gold belt buckle.

"Just a sec," he said. He wriggled out of my grasp and went to the soundproofed door that led to Frieda's floor above. He locked it and turned to me. "I've no idea why you showed up tonight, but I'm damn glad you did. For a whole pisspot full of reasons."

"Me, too, Larry. Me, too."

It wasn't the best sex I'd ever had. Larry was drunk and kept bursting into tears and telling me I was a fool to have anything to do with him. And there's always the clumsy aspect of not knowing what your partner likes or dislikes or wants to do next. I just tried to take it slow and easy, to show him I cared.

And when we were done, I settled him in his bed (not that stupid couch!) and left before he asked me to. I knew he didn't like to sleep with people.

#

April 30, 2080

It took creative scheduling, but some prominent members of the academic branch of the Ripper Council arranged a conference in New York where Nate, Danny, and Layla Bassali, the chair of Yale's history department, presented the evidence that showed David Greenbaum *was* at the opening of *The Cradle Will Rock.* Five participants were watching through computer links, but everybody stayed attentive during the presentation.

"Intriguing, Dr. Greenbaum," said Hideo Dobashi of UCLA. "Pity you didn't spot him while you were there. Your instincts were good, but your execution was lacking."

Nate swallowed his fury. "My brother's smart. He literally hid in the shadows."

The synthesized voice of Jack Szelong rang out. A veteran Ripper from Oxford, he was nearly one of the field's early fatalities while covering the 1956 Hungarian uprising. "As his brother, you might have had a chance of convincing him to turn himself in. Could a stranger succeed without using force? I'm having trouble imagining a Ripper dragging him across the country into Yosemite Park. It's not as if law enforcement from our time could explain the situation to the police then!" On the screen, he shook his scarred, grizzled head.

Andrea Schellenberger of Leipzig, the branch president, fiddled with something out of sight. It clicked, registering her impatience. "Let's face it. It was a huge gamble, sending Dr. Greenbaum back not once, but twice, to look for his brother. We're not wasting any more resources on this."

Nate bit his lip to cut off his response. *You're already pissed off because one of your team leaked the truth about Splinterverses to the press. I'm not going to get any love from you, Andi.*

But Layla Bassali jumped to his defense. "With respect, ma'am, his trips were completely professional and productive. The sponsoring firms were thrilled with his results and he did valuable research in his own field. The time he spent looking for his brother was above and beyond his regular mission."

Click click click. "Yes, yes, of course, no offense meant."

Galadriel Child of Northwestern, silent until now, cleared her throat. "There's another issue. We're still learning about the Splinterverses. We know David

Greenbaum did something in spring 1934 to create one, and that he and Nathan Greenbaum were both at this Broadway show, in the 1937 of this Splinterverse. They did not meet, however."

Schnellenberger clicked irritably. *Ja, ja.* Get to the point, Professor Child."

"Unless a truck killed Greenbaum after he left that theatre, he's still alive in this Splinterverse. Right? Well, maybe it's a good thing Nathan didn't find his brother. Maybe that would have created a Splinterverse of a Splinterverse. Who knows what might have happened then?"

That set off furious denials from the four theorists present, the details whizzing past Nate's head. He didn't like the notion that he might have been stranded in a Splinter-splinterverse. *No way I'm telling that to Isis!* The theorists didn't think it was likely, but even so…

"Professor Child's notion is one we considered—carefully, I assure you!—and rejected," said Josef Glück of Bern. "The data we have from SV-1 and SV-2 show that—"

Schnellenberger finally put a stop to the hypothesizing. "That's enough, everyone. Thank you for all-you've done, Dr. Greenbaum. You are a valued Ripper indeed. But despite this new evidence, which we will pass on to the entire Council, I believe we will be looking long and hard at all future visits to Splinterverses."

Sitting at Nate's side, Dobashi muttered, "How's she going to convince the French of *that?*"

The meeting ended. On the train back to New Haven, Nate thanked Layla for her support.

"You deserve it. None of this is your fault and everybody keeps forgetting you've lost a family member, too. But, Nate, maybe you and Danny should have kept this data to yourselves."

"I'm an historian! Suppress facts? Are you crazy?"

"You've annoyed them. They don't want to think about your brother again. The Splinterverses alone are a headache. You may have trouble getting approval for future trips—the ordinary kind, I mean."

"Screw them," said Nate, looking out the window at the pouring rain. "I've already spent too many months stuck in the past, away from my family."

#

From the diary of J.D. Taylor, February 20, 1941

I've been with Larry a couple of times since that first night. Once at his place, once at the Algonquin. We dined in the Rose Room, toasting the spirit of the Round Table, then went upstairs to a room I'd taken. Afterwards, I wanted to see Larry home safely, but he said we shouldn't go down to the lobby together, for appearances' sake. Later, I heard he was drinking at Ralph's until closing. Sigh. I've got a lot of work ahead of me.

Cole Porter's new show, *Dude Ranch,* opens tomorrow night. Never heard of it? Me, neither. In the world I left, Porter's *Panama Hattie* was the big hit of the fall 1940 season, with over five hundred performances. But here, Cole spent last spring horsing around—in more ways than one—in Wyoming instead of writing *Hattie.* Sam and Bella Spewack concocted a libretto about boys and girls at play in the Wild West, and Cole, drawing on his experiences (well, some of them, anyway), came up with the score. It sounds really stupid, but *Hattie* was dumb, too. Because I don't know how it will do, I'm not backing *Dude Ranch.* I'm sticking to known winners *(Pal Joey, My Sister Eileen, Arsenic and Old Lace),* so I'll have money to gamble on Taylor Productions.

Will this world ever get a *Panama* Hattie? I don't know. Clearly, ripples from my intervention keep spreading through the Broadway pond. I could produce this world's *Panama Hattie,* but I'd rather do other things. My one regret is this world won't hear the show's terrific torch song, "Make It Another Old-Fashioned, Please." I'll have to keep it as a secret pleasure on my Ally.

The main thing is, Cole's healthy and happy and writing songs, if not the same ones he wrote while crippled and in agony. God, I nearly had a heart attack when I read "songster Cole Porter to spend vacation at Wyoming ranch" in Walter Winchell's column last year. Thank goodness, the Wyoming horses were nice beasties.

#

From the diary of J.D. Taylor, June 14, 1941
I'm spending more time with Larry, becoming an almost-permanent fixture at the Ardsley. All the doormen know me. Maybe they smirk behind my back, but I tip well, so they stay quiet. I can't stop Larry from drinking. The busier he is, though, the less plastered he gets. I've got to know his sister-in-law, Dorothy. The two of us plan frequent events with hordes of Hart cousins. Larry loves being with a crowd, which explains why he haunts the bars and restaurants of the theatre district, but he's also a family man. Kiddie birthday parties, school plays, giant family dinners—he enjoys them all.

We go to boxing matches (ugh) and baseball games. He's a Giants fan, even though they stink. Growing up with Nate, I understand baseball pretty well. Last week, we saw DiMaggio, who's begun his famous streak. I used my knowledge of the future to make a good-sized bet with

Larry's financial manager, Willy Kron. "He'll go over fifty games," I breezily predicted. "I guarantee it." Larry whistled in amazement.

"Never happen," Kron said. "Five hundred bucks." It's unethical of me, but Kron is a scumbag, so I don't care.

Larry and I also listen to operas, go to shows (and then analyze them), and play endless card games: gin rummy, pinochle, poker. I distract him other ways, too. I don't always succeed; sometimes—as happened in my original universe—Larry just vanishes. To drink himself blind, to grab an anonymous fuck—who knows? But I don't think he's as far off the deep end as the erratic, disheveled Hart of 1941 I've read about.

What he really needs are medications that haven't been invented yet and therapy, which he vehemently refuses. But I'm trying to give him some kind of stability.

#

From the diary of J.D. Taylor, June 30, 1941
After *Dude Ranch* turned out to be a hit, Cole Porter vacationed in Hawaii. Now he's writing a score for a Warner Brothers film set in Gay Nineties San Francisco. Perfect for Cole: lively locale and scandalous characters. He'll put the Hays Code to the test. However, this film means this world won't get a fall production of the comedy, *Let's Face It*—a big hit for Danny Kaye, though not one of Cole's better scores.

But it also means Dorothy Fields, who wrote that libretto, is available for me. She and Vincent Youmans and—get this!—freakin' Eugene O'Neill are collaborating on my next production, *Connecticut Summer*. It's based on O'Neill's best-known comedy, *Ah, Wilderness!* The project was Vince's idea; he went to see O'Neill in California and talked him into it over many, many drinks.

I'm excited about it, though, there are more Time Travel Repercussions. This musical means it's highly unlikely that David Merrick will produce Bob Merrill's *Take Me Along,* based on the same property, in 1959. I've made a note to myself to find something for Merrill, who's underrated, so he doesn't end up starving eighteen years from now.

A bunch of us, including Larry and Dick Rodgers, are invited to George's tonight. He wants our opinions on his new symphony. More likely, he wants to show off, but I don't mind. I get to hear unheard Gershwin; how cool is that?

#

From the diary of J.D. Taylor, October 28, 1941
Connecticut Summer opened last night at the 46th Street Theatre, where *Panama Hattie* would have been playing in my home timeline. I wish I'd directed it; I'm unhappy with some choices George Abbott made. How arrogant is that, complaining about one of musical theatre's icons? I guess our backgrounds are too different. Abbott helped musical comedy evolve, while I've seen decades build on his work. Sure, comedies need a fast pace, but I suspect the actors (Dennis King and Charles Butterworth as the dad and the lively uncle; Betty Garrett and Alfred Drake for the young lovers) will collapse after a month of this.

I do love the score, especially King's second act ballad. It's musically more complex than Merrill's *Take Me Along,* and the nostalgic sentiment of Dorothy's book went over well. In the troubled early forties, the early century's simplicity seems desirable, as Dick and Oscar will discover with *Oklahoma!*. I was hoping O'Neill would come East for the opening, but he didn't. I'm disappointed, but I guess there's no way I could tell him I wrote my senior honors thesis on *Long Day's Journey Into Night.*

Larry, who's just over bronchitis, enjoyed the show. Afterwards, he hugged me at Sardi's. I wanted to pull him close, no matter what anyone would say—but, of course, we kept it decorous. "Good one, David! I hope Dick and I can match it in the spring."

"The Greeks and Amazons story?" In my world, *By Jupiter* was the duo's last original show.

He wiped his watering eyes with a big linen hanky and blew his nose. "That's the one! Makes a better musical than Ferber's *Saratoga Trunk;* that's what Dick wanted to do. This story's naughty—and how! The Boston city fathers will have kittens. We're doing the adaptation ourselves."

"Well, you know you can count on me for anything."

He rubbed his hands. "Ah, I leave money matters to Dick and Willy. They'll hit you for some indecent amount."

I put a hand on his shoulder. "That's not what I meant, and you know it."

"Sure, sure." He didn't look at me, but over at the bar. His eyes were glazed with what my dad called "the thousand yard stare." "I'm going for another. Want one?"

I shook my head. Part of me was thrilled about *By Jupiter,* which featured one of my favorite songs, "Nobody's Heart." But while working on it (or being forced to work on it), Larry will drink so much, he'll end up in the hospital three different times before the opening in June. Can I do anything about that? I don't know.

Chapter 12

"Praise the Lord and Pass the Ammunition."
—Frank Loesser

From the diary of J.D. Taylor, December 7, 1941

It's Pearl Harbor Day. I woke up early this Sunday morning, knowing the world will be a different place by the afternoon. I jogged around Washington Square, working up a sweat despite the bitter chill. Joe Gould, bundled in an overcoat that looked like brown swiss cheese, whooped encouragement every time I passed Garibaldi's statue.

"Here comes Bronko! Look out, kids," he called to his pigeons, "You'll be squashed squabs if you don't heed my warning."

Panting, I stopped and pulled money from my pocket. "Joe, that coat's a disgrace even for you. Go buy a new one at Wanamaker's winter sale. And if I see you spent this on gin, I'll stop any future contributions to the Joe Gould Fund. I mean it."

"Very well, you tyrant." Joe hopped off the bench, scattering more of his feathered friends than I'd bothered.

Good. No weird observations today. Guess he's more sober than usual.

I returned home for a round with my jump rope and punching bag, a shower, and lunch. I overheard Leo and two of his pals from Columbia chattering on their way to the football game. I tried working on a song, but I couldn't concentrate.

If I can't be creative, maybe I can be productive. I grabbed a taxi to the office, where I reviewed Mabel's accounts, checked the grosses for *Connecticut Summer* (fair) and the tour of *Young Man With a Horn* (not in the South, obviously, with segregation still horribly in force). I looked at my watch every ten minutes. Alan McDermott noticed. "You okay, David? You seem kind of tense."

"Headache, sour stomach."

He stuffed the Sunday papers he'd been studying into a desk drawer. With a new baby, he doesn't haunt the office as much as when I first hired him, but Sunday's important for publicity. "Want me to get some bicarb at the Rexall? I need to get diaper rash goop for Bobby. His bottom's red as a clown's nose, poor tyke."

I tossed him a quarter. "Thanks, Alan. Maybe it will help." *But I doubt it. It's hard waiting for all hell to break loose.*

The other offices at the Music Box were empty and silent. The current tenant at the theatre downstairs, a Kaufman and Ferber turkey called *The Land Is Bright*, didn't have a matinee scheduled, so none of their company was here yet.

Alan hadn't come back yet, but I didn't have to check my watch to know it was two-thirty. A kind of muted buzz began outside. I glanced out the window to see people pouring out of buildings onto 45th Street. They stood in clumps, talking and gesturing, not striding purposefully like typical New Yorkers. Phones began ringing in offices down the hall. Footsteps thudded on the stairs and McDermott crashed through the doorway.

"Jesus! David, the Japs have bombed our base in Hawaii! We're in the war!"

#

From the diary of J.D. Taylor, December 8, 1941

I was about to write in my diary when Frannie knocked on the door. "Leo's late for dinner," she said. "He should be here by now. He doesn't have afternoon classes on Mondays." The light picked up the gray in her black hair, the worry lines around her eyes.

"He's a big boy, a sophomore. It's only seven."

She looked at my kitchen. "Have you eaten yet? Come over, please, I'm going cuckoo waiting for my rotten kid."

I'd planned on El Chico's, but Frannie was on edge, like everybody else. "Sure. I'll bring the vino." I grabbed a bottle of *vin très ordinaire* and followed her next door.

We ate and drank. I tried to make small talk. Maybe she felt better that I was there, but she mostly ignored me. Her ears were tuned for Leo's key in the lock.

When he came in at half-past, she jumped as if she'd been stung. Leo grinned as he hung up his hat and coat. "Sorry I'm late. I'm starved!"

"Where have you been? I was worried."

He piled spaghetti and meatballs on his plate and slid into his chair. "Let's see. I went to my English lit class at ten, since the old codger wouldn't cancel even though most of the college did. He kept droning about Mr. Gradgrind and got sore because nobody did last night's reading. Sheesh! Then we all crammed into the Union to hear the President's speech." He took a gulp of wine and shoveled pasta into his mouth. Frannie and I waited.

When Leo kept eating, Frannie said, "Well? I heard the speech, too—hours ago."

He drained his glass, not looking his mother in the eye. "Yeah. Then a bunch of us went down to the Naval Recruiting Station on Church. Gee, there must have been

301

thousands. They had to turn guys away." Again, teeth flashed in his olive-skinned face. "But not us. Me, Ron Ebert, Jimmy Gates, and Shelly Bergman all signed up. They recommended me for radioman, since I already know Morse code. Mr. Youmans taught me during *High Flyers*. I was learning the light board, and we got to goofing around one night. He said he learned it in the Navy in the last war. I report for boot camp next week. More *vino?*"

"*Madonna mia,*" Frannie breathed. "You're only nineteen! You don't even have to register yet!" She ran to her room and slammed the door, but her muffled weeping filtered through.

Leo shifted in his seat. "They said all the mothers do that. You think they'd expect it. I mean, we're at war."

"You're her only child. It's natural."

Leo stared into his goblet. "Well, I know you'll take care of her while I'm gone, Mr. Taylor." He didn't say more, but the words hung in the air: *And if I don't come back.*

"Sure," I said. "She'll be fine. Say, Leo, maybe it's time you called me David. You're not a schoolboy any more."

"That's swell...David." He finished his meatball, wiped his mouth and stood up. "I guess I'll talk to her."

"Good luck." I shook his hand. "Let me know if I can help."

Maybe it won't be too bad. Maybe he'll get assigned to the Donald Duck navy and patrol the coastlines. Something safe.

#

From the diary of J.D. Taylor, May 17, 1942
Leo's serving on the *U.S.S. Honolulu.* The encyclopedia on my Ally says it did convoy duty and Alaskan patrols this year,

then saw heavy action in the Pacific for the rest of the war. I hope he comes through. I'm also worrying about Alan McDermott, who's joined the Marines, and Hank Ito—now assistant chef at the Golden Eagle—who's in the hospital after some of his fellow Americans beat him up.

I'm in Boston, with the *By Jupiter* team at the Ritz-Carlton. My room's on the floor just below Larry's, close by the stairwell, which has been handy. The last six months have been...interesting. As in the history I knew, Larry spent January drying out in Doctors' Hospital and working on the show with Dick. But I've kept him in better order; getting him to eat regularly and sleep more, so he didn't get bronchitis again. Yay for Team Greenbaum!

My relationship with Richard Rodgers has been weird. Once it became obvious Larry and I were lovers, he recoiled as if I had leprosy. I could be a gay investor in his shows, but bed his partner? No way.

He changed his mind when he saw how hard I tried to make Larry work on *Jupiter*. I didn't always succeed; sometimes Dick called and I had no idea where his lyricist was. "Well, thanks for trying," he'd say. "This is the shit I've tolerated for years." At least Larry's written all the lyrics this time.

Getting a second apartment—in the Westwind, an orange-brick lump on Amsterdam and West 93rd—was a brilliant idea. Even though there was soundproofing between his part of the Ardsley place and Frieda's, Larry liked having somewhere we could be together. He still went back to the Ardsley (and Mama) to sleep. I agreed, saying I'd preferred my Village place, too. Then we'd take a taxi— or walk the few blocks, if the weather was decent—and, like an anxious parent, I'd watch him go into the Ardsley lobby. Only then would I head back to the Seville Studios.

I expect he drank when he got upstairs. Or maybe he waited until my taxi drove off before sneaking back down and going to a bar. But I'm making *some* progress.

#

From the diary of J.D. Taylor, June 28, 1942
I've been amazed at how the war affects damn near everything, from groceries and travel and news to the never-ending worry about loved ones. So, to paraphrase a cliché, what did you do in the war, Davey? For starters, I had trouble registering for the draft. Rabbi Epstein in San Francisco had to sign an affidavit that I was the baby son of the Cohen family he knew in 1905, whose birth records burned in the quake the next year. If anybody wanted to get fussy, they could punch that story full of holes, but at thirty-seven I'm on the far end of the draft pool.

I've been helping at the Stage Door Canteen since it opened in March—playing in the band, washing dishes, making coffee and cocoa. This month, I've been working with Moss Hart and producer Kermit Bloomgarten, entertaining at factories and shipyards. We're doing a series of skits and songs called the *Lunchtime Follies* (since they're running round the clock, lunchtime can be three in the morning!). I wrote the lyrics for a song about welders for an upcoming show; Kurt Weill's doing the music, which boggles my mind. I mean, *Kurt Weill.* The sad thing is, when the song goes into the *Follies,* Kurt can't watch the performance. As a "resident alien," he's not allowed to enter the shipyards.

This is the kind of thing I figured I'd be doing during the war years. Maybe I'd do some USO shows, too. But Vince Youmans just turned up with an amazing proposal.

I was finishing my shift at the Canteen, bussing tables and watching a teenager named Lauren Bacall twirling on the floor with a pimple-faced G.I. not much older. The band was playing "Goodnight, Sweetheart," their traditional closing number, when Alfred Lunt tapped me on the shoulder. "Youmans is waiting for you in the office when you're done."

"Thanks, Alf." I finished clearing the tables, wondering what Youmans wanted. I took my tray of dirty dishes to the kitchen, where Hume Cronyn took it with a groan. I hung up my apron and went to the office. Vince was shooting the breeze with Tallulah Bankhead, who'd been singing for the boys earlier. She's one of the few women who could match him drink for drink. When he saw me, he gave her a quick peck.

"You're a doll, but I need to talk business with David. Another night."

"Ta, dahling." She skittered out into the mild summer night, heels clacking.

We shook hands. I was pleased to see Youmans had a pot belly. The gaunt composer of Colorado Springs was long gone. "Sardi's," he said, jerking a thumb.

It wasn't a long walk; the Canteen was in the basement of the 44th Street Theatre, with Sardi's next door. Vince led the way to a back table under caricatures of Al Jolson and Ethel Merman. Carlo, the head waiter, materialized out of the gloom, menus in hand.

"What can we do for you, Mr. Youmans?" asked Carlo. "A gin rickey? Excellent. Mr. Taylor—a Bronx?"

"Coffee, please," I said. "What's up, Vince?"

Youmans passed his hand over his sleek hair. "You know that show Irving's doing for the army?"

"Who doesn't?" During the First World War, then-Private Irving Berlin put together an all-soldier revue, *Yip*

Yip Yaphank, to support the building fund at Camp Upton. After Pearl Harbor, he approached the Army about doing a sequel. *This Is the Army* would open on Broadway this July, play sold-out houses for three months, then tour the country and military bases in the war zone. Oh, and it got a film version, too. It would raise millions for the Army Emergency Relief Fund.

"I was in the Navy for the last war," Youmans said. "Most important time of my life! So I naturally tried re-enlisting for this one." He bristled at the look I gave his forty-two-year-old carcass. "Yeah, I did! I'm in great shape. But they rejected me when the x-rays showed the TB scarred my lungs. Isn't that a bitch? Haven't been sick in almost eight years, but the TB's still fucking up my life."

The Minarcin couldn't help that. Sorry, Vince.

Carlo brought our beverages; Youmans took a long drink. "Since I can't serve, I want to do a revue for the Navy—an all-sailor revue. Will you help?"

"That's a great idea, but I don't have Irving's clout. When his team has problems, he just dials General Marshall to pull strings. Plus, he's done this before."

He waved all that away. "Ah, but FDR used to be assistant secretary of the Navy; he's got a fondness for swabbies. I think he'll get behind this."

"What do you want me to do?"

"That Taylor magic. Put it together—write the lyrics and sketches; I'm no good at that shit. You're smart. I saw what you did for *High Flyers,* and George told me how you handled things on *Young Man With a Horn,* diving in and directing when Connelly wasn't getting the job done."

"But I don't know anything about the Navy!"

"I do. And we'll go to the bases, visit some ships, talk to the boys."

An idea hit me. "Hey, I do know one sailor. Remember Leo Spinelli, the gofer on *Flyers*? He's on Alaskan patrols right now."

"Perfect! He's a great boy; you pick his brains. This is going to work! I'll start calling people tomorrow. Will I see you at Irving's opening?"

I shook my head. "I'm scheduled at the Canteen that night. I'm going next week."

Youmans drained his glass, licked his lips. "Take notes. We'll see what Berlin does and then do it better. The Navy way!" He grinned at me.

I chuckled, thinking of a song Irving hadn't written yet: "Anything You Can Do." "It sounds promising, Vince. I'll definitely commit to the sketches. But maybe somebody else should handle the lyrics."

Youmans frowned. "Like Larry Hart? Listen, David, it's all over town that you're screwing him. But when he's not with you, he's out of control. Since *By Jupiter* opened earlier this month, he's been celebrating nonstop. This project means a lot to me; I don't want that little drunk fucking it up. Besides, what will Dick say?"

"Who cares? Dick's thinking about a project Larry doesn't want to do. You hit the nail on the head, though: I'm trying to save Larry from himself. He's too good to lose to drink." *You too, Vince.* "I promise—if Larry doesn't come through, I'll write whatever lyrics you need. But this could be the perfect show for him."

He leaned back in the booth, considering. "Well, when he's on his game, there's no one better. Let's do it."

#

307

Larry, Vince, and I have been working all summer on *Anchors Aweigh*. Hart was reluctant at first, but I finally persuaded him it was the best way he could contribute to the war. That we'd do plenty of travel—okayed by Navy brass!—also appealed. He adores the West Coast.

We began in New York, interviewing officer candidates at Columbia University, WAVES at Hunter College in the Bronx, and trainees at the Brooklyn Coast Guard center. Then we toured the Great Lakes base near Chicago (where Vince was stationed in 1917) and the ones in San Diego and San Francisco, visiting dozens of ships. I worked out a rough arc: two brothers enlist, go through training, then John is assigned to the Atlantic theater while Jeff goes to the South Pacific. That helped Larry focus his energy; the more details he had, the better his lyrics. He'd take one of Vince's lead sheets, with the basic melody of a song, and work away from the piano. It reminded me of Ramon's skill at jigsaw puzzles, the way he had a sixth sense for the right lyric, fitting it in place.

Here's Larry in action: last month, at the Great Lakes base, we watched some raw recruits learning to pack their sea bags. Not easy, it seemed. "There's a song in that," Larry announced. He held his pad against the wall and started scribbling. Sailors hurried past on their way to classes, but Larry ignored them. Fifteen minutes later, he said, "Here, how's this?" and sang "The Sea Bag Rag" in his high, raspy voice.

It was a mini-three act comedy, detailing the trainee's initial confidence ("Packing your sea bag, nothin' to it!"), his frustration getting his belongings properly stowed; and his final triumph—a correctly packed sea bag, with his name stenciled on it in black block letters.

Youmans fell out laughing. So did the junior officers who were our guides. "You got it, Larry! That's on the money!"

Larry beamed. He hated being forced to work, but he knew how good he could be, and the songs for this revue are top-notch Hart. "Watching for Wolves" is about Atlantic convoy duty and the ever-present danger of U-boats. "The Spirit of Pearl" shows the resolve Jeff when he sees how Hawaii recovered after the Japanese attack. The obligatory drag number, "The WAVES on the Shore," is comical and naughty, yet still gives a shout out to the women's unit. "Scrapin', Paintin', Loadin', Drillin'" is a wry commentary on sailors' daily duties.

Leo provided much of the fodder for Larry's mill, sending letters full of details from a young seaman's perspective. His latest letter was different, though:

Dear David,

Done pounding the Japs up north; back to tropical climes. We inducted the 'polliwogs' crossing the equator for the first time (I did it this spring), and I wrote up as clean an account of the 'shellback' ceremony as I thought you could stage for a Broadway audience. The USN isn't exactly a Sunday school picnic! But then I couldn't help myself. My notes turned into a song, which I've attached. My mates think it's pretty funny. Maybe Vince and Larry can do something with it.

The piece was a riot, including a rousing chorus for "King Neptune," the senior officer conducting the ceremony. I wanted to keep it, but I wondered what my colleagues would think.

We met at Larry's and I played "Shellback" for them. Larry slapped his thigh in glee. "Let's use it! I couldn't do better. Plus, it's one less number to write."

Vince studied Leo's music. "I like it, too, but I'm never happy to see another composer's work in a show of mine. I had to put up with that shit when I was starting out; I know you and Dick did, too." When Larry began to protest, Youmans held up his slender hand. "But this show's different. Sailors will perform it. It's fitting that one number should be by a serving seaman. Besides, Leo's a good kid."

After our research trips, we'd settled into a pattern of working at Larry's every afternoon. I played den mother, supervising two sometimes fractious Boy Scouts. Larry goofed off whenever he could, with or without booze, and it took time for him to adapt to Vince's methods. He'd spent twenty-four years working with Rodgers. Vince, on the other hand, never had a regular collaborator. They had to adjust to each other, and Vince needed to work faster than his usual.

With the Navy's help, we searched enlistment records for sailors with theatrical backgrounds for cast and crew. Eddie Albert, who'd been in *The Boys From Syracuse,* will play Jeff. We pushed to get Leo assigned to the show, and might have done it had he been an ordinary seaman closer to New York. But the bureaucracy wouldn't approve transferring a Radioman Second Class from Samoa for a Broadway show. Damn.

#

From the diary of J.D. Taylor, December 7, 1942
Youmans worked like a demon and Hart did, too, since yours truly has been glued to his side for weeks. Here we

are, at the Broadway Theatre (recently vacated by *This Is the Army*), opening on the first anniversary of Pearl Harbor. A Monday opening is unusual, but appropriate here. The applause after "The Spirit of Pearl" was like *nothing* I've ever heard. Even Larry, pacing at the back of the theatre, looked astonished. Vincent was in heaven; this was his baby, all the way. If his libido had missed the presence of chorus girls during rehearsals, he clearly intended to make up for lost time. His date was a slinky brunette who draped herself all over him. At Sardi's afterwards, she was groping him in a booth. A bold wench, since he was surrounded by well-wishers the whole night. I missed Boots, who'd divorced Vince late last year over his boozing.

My guest was Frannie, absorbing praise for "Shellback" to pass on to Leo. We hope he's okay; there's been action near Guadacanal this week, though the papers never mention details like ships' names. Speaking of the papers, we got pretty good reviews. Sure, the critics softballed us; who's going to badmouth a show for the Navy Relief Fund?

The only drawback of the evening was a snotty comment from Richard Rodgers. After congratulating Larry, he pulled me aside for a private word "Impressive, David. I couldn't imagine anyone else having the gumption to work with my blight of a partner. But then, I guess you have ways to persuade him to finish a lyric that I'd never stoop to." In case I was slow on the uptake, he stared at my crotch.

I almost decked him, right there next to the caricatures of Texas Guinan and Sophie Tucker.

Except he and Hammerstein are busy writing *Oklahoma!*, and if I fractured Dick's nose, maybe this world wouldn't get "People Will Say We're in Love." Not to mention that I was a major backer, to the merry tune of fifteen grand. But I was tempted, believe me.

I didn't let him see how mad I was. I went to greet Kitty Carlisle, who was chatting with Kay Swift: a Gershwin's Ex-Girlfriends' Club. But I got another Bronx cocktail first.

#

From the diary of J.D. Taylor, December 21, 1942
Following *This Is the Army*'s example, *Anchors Aweigh* will play three months, then tour cross-country before heading overseas to entertain the boys. Vincent's going with the show, and he's as excited as hell. Larry, Dorothy, and Frieda are vacationing in Florida; I've heard bad reports about his drinking and making scenes in restaurants.

It's so hard. He knows he did good work on *Anchors*, even if it took prodding. Yet as soon as the shackles are off, he's out on a binge, same as in my home timeline. I need to talk more with Dorothy and Teddy. This spring won't be easy, with both the huge success of *Oklahoma!* and Frieda's death.

And in local news, our own Village bohemian, Joe Gould, is famous. Joseph Mitchell wrote a profile of him for the *New Yorker,* "Professor Sea Gull," and the little guy has been basking in glory all month. He still weirds me out, the way he looks through me, but I'm glad for him. Contributions to the Joe Gould Fund are way up, it seems.

Speaking of money, Leo's latest paycheck has squared his debt to me for helping out after Sergio died. As if I cared. But Leo's pleased, as he should be.

#

From the diary of J.D. Taylor, January 6, 1943
Letter from Leo: his language was vague to avoid the censors, but it seems his ship *was* part of that action last month, but came through unharmed. Whew.

I've got a new project for Larry, from an unlikely ally—Doc Bender. Doc isn't the party boy of years past. Since his brother died in early 1940, he's cut back on his carousing. He's still a slimy pimp, but he actually found a property with possibilities. This one nearly got off the ground in my world, but Bender couldn't find a producer and Larry was too drunk to work. Taylor Productions may lose money, but I'll make sure *Miss Underground* gets staged…*and* that Larry finishes the lyrics.

Bender's calling it "an adventure with music," featuring Nick Malden, an American secretly working for the Resistance in a circus in German-occupied Paris. His rich relatives send a woman detective, Susan Jones, to bring him home, only the Gestapo is after her, too. Hijinks ensue. The composer is Emmerich Kalman, who fled Vienna and Paris just ahead of the Nazis he'll be musically mocking. He's best known for operettas, but capable of a playful, melodic score. Paul Gallico's handling the book, and the rest of the gang is top-notch, with Balanchine for choreography, Boris Aaronson for design, and—this is what clinched Larry's commitment—Vivienne Segal as Susan. He adores her, and I mean that literally. He's even proposed several times, though I can imagine how *that* would have turned out. With all that talent, *Miss Underground* should make solid wartime entertainment, even if it won't change musical theatre history.

That's up to Dick and Oscar's show about the cowboys, the one opening at the end of next month.

#

Larry and I have our ups and downs. He's thrown me out twice, screaming drunken curses at me. Once I went home.

313

The second time, a couple of days ago, I hung around near the Ardsley's lobby. Thirty minutes later, I spotted Larry leave, weaving perilously.

I followed him into Central Park, heading towards one of the ever-present sailors. It was freezing, but they were still there, looking for action. Someone once described them as "vanilla cup cakes" in their gleaming white caps. Gay beacons, bobbing along in the shadows of the trees.

I easily caught up. "Larry, don't," I said softly. "Come home with me, to the Westwind."

He whirled around, almost falling over. Clearly, I was the last thing he expected to see.

"You don't need to look for it here," I said. "You got me."

"Why are you doing this?" he wailed. "You can't possibly want to be with me! Nobody in his right mind would want to be with *me!*" He fell to his knees, sobbing.

"Well, then, I'm certifiable," I said, squatting and putting my arm around his heaving shoulders. "Here's a clean hanky. Come on. I want to show you something." I got him to his feet and propelled him out of the Park, deflecting the attentions of two sailors. We crossed Central Park West, but instead of returning to his place, I flagged a cab. "Eleven Cornelia Street," I said.

"No, no," Larry mumbled. "Gotta go home. Mama will worry."

"I'll call Mary." I shoved him in the back and climbed in after him. He slumped against me and passed out almost instantly. What he thought he could accomplish with a sailor, drunk as that, was beyond me. At that hour, we got to the Village quickly. I tipped the cabbie well, and he helped me slide Larry out. I carried him into my apartment, trying not to bother my neighbors. I plopped him on my bed, leaving a towel and a basin near his head. I took a spare pillow and blanket into to the living room, where I dialed the Ardsley. "Mary? David Taylor. Sorry for the late call, but Larry didn't want Frieda fretting. He's sleeping it off at my place in the Village."

Forties technology was lousy, but her long breath came through clearly. "Thanks, Mr. Taylor. I'll tell Miz Hart in the morning."

I was too keyed up to sleep, so I made tea and poured some of my sugar ration in it. I curled up in my chair, and read the papers and letters from Leo, Alan, and Adam, who was touring in a USO show. Larry snored. The radiator purred.

It was almost four when I heard him stirring. He stumbled into the bathroom. I went to the piano and began singing one of my favorite Rodgers and Hart songs: "You Have Cast Your Shadow on the Sea."

He came to the doorway, puzzled. "You're too much, Davey boy. I ought to charge you with kidnapping."

"I invited you here. You didn't object."

"Hell, I wasn't conscious!" He went straight to my bar and poured himself a drink. I knew better than to argue. "I don't remember much, but I do remember asking you why you followed me. You didn't answer."

"I was worried, Larry. I care. I'm a fool, but I do." I stopped playing Rodgers' melody and pointed to Ramon's photo. "See that guy? Ramon Abarca was the love of my life, my partner, the man I wanted to be with, forever." I didn't mention raising kids, though I'd wanted that, too. Gay marriage didn't exist in this era; the notion of two gay dads would have been even more fantastical. "But I lost him to drugs. So gifted, so warm, so funny, *so stupid.*"

"He's handsome. Like you." He gestured at his rumpled, smelly clothes. "If you can catch people like that, why bother with an ugly runt like me?"

"You're missing the point." I resumed playing, switching to "My Funny Valentine." *Appropriate underscoring, with those lines about looks.* "Yes, Ramon was an Adonis and you're not. But, Larry, *talent* is beautiful, too, and you're a fucking genius. Your lyrics have inspired me for years. Watching you create new ones has been one of the greatest joys of my life. I want to do that for a long, long time. Though I love what you're doing with Emmerich, I've been thinking maybe we could tackle something *together,* something big and bawdy, like *Tom Jones.*"

That got a reaction. "Huh. I've always thought that deserved to be a musical. Got a good comic role for Teddy, too."

I know. I've read five biographies of you. I shifted my underscoring to "Bewitched, Bothered and Bewildered," which aptly described my state of mind with Lorenz Hart. "Larry, we'll do *Tom Jones.* I guarantee it. Now be an angel and come to bed with me."

He took another swig and set the glass down. A moral victory for me: it still held a finger's worth. "Kccchhhkk." He cleared his throat in that way of his. "You're loony, but all right."

#

From the diary of J.D. Taylor, March 31, 1943
Opening night of *Oklahoma!* at the St. James, a night that changed musicals forever. The show was everything I'd read about—glorious, with a warmth that radiated from the stage, sweeping over the entire house. I'm here with Mabel, since Adam's still touring. Larry escorted Frieda. I saw him embrace Dick at Sardi's, telling him "This show will be playing twenty years from now!" He left early, not wanting to steal the limelight.

I'm worried about the next few weeks, not just how Larry will cope with the raves for *Oklahoma!*. *Miss Underground* starts tryouts in New Haven in two days. That's stressful enough, but Frieda Hart will take ill and die on the twenty-fifth. A rough road ahead.

#

From the diary of J.D. Taylor, April 27, 1943
Miss Underground is in good shape. It doesn't need major rewrites before it opens on Broadway on the thirtieth. That's good, since Frieda's hospitalization had Larry hurrying back home on the seventeenth. I did, too, to keep an eye on him. He and Teddy and Dotsy haunted the hospital until Frieda died a week later. Larry drank all the time. I tried to slow him down, but no luck. Mostly, I made sure he wasn't alone, coming back to a dark, empty apartment. I really think that's what doomed him in my old world—being alone. He'd shared a room with his brother until Teddy got married in 1938; he never lived apart from his mother.

Teddy had to handle the funeral arrangements. It was hard enough getting Larry to the services. Even as the Hart clan piled into cars, he tried running off to a bar. But I was on his tail.

"I can't go, David!" he said, working himself into a panic attack. "I can't."

"You have to be there, Larry," I said, pulling his arm. "You can't leave Teddy in the lurch."

"He's got Dotsy."

"You've got me," I said. His eyes overflowed, so I passed him a hanky. I'd started buying his favorites, made of Irish linen. It took a while, but I settled him down. "Let's go."

Dorothy and Teddy were clearly relieved when Larry's chauffeur pulled up in front of the chapel. The brothers tearfully embraced and entered. I hung back, standing in the rear. Though people knew about us, this wasn't the place to broadcast that. Following the interment at the Hart plot in Long Island, I hustled back to the apartment with Big Mary before the family did.

"Come on, Mary," I said. "We're going to work." She gave me a look, but brightened when I headed for the kitchen. I'd been around the Harts enough to know the German-Jewish fare they favored. Frieda was famous, with Mary's help, for cooking enough to feed an army. By the time the Harts got back, the whole place smelled of simmering cabbage rolls and potato kugel. I had *The Magic Flute,* one of Larry's favorites, playing softly on the phonograph, and I'd tided the living room, too.

The Harts took it all in: the sights, the sounds, the familiar smells. "I think Teddy and I will rest a bit," Dotsy said. "Thank you for everything, Mary, David." Taking her husband's hand, she headed up to Frieda's room.

Larry, however, seemed on the verge of bolting again. In the history I knew, he did. He got smashed at a bar, and came back with six "friends" who partied all night, to the disgust of Teddy, Dorothy and Mary. *Not tonight!*

"Hey, Larry," I called from the kitchen. "I think this sauce needs more vinegar, but Mary doesn't. Come decide." Mary's lips twitched; she'd said no such thing.

But it worked. Larry got a drink first, but one from his own bar (bottles I'd slightly diluted, feeling like a character out of *A Long Day's Journey into Night*), and he wandered over to sample our fare. Every time he started to look lost and frightened, I found something to occupy him—opera, gin rummy, songs on the piano. Anything to hold back the silence.

Dinner was a quiet affair, and when Teddy and Dorothy left for their own place I gathered Larry into my arms. He was drunk, but not incoherent. "What'm I gonna do, David? She was everything. And I was such a rotten son."

"Bullshit. She started in a Lower East Side tenement, but thanks to you she ended in an Upper West Side penthouse."

He wept, drank more (I didn't argue, not today), and eventually passed out. I carried him to his room, undressed him, and curled up on the couch. Close as we'd become in the last three years, he still didn't share his bed for sleep.

#

From the diary of J.D. Taylor, June 18, 1943

Frieda's death has been tough on everyone, but there've been a few rays of light in the gloom. Larry's love for Vivienne Segal, my constant presence, and bringing *Miss Underground* to its opening kept him from plunging into alcoholic paranoia. The production's a hit, with Segal outstanding as the sharp, sarcastic lead, delivering one of Larry's acerbic masterpieces, "Do I Love You? (No, I Do Not!)." I'll claim credit for toning down Gallico's jokey script, and for insisting Larry and Kalman address the feelings of the circus performers escaping the Nazis with the heroes. "What We Leave Behind" isn't as good as "The Last Time I Saw Paris," but it gives some heft to a lightweight show.

Since Oscar is working on his *Carmen Jones,* the all-black updating of Bizet's *Carmen,* Dick, as he did in my timeline, came to Larry with a proposal to update their 1927 *A Connecticut Yankee.* Except there Dick's bait for luring Larry was writing killer numbers for Vivienne Segal as Morgan le Fay, and here she was singing Hart lyrics in our show.

But Larry agreed anyway, touched by Dick's attention. And who knows? Maybe *Miss Underground* will close by the time they finish the revisions.

The other good news comes from Vince Youmans. He and the *AA* tour are in the South Pacific somewhere; censors frown on mentioning locations. Here's his latest:

Dear David,

Well, we're safely installed at one of the bigger bases, after traveling in a convoy with some truly SLOW ships. No chance to do laundry for days—peeyew!

We're staging the show as often as possible, wherever it's possible, and for damn near anyone. The U.S. Navy comes first, but we're performed for the Limeys and Aussies, Red Cross staff, and a cut-down version for hospital wards, too. Crowds like you wouldn't believe— six or eight thousand sometimes, packed onto benches, perched on tops of trucks, hanging from fucking trees. They're so happy to see us, they devour every number and sketch like starving men at a Thanksgiving dinner. The cheers, the applause, the love! I've never seen anything like it. I swear, I'm spoiled for New York. A single U.S. sailor is worth more than a hundred Manhattan fat cats.

It rains all the damn time, though. Our clothes and costumes get moldy. The food is unspeakable. There's not enough booze or women.

I'm having the time of my life.

The best show was the one we did last night, with dozens of the Honolulu's *crew there. I took Leo to meet the cast before curtain. He was over the moon. Still as skinny as a stick; says the radio rooms are so hot, he sweats off any muscles. "Watch the show from the wings," I suggested.*

"Nope, I'm sitting with my mates," he said.

"Well, sit on the aisle, because we're going to give you a spot after 'Shellback.'"

Heh. We did better than that. His captain, a good egg, was in on it. "Shellback" is one of the show's favorites—especially here! After the number, I came out and told the audience that the songwriter was one of their own, RM2 Leonard Spinelli. Leo stood up and the crowd roared. I beckoned him to the stage, but he refused until Captain Thurber stepped out of the wings and shouted, "Get your ass onstage, sailor! That's an order!"

The boys chanted, "Sparks! Sparks!" as Leo trotted up the aisle. (Radiomen get called that, from the lightning bolts on their rating insignia.) Leo explained how he came to write the song. With a cheeky grin, he said, "Of course, that's the clean version." That could have been an invitation for trouble, but Thurber was copacetic. He waved Leo to the piano where he sang some truly filthy verses and earned an S.O.! I've included them, since Larry will love them.

Afterwards, I brought him back to my room for a drink. We're in a small, spartan barracks near the docks. Leo didn't take more than one little swig. "I'm on duty at oh-four-hundred," he said, wiping his mouth on his sleeve. "Besides, I'm still drunk on that applause. Who needs whiskey?"

Vince included a photo of the captain, himself, and Leo standing on the stage, palm trees in the background. I'm copying it for Frannie.

#

<u>October 29, 1947</u>
Sitting at an outdoor café veteran Ripper Margo Guerrera tilted her head back and let the fall sun warm her face.

It was only around twenty-one degrees Celsius, a typical October day in Mexico City, but after enduring Britain and Denmark in one of the coldest winters on record, she appreciated it. Except for a side trip to Roswell in July, filming stupid weather balloons to pay for her SlingShot, she'd spent most of her year in SV-4 1934 freezing her butt off. *If I'd gone into art history like Mom, I wouldn't have got frostbite in Wales. Or been soaked to the skin for weeks on end in Kent. Or had to fend off horny Danish sailors, while seasick, shivering, and trying to take readings. Art historians have it knocked.*

Margo could have gone back to 2082 after covering the Fort Lauderdale hurricane in late September, but decided on the trip to Mexico City for her mother, who'd specialized in Mexican muralists. Today, she planned to attend an exhibition of David Alfaro Siqueiros' work. As a bonus, Diego Rivera would be there. Margo didn't have a chance of meeting either man, but she intended to film the presentation and exhibit for her mom.

She drank her coffee and watched people milling in the plaza, the smoke-belching cars crawling through narrow streets. She'd already visited (and filmed) most of the important murals, especially the ones that would be damaged in the 1985 and 2057 quakes. The vibrant colors amazed her; she'd seen them all her life, but after decades of filthy air darkened them.

Knowing the exhibit would be jammed, she got to the Palace of Fine Arts early, elbowing through the throng. The museum's director spoke, as did Siqueiros, but Rivera's companion, the sexy film star, María Félix, drew the loudest cheers.

Margo squeezed her way through the exhibit, recognizing many of the paintings as old friends. Other kids grew up with superhero posters; her bedroom had the weird masked figure of *Nuestra Imagen Actual,* reaching out with open palms. She shuffled along, moving from one piece to the next, trying to get good coverage of each one.

Then she stopped. Hanging opposite *The Devil in Church* was a work oddly out of place: *George in an Imaginary Concert Hall.* Margo knew it well; Siqueiros painted it for George Gershwin, shortly before the composer died. It featured Gershwin, seated at a grand piano in a crowded auditorium. The faces in the first few rows were those of people important in Gershwin's life, including Siqueiros himself.

That's weird. I guess Gershwin's heirs loaned it for the exhibition. She leaned forward, pushing past a sweaty gentleman with a walrus mustache. *"Con permiso,"* she murmured. Sure enough, there was a cardboard card below the painting: *from the collection of George Gershwin.*

Margo knew meteorology. She knew a fair amount about Mexican art. She wasn't sure if that sign was correct, but something about the picture bothered her. The composer looked right. The three tiers of the hall looked right. The dozens of tiny faces? *Maybe...*

She filmed it from every possible angle. *I wonder what Mom will say.*

#

From the diary of J.D. Taylor, June 20, 1943
Ever since Frieda's death, Willy Kron, Larry Hart's accountant and financial advisor (I use the term loosely; I think he stole for years), has been pestering him to change his will, fire Mary Campbell, and move to a cheaper place. "Lack of funds," he told Larry. In the world I left, Hart was in no position to argue, and drank himself to death in an empty, unfamiliar apartment.

Enter David Greenbaum, time traveler and professional meddler! Dolly Levi has nothing on me. When Larry mentioned Kron's comments, I phoned the schmuck. He's hated me ever since I took him for those five hundred bucks over DiMaggio's streak. "How can Lorenz Hart have money trouble?" I asked. "His income was over two hundred grand last year."

Kron coughed on the other end of the line. "You know how careless he is with money—buying drinks for everyone at Dave's Blue Room and Ralph's."

"Unless they've drastically raised prices, I'm not swallowing. Two hundred grand worth of drinks? Since I've been working with him—"

"You mean screwing him!"

"I've published a song with him, did the sketches for his Navy revue, and produced *Miss Underground.* I've invested in Hart productions since 1936 and will keep doing so. Personal relations don't enter into it."

"What do you want, Taylor?"

"First of all, Larry agrees with you about a new place. The Ardsley has too many memories. But Mary stays. She's been with the family twenty years. Larry needs her."

"Too much money!"

I fiddled with a pencil while he spluttered on about Larry needing to borrow from the bank. "You keep saying that, but you don't seem to be able to show Larry where all his dough's gone. Expect a visit tomorrow from Mabel Finkelstein, CPA. She's going to check your figures."

He howled. "What? That's an insult!"

"Larry wants answers, and Mabel's terrific at explaining things. Oh, and Larry also agrees with you about getting a new will."

"That's the first sensible thing you've said."

"So he got one yesterday." *Bombs away!*

"What?"

"At Nicholas Santino's office. There's a copy in the mail to you."

"With yourself as chief beneficiary, I'm sure." His voice was cold as ice. "You lousy fag, if ever there was a case of undue influence, this is it!"

I ignored the name-calling. "I'm not a beneficiary. You are, though. Larry insisted." *Though it's not the thirty per cent you finagled in the other June 1943!* "I think you'll find everything in order." Oh, I made sure of that, bringing a cold sober Hart to Nick's office, where two doctors checked him out and watched while the lawyer went over the will's details with him. Impeccable, highly respected doctors, too. One's a former Navy man, now in the War Department. His son-in-law is in *Anchors Aweigh*. The other's an egghead at Columbia.

I didn't stay past the doctors' introductions—nope, no undue influence here! I waited at Dinty Moore's, where Larry and Doc Bender met me for lunch. And yes, Larry did drink there, having been dry all morning. At least I got him to down soup and a sandwich, too.

Kron could discover these details for himself. For now, he just swore at me. "You queer bastard, you'll regret this."

Oh, I don't think so. "Lovely chatting with you, Willy. Let me know what you think of Mabel. She's one sharp cookie." Smiling, I hung up.

I've changed history in this world in different ways—with my bag of medicine from the future, with my cash producing shows that never existed, talking to piano movers and stable boys. But this is the first time I've done it with a lawyer. I hope to keep Larry alive for years, but when he does pass, this makes sure that Teddy and Dotsy and their descendants, including a son who'll be conceived this fall, keep control of Larry's copyrights.

Dick Rodgers will be pissed, but there's *no way* anyone's going to make Larry get another will. I had a bitch of a time getting him to Nick's, making sure he was sober as a judge, and I only did it because of his love for his brother. As we headed out of the Ardsley yesterday, he said, "You know, David, *everything* I've done in my life was for my mother and my brother. Now it's just Teddy."

"Which is why you've got to do this. For Teddy and Dorothy."

He rubbed his freshly-shaved chin and gazed up at me. "Know what I hate about you? You're always right. Let's get this fucking document signed and then I never, ever want to think about it again."

#

From the diary of J.D. Taylor, July 18, 1943

I was at George's this evening, listening to the tunes he and Ira are writing for Moss Hart's *Winged Victory,* a show benefiting the Army Air Corps. Unlike *This Is the Army* and *Anchors Aweigh,* it's a play with music. The Gershwins have written just four songs, but they're "cherce," far more likely to be remembered than the ones in my timeline's *Winged Victory.* They've also started on songs for the *Cavalcade of History,* a project with Kaufman and Hart for the Theatre Guild for next spring. That's one that the brothers were considering in the late thirties of my old world, so you can bet I'm backing this baby. I feel like its midwife.

We've also begun discussing a revival of *Porgy and Bess.* In my world, Cheryl Crawford produced one in 1942, but that had the impetus of Gershwin's early death behind it. Now he's over there, laughing and playing. But I'm going to get that show on the boards again, so people will realize what a treasure it is.

Sitting on George's couch, listening to fresh Gershwin tunes, a beer in my hand, I was relaxed and happy. Keeping tabs on Larry drove me nuts. I found a new apartment for him and Big Mary (wonder of wonders, Willy Kron "remembered" some additional Hart accounts to cover her wages; Mabel scared the shit out of him!). It's at the Osborne on West 57th, closer to the theatre district and familiar neighborhoods than the distant Delmonico, his last lonely home in that other world. Best of all, it's just a few blocks from Teddy's place.

Right now, Larry and Dick are at Rodgers' place in the country, revising *Connecticut Yankee;* it was nice being off-duty. Don't get me wrong. I love the guy and would do anything to save him from himself, but there are times when it's like Ramon and the fucking Tantalus-3 all over again.

Then the phone rang. George's valet, Paul, answered it. You can always tell when people get bad news, just by the way their body language changes. I simply didn't think it would be for me. But Paul said, "Yes, ma'am. He's here. Mr. Taylor, could you come to the phone, please?"

George, caught up with his playing, hadn't noticed, but ever-observant Ira did. He gestured for his brother to stop.

I took the receiver. "Hello?"

"David! Thank goodness, I found you at last. I've called a dozen places!" It was Mabel Finkelstein, normally the most unflappable of women.

God. Did something happen to Adam, with the USO in England? "Hey, Mabel. What's happened?"

"Frannie got a telegram. Leo was badly wounded in that battle in the Solomons last week. No more details. She's hysterical."

"I'll come right home." I relayed the news to the brothers, who went into action. Ira had the doorman get a taxi, while George poured me a stiff one.

"Drink it," he ordered. "You look pasty-white under that dark beard. Now, I'm betting that young man will pull through just dandy. Say, isn't Junior still out that way? Maybe he can help."

I downed the drink and looked at George in confusion.

Ira translated, "He means Youmans."

"Oh! That's a damn good idea!" *I'd forgotten the silly nickname.*

Considerate as ever, both Gershwins saw me into the cab. "Call us with any news," George said. "Leo's a great kid."

When I got to the Village, everything was dark at the Spinellis', but I could hear voices at the Finkelsteins'. *I need some aspirin before facing two distraught women.* I went inside and discovered a telegram on the floor—from Vincent Youmans!

LEO HURT JAP ATTACK STOP
EYE INJURY AND FEVER BUT STABLE STOP
TELL FRANNIE DONT WORRY IM ON JOB
YOUMANS STOP

I forgot about the aspirin and ran next door.

#

From the diary of J.D. Taylor, September 10, 1943
Vince was as good as his word, updating us on Leo's condition and even staging a special production of *AA* for his ward. Leo lost his right eye, but he'll live. They've just transferred him to Hawaii. With luck, he'll be back on the mainland soon, so I've sent Frannie out West. Rabbi Epstein found a family to house her; you can't get a hotel room in San Francisco.

I've had one short letter from Leo, written in an unfamiliar, feminine hand.

Dear David,

Lucille Ambers, the best nurse ever, is writing this for me. I have to thank you for saving my life, because you taught me how to swim in the pool at the Y, all those years ago. The Jap torpedo hit us in the starboard bow. As dumb luck would have it, I wasn't in my cozy, overheated radio room, but on the deck. I don't know what hit me, but into the drink I went, bleeding like anything. I could barely see, but I stayed afloat until the guys fished me out. So, thanks.

Leo

P.S. Don't tell this to Ma.

That got me thinking. Did I somehow change this world's history *again,* teaching Leo how to swim? Maybe. Of course, if he didn't know me, he wouldn't have been working on *High Flyers,* where Vince taught him Morse code, which put him on that ship...

I guess I changed Leonard Spinelli's life the minute I moved to Cornelia Street and Frannie came over with that casserole.

#

From the diary of J.D. Taylor, September 29, 1943
Leo and Frannie are back. Leo's wearing a big black patch over the ruined socket, but the red, raw edges of the wound are still visible. It's like *The Phantom of the Opera* for real. I'm also worried about things like PTSD, but he seems to be doing well. He told me he saw enough horrible things to know he's lucky, in spite of what happened. I've got him

doing light chores at the office and helping at the Stage Door Canteen, but he wants to do more. He's trying to convince Navy brass to let him return to duty, here in the States. "My ears are fine," he said, washing coffee cups at the Canteen. "I can still work a radio. Or maybe they'll let me help Vince with the *AA* tour. Damn it, I can't spend the rest of this war sitting on my ass!"

"Don't let Frannie hear that. She's wearing out her rosary, thanking God your war is over."

He smacked me with a wet dishrag. "Bullshit. I ain't done yet."

#

From the diary of J.D. Taylor, November 27, 1943
In my home timeline, Larry Hart, battling depression, alcoholism, VDs, respiratory ailments, and even a sprained ankle, still wrote lyrics as good as those in this prime for the updated revival of *A Connecticut Yankee*. But he completely lost it on opening night. He went out in the rain at intermission, got blotto, and raised a ruckus at the back of the Martin Beck. Dick Rodgers had him ejected, and Dotsy Hart took him to their place to sleep it off. He vanished by morning. Fritz Loewe, whose composing career was just starting, found him passed out in a gutter, chilled to the bone. A few days later, he died of pneumonia.

Well, thank God and the SlingShot, that didn't happen here. With Vivienne Segal still playing in *Miss Underground,* they cast Charlotte Greenwood as Morgan le Fay—a splendid substitution. Dick Rodgers *really* doesn't like me after the business with the will in June, but he appreciated my keeping Larry on track as work on the show progressed. *Connecticut Yankee* won't be a big hit, but it wasn't in my history, either.

The real happy news is in the Hart family. Dotsy and Teddy had been married for six years without kids and concluded she was barren. On the day Larry died in my timeline, Dorothy learned what she thought was an ulcer was really a baby. They named the kid Lorenz Hart II, in honor of his late uncle. I hoped that they wouldn't be applying that particular Jewish tradition next summer, but had to find some other handle.

Larry was ecstatic about the baby. "I'm going to take him to Giants games! The zoo! Europe, too, if this fucking war ever ends!" Rubbing his hands, he paced up and down in our private den of iniquity on Amsterdam.

I sat with a cup of lousy coffee on our couch—a floral monstrosity unlike Larry's stunning Belgian furniture or even my modest Village furnishings. But neither of us cared what the Westwind apartment looked like. It was a hideaway, not a place to entertain. The larder was usually bare, but Barney Greengrass was right down the street.

"You're not taking him *anywhere* if you don't take better care of yourself," I said.

"Shit, I can stop drinking any time," he declared.

I snorted. "Then do it. This tyke's going to need his uncle. Teddy's a terrific talent, but you know what an actor's life is like." *And his size makes him hard to cast, as you know.*

"He's in a hit now!" Larry said with fraternal pride. *One Touch of Venus* was a smash for Kurt Weill and Mary Martin, who played the goddess come to life. Teddy had a supporting role—not big, but steady work for months. I'd invested heavily in it.

"But before *Venus,* he was touring the country, staying in crummy hotels. That's a tough way to raise a family. Ask Eugene O'Neill." *Dirty pool on my part.* Generous Larry constantly offered to pay Teddy's bills, but, understandably, his brother was proud of making his own way, even when times were tough.

"My nephew will only stay in five-star hotels!" Then he sneezed, a wet, snotty explosion—his usual sort.

I waited a beat, then said, *"Gesundheit."*

He dabbed at his nose and laughed. "You're a goddamn wonder, David. Always looking so far ahead, like you have your own fucking crystal ball down there in the Village. Me, I can barely keep my appointments for next week straight."

Whoa, Larry, change the subject. In my nine years here, I've had folks question my accent, which is still a little off for this era. I've dodged queries about my imaginary family and my time in California and Mexico. I've even fended off Joe Gould's constant loopy remarks about my being "a man out of time." But you're the first person I've let get close. Just not close enough to know my biggest secret..

He poured himself a drink and sank onto the couch at my side. "Look, David, I need a break. With *Miss Underground* and *Yankee* and ... Mama ... Well, I got to get away for a bit. Usually, I go to Miami, but we had such a crappy time last year, I was thinking of Mexico. Then we'll tackle *Tom Jones,* like you said. You'll see what a good boy I can be."

Bullshit. You'll get wasted in Taxco and fuck boys at the cantinas, then come home and go on drinking. But at least you've accepted the new project and you're excited about the baby.

"Some day, Larry, *I'd* like to take you to Mexico."

His brown eyes widened, just a tiny bit, as if my words scared him. *Why? Because my presence would be inhibiting? Oh, I've seen that before. Ramon once nicknamed me PP— for Party Pooper. He only stopped calling me that because Bertie started doing it, too.*

Larry recovered quickly. "Sure, that'd be great. I know you savvy the lingo. But, listen, you're not taking this city boy to those backwoods villages, like you did with George a while back."

"George was born in Brooklyn. He's as much of a city boy as you are."

"With more energy than any four people I know. But he told me he was never so tired as on that trip. Worn to a nub, he said."

That wasn't Mexico, that was the medicine that saved his life.

"Okay, no Indian villages. But you'd like Veracruz."

He pursed his lips, thinking. "Any of Ramon's family out there?"

Probably his great-grandparents. "None that I know." *What on earth made you say that, Larry?* I jumped up and got a Blatz from the fridge. "I'll wish you a Happy New Year now. Safe travel, come back refreshed, and we'll spend the spring 'Fielding' a new show."

Larry adored bad puns; he laughed louder than the joke deserved. He lifted his own glass. "Death to the enemy and cheers to Baby Hart! May he be born in a world at peace!"

That will take another year, but it will happen.

#

From the diary of J.D. Taylor, June 28, 1944
I've been pretty happy lately. The war news is great; the invasion of Normandy progresses. Larry and I have nearly finished the score for *Tom Jones,* with a projected October opening. Lots of wordplay and puns, farcical situations, swashbuckling adventure, and, of course, sex. But the tone is more playful than raunchy—there are limits to what this era will stand. I want to use some period instruments for the orchestrations, the sort of thing I wish I could ask Bill Daly about. As it is, Larry thinks my music is … different. He

listened to the latest, then shook his head—half-admiring, half-perplexed. "Where do you come up with this stuff? In Mexico? Maybe I'm too used to Dick, but, damn, your melodies don't sound like anybody else's!"

That worried me, but only for a while. At first, I tried holding back my modern (as in late twenty-first century) sensibilities, but I hated what I was doing. I'm used to less rigid structures, more dissonance, more tonal experimentation all around. I finally realized I had to write music the way I'd always done, damn the consequences. My music sometimes baffles Larry, but the difference between my approach and Richard Rodgers' also stimulates him.

Leo likes what I've been writing, too. He's in Washington, transcribing coded messages. With his injury, he could have gone back to Columbia, but he doesn't want to until the war ends.

So *Tom Jones* is going well. Maybe it will be too unusual for 1944—we're planning a lot of rapid-fire scene changes, making the audience use its imagination—but Taylor Productions can live through a failure. *Miss Underground* barely edged into the black, but I'm raking in the dough from *Oklahoma!, Carmen Jones, Something for the Boys, One Touch of Venus,* and the Gershwins' *Cavalcade of History.* I'm also backing the plays *Ten Little Indians* and *I Remember Mama,* both of which will have long, profitable runs.

George Gershwin's alive, working on another symphony, with plans to join Ira in L.A. for a movie later this year. I'm producing the *Porgy* revival in September; can't wait for that! Cole Porter has two good legs, and, while his career hasn't matched the one in my home timeline, I've mostly liked what he's done. The *Barbary Coast* film was a delight, especially Ann Miller's "Shanghai Me" number; *Dude Ranch* was moronic, but four songs are destined for the Great American Songbook. Porter's lyrics are always brilliant, and there's a greater variety to the music he's writing here—maybe because he's not in constant pain. He's doing a show set in Prohibition Chicago this fall, *Speakeasy.* Vince Youmans is healthy, touring with *Anchors Aweigh* in the war zones. We've exchanged some letters about future properties. Jerome Kern's still working in Hollywood; I heard he was ill in 1942. Maybe saving his piano helped him, maybe it didn't. We'll find out next year, I guess, when he has that stroke or doesn't.

My ongoing worry is Joe Gould. Following the *New Yorker* profile, he's become a kind of tourist attraction. He sits in a booth at the Minetta Tavern, scribbling additions to the *Oral History* in his nickel composition books, delivering lectures, and translating poetry into sea gull, while the visitors gawk. And contribute to the Fund, of course.

Why should that bother me? Apparently, Joe endlessly rewrites many of his essays. His favorite topics are the death of his parents, the dangers of tomatoes (this from a man who eats "soup" made of ketchup and hot water), and his time on a Chippewa Indian reservation in the teens. But Karl Sundgaard told me Joe passed out in the Golden Eagle recently. While he and Skip were waiting for the doctor to come, they picked up Joe's scattered papers. "Now he's writing about you, Dave," said Karl. "Well, not exactly you—I remembered he calls you Bronko. Says you don't sound like anyone he's ever heard in all his travels, and that you magically appeared in his path one night and flattened him. Calls you the 'man out of time.' Isn't that a riot?"

"Hilarious. Can't you hear me laughing?"

"Well, we thought it was funny."

Bad enough Joe makes freaky comments like that to my face. I don't exactly know what this crazy *Oral History* is, if it will every be published or not—there's no record of it in my Ally's encyclopedia—but I don't want to be part of it.

I took a cab to the office. Taylor Productions could have moved to spiffier digs by now, but I like the Music Box. We have expanded from our original three rooms, though. Mabel and her accounting staff are in two of those. Frannie does day care in the third, while the main staff has taken over much of the floor above them. Some folks have criticized me, since not everything's centralized, but what does it matter? We're connected by phone lines and only separated by a staircase. I've got a weird reputation for not caring about appearances; I mean, on-site day care, in a producer's office?

I checked in with Mabel, who was still looking green. "Bad morning again?" I asked.

She wearily shook her head, never looking up from her adding machine. "Sadie and Ike wanted eggs for breakfast. I cracked them in the bowl and the cussed yolks kept looking at me. Next thing I know, I'm in the bathroom, watching the coffee with my darn sugar ration in it disappear.'"

Sadie, now six, was sharpening the pencils. She looked like a feminine version of her father, with Adam's lithe limbs and almost feline features. "Poor Mom. I made the eggs myself."

"They were icky!" Ike declared. "Come on, Bobby, let's go ask Mrs. Spaghetti for something *good* to eat." At almost five, he bossed the smaller children, including Alan McDermott's lad, who was not quite three. All told, Frannie had six in charge, offspring of Taylor Productions' managers and staff. I liked it. I missed my nieces and nephew.

I clumped up the stairs to my office. My secretary, Jeanette McDermott (Alan's sister), gave me the mail, but I fixed my own coffee. A secretary is not a toy. I intended to work until noon, lunch at Dave's Blue Room with Moss

Hart, then try to get Larry to finish the lyrics for the sly Lady Bellaston, one of the last numbers for *Tom Jones.*

But I'd barely picked up my mail when Jeannie buzzed me with a call. "It's Mr. Albert, sir, from London!"

Eddie? What's gone wrong with the tour? They got past the U-boats to England; everything should be fine! I punched the button on my phone. "This is David Taylor."

"Mr. Taylor! I've got the most awful news! Mr. Youmans was out shopping—we needed some new props—and the Nazis bombed the market! He was killed instantly."

Chapter 13

"He Loves and She Loves" —Ira Gershwin

From the diary of J.D. Taylor, September 22, 1944

We're on tryouts with *Tom Jones* in Baltimore's Ford's Theatre. Work has been a blessing and a curse. A blessing, I'm so busy, I mostly dwell on Vince Youmans' death in the wee smalls. A curse, I'm always up then. I'm exhausted and constantly sick.

Larry hasn't been much help. Oh, he feels for me, since he can see how upset I've been. Aside from *Anchors Aweigh,* though, he was never close to Youmans. Hard drinkers and fantastic talents both, but little in common beyond that. And he's still mourning Frieda, and doesn't know how to handle someone else's grief.

I came from 2079 with a bottle of Minarcin to save Vincent Youmans, and the fucking Nazis got him. It wasn't supposed to work that way. I'm grieving not only his death, but the deaths of the dozens of great unwritten songs. Shit, he lived longer with tuberculosis—April 1946.

So here I was again, miserable at one in the morning. *Tom Jones* needs drastic cuts, so director Rouben Mamoulian, Larry and I stayed late after tonight's performance, slicing away. Larry wasn't well; his dinner had given him the trots.

I finally sent him and Mamoulian back to the hotel to get some sleep.

Alone with the ghostlight and a family of bats (this theatre is over seventy years old), I stayed at the piano, revising the opening comic ballet that recounts Tom's early life through Jack Cole's dazzling choreography. Although the show wasn't going as I'd hoped, working with Jack and Rouben was a joy.

The night watchman, an African-American with a hook for a hand, entered the house, making me jump and the bats squeak. "Sorry t'bother you, suh, but there's a gent at the stage door. Says he come up from Washington. I told him you was workin', but he says, 'I know. I'm here to help.'"

"Is he wearing an eye patch?"

"He shore is."

"Then let him in."

Moments later, Leo came jogging in, a duffel bag over his shoulder. I hadn't seen him since the spring, when he surprised Frannie for her birthday. "Hey, David! How's tricks?"

"Shitty. The show's in trouble. I'm not happy with the cast, and it's running over three hours!"

He threw down his bag. "I'm yours for the weekend, if I can help. Just give me a flat space to bunk."

I kept playing the damn ballet while we talked, half my mind trying to find places to trim. "You're with me. I'm just amazed to see you."

"As if I'd miss tryouts! Mabel told me which hotel, and I bummed a ride with some buds who were dropping another guy here on their way to Annapolis. I saw Larry in the lobby—he looked wasted, but he says it was bad crab cakes. Hope he does better than President Harding! He told me you were here, so I walked over."

"In the middle of the night?"

He shrugged. "It's nothing." He sat on the edge of the stage, legs dangling, and began flipping through my heavily annotated copy of the score. The scars around his eye patch looked pink and shiny. They'd reconstructed the socket for a glass eye, but he preferred the patch—people didn't stare as much.

His fresh approach helped. He saw things I hadn't noticed because I'd been staring at the same measures too long. We finished up and took a taxi to the Emerson Hotel, where I badgered the night clerk for a cot. Not easy— the Emerson was stuffed with military personnel—but I got one.

Leo was making up the cot with GI corners when I came out of the bathroom in my pajamas. "I've a spare toothbrush, if you need one," I said.

He gave me a double take. "God, I couldn't tell in the dark theatre, but you look like hell."

"No sleep, too much to do, and I keep thinking about Vince. I feel responsible."

Leo smacked his pillow like he wanted to smack me. "That's garbage. First of all, *Anchors* was his idea. He would written it, even without you and Larry."

"Maybe."

"No maybes. He wrote better songs for *No, No, Nanette* and *High Flyers,* but he was prouder of *AA* than everything else he ever did. You didn't see him on the tour. I did. He loved every minute, even the heat and the mud. He loved making the guys laugh. He told me that made him feel like he'd been awarded a Navy E."

I got that particular reference from the newspapers, but also from a lyric in the upcoming *On The Town.* The government granted the E awards (Excellence in Production) to industries aiding the war effort.

"I was just a kid on *Flyers*. Vince was nice to me, but I saw he could be a jackass. He picked fights and was mean to Boots and drank too much—like my dad, though Pop didn't chase skirts. Vince thought anybody who disagreed with him was not only wrong, but an idiot. Not an easy guy to like. I think you deserve credit for handling him so well. You got good work out of him."

But I should have got more! Years more!

Leo hadn't finished. "He wasn't a happy man. He wasn't a generous man. He was full of himself. But, David, he was happy on the tour. He was kind and considerate. That was a different Vincent Youmans out there. When he wasn't working the show, he was playing songs for the wounded or lending a hand with the USO folks. When I got hurt, he spent every spare minute doing stuff for me and the fellows in my ward. It got embarrassing! It's a rotten shame the Krauts got him, but he was doing what he loved. I'm guessing if you offered him a choice of deaths, he'd pick that one in a heartbeat. Sure beats death by consumption—he once told me he thought that would get him." Leo yanked off his sweater and buttoned up his pajamas. A network of thick and thin scars patterned his right shoulder. He picked up his Dopp kit, a present from the Finkelsteins on his eighteenth birthday, but paused in the doorway.

"I feel lousy 'cause he's gone, too. We've lost thousands of talented people. But blaming yourself? Bullshit. Vincent Youmans was exactly where he wanted to be. It's the Nazis' fault for dropping a buzz bomb on that market."

He shut the door behind him. I heard water running, gargling. A few minutes later, he came out. "Hey, did you even hear a word I said?" he asked.

"Yeah. I appreciate it. I'm still trying to imagine a happy Youmans."

"Ask any of the guys in the revue. Stop kicking yourself, boss man. You got enough things to haunt your nights, like cutting another twenty minutes from this show." He tossed his eye patch into his Dopp kit, giving me my first look at the wound in months: ugly, but no longer gruesome. "Taps, taps, lights out, all hands turn in to your bunks."

"Aye aye, sir," I said, clicking the lamp switch. I had twenty years on him, but he was clearly in charge tonight.

Leo made a compelling argument. I still felt terrible. If I hadn't cured Youmans, he wouldn't have been in London.

But... he also wouldn't have written *Anchors Aweigh,* a show that raised thousands for the Navy Relief Fund and brought joy to so many servicemen, and apparently to Youmans, too. *Connecticut Summer. High Flyers,* with the great anthem, "Challenge." The "Caribbean Concerto." In the world I left, Vincent Youmans did little after the success of *Flying Down to Rio* in 1933 except drink and aggravate people. He produced a revue that didn't even include one of his own songs. The studios considered making a movie of his life in 1945, but he sourly acknowledged he was a has-been, that no one even knew his name any more. The film exec denied it, asking his secretary, "Do you know who Vincent Youmans is?"

"Yes! The bandleader!" she said, thinking of Vincent Lopez.

The movie was never filmed; a bitter Youmans died a year later, shortly after Boots divorced him.

In this world, Vince not only created so much more, but the entire nation, including FDR, a fan of *Anchors Aweigh,* recognized his death. Maybe Leo was right. Like Achilles, Vincent probably would have picked the life that was shorter, but full of glory.

I slept better than I had in weeks.

#

From the diary of J.D. Taylor, October 18, 1944
Well, the cuts and revisions didn't help. *Tom Jones* will
be lucky to last through January. Our notices were wildly
uneven—as is the show. Arlen and Harburg's *Bloomer
Girl*, a comedy about an early suffragette (Celeste Holm—
hilarious) during the Civil War, fared better with the press.
So did the revival of *Porgy and Bess* (fascinating to see
the cuts George and DuBose made, after reading over a
century's worth of "experts" on that very subject!). Then
those talented youngsters, Jerome Robbins, Leonard
Bernstein, Adolph Green, and Betty Comden, will make
their smash debut in December with *On the Town*. I've got
money in both new shows, and I'm lead producer on *Porgy*,
thank God and the SlingShot, but they'll crush poor *Tom*.

Part of the reason we failed is the subject matter. Though
it's a classic and we toned down the raunch, prudes objected
to the bastardy. Part was my music, which some critics found
"off-putting," though Larry's witty lyrics drew praise. We did
our best to write for character and the demands of the plot.

But the biggest reason was the cast. Our comics were
terrific. Too terrific. With Teddy and Hope Emerson as the
Squire and his sister; my old pal from *Anything Goes,* Vivian
Vance, as the lively wench, Molly; and Zero Mostel as Tom's
rival, Bilfil, we had a comedy blockbuster. Unfortunately,
we had Harry Stockwell in a lead that needed Gene Kelly
(gone to Hollywood) or John Raitt (whom I couldn't cast,
since he'll star in *Carousel* soon) or Hugh Jackman or my
boyhood crush, Rajiv Anand (neither born yet). Stockwell
was earnest, but not sexy and winning, and he couldn't
hold his own with the comics. Mostel in particular mopped
the floor with him.

Hell, we tried. Jack Cole's dances are magnificent, especially the opening; Mamoulian's staging sparkled, despite the complex plot; and I got to write a score for Larry Hart. I did some creative things with underscoring that a few critics and colleagues noticed, too. Praise from Kurt Weill—wow!

Hollywood's next—Columbia bought *Miss Underground* and I'm a consultant on MGM's upcoming Vincent Youmans biopic.

#

From the diary of J.D. Taylor, November 7, 1944

Los Angeles. My first experiences with the unreal world of the movie studios. Larry, however, was an old pro. "I love this place," he chortled as our driver sped along Hollywood Boulevard to Columbia Studios. "Just think, it's freezing back home. Here, it's warm and breezy in November."

"Santa Ana winds, kicking up tons of goddamn pollen." I had allergy problems when I came here with Ramon, but I had decent medicine then.

Larry ignored me. "I even loved it when Dick and I worked here years ago. Well, except for the earthquake in 1933. That scared the crap out of me. I pitched Dick's piano stool through our bungalow's window and jumped after it." He waved his cigar at the palm trees. "But, damn, everything else is jake! Dotsy and baby Max should visit us. This is a better climate for the little *pisher*."

Our driver, Ned, pulled into the lot on Gower, got passed by the security guard in his little booth, and dropped us off for another day of cinematic stupidity. They're filming *Miss Underground* in a big hurry because of the good news from Europe. Studio head Harry Cohn worries that if we beat the

Nazis too soon, nobody will want a musical about escaping German-occupied France.

Emmerich Kalman was supposed to come, but he broke his leg in a fall, so I'll do any new music. But they keep cutting songs, not adding them. Gallico's script vaguely resembles our original.

The cast is good, though. Since Vivienne Segal is a mere stage star, they cast Rita Hayworth (who will end up getting dubbed) and Gene Kelly, reunited from the recent hit, *Cover Girl*. Side note: it wasn't the *Cover Girl* I know. Ira Gershwin did the lyrics to Jerome Kern's music for that one, but Ira was happily working on *Cavalcade of History* with George. Johnny Mercer did the honors on this *Cover Girl*. Oh, they're good songs—Mercer's no slouch—but dang, it was freaky hearing different words to the music for "Long Ago and Far Away.")

So I've been champing at the bit. Larry adores doing nothing. Not me. They don't need me at MGM as a consultant for the Youmans' biopic, either. Like all the movies of this era about composers' lives, it's fictional blubber on a skeleton of facts. For instance, they've got Vince on a destroyer, launching torpedoes at Germans in the first war, which becomes the inspiration for *Anchors Aweigh*. Bullshit.

Our days start with the short drive from the Roosevelt Hotel to the studio. Once I suggested walking, since the weather's so nice: heresy! Standing around, some filming. More standing. More filming. A break for lunch, more filming, then parties. Lots of parties. Larry goes to them all, then hits the gay hot spots in Malibu and Santa Monica. Not my scene; the only parties I enjoy are the ones at the Gershwins'. I cherish any chance to see George and Ira and hear their latest.

Today, after three hours of listening to the Hays Code sanitizing Larry's lyrics, I glumly stood in line at the Columbia commissary. Larry had run off to some bar on Hollywood Boulevard. I took my ham sandwich, greasy fries, and Coke to an empty table. I had clout in New York. *Here, I count like those extras in togas at the next table.*

I ate my lunch, yearning for Manhattan, when two young women approached me. "It's Mr. Taylor, isn't it?" asked one.

I stood up. "Guilty as charged. But I'm afraid you're one up on me."

They were both brunettes—not starlets, but office workers or staff. The one who had addressed me was younger than her friend. She smiled. "I'm not surprised. I was a girl when we last met, down in Mexico."

"Amelia Küster!"

"It's Custer now, like the general. No umlauts! Strictly American! This is my roommate, Sylvia Levitt. She's in Costumes; I'm in the typing pool. May we join you?"

"Please."

Amelia pressed Sylvia's arm, leaning into her friend with excitement. "Mr. Taylor looks like Cary Grant under that beard—simply dreamy. I met him at sea, on my way to our ranch in Mexico. He came back the next year, but *Oma* and I had already moved here. I was so sorry I missed him! He used to send me movie magazines; I'd sleep with them under my pillow, just because he touched them. Silly, wasn't I?"

Sylvia rolled her dark brown eyes. "What's with the past tense? A pleasure to meet you, Mr. Taylor. I liked 'Second Chances' very much."

"Thank you. That song means a lot to me." *More than I can tell you.*

The commissary food was still awful, but chatting with them turned it into a great lunch. Amelia's father was still

346

growing fruit in Anaheim; her grandmother Helga had died in 1939. She took secretarial courses after high school, and had been working for Columbia for two years. "I kept drinking sodas at Schwab's, hoping to be another Lana Turner, but I just got fat. So! I'm a typist. I know life could be worse."

Sylvia knew that, too. She was thirty, with high cheekbones and a mass of curls, a New York native whose parents had moved west after their retail business failed in the Crash—"like Jewish Joads, in a Model T held together with baling wire." She married in January 1940, only to lose her pilot husband and toddler son three years later. "A bad time," she said, pursing her bright red lips. "I had some pretty gloomy thoughts then, but I figured Harv would have wanted me to get on with life. I can look at women with husbands and babies and not cry. I can enjoy good food and parties and dancing." She shrugged. "You survive, or you don't." She poked Amelia in the ribs, making her squeak. "Getting a crazy Kraut for a roomie actually helped. She's so bubbly, she's like walking champagne."

Parties! Dancing! "Are you two free this Saturday night? I have some friends who throw a bash most weekends—very casual. You'd be welcome."

"Of course!" Amelia said, without hesitation. She'd worked on losing her accent—not a good time to sound German—but it came out "Uff course!"

Her roomie hesitated. "Mr. Taylor—okay, David—you're a Broadway producer, a songwriter. We're nobodies. Who are your friends, and why should they want us?"

"Because they're good fellows. Because they'd say any friends of mine are friends of theirs. Because they've got plenty of room. Because you're pretty, smart young women. Besides, the host owes Amelia's family a favor." I sipped my flat Coke before delivering the capper: "It's at George

Gershwin's. As Amelia said, her family let me stay at their *ranchero*. When I came back the next winter with Gershwin, the invitation was still open. I'm certain George would love to repay that hospitality."

Amelia tugged at Sylvia's sleeve. "Say yes! I'll *die* if you don't want to go."

"Such dramatics! *Nu*, Mr. Broadway Big-shot with the Famous Friends, make with the details." She shook her head as Amelia bounced with eagerness.

I scribbled several phone numbers on my card, and handed it to Sylvia. She gave me their number and address in return. "I'll pick you up at seven," I said.

Sylvia mimed wiping her forehead. "Whew! I can imagine Gershwin's reaction to Harv's 1934 Chevy coupe with the crunched fender in his driveway."

#

From the diary of J.D. Taylor, November 11, 1944

With an impudent grin, Larry declined the invitation to George's. He and Gene Kelly were going out on the town. "Have a good time with your young ladies, you fabulous sonofabitch. Who knows? Maybe wedding bells are in your future." In perfect imitation of Al Jolson, he sang, "You Made Me Love You."

"Oh, for God's sake, Larry, grow up!"

He waggled a finger at me, laughed loudly (really, the only way he did laugh), and went across the hall to his own room for a second shave. The thing is, he might not have been teasing. He'd proposed to at least three women himself; he'd loved many deeply, if not sexually. I sometimes wondered how gay he was: if were men just a substitute, since no woman would want him as a partner. In the forties, men and women were *supposed* to get married.

Those who didn't got called "mama's boys" and spinsters. Larry's mother had hoped he'd marry and have kids; he felt guilty disappointing her. Would he have tried to make it work if Vivienne Segal or Nanette Guilford said yes? Did he drink so much his last year to fill up the emptiness in his life? His friends and family were busy raising kids, while he lived alone, haunting 45th Street bars.

Well, I've spared him that. How does he thank me? With smart-ass comments. Fine, go play cards till dawn, Larry. We'll see who has a better time tonight. No contest. I get to listen to Gershwin, so I win.

I adjusted my tie, put on my coat and hat, and took the stairs to the lobby, where I gave Ned the address. The girls' apartment on Lankershim was on the grimy side, but I'd lived in worse in the Village. They came down when I buzzed, decked out in terrific mid-forties frocks with sheath skirts, their hair flowing in long, soft curls. Amelia's dress was golden yellow, with tiny black dots; Sylvia's a deep royal blue, with a shiny pale blue lining that flashed as she climbed into the town car, showing off nice gams. I'd always thought this was a great time for women's clothes. It was fun to see it around me, every day, not just in books or screens.

"You're *sure* this is okay?" Sylvia asked as Ned turned onto Sunset Boulevard.

"Mwah-hah-hah," I cackled. "I now reveal my evil plot. I snatch girls for the white slave trade while dining at the Columbia commissary. Seriously, quit worrying. George is delighted."

"I feel like Cinderella going to the ball," Amelia said. "Except for these old shoes. Darn rationing!"

I resisted a joke about fairy godmothers I might have made with Rose and Zanzi. Still, I felt like a conjurer as Ned pulled up the long driveway and they gasped in amazement. Ira and Lee still had their place over on Roxbury, but tonight's gathering was at George's new mansion on Bedford Drive.

"Wow!" said Sylvia. "Does Daddy Warbucks live here?"

"If it's any consolation, I feel funny here, too—until I start talking with the brothers. They're the same in Beverly Hills and a Hell's Kitchen rehearsal hall."

Paul Mueller, George's assistant, opened the massive door on cue. "Mr. Taylor, welcome. And this must be Miss Custer and Mrs. Levitt? May I take your coats and hats? ... Thank you. I'll let Mr. Gershwin know you're here."

About twenty people milled around in the big living room, drinking and talking. Fred Astaire, a longtime pal of George's, played the piano; Paulette Goddard, yet another of George's ex-girlfriends, chatted with Gary Cooper. Jerome Kern was playing poker with a leggy blond gal and two middle-aged men. The girl was stunning, yet Kern stayed focused on his cards.

The bartender fixed me a Bronx and made the ladies daiquiris. We stood there, sipping, taking it all in. I thought back to my first visit to George's, when I was as overwhelmed as my companions tonight. *My God, more than ten years ago!* Then Gershwin came clattering down the long, curving staircase, spiffy in a navy pinstriped suit.

"David! You're looking swell. Please introduce me to your friends."

I did the honors. Amelia looked ready to hyperventilate, but seeing that the great composer was flesh and blood settled Sylvia's nerves.

George clasped Amelia's hands in his own. "I owe your family a debt, Miss Custer. My visit to Mexico was wonderful, thanks to David, my marvelous guide, and thanks to your family's generosity. I have something for you. Lee! Where's that score I signed earlier?"

Leonore, Ira's wife, called from the kitchen: "On the mantle."

George sailed through the crowd, tossing off introductions. Then he hushed everybody and gave Amelia a copy of the score for his upcoming Aztec ballet. "Eddie Warburg and I started planning this at Miss Custer's family ranch near Veracruz in 1935. It's taken too long to finish, but you'll see it on the big screen next year. Fred will fly around on poles and play a masked jaguar, and Tilly Losch will be the maiden princess. It'll be killer diller! So, Miss Custer, these are for you, with Gershwin's thanks." He handed her the score and a tiny box. She fumbled awkwardly, so Sylvia took the score, letting her open the box. I caught a flash of gold against white velvet: a stunning brooch.

"The notes on the pin are from the ballet's opening movement," George explained.

"I hardly know what to say," Amelia said. "Thank you!"

"No, thank *you!*"

Sylvia tucked the score under her arm, and pinned the brooch on her friend's dress. "There you go. *Très chic.* I wish *my* parents owned a Mexican ranch! They started with a dry-goods store on Second Avenue and ended up in Van Nuys. Though you're welcome to visit my uncle's chicken ranch in Winnetka, Mr. Gershwin. Best eggs in the Valley."

"Second Avenue!" said George. "Gee, we lived on Second. A million other places, too. Ira and I once tried remembering all of them: Grand, Eldridge, Chrystie, Third. I was born in Brooklyn, but we mostly stayed on the Lower East Side. Poppa had a different job every year, so we kept moving."

"At least your father had a job! We moved plenty, too— escaping people we owed money to. Finally, we figured they might not find us in California."

George grinned and waved for them to the couch. "Momma's wedding ring went in the pawnshop a few times, but we did okay. Hey, Ira! Lee!" he called. "Mrs. Levitt used to live on Second Avenue. How 'bout that?"

Before long, the four New Yorkers were talking about old neighborhoods and calling each other by first names. Amelia and I, after ten minutes with nothing to add to the "Do you remember ... ?"s, headed for the bar.

The bartender was on his break, so I fixed them myself. Amelia took hers, smiling at the foursome. The Gershwins were laughing at something Sylvia said. "Listen to that! Just think, she nearly didn't come. She's having the best time. I'm going to tease her about this for ages. Oh, dear heavens, Fred Astaire is coming over! What can I say to him?"

"Try 'hello,'" I suggested. I moved away to give the star-struck young woman a chance with one of her idols. A fresh Bronx in hand, I looked back at the couch. Ira slouched comfortably, his fingers entwined on his tummy, with Lee at his side, smoking a cigarette. George perched on the overstuffed arm, grinning down at Sylvia. *She does look like she's having a ball. They all do. Ira's usually not so perky at parties; he likes to lurk in corners.*

And George ... looks happy. Very happy.

Interesting.

#

From the diary of J.D. Taylor, December 10, 1944
George sent flowers to the girls the next day, candy the next week, and an enormous turkey and fruit basket for Thanksgiving. He made Paul Mueller drive up through the Sepulveda Pass to buy eggs at Sam Weinstein's farm. He invited them—and me, too—to play tennis, come for dinner, go horseback riding *(Oy! Horses again!)* at Astaire's

place in Chatsworth, and go to the USC-UCLA football game. But Amelia and I just came along for the ride. George's attention focused on Sylvia.

I was worried at first. I'd never seen George be anything but a gentleman, but he was sixteen years older and filthy rich.

Not to worry. Sylvia had brains and a solid sense of self-worth. When George complimented her dress, she said it came from "that fabled fashion house, Chez Weinstein." He didn't catch on, so she tapped her chest. *"C'est moi,* dearie." When George played a charming little waltz, "written just for you, Sylvia," carefully inserting her name in the lyric, she called him on it. "Honestly, George, how many girls have you played that for? Emma, Charlotte, Peggy-Ann? What do you do if she's named Esmerelda May? Or Theresa Conchita Guadalupe? Does that throw off the rhythm?"

George, at the piano, did a double-take: *this approach never bombs!* It didn't help that Ira was giggling, three feet away. "'Who is Sylvia?'" he quoted.

George could always tell when Ira was being literary, and leaped at the chance to change the subject. "What was that?"

"It's from *Two Gentlemen of Verona,*" I said, trying to help. Both brothers were red-faced: Ira from laughing, George from embarrassment. "Proteus' love poem." *Not Albee's goat!*

George recovered nicely, though. Two days later, he sent her a song by special delivery, adapting Shakespeare's words. His firm hand on the cover sheet read: *You're right. I was cheating with that waltz. This one's the real McCoy, and if you don't believe me, ask Ira. I wrote it in front of him Sunday night, after he showed me the piece in Shakespeare. Franz Schubert used the same verse, but I hope you'll forgive me for that.*

He'd dated movie stars and owned mansions. She'd lost a child and shared a crummy North Hollywood studio apartment.

Could this work?

#

April 26, 2082

Department staff meetings! Worst torture ever devised. Nate rose from his seat and stretched, managing to contain a yawn until Layla Bassali's back was turned. *She's a decent chair. Meetings were even worse before they hired her. They're still a waste of time, though.*

He gathered his things, grabbed another coffee from the break room, and hustled to his office two floors down. His next class didn't start for ninety minutes. *A good chance to work on the book, if I can wake up.*

He hadn't got very far when his phone rang. A smiling Latina woman in her late thirties was on the other end. "Professor Greenbaum? Margo Guerrera, Arizona State. I've just come back from SV-4 1934 and I've got something to show you. It's kind of weird."

#

From the diary of J.D. Taylor, February 14, 1945

I took a train east when the films ended in December, squeezed among dozens of soldiers. Larry zipped down to TJ for so much sun and fun, he needed to check into Doctors Hospital to dry out when he got back. Dorothy Hart railed at me for not going with him. I thought about it, but he's easier to handle after his wild winter trips. They blow off steam, even if they're hard on his liver.

Besides, I had tons of work to do. Cleaning up after *Tom Jones* flopped was grim but necessary. I had already put money in this season's upcoming hits: *Carousel* and *The Glass Menagerie,* obviously, but also Romberg-Fields' *Up in Central Park*—a smash, but one forgotten in my era. Now I was lining up fall prospects. I intended to back several plays, including the Pulitzer winner, *State of the Union.*

I was also dickering with Fox over a film version of *Connecticut Summer,* writing a libretto based on *The Canterbury Tales* with Larry, and reading plays and books for future projects. *Got to keep that man busy.*

Around lunch, I went down to accounting to check with Mabel. Though *Ladies First* flopped on Broadway, we're doing well licensing community productions—a good show to stage when all your male actors are in the service. As I expected, "Go Far" has had several hit recordings.

Mabel was in the day care, changing three-week-old Shirley's diapers. Red roses on her desk reminded me what day it was. *Ramon's favorite holiday, that old Latin softy, but not one Larry likes, even if he wrote "My Funny Valentine." When I gave him a valentine in 1942, he looked nauseated.*

But I could buy a card for *someone.* I dashed over to the stationer's for a big red heart with a flocked striped kitten on it. Mabel was on the phone when I got back. I wrote FOR SADIE, LOVE FROM UNCLE DAVID in big block letters and handed it to her. But Mabel was listening avidly and didn't even glance at it.

"He's here now, Mr. Gershwin. *Mazel tov!*" She handed me the phone, her eyes bright.

"Hello?" I said. Static crackled; both Gershwins were still in California, and the connections weren't always the best.

"David! It's George. I wanted you to be among the first to know, since you were the matchmaker, like in the old country. I proposed to Sylvia this morning and the damn fool girl said 'Yes.'"

#

From the diary of J.D. Taylor, March 12, 1948
It's been an eventful couple of years. Sylvia Weinstein Levitt insisted that George wait until the end of the war before having the wedding. He tried for V-E Day, but she was adamant. The invitations went out in late August 1945, and they got hitched six weeks later. I was there, close enough to the *chuppah* to see the suave, confident Gershwin sweating bullets. Sylvia was the cool one; she'd done this before.

I cornered Ira at the reception. He was smoking his pipe behind a pillar, watching the dancers swirling in Ambassador Hotel ballroom. "Ira, did you ever think this would happen?"

He ran his hand over his round chin, thinking. "Years ago, there were a few times I thought George *might* marry. But I'm glad he didn't. He wasn't ready for marriage then; his music meant more to him than anything. He's slowed down, got a wider view. He's matured...no, that isn't the right word." The master lyricist searched for the proper term. "He's more *settled* now. Frankie says he's more rounded; that fits, too. And he definitely wants a family. He's older than she is, but Sylvia's the experienced one there. Yes, I think she's a fine choice for my brother: warm, smart, not fixated on her own career."

Was that aimed at Kay or Kitty or any of George's other exes in the entertainment world? George didn't mind women having careers—look at how he helped Kay and Ann Ronell and others—like most men in this era, he didn't entirely approve of mixing careers and motherhood. What he really disliked were cheap, coarse women. While Sylvia

*was used to "making do," there was nothing cheap about
her. Class, all the way. Just look at the way she's holding
her own, chatting with her uncle Sam-The-Egg-Man and
Edward G. Robinson.*

I grabbed two champagne flutes from a passing waiter
and handed one to Ira. "To the Gershwins," I said. "All of
them."

A slow smile from the older brother. "To the Gershwins.
And their friends."

That warm fall night in L.A., I thought this marriage
had to be the craziest result of my meddling. Then word
spread that the Gershwins were having a blessed event in
late summer, 1946. Morris Michael Gershwin, named for
George's late father and Sylvia's grandfather, was soon
followed by Ruth Mary Gershwin (honoring her aunt and
his grandmother) in December 1947. Oscar Levant tells me
they're planning a third, even though "all this fucking is
delaying the Santa Fe opera. How's he supposed to finish
when Sylvia keeps dragging him into the bedroom?"

I'd hoped George would tackle this opera, based
on Lynn Riggs' *The Lights of Lamy,* a project he'd been
looking at the year before he died. It centered on Mexican
and American relations in the Southwest, including some
sly satire on the Santa Fe art scene. Taylor Productions is
backing it for spring of 1949—I can't wait.

But the notion of George Gershwin creating *children,*
not just music? Ira never had kids, but sister Frankie and
brother Arthur had talented offspring. I wonder if I'll live
long enough to see what Morris and Ruth can do—this
blending of DNA that exists because I stole a time machine!
Every time I see them, I get shivers. Morey looks like a
mini-George.

Meanwhile, my Broadway Revival Project continues,
both good and ill. Larry and I tried our luck with English

literature again in early 1946. *The Canterbury Tales* was a surprise hit, but our adaptation of Philip Barry's *Holiday* flopped last fall. Too brittle for a musical, and we fought all the time writing it. We're taking it easy with the next one, adapting the recent play, *The Corn is Green*. Audiences will probably balk; a play can address poverty and unwed motherhood, but a musical? Still, I've got some ideas for character motifs and Larry's pumped about tackling a serious show. Thanks to me, he's seeing the growth of musical drama in the late forties, a trend led by Dick and Oscar, and it's inspiring him.

My rescuing Jerome Kern's piano didn't help him: he gained only four weeks before his fatal stroke. But that makes this timeline's *Annie Get Your Gun* is slightly different, since Kern and Dorothy Fields had finished two songs. As in my world, Irving Berlin stepped in, but he kept Kern's numbers in tribute. The show is still a smash, but I'm not a fan of the new songs. Frank Butler was my first serious lead, so it's a sentimental favorite.

Annie's rehearsal pianist was one Leonard Spinelli, who was finishing his degree at Columbia. He was tickled when he remembered I also got started as pianist in a Merman show. He's taken summer courses in orchestrations and arranging from Ted Royal at Juilliard, and has worked as an assistant arranger and copyist on several shows, including Rodgers and Hammerstein's experimental *Allegro*. He's plugging away at a score of his own, but won't show it to me yet.

Gershwin finished his film contract by the end of 1945 and took Sylvia on an extended honeymoon in the West Indies. Then he wrote a quartet for his firstborn, finished shortly after Morris' birth. It's Mozartian in its simplicity, but the rhythms are pure Gershwin. I've driven Larry mad, playing the record constantly. When that happened with Ramon, I could put on headphones. Home audio equipment here isn't up to that. Leo's nearly as obsessed with the piece as I am. Even better, George has promised more works like it in the future; he says Ruth deserves one, too, but Daddy has to finish *The Lights of Lamy* first.

Every new Gershwin work is an unexpected treasure, as he composes the music denied him in my world. It's different for Cole Porter. Once I kept him from riding that cursed beast, his life changed not just physically but personally and musically. After Linda left him, everything he's done has been either slightly different from the what I knew *(DuBarry Was a Lady, Something For the Boys)* or new *(Dude Ranch; Barbary Coast, Speakeasy,* set in Prohibition Chicago, which managed a modest run in 1944; and *Glamour Gal,* about an Atlantic City beauty contest—a ghastly mess).

In my 1948, he was washed-up, his last three works all failures. Hollywood released a biopic of him, with Cary Grant as Cole—standard movie haigiography. All the same, the producers of *Kiss Me, Kate* hesitated over hiring him and backers were worried *Cole Porter—he's ancient history!*

Well, no film like that here, not with a divorced lead, not without the tragic injury to add pathos. Especially no biopic for a composer arrested on for lewd conduct. Oh, Cole and the other famous gays at that Malibu orgy got the charges dismissed, but that naughty night had saddled him with a worse reputation than "has-been." His position and talents are too strong to turn him into box office poison, but he's not in good odor just now.

I intend to get things back on track so he can write *Kiss Me, Kate,* his masterpiece. As soon as rumors of the project began buzzing, I invited producer Arnold Saint Subber to lunch at Keen's Chop House. Over a plate of mutton almost as big as a breadbox, I said: "You'll get sixty-five grand from me, but only if you hire Porter for the score. He's perfect."

Frowning, Saint Subber plucked at the sleeves of his brown suit, revealing skinny wrists. He was a young man as gay as Porter and I were, with a elfin charm much like Cole's. But producers have to consider the whole picture: *Will audiences stay away if they think the songwriter's a pervert?* "I love Coley, but I was hoping you were offering me Hart and Taylor. I adore your music—so stunningly unique!—and Larry's already had a hit adapting Shakespeare with *The Boys From Syracuse.* You two could work wonders with this."

Flattering, but no thanks. I sipped a musty ale, one that could stand up to the mutton. "We're committed to *The Corn Is Green.*"

Saint Subber glanced upwards, either seeking divine aid or studying the hundreds of churchwarden pipes dangling from the Chop House's ceiling. The light reflected strangely on his cheekbones, reminding of a boy I dated in college. *What ever happened to you, Bailey, with your so-kissable face?*

Saint Subber jolted me out of my musings. "We've also been considering Burton Lane. He's on fire after *Finian's Rainbow!*"

No, no, no. "Seventy grand, in your hands tomorrow, but only for a *Shrew* with Porter." *You're sweating for backers, Saint. This is the first show you've ever produced, you little virgin. Come on, baby, you know you want my big sexy wallet.*

"Um." Pause. "I'll talk to the Spewacks and call you in the morning." Bella and Sam were writing the libretto.

"Okay. I suspect they'll like it. They've worked with Cole before." I leaned back in the big leather booth, pushing my plate to one side. Mutton was tasty, but I was counting calories these days. Middle-aged Greenbaum men pile on the pounds—Nate got plump despite his Ripper workouts. I ignored the salad, too—the iceberg lettuce looked more like an actual iceberg than a plant. Then I waved for the check, to Saint's surprise. I meant business.

#

May 2, 2082

The Greenbaums went to Manhattan for Rose's birthday: a celebratory breakfast at Katz's. Hannah, who liked sleeping in, silently stumbled along, but Bertie made enough noise for three as they came out of the subway station. "So, Dad, we get the answer to your big mystery at last?"

"Yup. Because Rose needs to hear it. It's ... fitting."

Isis smiled at her husband. "I'll say. Look, there's Rose, just inside."

She looked tired, but glad to see her family. "It's been a long week," she admitted. "Rehearsals for _Citadel_ aren't going well. I'm playing the younger sister, with that scary second act ballad. The only thing that reassures me is everyone else is terrified of their songs, too. T.K. Singh was a genius, but his music is so hard. Please, distract me with coffee and pastrami and eggs."

The family ordered their meals, showered Rose with gifts, including a new Ally, and then Nate got out his own device. Bertie sat up straight, suspecting something was coming; Hannah gulped at a second cup of tea. Nate and Isis exchanged looks; they'd been sitting on this for days. "So, Rose," said her dad, "this week I heard from a Ripper who'd been to SV-4."

"Uncle David's world? Oh, my God! Did she see him?"

"She was collecting climate data in that world's 1947, but she's also interested in art. Ever seen this painting?"

Rose looked at his Ally: a multi-tiered hall, a crowded audience, a man at a concert piano. "No. Is that Gershwin?"

"Yes. It's called 'George in an Imaginary Concert Hall,' by Mexican painter David Alfaro Siqueiros. Gershwin asked for tiny cameos of his friends and family in the audience." Nate enlarged the image. "Here's Ira and his wife, other siblings, parents, cousins, Kay Swift, Oscar Levant, even Siqueiros himself. It's a fantasy scene, since some of the people here are dead, like Gershwin's father and his friend, William Daly."

"What are the blobs behind Daly?" Bertie asked. "Martians?"

Nate shrugged. "I'm a social historian, not an art historian. The Ripper said Siqueiros liked surrealism. For all I know, they *are* aliens."

"Okay, Dad, I'm hooked," said Rose. "What else did she say?"

"This painting's at the University of Texas at Austin." Nate clicked his Ally and handed it to his daughter. "But *this* was the one she saw in Mexico City, in August 1947 of the Splinterverse."

"Looks the same," she said, peering at the screen. Her siblings leaned in, straining for a glimpse.

Nate took a deep breath. "Check out the second row."

Hannah suddenly squealed. Waitresses and customers stared. "It's Uncle David! With a beard and glasses!"

"Oh, my God! You're right!" said Rose, enlarging the section with the bearded man. "You can see how much taller he is than Oscar Levant."

Bertie pounded on the table. "Aw, ya-whoo! It's him!"

Rose couldn't stop gazing at the tiny caricature of her beloved uncle. *So far away in another era. Another world.* "You know what this means? Uncle David not only met Gershwin, he got close enough to go into this painting."

"A fast worker," said Nate. "He got there in 1934; this was painted two years later. Though we're still puzzled about why it was in that exhibition in the Splinterverse. In our world, after George's death it hung in Ira's house until he bequeathed it to Texas."

Isis said, "Maybe Mexico's the key. The artist is Mexican; David knew Mexico; Gershwin met Siqueiros there; and that bum your dad met in the Village said something about 'Bronko' going to Mexico, too."

Nate finished his lox and eggs. "No way to know. What's definite is that David *did* get involved with the theatre crowd. Gershwin died in 1937, but plenty of the people in this picture lived long lives. Any Ripper in that damn Splinterverse could contact Ira Gershwin and ask, 'Who's the guy in the second row?'"

His intensity alarmed Rose. "Then what?"

"You know, honey, after David pulled his stunt, I wanted to drag him home and bang him over every rock between New York and Yosemite. It was horribly dangerous. It embarrassed me and my field. Worst of all, he involved you."

"By accident! Even at the end, Uncle David was ready to chuck it to keep me out of it." *I convinced him to take me into the lab.*

"But now I'm just pissed at the idiot Council. Never thought I'd agree with the French Rippers-they're narrow-minded zealots obsessed with their funzone—but these new restrictions are asinine. Professor Guerrera only got permission because she needed more data from early 1947 storms and couldn't go back to our own 1947 a second time. And their 'safety precautions' have added to the cost of each trip. Funding was always the toughest part, anyway." He sighed. "I wonder if I'll ever get to go on another trip."

"Wow," Rose breathed. "Uncle David became George Gershwin's friend." The image suddenly blurred. *Damn it,*

I'm crying in this stupid deli, just like when Dad told me about the apartment.

To her surprise, her father honked his nose, too. "Hey," he said, "don't look so shocked. I may be furious at David, but nobody knows better than I do how much Gershwin meant to him. I was there the first time he heard the 'Rhapsody in Blue.' It was...an epiphany. For once I completely agree with Bertie: aw, ya-whoo!"

"Best birthday ever," said Rose.

Chapter 14

"Glad to Be Unhappy" —Lorenz Hart

From the diary of J.D. Taylor, August 13, 1948

It was going so well! Things are decent with Larry. Not great, but decent. We fight, sure; that's become routine. He finds me too disciplined, controlling, a wet blanket, while I hate his carousing—the same things Ramon and I argued about. But, like Ramon, he appreciates that I'm solid as Gibraltar. And we're doing damn good stuff on *The Corn is Green.* I've never seen Hart lyrics with so much... heart. We've signed a fantastic cast, too: Lotte Lenya as Miss Moffat, the teacher determined to help a young Welsh miner (Jeff Warren, a fine tenor) go to Oxford, and Joan McCracken as the village girl with her hooks in the lad.

Other good stuff: Leo showed me his first score last week. Most of it will end up in his trunk, but there's promise in the rest. Thursday I had dinner with Kurt Weill, who's composing a daring flop, *Love Life*—he's next on my Project. This morning, the radio played Peggy Lee's cover of "Magic" from *Young Man With a Horn,* one that never fails to make me smile. I discussed new investments with Mabel, including *South Pacific*, then spent the afternoon in the office's music room, wrestling with the first act finale for *The Corn is Green.* I hoped Larry would like what I'd done. *Any time I impress him, he writes faster. That's where Dick had a huge edge on me. I have to sweat to turn out a decent melody.*

It was only in the mid-eighties, but late-afternoon showers made things muggy. I needed to change before my dinner meeting with Larry at La Pavilion. I was looking forward to every bite, from the caviar on toast to the famous "veiled pineapple" in liqueurs over ice. Personal service, too—Larry and Henri Soule were pals. I clicked on the radio and changed into one of the spare shirts in the office. The usual dreary news (Truman blasting Congress; Cold War woes) couldn't dampen my good mood. I kept humming the new finale as I fixed my cufflinks.

Then the damned announcer said in his resonant baritone, "News flash from Los Angeles. Composer Cole Porter has been killed in a boating accident off the Santa Monica pier."

Water-skiing, actually. Fifty-seven years old, and he decides to try water-skiing. I saved his legs so he could break his fucking neck. Really, I should have expected it. Cole was always active, from racing speedboats in Venice's Grand Canal to climbing Machu Picchu. Losing Vince was tough, but I could console myself thinking he'd created things he never did in my timeline. But Cole wrote scores until he finally lost one of the maimed legs in 1958: *Can-Can, Silk Stockings, Out of This World, High Society.* I'd assumed he'd do at least that much work.

Shit. How much of Kiss Me, Kate *is finished?*

#

From the diary of J.D. Taylor, August 21, 1948
The theatre is a family. Families pull together when they lose one of their own, and they don't come bigger than

Cole. It was different when Vince died. That was wartime. And let's face it: Vince, for all his talent, was a prick. While Cole could be aloof, he could also be charming. People felt his loss. The recent sex scandal? Forget it. His funeral was private, at the family plot in Peru, Indiana, but in New York Vinton Freedley and Moss Hart commandeered the dark Martin Beck Theatre and assembled a memorial concert in a week's time.

In my world, Porter left instructions that he didn't want such an event. Not here. The cream of Broadway filled the seats behind Porter's elderly mother and ex-wife Linda. His friends and colleagues—Irving, George, Moss, Dick and Larry, Noël, Monty Woolley—all spoke about what Cole meant to our world. I declined the invitation to give those who knew him better more time to speak. I did play the piano for Alfred Drake and Patricia Morison, our leads in *Kate*, who ended the concert with one of Porter's last songs, the poignant "We Shall Never Be Younger."

I expected they would dim the lights on the Great White Way for him, but apparently that tradition hasn't started yet.

#

From the diary of J.D. Taylor, August 23, 1948
Arnold Saint Subber is freaking out. I can't blame him. As the only notable backer, I've seen the current state of *Kate*. I also know just what the finished show looks like. That's both a plus and an minus. I can't simply say, "Hey, cut those numbers, add these, revise the ending." Musicals are like gardens: they're organic, shaped and pruned by the creative staff. However much I want to, I can't use my Ally to produce the final script like magic. Cole nicknamed me

"Wizard," but that would be beyond Merlin, Gandalf, and Harry Potter.

Rehearsals start in mere weeks, with tryouts in Philly ("Another Op'nin', Another Show," for real!) on December 2nd, and then it's the New Century on the 30th. I'm going to do the needed songs, telling the Spewacks and Subber that "Cole had discussed possible melodies" with me. Bullshit, but nobody can prove it.

So I hope I can make a *Kate* that's close to what it should be. Unfortunately, *The Corn is Green* is scheduled for late April. And Larry balked when I wanted to delay it for *Kate.*

We were in our den of iniquity at the Westwind, still maintaining the fiction of our independent lives. Larry has taken a larger place at the Osborne, now neighbors with Leonard Bernstein, but I'm still at the Seville Studios. a big Broadway producer with a small Village flat confuses people, but the place means too much to me. I see Ramon in the sculpted wall reliefs, in Washington Square, in the dormered windows, in the familiar historic buildings— not as historic as they'll be decades from now, of course.

The Westwind's original hideous couch was gone; Larry sat on a brass-studded leather sofa, his stockinged feet on the matching ottoman. "I know you've got piles in Cole's show, but we've got responsibilities with *The Corn Is Green.*" He puffed on his cigar.

Lorenz Hart talking about responsibility? Ha! "*Corn* can go more slowly," I said. "You always complain I push you too hard. Besides, I think I can finish *Kate*'s score without much trouble."

That too-large head on the small frame cocked to one side, eyeing me suspiciously. "'I?' What's with the single person? You putting me on an iceberg?"

Oh, God. How can I explain I don't need a lyricist?
"Well, it's going to be a rush, crazy as hell."

He wasn't buying it. "How is that different from any other show? I've been in this biz since you were wet behind the ears, kiddo. You're contradicting yourself, too. Either it's 'no trouble' or it's a 'crazy rush.'"

"My dough's on the line, Larry. I should handle it."

"It's fucking Shakespeare, David. I did the first Bard musical, you know." He knew something was going on. This wasn't the David Taylor he'd known for years: hovering over him, saving him from himself, coaxing him to work. "I thought we were a team," he said, his voice full of pain.

Shit! "We are, baby, we are," I said, moving to the couch, slipping my arm around him. "In every way. I'm just trying to spare you headaches. You could revise *Corn*'s second act while I tackled *Kate*."

Move. Countermove. He slapped my hand away. "What's up, Davey? You keep me on a tight leash; you don't let me roam free. Not with our own plays. You got some reason you don't want me along for this one?"

Yes, but I can't say why. Think, Greenbaum!

Okay! Here's a plan: I know what you'll do to duck work. I'll let you come along, then when you're drunk in some Philly bar when I'm "composing" those last-minute additions, I'll "write" the lyrics, too. Just like Dick did when you weren't around. "Of course I want you, if you're game," I said. "I'm meeting Saint Subber and the Spewacks tomorrow at nine at my office. Okay?"

It was far from okay. "Nine, huh. All right." He stubbed out the cigar. *I should empty the ash trays. Larry never does.*

I tried smiling, though I felt uneasy. "Kiss and make up?" *Ah, the old Distract Him with Lust ploy, a game I'd played countless times with both Larry and Ramon. Especially Ramon. But I was younger then.*

369

"Sorry. I need to make it an early night." He grabbed his hat and coat, and vanished into the summer night, leaving me to wonder exactly how much hot water I was in.

#

From the diary of J.D. Taylor, September 3, 1948
Damned if Larry wasn't at the Music Box the next morning, with candy for the kids in the day care. Freshly shaved, sober, cardboard cup of coffee in hand—who was this guy? Saint Subber and the Spewacks, who loathed each other and disagreed about *everything*, were thrilled to have him on board. I don't have much reputation as a lyricist.

The thing is, while I didn't want him there, he *was* hugely useful. I mean, he's Lorenz Hart: brilliant, with keen dramaturgical sense. He saw right away that we needed less Shakespeare and more of the Fred-and-Lilli plot; that the secondary female needed her own number; that "We Shall Never Be Younger" was too sad for a zippy comedy, even if it was a success at the memorial. Guiding *Kate* where I wanted it to go was going to be hard any which way. This was worse, because while I could agree enthusiastically with Larry and the Spewacks when their intentions matched mine, it was different when Larry suggested something that didn't. His ideas were smart, based on his years of experience. I couldn't say, "But this isn't what Cole wanted." Not unless Madame Arcati could suddenly produce Porter's ghost in a séance.

As the meeting ground on, Larry got pissed when I deflected yet another of his proposals. "What's wrong with that?"

"It will work better this way. I'm sure of it. I guarantee it."

He rolled his eyes. "You guarantee it. Damn! It's like you've already decided everything, and the rest of us are along for the ride."

Um. Yeah.

At the end of the day, I promised to work on the new comedy number for the second female lead. "We should emphasize that while Lois plays around, she's still true to Bill, in her own fashion," I said, carefully planting words from Cole's lyrics.

Larry rubbed his hands. "Now you're talking! That will balance her character against the lead. Get me the tune, baby, and you got it. Let's go to Downey's. It's been ages since those sandwiches, and I've got a helluva thirst."

It's like a horrible experiment in reverse psychology: Dick Rodgers and I fought for years to get Larry Hart to buckle down and work. The one time I don't want him around, he turns into a goddamn eager beaver.

#

From the diary of J.D. Taylor, September 30, 1948
That first number, "Always True to You (In My Fashion)," went smoothly. I'd given Larry the basic idea, developed it more when I handed him the lead sheet ("Damn! That was quick, David!"), and let him go to town. I even inserted some more of Cole's lines in late revisions. It's not the same song, but it's a successful comedy number. Why not? Larry's a master. Ditto for the number for Lilli-as-Kate, "I Hate Men." Not to speak ill of the dead, but Larry topped Cole here. The number's already going over in rehearsals; Cole's version didn't work until tryouts, aided by the bit where Pat Morison slammed down her tankard each time she sang the title line.

In the end, my demands were too many, too specific. I'd already hurt Larry with my initial reluctance to take him on. He noticed I was writing music with a flair I'd never shown before, rejecting other people's advice. That led to a nasty quarrel over one of Cole's most romantic songs, "So In Love." It's a critical late addition, for it provides the show's one bit of painful emotional honesty amidst all the comedy. Cole used his favorite minor key to set the tragic tone, and his lyrics are devastating, full of longing and bitter realization.

This week had Larry busy with "I Hate Men" and several Hart family events, so I figured he'd be happy I did the honors here. I invited him over to the Westwind to hear it. I had tidied up, put flowers in the vases and champagne on ice, candles on my piano, warmed up my voice. When his key turned in the lock, I couldn't *wait* to sing it. "Sit down, honey," I said, "and feast your ears on this one."

"Okay." Larry fixed himself a drink and sat down to listen. He registered surprise when I began singing, not expecting it. Then, despite my rattling the rafters with one of the most romantic numbers ever written, he sipped his whiskey in silence, his features still. I was irked.

"*Nu?*" I asked. "I thought we could give this to Lilli in the first act, to show how much she still cares for Fred, then he reprises it late in the second, when he thinks he's lost her."

"Oh, it's a killer. But where did it come from, David? You wrote it practically overnight, and it doesn't sound like you *at all.*"

"Does it sound like Cole?"

He stared into his drink. "Yeah. The minor key—Cole said his secret was writing 'Jewish music'—and those tormented lyrics. Sex, pain, thwarted desire. That's Cole."

I closed the piano lid, pleased. "Good. As I told Bella, I had chatted with Cole about what the show still needed. I've worked off those notes."

He pounced. "When? When did you talk to him? He'd been in California most of the summer. If I look at your phone bill, will I see long distance calls? And why were you two having gabfests, anyway? Sure, you're the main angel, but you never got involved with *Oklahoma!* or *Brigadoon*."

"What's with the third degree?"

He jumped up and started pacing around the room. "You've been acting queer, like Mussolini, making everyone follow your orders. You're pulling melodies out of thin air, ones nothing like anything I've ever heard from you. And I think you're lying about talking with Cole. See, I spent some time with Cole when we were in Los Angeles. He wanted me to dish the dirt on you. I gather you once turned him down flat—in public!" He stopped pacing and made his throat-clearing noise. "Kkkkkhhhh. Seriously, David? Instead of elegant Cole Porter, you ended up with the ugliest runt around? You're dumber than I thought."

"If I'd gone with Cole, it would have been for a week at most. You know that's not me." A horrible tight feeling began to fill my chest.

He nodded. "Yeah. But you pissed him off. He admired your talents, but *he did not like you.* Not one bit. He asked me what on earth I saw in you." For the first time all evening, he smiled—a truly evil grin. "I told him you had a dick like a Louisville Slugger. Oh, God, the look on his face!" The memory left him, and he got serious once more. "But that's why I don't buy it. I can't imagine Cole chatting with you over this score. Or anything else."

Shit, shit, shit. "All right, I exaggerated. But I do have a feel for what he would have composed. He worked harder on this show than any other—revising, rewriting, improving. We owe it to him to make the score the best it can be."

Larry wandered over to the piano and looked at my lead sheets for "So In Love." "This a solid number, a fine Porter pastiche. But you haven't given me any *answers*, David." He jabbed a stubby finger at the paper. "Look at this! It's clean, like it jumped out of your head, like Athena from Zeus. You're Mozart—music from brain to hand without hesitation. Yet here's 'The World Beyond' from *The Corn Is Green*—full of pencil marks and smudges! What's going on, David?"

I damn near told him. He was closer to me than anyone in his world. I had come to love him, for all his aggravations. Not the way I loved Ramon, but I'm not that person any more. I doubt I'm capable of that white-hot intensity for anything, let alone anyone.

He'd understand the concept. He'd even done *A Connecticut Yankee*. But would he understand my motivations, or be pissed at my playing God? What would he say when he learned that he'd been dead for five years in my world? Would he keep my cover?

Instead, I fumbled about with lame explanations about rewrites. He knew I was keeping something from him; he just didn't know what. Our relationship—fragile from the start because of who he was, who I was and what I knew, idiotic twentieth-century constraints—had taken a big hit.

"I like the number," he finally said. "Wherever it came from. I'll see you at rehearsal tomorrow, see what they do with it. Good-bye, David."

The door shut. I stared at it, disbelieving. In trying to keep Porter's score, had I lost Larry Hart?

#

From the diary of J.D. Taylor, December 31, 1948
Larry soldiered on through rehearsals and tryouts, teasing Harold Lang about his oversized and bejeweled codpiece, devising last-minute sassy lyrics for Lang's "Bianca" solo, and paying bar tabs for half the company in Philadelphia. To the rest of the world, he was the same old Lorenz Hart.

But he wouldn't answer when I tapped on his hotel room door. He hung up when I phoned. When we were together, Larry made certain someone else was there.

Last night, *Kiss Me, Kate* opened to triumphant reviews, but I couldn't enjoy them. As soon as they were in, Larry thanked the company and left for Miami.

#

From the diary of J.D. Taylor, May 5, 1949
Our relationship began with poetry. It ended with a line of Shelley's. After his winter vacation, we worked steadily on *The Corn Is Green*, but we might as well have been assembling a tractor. Larry did what needed doing and stayed sober when he needed to, but the joy in the craft was gone. Yet whatever the reason—sobriety, determination, the example of the other great shows of the decade—it's some of his best work ever. He showed up at my office today, handed me a page of revised lyrics, and bluntly said that after the show opened next week, our partnership was over. We were through as a couple, personally and professionally.

I couldn't believe my ears. "Because I wrote those lyrics for *Kate*? You're dumping me for that?"

He's lost more of his hair lately; the overhead lights reflected off his shiny pate as he shook his head. "That's the tip of the iceberg, and you know it. I always felt there was something different about you, and I've finally figured it out. There's a part of you locked up so tight, nobody can even peek at it. You've seen me coming apart at the seams, and I thank God you did. You helped put me back together. But I've never even come close to cracking that shell of yours. All these years—I still don't know who you are or anything about your background. I never will. I trust you, but you plainly don't trust me. If you did, you would have told me the truth about the *Kate* songs. You didn't want me involved at all."

I spread my hands. "I can't explain. It's... complicated. I committed a crime coming here; I betrayed my brother; I left everything I knew and loved to be here. With you. With George. With Vince. With all the others. But I can't tell anyone."

"Shit, David, you sound like Pinza's character in *South Pacific*, full of dark secrets. Do you think I care what you did then? It's *now* that matters!" He put on his hat and went to the door, but didn't open it. "I never understood why you stayed with me this long. Every day, I'd wake up thinking, 'Today's the day he throws me over.' Because I figured my life had to be like that old song of mine, that 'Nobody's Heart Belongs to Me.' I never thought I'd be the one saying good-bye to you." He barked a short, rueful laugh. "Funny, I'm older, yet it always seemed like you were in charge of whatever we did, everything from the shows to family picnics. Maybe it's time I grew up. 'Tomorrow to fresh woods, and new pastures,' as Shelley says. See you at rehearsal."

I was an ogre at rehearsal. Jerome Robbins at his worst had nothing on me. His cast let him walk backward into the orchestra pit one infamous day, without a word of warning. The *Corn* cast was ready to hurl me in the pit. Leo, my m.d., finally dragged me outside. "Boss man, I don't know what's gotten into you, but snap out of it."

But I didn't rein in my temper until Lenya said I reminded her of Brecht ("Always screaming, you know?"). To everyone's relief, I dismissed the company.

Then I went to a bar or two. Maybe more. I lost track. At Gallagher's, I slugged a schmuck who said something about Larry. I know it was Gallagher's, because I got a great look at that wood plank floor.

Fritz Loewe, who'd been a boxer in the twenties, saved my ass and took me home, but I don't remember much. I'd lost Vince to the Germans, Cole to a freak accident, and Larry to my own stupidity.

#

June 26, 2083
Rose hurried past her fellow cast members in usual post-curtain chaos at the Delacorte Theatre. She'd had an unexpected text from her folks to meet them at the box office—they'd brought a guest to the performance.

Who's so important that they came down on a weeknight? The place was packed; *A Midsummer Night's Dream* was always popular, and movie star Lucas Zuber as Bottom made every night a sell-out.

Finally, she spotted them. Nate, preparing for a new Ripper trip, had grown a handlebar mustache suitable for the 1890s. Isis, in a floral skirt, was talking to a woman who looked vaguely familiar... Lt. Mickey Mertz! *What the hell?*

"Hi, guys," Rose said. "Did you like the show?"

Mertz harumphed. "I almost said no, since it's Shakespeare—yuck! But I loved it. I didn't know it would be so funny, but Luke Zuber makes you laugh just walking on stage."

"I suppose you're wondering what this is about," Nate said. "Well, we are, too. Lt. Mertz has uncovered a tip relating to David. Since she's moved to Queens, we decided to get the news in person—with you. Your siblings will have to find out second hand." Hannah was at an intensive science camp and Bertie was on a school tour in Japan.

"So you and Mom haven't heard this yet?"

"Nope. Aren't we considerate? Let's get some chow."

Rose led the way out of the park, heading for a café where a friend worked. It would be jammed, but Ollie would get them a table. Along the way, they talked about the play. Her role, Robin Starveling, wasn't large, but she was learning plenty from talents like Zuber, Patty Kim, and Nigel Collingwood. "Nigel played Lloyd Douglas in *Versailles*; he remembers Uncle David and Ramon," she said. "He said he tried to steal David away, but 'failed miserably.'"

"David had two passions," said Isis. "Musical theatre and Ramon."

At the Glowing Mushroom, Ollie squeezed them in the back, where they ordered Ukrainian appetizers and drinks. Nate stuck with beer, but the ladies tried Foggy Days in Kyiv, a concoction of blue curaçao, vodka, and lemonade. "Drink two, and you're worse than foggy," Ollie warned.

Mertz seemed more relaxed than when she was investigating the case. "I'm a consultant now. Less pressure. But my crowd in New Haven called me when Shanta Gholkar got busted."

"Shanta got arrested?" said Isis. "That's the best news in months."

Mertz had moved up to a Kumi 500, nothing tech-savvy Bertie would want, but a decent device. She set it up for the Greenbaums. "Dealing Tant-3 and naughty financial games. Here's her statement. It raises more questions than answers."

On the screen, Shanta glared at the camera. Her voice was harsh. "I couldn't say anything before, since the bastard was threatening me. Now, who gives a fuck? That guy who stole the SlingShot, David Greenbaum, made me get him some drugs. Very specific drugs."

Off camera, a detective asked, "Tant-3? He took Tant-3 to back in time?"

"No." Shanta rolled her eyes. "David hated Tantalus. No sympathy in *his* noble soul. He knew my dad was a doctor, so he had a list of things he wanted. Dad said they were antibodies and vaccines for certain tumors."

Mertz paused the recording. "Was your brother ill?"

"Not that I knew," said Nate. "He'd just lost his husband to Tant abuse."

The interview resumed. "I asked him if it had to do with Ramon Abarca, his dead spouse, since he had just been to Mexico. He said, no but a young man would die without them." Shanta shrugged. "I don't know who he meant, but I'm already in shit creek, and my dad's dead. *You* make sense of it." The screen went dark.

Mertz said, "We got nothing in Mexico, but we finally got security footage of Greenbaum in Hong Kong. He goes into a building and come out with a bag—a place known for selling black market Boost."

"The stuff for cancer patients?" asked Isis. "They're taking forever to approve it here, but I hear it works wonders."

Rose suddenly felt woozy, but not from her cocktail. "Oh, God. It all fits. The drugs, the painting, everything. Uncle David told me he wanted to 'make a difference.' So he took cancer drugs and Boost to 1934. He couldn't save Ramon, but I think he saved George Gershwin."

\#

From the diary of J.D. Taylor, July 20, 1949
It would be nice if I could report that Larry did "grow up." Instead, he partied, visited Havana, and talked endlessly about future projects. He sounded out composers, from Fritz Loewe (then estranged from Alan Jay Lerner) to Burton Lane, but everyone was wary, even though *The*

Corn Is Green is a hit. He rebuffed my attempts to get back together.

Dotsy and Teddy blamed me, but I got a sympathetic call from Dick Rodgers. "He's a genius," Dick said, "but a permanent source of irritation. The first part is why I put up with the second part for so long. I'm surprised you got as much out of him as you did. That trio at the finale of *The Corn Is Green,* with you pulling the motifs together and Larry weaving in all the stuff from earlier in the show...it made the hair on my arms rise up. Brilliant. Don't beat yourself up about him. Move on."

Well, I had to. Even though I was miserable, I needed to decide what to do about Cole Porter's unwritten scores. His next show after *Kate* was 1950's flop, *Out of This World.* Some good songs, crass humor, and not much else. After that, *Can-Can* in 1953, a smash featuring the debut of Gwen Verdon. Since I needed to start working on saving Kurt Weill, I decided to shelve *Out of This World* for now and worry about *Can-Can* later. I buried my gloom in planning.

I'd worked with Kurt on that number for the *Lunchtime Follies* and had money in several of his shows (including this fall's *Lost in the Stars*), but I've got to know him better recently. He was thrilled that Lenya finally had a successful starring role in *Corn.* Though he stayed busy (eighteen-hour days!) writing his own show, he came to many of our rehearsals. Leo and I picked his brains whenever we saw that short figure in gray flannel standing at the back of the theatre. He was a born teacher. Leo, who'd loved his work since *Johnny Johnson*, had a new hero.

I cashed in another connection, too. Weill and Alan Jay Lerner's fascinating flop, *Love Life*, had just closed. In my timeline, a musicians' union strike prevented a cast album recording. I reassembled the cast after the strike and produced it myself—a small run, but it's preserved. An album does more to keep a flop in theatre buffs' memory than anything else, and this show was too innovative to be forgotten. Along with Rodgers and Hammerstein's *Allegro*, it's the forerunner of the concept musical. I knew Lerner casually. I'd backed his first hits, and he was an acolyte of Larry's early in the decade, hanging out at the Lambs Club and going on benders with Bender. I used the album to stay in touch, and wangled an invitation to his place on an July afternoon when Kurt, his neighbor, would be there, too.

Weill had an engaging smile and large eyes behind round steel-rimmed glasses. Like so many in this era, he smoked like a chimney. He stubbed out butts as we sat on Lerner's patio, drinking beer and discussing musicals. He had a brilliant, analytical mind. I loved the conversation, especially when he began dissecting the flaws in Berlin's *Miss Liberty* (ouch!), but Alan finally said, "Enough shop talk! Who's up for tennis?"

Like Gershwin, Kurt was intensely competitive. Maybe that's why I'm a decent composer, but not a great one. I lack a killer instinct. Weill took a final pull at his beer and grinned. "I accept your challenge."

They began playing in the ninety-degree heat on Alan's beautiful court. I watched, biting my lip. *Advance knowledge is hard to bear.*

Alan was a vigorous man who still had a collegiate air in his early thirties. He had no problem slamming shots over his older opponent's head. Kurt chased them every which way, cheerfully cursing, his short hairy legs pounding over the court.

Then, as I knew he would, he crumpled to the ground, knees buckling.

I was at his side before Alan even realized anything was seriously wrong. "I am okay," Kurt gasped. "I just...fell. Don't tell Lenya!"

He was clammy and ashen-faced, breathing rapidly—far from "okay." I scooped him up—he was only about five-three—and carried him to the patio, where I loosened his clothing. I looked up at Lerner, who was anxiously biting his nails. "Alan, you got any aspirin in the house?"

"This isn't a headache, David!"

"Trust me. Go get it." *I have some in my pocket, but this looks more natural.*

Lerner gave me a funny look, but ran into the house, quickly returning with a bottle of Bayer. Even after fifteen years here, I still keep expecting child-proof lids. I unscrewed the top and took out a pill. "Kurt! Chew this—slowly. I know it tastes like hell, but do it."

He was in no position to argue, but he did grimace at the bitter taste. Alan still looked puzzled. "Aspirin?"

"People have used willow bark for centuries," I said with a confidence I didn't feel. Even knowing Kurt would survive this, I still felt shaky. "Aspirin helps with blood flow. It certainly can't hurt."

It took a while, but he began to get some color into his cheeks. He got feisty: he wanted a cigarette, a beer, some water. I vetoed them all so the aspirin could work. "We should take you to the hospital," I said. "You need a doctor."

"I haf a doctor here," Weill said with a slight smile. "The renowned Dr. Taylor, with his miracle pills from Bayern. I know what my doctor will say: my blood pressure is too high, I work too hard." His features twisted in pain, but not from his chest. "But what else can I do? The work—always the work!—comes first. I know the consequences. My dearest brother, Hans…"

Lerner murmured in my ear, telling me what I already knew: "Hans died two years ago. Heart attack."

We moved him inside and settled him to rest with a light blanket. In the end, he promised he would get a check-up if we didn't tell Lenya about his collapse. "She would be so upset. Let us keep her ignorant of my little mishap."

#

From the diary of J.D. Taylor, October 9, 1949

Despite our split, I kept suggesting projects to Larry. He kept saying no. Word finally spread that he and Emmerich Kalman, from *Miss Underground,* were teaming on the romantic story of *Marinka.* This amused me; in my world, Kalman recycled music from the unproduced *Miss Underground* for this show. I wrote to wish him well, promising to back it, though Larry Hart was the last man I'd pick for a lightweight nineteenth-century operetta. I owed him. I was happy he was working, even without me.

Marinka didn't get far before Larry ended up in the hospital—cancer of the liver. Dotsy Hart called me October fifth. "He's going fast, David. He's asking for you."

In a weird coincidence, Larry was in the same wing of Mount Sinai as when he'd had pneumonia ten years ago, when we revised that song of mine—the first time we'd worked together. Hart and Taylor. A partnership that should have lasted longer.

It was easy to find his room; the World Series was blaring from a radio. "Hey," I said in the doorway. "Who's winning?"

He looked dreadful, his flesh tightly pulled over his bones, except for his distended abdomen. His skin and eyes had a yellowish tint. Still, teeth flashed under his heavy beard. "You fabulous sonofabitch," he croaked. "It's the most fantastic pitchers' duel in fucking history. Nothing-nothing in the seventh."

"No score, huh? So I haven't missed a thing!" Lame, but it got a laugh. I was glad he could still laugh.

Dotsy and Teddy were seated by his bed. They pressed Larry's hand and slipped out, leaving us alone together.

"Last time, you brought knishes," Larry said. "You're slipping, baby. But it's good to see you." Tears filled his eyes. "God, I wanted to see you before. I haven't been this miserable since Mama died. I never realized how you filled up all the empty holes in my life until you weren't there. I'm such a fucking idiot."

"Me, too," I said. I sat on the bed and embraced his skinny frame, and we both cried for a long, long time. He lifted his head from my shoulder only when the radio announcer went bonkers over a walk-off homer by Yankee Tommy Henrich in the bottom of the ninth.

"Damn! Wish I could have been there," he murmured. He sank back into his pillows, brooding. "Wonder how it will end?"

"Yankees in five," I instantly said. It just popped out. Nate drilled Series stats into me the way I babbled about Tony winners to him.

He looked at me—a long, penetrating look. God knows *what* he was thinking. "You sure?"

"I guarantee it." I'd never been wrong when I said that. Not once. He knew it, too.

A slow smile spread over his face. "Uh-huh. That's good to know. Can't have those Bums as the toast of the town."

He fell asleep. For the next four days, I left the room only when they were doing things to him. I didn't care what anyone thought, aside from Teddy and Dotsy. Leo brought me food and fresh clothes. I moved in a piano, and played and sang his songs until I was hoarse. I'd read about Larry's last days in my timeline: hallucinating, frightened and alone, ripping at his I.V. This wasn't easy, either, but at least they kept him well-sedated, and Teddy and Dotsy were at his side. He'd drift in and out of consciousness, smiling when he recognized a tune. He was more alert this morning when Dick came, and took his turn at the piano, playing everything from "Manhattan" to "I Could Write a Book."

Larry knew the end was coming, and it was starting to get to him. "Fuck it!" he suddenly gasped. "What have I lived for?" Dotsy tried to take his hand to console him, but he batted her away.

Dick abruptly stopped playing. His wife, Dorothy, hovering in a corner, looked pained—at the profanity, not the despair in Larry's voice. She opened her mouth to say something, but I wasn't having it. If these were Lorenz Hart's last moments, I didn't want the voice of someone who despised him in his ears. I strode to the foot of the bed, right in front of him.

"What for? I'll tell you what for. Look at me, goddamn it. You lived so you could write lyrics for Dick and me. No one lives forever, Larry, but your songs will. *That's* what you lived for."

He blinked. "Oh. Oh, yeah."

"People will be singing your lyrics decades, even centuries, from now. *I guarantee it."*

Doped as he was, he remembered what I'd said about the Series. "Uh-huh. That's...good to know."

Those were his last words. He never regained consciousness: didn't hear the Yankees win in five, didn't feel Teddy and Dotsy holding his hands, didn't hear me singing "The World Beyond" from *The Corn Is Green* at the very end. It's a song about a boy seeking a better life through education, but, it makes a damn fine eulogy.

Chapter 15

"I Ain't Down Yet" —Meredith Willson

From the diary of J.D. Taylor, December 6, 1949

Happy birthday to me. And it is. For all that I miss Larry's endearing chaotic presence, I'm content. I don't blame myself for his death. He'd been abusing his liver since his teens. I do regret the final months of our separation; I should have been with him the whole time, not just at the end.

The Spinellis and Finkelsteins think my birthday's in March. They still joined me for scallopini marsala at Lee Chumley's, nestled snugly by the open fire in the front room. Joe Gould was tucked away in a dim corner, nursing a beer. Sadly, he's not the character he used to be. He's cranky and rude, even to old friends. I had the waiter bring him a New England boiled dinner. Maybe a taste of his childhood will brighten his day.

#

From the diary of J.D. Taylor, December 7, 1949

I completed another step of my Project today. I invited Lenya and Kurt for drinks at Sardi's after tonight's performance of *The Corn Is Green*. It's still playing to great houses.

Lenya was in her usual impish mood, rumpling my hair. You haven't lived until Lotte Lenya tousles your hair. Kurt looked on indulgently, either because he knows there's no stopping her or because he knows I'm no competition. He urged me to keep creating shows, despite losing Larry: "You do fine lyrics on your own. Broadway needs you."

"I'm flattered, but I think I'll stick to producing. I hear you and Maxwell are thinking about *Huckleberry Finn*."

The lights reflected off the thick glasses. *I'd hate to play poker with him. He's unreadable.* "You haf good ears. We've said little about it. Lenya, haf you been telling tales?"

"Me? Not a word, Weillchen!" She looked innocent as a lamb. As far as I knew, this time she really was.

"It's on the Rialto," I said. "I assume Playwrights' Company is behind you?" This was a group consisting of Anderson, Robert Sherwood, Sidney Howard, and others. Weill was the only composer.

He shrugged. "Backing is always such trouble, but, yes, we hope so."

"The last thing you need is trouble. I want to put something unusual to you—a two-part deal. I'll co-produce *Huck* with Playwrights, and put up a hundred and ten grand." *That's more than the whole budget of Weill's recent* Lost in the Stars*, but that was a sparse production. A gamble, but he has to take it. Besides, I believe in the show.*

The outrageous amount got their attention. They weren't starving, but their finances were iffy. Weill whistled softly; Lenya grinned, showing the famous gaps in her teeth. Then Kurt said, "And the second part? Is there a sting in the tail, my friend?"

"Four grand to you, personally, for following certain instructions, plus another thousand to an Israeli charity. I know your folks live there."

"Yes. They got out in time, thank God. So, what are these mysterious instructions? I must entertain your dinner guests every Sunday night? I must wear polka-dot underwear?"

Lenya giggled. "You would look charming. I will buy some tomorrow."

I reached into my pocket and placed two bottles on the table. One was St. Joseph's Baby Aspirin, one was full of Gulsrudix, the top statin-beta blocker combo of my era. "I'm worried about your health."

Weill scowled, expecting me to hit him with his collapse on Lerner's tennis court. Instead, I went on, "Your brother died young; I don't want you going that way. I know a doctor in Mexico City who recommends taking small doses of aspirin every day for heart conditions. He also concocted these supplements. I got some for Larry, but he was too far gone, but Boots Youmans can tell you how I helped Vince's TB, years ago." *See? I've got references!*

Weill examined the bottles, perhaps thinking of the aspirin I gave him in July. He set them down next to his highball. "Is that all?"

"No. Let someone help with the orchestrations. Don't flinch, Kurt. Yes, you're a master, but it's a crushing demand unless you can afford to spend months doing it, like George did with *Porgy*. If we want a fall opening, lighten your load. You can still have final approval over the arrangements."

He wasn't happy. "I do not like people telling me what to do."

"I'm not. It's a contract with specific terms. If you don't like it, say no. Go home, talk it over."

Lenya said, "Let me get this straight. You would *pay* Kurti to take some medicine and not drive himself mad orchestrating until four in the morning? You are some kind of looney!"

"Yup."

Weill stubbed out his cigarette. *If I could, Kurt, I'd make you quit those cancer-sticks, too, but I know you won't.* "Come, Lenya. David, I will call you Friday." He stood up, staring at the bottles on the table. Lenya scooped them into her purse. *I think she's on my side.*

#

From the diary of J.D. Taylor, December 8, 1949
Opening night party for *Gentlemen Prefer Blondes* at the St. Regis Roof. It's a smash, of course, so I'm a happy angel. Film footage doesn't do Carol Channing justice. "Larger than life" was made for her. I wandered about the ballroom, drinking champagne and people-watching: George Kaufman and Heywood Broun in animated discussion; Ethel Merman loudly laughing with Bea Lillie; Noël Coward congratulating his former partner, Jack Wilson, the director: "Jack, my dear boy, it's a triumph. The music's no good, of course, but thank heavens, your Amazon carries the show."

The orchestra alternated between Styne's score (which I admire, even if Noël doesn't) and actual twenties numbers, including the Charleston. The crowd ate it up. I took to the floor, cherry-picking for all I was worth, with George Abbott on one side and Lily Pons on the other. Abbott can really dance. My right knee ached afterwards.

I was heading for some more champers when someone tapped my shoulder: Kurt. Like Coward, he wasn't impressed with the frothy production. But then, his twenties were Weimar, Reds, and Nazis. "This show is a piffle, a nothing. Stupid, but amusing. My *Huck* will be much more. I agree to your proposal."

"I'm glad."

He held up a warning finger. "But when it is done, I shall do as I please."

"Then I'll just have to come up with a new proposal."

#

From the diary of J.D. Taylor, April 4, 1950
I have no idea how long Kurt Weill will live taking baby aspirin and sixteen-year-old medicines from 2079. But I'll treasure each day and each note of *Huck Finn* he finishes. In my timeline, he died yesterday. Here, he and Maxwell are going gangbusters. Opening night is November 3rd at the Majestic. We've signed Weill veteran Todd Duncan (the original Porgy) as Jim, Burgess Meredith as the Duke, and I convinced everyone to accept a young Welshman for Huck, a fellow who had a supporting role in Olivier's recent *The Lady's Not for Burning*. He's not a trained singer, but his voice is one of the most musical I've ever heard, and he's a natural actor. Kurt coped with Gertie Lawrence's vocal weaknesses, and Richard Burton has more range than she did. He's twenty-four, so at first glance, he's too old for the part. But if anyone can pull it off, he can. I can't wait.

I might be able to delay Oscar Hammerstein's stomach cancer with a regimen of baby aspirin, but I can't make the same kind of deal with him. Weill needed money; Oscar's rolling in it. There are limits to what one mad time traveler can do.

#

September 19, 2083
Lieutenant Mertz had her contacts investigate Shandra's claims; she'd covered her tracks, but her dad was less thorough. Dr. Gholkar had indeed obtained drugs that, in the words of one expert, "were commonly used to treat brain tumors." When Rose heard, she danced around the room,

squealing about the wonders of a world where Gershwin lived. "Who knows what he might have composed? God, if Uncle David pulled that off... "

Nate hated to bust her bubble. "Sweetie, the idea makes sense. We know the drugs. We know David's Gershwin obsession. We have that painting, which, by our accounts, never left Ira's home until his death in 1983. But how does an unprepared time traveler get close enough to one of the biggest celebrities of the era to give him a week's worth of powerful drugs?"

They were in David and Ramon's apartment, now Rose's; Nate had spent the night while doing research in Columbia's special collections. Rose had kept David's furniture, hung a mobile of neon green fishes (a gift from Zanzi), and added a wall collage of photos, many of them of her uncle. She stuck out her tongue. "Don't underestimate Uncle David. Maybe you need a Ripper's specialized training for accurate historical studies. But I'll bet anything he knew what *he* wanted to do and how to do it. Maybe he couldn't survive 1892 Pittsburgh, but he could handle thirties New York, in musical theatre. He's a planner. I still find his Post-It notes in the sofa cushions! Think of the way he prepped for a role or researched his shows. If you two have one thing in common, it's research skills. If he went to all that trouble to blackmail Shandra, I'm convinced he'd find a way to get the drugs in Gershwin, even if he had to hire Al Capone to kidnap him."

Nate snorted. "I'm picturing my brother with mobsters. Right. And Capone was already in jail by 1934."

Rose sipped tea from her faded *Carnival* mug. "The thing is, now that we have some idea what he did, I can't stop thinking about it. I want to hear unheard Gershwin!"

"Yeah, that'd be neat. But God knows when somebody's going to that Splinterverse again. Damn funding. I'm sick of being grateful to sleazy outfits that want blood and guts and gore, just so I can do my proper work." Nate's recent trip to cover the Homestead Strike was underwritten by a film studio that demanded a recording of the shoot-out with the Dalton Gang. Next to that, covering Dillinger's ambush was easy.

"When we were little, Hannah and Bertie and I were convinced that 'funding' was a swear word."

"Well, it is! Thanks for putting me up, honey. We'll see you when *Crossing the Rubicon* opens next month. Break a leg." He kissed the top of her head and left.

Rose muttered to herself. "Funding. Hmm."

#

From the diary of J.D. Taylor, June 28, 1950
Well, I didn't see this coming. I'm having trouble getting used to the Cold War. Everybody's talking about the Soviet threat and the end of the American Way of Life. To me, it's high school history. Here, the Hollywood Ten got blacklisted, Tail-Gunner Joe rants about Commies everywhere, and companies are requiring "loyalty oaths." The Korean War has got things hotter. But I know how everything plays out, so I stay weirdly detached.

But I am *steamed* about a pamphlet called "Red Channels," put out by a right-wing journal to resist the Communist takeover of American broadcasting. That's the first step, followed by general upheaval and civil war. Anybody who lives through the purges will learn Russian.

"Red Channels" lists a hundred fifty-two entertainment figures with suspected Communist ties, including Marc Blitzstein, Leonard Bernstein, Will Geer, Lillian Hellman, Dorothy Parker, Burgess Meredith, Harold Rome, Lena Horne, Yip Harburg, Orson Welles, and ... *George*

Gershwin. A few of them had been actual members of the Communist Party; others, like Horne, were nailed for things like supporting a South African famine-relief program! Haven't the idiots behind this ever read the Constitution? I don't like the Soviets, either—they're ruthless, bloody monsters—but last time I looked, the CPUSA was a legitimate political party. These people are so clueless, they asked Yip Harburg if his song, "Happiness is a Thing Called Joe," meant Stalin.

George got listed not least because he's connected with David Alfaro Siqueiros. He commissioned a portrait from him and supported the New York-based Siqueiros Workshop, which created art for the Communist Party's presidential candidates in 1936. He even bought a Siqueiros work called "Proletarian Victim"; how pinko is *that?* In the thirties, he also belonged to the Workers Film and Photo league, a leftist organization devoted to promoting social change through the arts—clearly suspicious.

Some people listed in "Red Channels" will move to Europe. Some will testify against others, ruining friendships and causing lifelong rifts. The lesser lights will struggle for years finding work in Hollywood. The stage community is more forgiving. In fact, so many theatre folk started First Amendment protests against the Commie-baiting that right-wingers are calling Broadway "The Great Red Way."

I don't know how George is taking it. He and Sylvia and the kids will spend the summer in L.A. with Ira and Lee. He's secure enough to get through the Red scares, and Broadway, of course, will never turn him away.

But I just read that Joe McCarthy called his work—some of the greatest music ever written in this country—"subversive."

It makes me want to *scream.*

#

From the diary of J.D. Taylor, July 1, 1950

George and Sylvia stopped by the office. They intend to hit back against "Red Channels" in the Gershwin way. George wants to do a show about the Bill of Rights, to "remind those bastards what this country's based on." I said of course I would back it, whenever he's ready.

#

From the diary of J.D. Taylor, November 4, 1950

I'm hung over from trying to match drinks with Richard Burton last night. A mistake; he's half my age, with a cast-iron liver. As I write this, I'm guzzling coffee in my living room, looking at my photos of Ramon and my folks and Nate and Isis and the kids, and, yeah, Larry, too. "Well, gang," I said. "I wish you could have been there. Brooks Atkinson called *Huck Finn* 'an American classic.' John Chapman said it's the best thing Kurt's ever done. Walter Kerr raved about Lenya as nasty Miss Watson: 'stern enough to make a saint turn mischief-maker.' Dick Burton's the hottest thing in town; thank God, he's signed for eight months, since Hollywood's banging on his dressing-room door. Ethel Merman's furious that we're stealing thunder from *Call Me Madam*. Ain't that somethin'?"

The smiling faces didn't answer. They never do. One of the biggest successes of this whole escapade, a Kurt Weill masterpiece, but I've got no one to share it with.

Oh, well.

The second best part of opening night was the standing ovation. Dick and Todd stood center stage while the orchestra reprised the finale, "Gonna Light Out For the Territory," and the rest of the cast assembled behind them. How I wish those highbrows from my home timeline who think Weill's Broadway output was inferior to his German work could have seen it. It's a magnificent score, especially Huck's soliloquy, "All Right, Then, I'll Go to Hell," when he defies his upbringing to free Jim. We're taking hits for strong language, but I don't give a shit. I told Kurt and Max to be true to Twain. It's time folks realized the American musical is a respectable art form.

The best part? During the party at Sardi's, when Kurt came up to me, beaming. "So! Haf you a new proposal for me, David?"

"I might. Do you have something in mind?"

"An opera. You know, Lenya and I had only just arrived in 1935, when I saw *Porgy and Bess* in rehearsals. I was astonished: that there could be a country where one could not only write such music, but where it was allowed to be played. I would like to do something equally ambitious. What do you think of *Moby-Dick*?"

I bit my tongue so I didn't automatically say the punchline from *Wonderful Town*. But Comden and Green wouldn't write it for another three years. "Sounds promising. Let's talk more."

"As proof of good faith, I shall continue to follow your prescription, Dr. Taylor," he said with that sly smile. "I might not haf agreed had I not seen what your miracle aspirin did at Alan's house. You know, during the war, Lee Gershwin gave me some vitamins that improved my rheumatism. Your pills are much better! My physician is most pleased with my blood pressure. And maybe that young man could help with the orchestrations again." Across the room, Leo, dark head tossed back, was laughing with Burgess, his friend since *Young Man With a Horn*. A buxom chorus girl clung to his arm. Though Frannie despaired, Leo hadn't settled down. He didn't lack for admirers, despite his ravaged face. The eye patch gave him a piratical air, and the beard he grew last year (in imitation of me!) adds to the impression.

"Sorry to disappoint you, Kurt. I'm producing Leo's first show next year."

He looked pleased, not dismayed. "There are other orchestrators. So! Even though he will be my competition on Broadway, I look forward to Leo's work."

Me, too.

#

From the diary of J.D. Taylor, April 5, 1951

Leo's chosen a novel from the thirties, *Disputed Passage*, for his first musical. Milton Lazarus is doing the libretto. Lazarus isn't my first choice, but he's personable. Unlike the movie version, they aren't sugar-coating the ending, including the Japanese attack on Nanking. It's gutsy writing a musical whose central issue isn't romance, but which philosophy a young doctor should follow: that of a unlikable, pragmatic scientist, or a kindly, holistic general practitioner. No, it's not *Allegro Redux*, though there are similarities. This material is better developed. The bitter scientist isn't only a foil; he's a character with depth, whose love of science has crowded out the possibility of other love. There's as much of a war within cold Dr. Forrester as in his protégé.

Great stuff, but not commercial. I don't care I'm flush from the latest hits of this Golden Age: *Guys and Dolls*, *The King and I*, *Call Me Madam*. And, by God, add *Huck Finn* to those! So I don't care if we lose money here, or with the controversial new Gershwin show.

George appeared before the HUAC this week. I didn't know how it went until both Gershwin brothers appeared at my apartment late last night. They were armed with salami and pumpernickel from Reuben's, so I supplied the Blatz, ready for a schmoozefest.

"I was there for five hours!" George said. "They started with Mexico, with Siqueiros and Rivera, and then brought up organizations I don't even remember. Even charities, like Russian War Relief."

"Nobody remembers we were allies then," I said.

"That turd from Missouri, John Rankin, really didn't like that the Moscow Theatre staged *Porgy and Bess* in '46. Damn Southern bigot. You could tell he was thinking, 'Arrest that commie kike who writes songs about *niggrahs!*' I wanted to scream, 'You scum, I've played the Lincoln piano at the White House for Roosevelt. Do you think *I'm* writing symphonies for Stalin? That's Shostakovich's job!'"

Ira said, "When the committee was investigating the Federal Theatre Program in '37, they asked Hallie Flanagan if Christopher Marlowe was a Commie and if Mr. Euripides' plays supported class conflict. They'll drag you in because someone's uncle thought you were wearing a red tie at a football game."

"I've been copying you, David, treating others on the 'Red Channels' list to meals, slipping them cash," George said, lifting his bottle in tribute.

"I'm just doing what Hammerstein's doing. Most generous soul on Broadway."

"It's time to move past handouts," said George. "They're done with me, in spite months of FBI snooping. They won't like my revenge. I'll foot half the bill to do this show. Are you in? Moss Hart will do the book and direct."

"You know Yip's new show is also a satire?" I asked. *'Flahooley.* Opens next month. He's taking aim at these clowns, too."

"Aim?" Ira laughed. "It'll be an A-bomb." Ira and Harburg had been pals since grade school.

"Or another kind of bomb?" George leaned towards me. "What have you heard?"

"Rumors. Yip made his views work in *Finian's Rainbow*, but he may have gone overboard here." *That's putting it mildly!*

"You got money in it? No?" George crumpled up his wax paper and tossed it neatly in the trash. "Let's see what Yip does, then take our shot. These bastards deserve all the hits we can dish out."

"I'm in." *I didn't back Yip because I knew his show would flop. But this is why I stole the SlingShot: to bring new Gershwin to Broadway.*

#

From the diary of J.D. Taylor, May 17, 1951
The brothers attended Flahooley's opening with me. They admired Barbara Cook and Yip's jabs at McCarthyism, but saw that the show was a hot mess. We had a brief meeting in ny office today before the Gershwins went west to work with Moss. I told them they had to keep the story first. "You want your audience to think, but you can't bludgeon them like Yip did."

Ira leaned back and smoothed his tie over his pudgy belly. "We're going all the way back to Magna Carta, tracing civil liberties through history. Themed revues are out, but I thought maybe a time traveler, like in H.G. Wells... David! You okay?"

I coughed violently. "Swallowed wrong."

"Or else one family, from England to America. You like that better? Yeah, gives continuity." Ira jotted in a small notebook. George played two songs they'd finished, which were promising. I approved, and sent them to California with my blessing.

H.G. Wells!

#

George isn't just backing his own show. He's behind Leo's
Disputed Passages, too. Rodgers and Hammerstein are the
chief examples of producer-songwriters, though I guess I'm
up there, too. With his sharp business sense, Rodgers has
noticed my track record. He cornered me at the opening
of *The King and I* in March; I had a solid ten per cent of
the show.

"Something odd about you, David," Rodgers said.
"Since *On Your Toes,* you've been an angel for nearly all
my shows. The only ones you didn't back were the ones that
didn't do so well, like *Higher and Higher.* I checked your
records, and while some things you personally worked on
failed—*Tom Jones* comes to mind—every production you
invested in became a big, fat hit." He puffed on a cigarette;
I couldn't help thinking of the hideous throat cancer he'd
get in a few years. "What's your secret? Do you do this well
at Saratoga?"

"I don't play the ponies. I've got good theatre instincts."

"Instinct told you to stay away from *Miss Liberty?* It had
everything going for it—Irving; Moss; Robbins; a book by
Bob Sherwood, who's got more Pulitzers than Carter has
liver pills; a half-mil advance—and it sank like the *Titanic.*"

I sipped my champagne. "Didn't like the premise."

"Hmm." Rodgers clearly wanted to press the issue, but
I escaped when Mary Martin wrapped him in a bear hug,
squealing about how she'd been so right about Yul Brynner.

That's not a line of questioning I want to face again. What
will Dick say when I don't invest in *Pipe Dream* in 1955?

#

Disputed Passage opened last night. It will probably close soon, with competition like Phil Silvers' *Top Banana;* Lerner and Loewe's *Paint Your Wagon;* and the Gershwin political satire, *We, the People.* That one features Howard Da Silva, Zero Mostel, and a bunch of other "Red Channels" names. But I love Leo's songs. He put such craft into each one; they shine like little gems, but he setting wasn't golden.

Edgar MacGregor's direction was leaden, and Lazarus' book dragged. I found myself waiting impatiently for each musical number. I wished I'd directed it myself, but I didn't want to push myself on Leo. MacGregor has been staging shows since the teens; a nice guy, but a dinosaur. But he gave Frannie steady wardrobe work for years, so Leo wanted to him to have a chance. The cast does its best, especially the amazing Walter Slezak as Dr. Forrester and the utterly gorgeous Anne Jeffreys as the American girl raised in China.

The audience seemed moved, even shaken, by the violent end in Nanking. But if we confused them, we flummoxed the critics. They slammed the production. Most of them stupidly took it for another *Allegro.* I was afraid they would. *Passage* took some chances, especially with Leo's songs, but it's a dramatic musical, not a concept show. It has more in common with *South Pacific* than *Allegro.*

No matter. Leo's first show is under his belt. He doesn't seem fazed by failure, either. "I'll do better next time, boss man," he said. "I'm just happy Kurt and George like my songs."

They weren't the only ones. Every songwriter I'd talked to admired them. In the lobby of the Broadway Theatre, I saw Oscar's young friend, a new college graduate named Stephen Sondheim, gesturing enthusiastically to his mentor. Broadway insiders agree: this Spinelli is a comer.

"How long do you think we'll run?" Leo asked. "I have lots of relatives; maybe the Spinellis and Santinos can keep us afloat for a month. Hey, babe! I've been looking everywhere for you!"

This was aimed at Jeanette McDermott. After years of sultry chorines, Leo found the girl of his dreams at home. Well, my office. Jeanette is a plump, funny girl with wavy auburn hair and, like her brother Alan, an insatiable appetite for theatre and books. I expect a wedding announcement any day. Frannie's more excited about the idea of grandchildren than about her son's first Broadway score.

"Alan's stupid leg jammed again," Jeanette said, frowning. "He had trouble on the stairs." Alan lost a leg at Tarawa, but at least he lived. Most of his squad didn't. "He needs a better prosthetic, because this one's junk."

"Damn! The crap he has to go through!" said Leo. "I'm lucky in comparison, just losing an eye. I can dance with my girl. So, Jeannie, what's that cra-a-a-zy song they're playing? Let's hit the floor! Spinelli can take whatever the critics dish out!"

The orchestra was playing the main ballad from *Disputed Passage*, "Finding My Road." A good song to build a future on.

#

From the diary of J.D. Taylor, February 5, 1952
I'm looking at the score for Porter's *Can-Can*, which opened in 1953 in my world. Given the struggles I had making a *Kiss Me, Kate* that came close to the original, I've been wracking my brains over what to do with it. *Can-Can* has typical book issues, and for every classic like "I Love Paris," there's a dud like "Maidens Typical of France."

In my timeline, it got started when Cy Feuer and Ernest Martin tried copying *Kate*'s success by having Porter do a romantic show set in gay Paree. Abe Burrows ended up doing the clunky book. He directed, too.

With these flaws, why should I bother? Because aside from five standards and an eight-hundred-performance run, it catapulted Gwen Verdon to stardom. She literally stopped the show. Ever since I landed back here, I've been looking forward to her "Apache Dance."

So I sounded out Feuer and Martin, flush from the success of *Guys and Dolls*; they're cautiously interested. I've had several lunches with Burrows, but he can't take it on yet. He's working on an Irish fantasy, *Three Wishes for Jamie*, and keeps trying to get me to back it. *Sorry, Abe, but what's the Gaelic for "turkey"?*

That leaves me struggling with the libretto myself. I'm reading books about *belle époque* France and the history of the can-can. No inspirations that fit with Cole's existing songs. The structure of the show is still the same: polar opposites meet, fight, fall in love. Add comic secondary couple. Heat and serve. *Oy.* And I'm uncomfortable claiming Cole's work as my own. *Kate* was different; it was practically finished and I gave Porter credit, based on our "conversations."

I feel better about other developments. Although *Disputed Passages* closed last month, Leo and Jeanette are getting hitched in June. He's got two numbers in the upcoming revue, *New Faces of 1952*. Some damn good youngsters there: Sheldon Harnick, Mel Brooks, Alice Ghostley, Carol Lawrence. After the honeymoon, he'll start his next score, which will be romantic but quirky—like Leo himself. He and his librettist, Dexter Rhys, are adapting the film, *The Ghost and Mrs. Muir*, about a young widow who moves into a house haunted by an irascible sea captain.

Dex is a buddy of Leo's from the Navy. I'd never heard of his work, so I looked him up on my Ally—a few radio and television scripts, nothing more. Well, in my timeline, Leo Spinelli wasn't a Broadway songwriter. Maybe this will be the making of him.

#

From the diary of J.D. Taylor, August 14, 1952
Kurt and Max's *Moby-Dick* opens in September at the Met. I'm principal underwriter for the production, with options on royalties and future performances. I'm proud to say it will make history: the Met's first mixed-race cast, three years before Marian Anderson broke the opera color barrier in my timeline. We kept true to Twain, so we couldn't do any less for Melville's characters. The crew of the *Pequod* has Africans, Indians, and Polynesians, and we wouldn't cast them with whites. We've signed William Warfield as Queequeg, young Brock Peters as Daggoo, and a boy soprano named Herbert Coleman (from Kurt's *Lost in the Stars*) as Pip, the doomed cabin boy. Joining them are Cesare Siepi as Ishmael and Robert Merrill as the demented Ahab. At first, the Met's higher-ups didn't want to hire African-American singers, though manager Rudolf Bing was with us from the start. I think *Huck Finn* changed their minds; the civil rights movement has adopted several of Kurt and Max's songs, including the stirring "This Time, Next Year." The publicity has been phenomenal.

I've only got another three months' worth of drugs for Kurt, dammit; then I'll have to tell him my Mexican contact died. As usual, he's plunged into a new project. Marc Blitzstein has been pestering him for years to do a new English translation of *The Threepenny Opera*. They don't always get along—Kurt thinks *The Cradle Will Rock* is watered-down Weill—but it's moving ahead—assuming we can cope with Brecht on the rights.

#

From the diary of J.D. Taylor, August 8, 1952
I'm still dragging my feet over *Can-Can*. Despite my tweaks the second act is still moronic. Leo has his own opinions about it, too. He came by my place this evening carrying his work for *The Ghost and Mrs. Muir*, only we ended up wrangling over *Can-Can*.

He hadn't seen any of it yet, he just knew that I was working on something "original" *(Ha!)* and French. While I was getting some beers, he found the *Can-Can* songs and started playing them. It felt like a weird flashback to 1934, with Leo at the piano while I puttered in the kitchen. Only he plays so much better than when he was stumbling through "Camptown Races."

I'd carefully hand-written all of Cole's music on lead sheets, so there wasn't anything to show that they weren't original compositions... except they weren't in J.D. Taylor's style. Not by a long shot.

As Larry had with "So In Love," Leo called me on it. "Boss man, what on God's green earth is this?" He played a few songs, then tried accompanying himself with the lyrics. Most songwriters are rotten singers; Harold Arlen, Johnny Mercer, and I are notable exceptions. Leo's a screechy tenor with a range like Gertie Lawrence's, from C to C sharp. He squawked a few verses of "I Love Paris" before mercifully stopping. He flipped through more sheets, staring closely at one especially idiotic comic piece. His surviving eye gave me a funny look. "Honestly, David? Can-can girls?"

I was standing there, sweating, and not just from the humid summer evening. I handed him a Blatz. "Yeah, can-can girls. Color, romance, fun. Solid hit material."

He took a swig from the bottle. "Doesn't seem like your sort of thing. What am I missing, some hook in the book? Give, give."

I flopped on the couch and described the story of Pistache, who owns the music hall where the scandalous can-can is performed, and how she wins the approval and the heart of the stern judge who wanted to close her down.

Leo finished his beer while I talked, got a second one, and drained that, too. He scratched his black beard, considering. "No offense, but it sounds... predictable. That's a word I never thought I'd use about anything of yours. I still remember the chills I got when you let me read the libretto for *Eclipse,* about the murder on the moon base. I was fifteen, and all I wanted for months was to see that staged. I acted out the whole thing on my model theatre. Shit, I still want to see *Eclipse!*" He pointed at the libretto. "Hard to imagine that the same guy who wrote *Eclipse* is scribbling about goofy sculptors and their naughty models."

"Leo, there's a reason *Eclipse* never had a major staging. I'd lose my shirt producing a dissonant, depressing dystopian disaster."

"Nice alliteration, but I know which show I'd rather see."

"You're a specialized audience."

He leaped up from the piano bench, gesturing like Frannie. "I grew up watching everything you did, seeing shows with you, analyzing what made them work or fail. I learned plenty at Columbia, but *that* was my real education. When you started producing, I felt proud to sweep your office! Being on the inside, seeing *High Flyers* and *Young Man* come together—there couldn't be anything better."

He laughed. "I've never told you this, but I wanted to *be* you. Uh, except with girlfriends."

"I'm flattered." My face heated. *I never thought of myself as role model material. And I'm glad Leo has different attitudes from Sergio.*

Leo continued: "I admit to being prejudiced, but I've always felt there was something a little different about every Taylor production, compared to other musicals. I don't know how to describe it. Daring. Freshness." He ran his hand through his thick black curls and had to adjust his eye patch. "I'm not explaining this well. It's the way you take chances, like doing a revue written entirely by women or casting Negroes in major roles. Your crazy staging ideas, like *Canterbury Tales'* opening number. Producing *Passages*, with a score by a rookie, tackling moral philosophy. Most producers would have slammed the door in my face! I know this is a business, but it never seemed to me that having a hit was important to you. It was about creating the best show you could. If the critics didn't get it, if it didn't attract big houses—you'd be disappointed, but I never had the feeling you regretted any of your flops."

"I don't. Success doesn't come just from the box office. If I were a betting man, I'd gamble that later generations would appreciate those flops. Sometimes a show flops because it's ahead of its time."

Leo went to the kitchen and grabbed a banana from my bowl of green Depression glass, the way he did when he was a teen with an impossible appetite. "Like *Rainbow* and *Porgy and Bess?* Their revivals ran longer than the originals. Hey, if I live long enough, maybe I'll see *Disputed Passages* revived! Whoa, that would be a kick!"

"Anything's possible."

He ate the banana in three bites, then went to the piano again. With a slender finger, he tapped the lead sheets.

"David, I'm sure *Can-Can* could be a hit, but it seems so boring! The music's terrific, with a good French feel; the judge's ballad could be a Billboard hit. But those lyrics, the dopey plot! I know I'm still getting my feet wet, but that's what I think. I hope I haven't hurt your feelings." He was nervous about speaking so frankly.

"If friends can't tell each other the truth, they're not really friends. In fact, I agree with a lot of that. You've given me things to think about. But what about *Mrs. Muir*? How's it going?"

He grimaced. "Shitty. I hate what Dex has been doing, but I don't know how to fix it. Can you take a look?"

"Of course." I took the papers from him. "I'll see what I can do."

"Don't forget my party's next week. Jeannie's baking a lemon chiffon cake."

"Wouldn't miss it for the world," I said. "Thirty, huh? Time *does* fly."

After he left, I studied the *Can-Can* lead sheets. *Am I doing the right thing in giving this world Cole Porter's songs under my own name? Or am I doing both of us—and my Project—a disservice?* The song on top was the ballad Leo admired: "It's All Right With Me." But was it ?

#

November 17, 2083

Rose took the subway uptown and hustled through pouring rain to an address on Lexington Avenue, a bland glass-and-steel office building with a polished granite lobby. A bored receptionist, his hair dangling in snakelike braids, didn't even look up as she shook out her umbrella. She crossed to the elevators, entered the car, and punched a button.

The Save Our Standards Foundation took up the whole fifteenth floor. The car opened onto a gleaming, gold and silver Art Deco reception area. Music was playing: an instrumental version of Berlin's "Let Yourself Go." Unlike the guy below, the gray-haired woman behind the counter greeted her immediately. "Hello, Ms. Greenbaum. Ms. Oakes is expecting you." She led Rose to an interior office door, which she opened. "Ms. Greenbaum is here."

"Bring her in!" said a rich, vibrant voice. Rose walked into the office. It continued the 1930s decor, though many photographs gave it a personal touch. She recognized many faces from twenty-first-century musical theatre. Philippa Oakes was a double Tony winner, but she'd spent most of the last three decades doing cabaret and promoting classic American standards. She was the Foundation's vice president, and its most public face. She smiled at Rose from behind her desk. So did a middle-aged African-American man with close-trimmed hair and a pencil-line mustache on his round face.

"Delighted to meet you, Rose," said Oakes. She was in her early seventies, but looked more fit than her younger companion. "Before I forget, let me say how much I liked your take on Dorrie in *Citadel*—quite refreshing. You clobbered that bitch of a ballad."

"Wow. Thanks so much. I grew up on your work, so that means a lot to me."

Oakes gestured to her companion; he and Rose shook hands. "Marcus Wheeler, our money guy. Since you said this involved dollars—a lot of them—I asked him to sit in. So what's this about? Usually, if I got an e-mail babbling about unknown Gershwin tunes, I'd pass it to an intern, since it's likely bogus. But you're a Juilliard kid with plenty of talent, like your uncle, so I'm willing to listen."

"You knew David?"

"I was cast as Carlotta in that *Follies* revival with him, but I tore my Achilles' tendon in rehearsal. He had such a promising future. A talented performer, and his score for *No Heroes Here* was so moving. What on earth made him run off in a time machine?"

Rose took a deep breath. "Well, my visit's connected to that. We've been piecing things together for years, and I think he went back in time to save George Gershwin."

"What?" The word exploded from Wheeler. "That's impossible!" Oakes shushed him.

Rose began her presentation. She'd rehearsed it in the apartment, with David and Ramon's photos looking on. She built the case brick by brick, every last detail. She fascinated Oakes from the start, but watching Wheeler's icy demeanor thaw was fun.

"So the portrait of David in that painting, and the fact the painting was in Mexico City in 1947, not in Los Angeles, shows he got close to Gershwin and something was different from our past. I can't see Ira letting Siqueiros have it for that exhibition, but George might have if he was still alive."

"God!" said Oakes. "What would he have written, given another decade? Or more?"

"I'm shaking at the mere thought," said Wheeler. "I'm like your uncle, a Gershwin fanatic my whole life. I used to curse God, 'Why'd you take him so soon?'"

Oakes said, "Obviously, we'd be *very* interested in unheard Gershwin, but there's no guarantee there is any. Your theory is convincing, but there's no proof."

"My dad always says the hardest part of being a Ripper is finding the funding. Could the Foundation back a trip to the Splinterverse to look for Gershwin songs?"

Wheeler and Oakes exchanged glances. "What kind of figures are we talking about?" the CFO said.

Rose couldn't bring herself to say. She clicked a link, turned the Ally's screen towards them. They both winced.

"If it were a sure thing, if we really knew Gershwin lived past 1937, I'd approve it instantly," said Wheeler. The emotion in his voice touched Rose. *He wants to do this. I know he does!*

"What if a Ripper brings back solid proof—recordings, films, newspaper clippings, sheet music—what then?" said Rose.

Oakes and Wheeler exchanged looks. "We'd have to talk to our board. This would be a gigantic investment, and God knows what kind of licensing issues there are," Philippa said. "But I'd argue it's totally worth it."

"Me, too!" said Wheeler. "We're dedicated to preserving American standards. What could be better than finding new ones to add to the songbook?"

"Get us proof," said Philippa Oakes. "And we'll go from there."

Chapter 16

"New Sun in the Sky" —Howard Dietz

From the diary of J.D. Taylor, November 20, 1952

Sad news. Joe Gould, the Village's own "little Professor," collapsed on the street last week—hospitalized with dementia and kidney trouble, among other ills. The poor guy hasn't been right for some time. The last long talk I had with him was this summer, when I treated him to Sunday breakfast at Charles's, over on Sixth. "What's with you, Joe?" I asked over a stack of fluffy French pancakes. "You don't seem yourself lately."

The rheumy eyes narrowed. Joe's cup of espresso (not "cowboy coffee," for once) paused on its way to his mouth. "I'm *not* myself," he said, biting each word las if it were part of his meal. "I've *never* been myself." The cup finished its journey; he thumped it down on the table. "What's more, *you've* never been yourself, either, Mr. Joseph David Taylor."

Gould had been weirding me out for for years with comments like that. This should have been more of the usual drunken rambling, but he was sober, coherent...

And I don't think he's called me anything but "Bronko" after the first week we met. It gave me the "cauld grue," as Jeanette and Alan McDermott's mum says. *What has he written about me in that stupid history he's writing?*

"I'm who I'm supposed to be, Joe," I said, trying to sound braver than I felt. "My name's on my door in gold letters."

"Sure," said Gould. "But they could have painted 'Harry S. Truman' on it, too. You're too tall for that role, though. Oh, *garçon!* Another madeleine, *s'il vous plaît.*" The staff here is exceptional, and instantly placed a plate of tiny shell-shaped cakes in front of him. He tucked in, smiling once more. Was it was the blood sugar or some strange Proustian effect that made him thoughtful? "You're saner than most, Bronko. You recognize the tragic isolation of humanity—indeed, you are more isolated than most—yet you resolutely pursue your essential purposes and do it well, by everything I've heard. Good for you. And thanks for the delicious food."

I have no idea what the hell *that* meant. I saw Joe a few weeks later, talking to the pigeons on Christopher Street. I gave him a dollar and he told me the birds would protect us from the Russians. When I made a joking response, he told me to go fuck myself.

I hope he pulls through, but a lifetime of boozing and sleeping on the streets has probably wrecked his whole carcass.

\#

From the diary of J.D. Taylor, March 5, 1953
Leo's criticism of *Can-Can* echoed in my ears whenever I tried working on the damn thing. It was more fun wrestling with *The Ghost and Mrs. Muir*—a live, evolving work, not a zombie show. I attacked Dexter Rhys' libretto with a red pen; he wasn't hopeless, just inexperienced. He sourly accepted my changes. Leo, however, was quite pleased. He asked me if I would direct *The Ghost* myself. Given how unhappy I was with the direction for *Disputed Passages*,

I agreed. Maybe it's the influence I had developing his theatrical sensibilities, but Leo and I ended up in sync about everything.

So this world will have Leonard Spinelli's second show, but not Cole Porter's (or "J.D. Taylor's") *Can-Can*. I mourn losing those great songs, but passing them off as my own would be wrong. They don't sound like me; *Can-Can's* a thoroughly conventional show, and Taylor productions are *unconventional*. Maybe that's what Gould meant by "pursuing essential purposes." Anyway, I'm damn proud of *The Ghost and Mrs. Muir*, especially the three dance numbers choreographed by Michael Kidd; Leo's character-rich songs (the hilarious "Blood and Swash," heartbreaking "Lucia"); and a few directorial touches of my own, blending historical eras. No subplot, no secondary characters, none of the touches expected in a musical from this period—the grown daughter has one number with her fiancé, but her best scenes are with her mother. Hell, I even adapted some tricks for the age make-up at the finale, when the heroine dies and the ghost of her beloved captain comes for her. No twenty-first-century silicone or plastics, but I came up with some substitutes. Our lead actress completed the effect by convincingly changing from arthritic granny to a lithe young ghost. She's a *whiz* at movement.

Oh, yeah, our terrific cast: John Raitt as Captain Gregg, Barbara Cook as the grown daughter, and the incomparable Gwen Verdon as Mrs. Muir. No "Apache Dance," but I'm betting she brings down the house when her character convinces a stuffy publisher to buy her book by explaining the entire plot…in dance. I'd worried that her career might fizzle without *Can-Can*—and we'd have no Lola in *Damn Yankees*, no years of collaboration with Bob Fosse. Silly me. Cream always rises to the top.

We open tomorrow night. I smell a hit.

#

From the diary of J.D. Taylor, March 20, 1954
My twentieth anniversary in this other timeline. Is that possible? Well, yeah. My beard's going gray. My gimmicky knee aches when I jog around Washington Square. Leo's thirty-one and looks more like Sergio every day, while his schoolboy features are taking shape on his baby son, Dave. (Yes, he's named for his godfather; his great-uncle, Nick Santino, joked that I used "undue influence.")

And my case of treasures—the works that wouldn't have existed if I hadn't stolen Nate's SlingShot—keeps growing. After the mixed reaction to *We, the People* (deliciously barbed, but too much preaching to the choir to succeed), Gershwin began work on his own personal reaction to the Red hysteria. His "American Rhapsody" (royalties promised to Veterans of Foreign Wars) debuted on Memorial Day last year. Curiously, that was the working title of the "Rhapsody in Blue" until Ira came up with the classic phrase. Like the earlier piece, it's written for piano with orchestra.

But America in the early fifties isn't the same place as America in the mid-twenties. The exuberant first rhapsody celebrated our "vast melting pot…national pep…and metropolitan madness," as the composer said. The second reflects the strengths of a nation that went through the Depression and won the war, but one less innocent. In the middle of the piece, an unsettling passage grabs the listener and shakes his sense of complacency. This land is vigorous, prosperous—but not without flaws. Then, in a dazzling burst of harmonic originality, the passage evolves into something completely different, almost futuristic. The "strength theme" slowly weaves back in, climbing to an optimistic finale.

414

I sat with Oscar and June Levant at "American Rhapsody's" Carnegie Hall premiere. "Know what that was?" he bellowed in my ear during the thunderous applause. "Pure Gershwin!"

George isn't the only busy boy. Kurt's supply of Gulsrudix has ended, but he's still taking baby aspirin, without any "deals" from me. He's exercising and bragging about his cottage cheese diet; I hope it helps. *The Threepenny Opera* was a success off-Broadway last fall, though Kurt and Marc nearly came to blows a dozen times. It's not *exactly* like the one I know, since Kurt was there. Now he and Maxwell are writing a musical based on the outrageous life of Nell Gwynn, the famous actress who was King Charles' mistress.

Following the success of *The Ghost and Mrs. Muir* (Gwen won the Tony!), Leo and I are tackling Thornton Wilder's *The Skin of Our Teeth*. It was the first play Leo saw after coming back to the mainland, and he's been obsessed with its absurdist take on life ever since. It will be a challenge—in my world, Kander and Ebb couldn't make it work—but we're trying. Leo's songs for the outrageous maid, Sabina, are hilarious. He's even written a short duet for the dinosaur and mammoth—nothing but roaring. I intend to use plenty of quick, almost cinematic dissolves, to keep the whole thing moving. No let-up, or we'll lose our audience.

It's just me and Leo; Dexter Rhys said he wasn't interested in doing the libretto. That was fine. It saved us from telling him we didn't want him. He was competent, but you need more than that on Broadway. He resented my rewrites, my direction, and my sexuality, though he never let Leo see that. I'm just glad I didn't have to axe the guy who helped save Leo's life.

We're aiming for an opening next January; our only significant competition will be *Plain and Fancy* and then

Damn Yankees in May, since Porter's *Silk Stockings* won't happen. I've decided to shelve all Cole's post-1948 works. It hurts, but I can't do them in good conscience.

#

November 24, 1963

Keevaughan Randall was exhausted—physically and emotionally. He'd been in SV4-1934 for five months, covering the civil rights movement. The high of participating in the March On Washington, though, was obliterated by Kennedy's assassination. But that was his devil's bargain for this Ripper trip: plant cameras on the motorcade route, near the grassy knoll, across from the School Book Depository. He didn't dare try placing any inside; as an African-American, he was watched everywhere in Jim Crow Dallas. And, the authorities would swarm the building afterwards, making it impossible to retrieve them later. *The conspiracy nuts would love that: alien technology involved in JFK's death!*

He hoped dinner would revive him; he'd picked up some burgers at a joint down the block and brought them back to his room. The hookers who worked the corner near the Ross Avenue Motel ("the South's finest colored motel") wanted to share his meal. They trailed him to the lobby door. "How 'bout giving us a little o' that, sugar? Aw, come on, baby. It's lonely out tonight."

He'd learned not to talk to them. They would latch on to anything to keep the contact going. He gave the pair a sad smile and slipped inside, away from the litter-strewn, smelly street. *No sex, but I'd really like to get smashed, forget the last two days ever happened.* A bottle of Early Times was buried in the dirty clothes in his suitcase. He fetched the tumbler from the bathroom and got out the whiskey.

Not enough left to get as drunk as I want. Damn. With a sigh, he turned the TV back on and recorded the live reports. He concentrated on the local stations' coverage, as the big three networks' had largely survived. At seven, however, he'd had enough of the hysterics over Jack Ruby and switched to ABC for the "Tribute to John F. Kennedy From the Arts," a memorial concert. A grainy tape survived to his time, but Keevaughan's gear could do better than that. Besides, the line-up was terrific and he was sick of the news.

He plumped up the pillow, finished his fries, and settled down to watch. Frederic March hosted. He recited the Gettysburg Address. Christopher Plummer and Albert Finney performed Hamlet's death scene; Marian Anderson sang spirituals. There were selections from the Bible, and Charlton Heston read poems by Robert Frost.

Kee watched without paying much attention; maybe the booze was getting to him after all. Then March announced, "Now George Gershwin honors the memory of our fallen leader with one of Mr. Kennedy's favorite pieces: the composer's own 'American Rhapsody.'"

Kee spluttered whiskey over his shirt. He'd been told to check for references to Gershwin in this Splinterverse. It was on his "to-do" list before he headed back to the SlingShot. But there, on the tiny black and white television, was a slender man in his mid-sixties, largely bald, with gray at his temples and in his thin mustache. He nodded to the conductor and sat at the piano. Kee was no musician. He could recognize the "Rhapsody in Blue" and his mom sang "Summertime" as a lullaby, but that was all he knew about Gershwin. This "American Rhapsody" was unfamiliar. But he'd been told there was a chance Gershwin didn't die young in this world.

More than a chance. There he is.

417

When the tribute ended, Kee went down to the night clerk, a bookish African-American, about twenty. When he saw Randall coming, he snapped to attention, sliding a textbook aside. "Yes, Mr. Randall? How can I help you?"

"Nothing, really," Keevaughan said. "I was just watching a tribute to the president where George Gershwin was playing. I had this weird memory that he had been ill or maybe died, so it was odd seeing him at the piano."

The clerk slid his hornrims up his nose. "Oh, no, sir. He just had a show open in New York, *Around the World in Eighty Days.* You know, the one where Louis Armstrong got that big hit, 'Imagine the Possibilities.'" He sang a few lines, doing a decent job of imitating Satchmo's growly tones: "'Anything one man can imagine, other men can make real.' Of course, Armstrong and Gershwin go way back to that jazz show, before the war." He laughed. "I might not exist without that show."

Kee prayed his Ripperglasses were getting all this, especially the melody. He couldn't carry a tune in a bucket. "How's that, son?"

"Well, Ella Fitzgerald's recording of 'Magic' was my parents' special song. I hear tell Mama used it to work her own magic on Daddy, snaring him before he went to boot camp. And here I am!"

"Well, thanks for putting my fading memory to rights," Kee said. "Guess I've got too much death and sorrow on my mind."

The smile left the young fellow's face. "We all do, sir."

\#

From the diary of J.D. Taylor, January 28, 1955
The Skin of Our Teeth opened last night. It may run; the critics mostly liked it, noting Leo's witty songs and

418

my direction. But who can celebrate while Kurt's in the hospital? He had another heart attack; although he's stable, the outcome's iffy. I wish the docs here knew more. His *Nell Gywnn* debuted last month—a modest hit, but as usual, workaholic Weill plunged immediately into his next project, adapting Molière's *The Doctor In Spite of Himself.* I'm driven, too—I've got meetings the afternoon after an opening night—but I don't have high blood pressure and heart disease. He should have taken a break, dammit.

#

From the diary of J.D. Taylor, February 22, 1955
Kurt's stabilized, but the quacks are trying to get him to take a vacation. This is like asking the sun not to shine. "Well, keep him away from the piano!" ordered his doctor. That's useless. Like George and Vince and Sondheim and MacGugan, Kurt works at his desk—the piano's in his head.

Leo and I are taking our next show slowly, since it's completely original ... and a subject that means a great deal to men of his generation. Watching Alan McDermott cope with his artificial leg; enduring people's sidelong glances at his own grisly scars; seeing men with hooks, missing fingers, disfiguring burns, and invisible injuries—all that inspired Leo to write some songs about vets dealing with life after the war. "I got the idea from your 'Red Sky At Morning,' the one where Larry helped with the lyrics. You said it was based on a shellshock patient."

We were having brunch at Leo and Jeanette's place, a cozy, cluttered apartment on East 51st Street. He'd die if he knew what rent here is in my era. Frannie and Jeanette were in the kitchen, toasting bread and scrambling eggs. I hoped Jeannie would be able to keep her meal down; she was expecting again. I sat on the floor with little Dave (I love being called "Uncle" again!), playing with his wooden zoo animals, while Leo described what he hoped to talk about in this show: "I don't want folks to think we're doing a musical of *The Best Years of Our Lives*! A great flick—it did a lot for handicapped vets—but we can go deeper. And darker. It can get dark, boss man." His single eye swung towards the window. He wasn't looking at the murky winter skies, but something I couldn't imagine. I'd never seen the elephant.

"You made it through," I said.

He shook his dark head, chasing away memories. "Thank God I had somewhere to go, something to do, or I might have ended like that joe in your song. But I'm afraid you're taking a big chance here, David."

"I don't care. I want to do it, so let's do it—and hope the audience goes along. What kinds of problems should we tackle? You're the veteran, so you have to take the lead. Interview Alan and other guys for ideas. What mattered most? What was hardest to overcome? Then we'll concoct some scenes, figure out a structure. It needs to be more than a song cycle or a revue like *Call Me Mister.* Let Jeannie help, because she knows shorthand and your handwriting is a disaster."

Leo frowned. "Some things fellows won't talk about with a girl around."

"I understand that. But half our audience will be women. Wives and mothers, whose loved ones who came back damaged. The show can't just be about the boys; we've got to look at them, too."

"You're right. A balanced show is a stronger show. Maybe Jeannie can do some interviewing on her own, get the feminine angle." He squatted by his curly-haired son. "What's that, sport? Got a tiger by the tail?"

Dave held up his chubby fists. "I got two!"

"And we've got two songs already," I said. "That's a good starting place."

"No, three: 'Red Sky.' Or do you mind using it?" He gave a wry grin. "One last theatre credit for Larry, huh?"

"Sure, but only if it fits. It's got to be natural." I put a blue hippo on my head. "Look, Davey—my new hat."

"Dat's *not* a hat!"

#

September 5, 2084

Philippa Oakes was as good as her word. The Save Our Standards Foundation shifted into high gear as soon as its board of directors saw (and heard!) the footage of Gershwin at the Kennedy tribute. Experts were analyzing the "American Rhapsody." Even the single line from an unknown Gershwin musical the motel clerk sang had them salivating. One fellow, an Ira Gershwin scholar, told Rose, "*Around the World in Eighty Days* was one of Ira's favorite books when he was young."

"Honestly, Mom, this guy talked like he knew Ira personally," Rose said over coffee and bagels at Katz's. "He had tears in his eyes."

"You were crying, too, when Dad screened that concert," Isis said. "We all were. My God, David did it. He saved Gershwin. Besides that 'Rhapsody' and at least two musicals, who knows what else there is?"

Rose stared into her big mug. "I wish Keevaughan Randall had gone to a music store. He could have found that Ella Fitzgerald record, maybe sheet music, too. Or cast albums!"

"Nate said Randall didn't have an easy trip. He got what we needed—proof of a living Gershwin. So once the Foundation gets things in order, they'll give your Dad the

421

green light." She smiled. "It's a few years past his specialty, but for some reason the Foundation won't let any other Ripper handle the job. Where on *earth* did they get such an idea?"

Rose looked as innocent as possible. "Beats me. When is he planning to go?"

Isis knew Rose didn't mean Nate's departure, but his target date. "It's still under discussion. If he goes later in the decade or in the seventies, there's a chance that there might be even more Gershwin to recover. On the other hand, Gershwin and your uncle aren't getting any younger. I think they'll pick 1964."

"Wow, that's so weird—Uncle David in his sixties."

"Hey, kid, nobody can stop the march of time." She took her daughter's hand. "You know, he might even be dead. Doctors didn't know so much then."

Rose gulped. "I know. I can even accept it, since he's been gone so long already. But forgive me if I hang on to my private notion of David Greenbaum, attending musical theatre forever."

"Cling away, sweetie," said Isis. "Now I know you're busy with rehearsals for *In the Bar of a Tokyo Hotel*, but if you have a chance, could you study 1964 musicals for your dad?"

"Of course."

That night, Rose started taking notes. It was the end of Broadway's Golden Age, with *Hello, Dolly!*, *Funny Girl,* and *Fiddler on the Roof* commanding record runs. Fascinating flops, too, like Sondheim's *Anyone Can Whistle:* only nine performances, but preserved in the hearts of musical buffs.

She didn't just study the shows; as the daughter of a Ripper, she knew to look at the larger picture. What else was happening on the Rialto? She was halfway through an article on how theatre attendance was affected by students burning their draft cards in Times Square when a comment caught her eye—something about the "untimely death of Marc Blitzstein earlier this year."

Thanks to David, Rose knew more musical theatre history than most of her Juilliard classmates. But she didn't know how Blitzstein died. A few clicks later, she had her answer.

Gershwin had a brain tumor. This is child's play in comparison! And Uncle David was interested enough in Blitzstein to attend The Cradle Will Rock. *I bet they knew each other.*

She clicked over to her phone. "Hey, Dad..."

#

From the diary of J.D. Taylor, January 19, 1956
We lost Kurt last week to one more coronary. He never really got over the last one. I felt uncomfortable at the service— would Lenya blame me for not having more drugs? But she was sweet to me. "We had what we had," she said with Teutonic fatalism. "I wish there were more of your Mexican pills, so I might still have my Kurt. But at least you had *some!*" She dabbed her eyes. "I also wish he had finished the Molière. It must bother him, knowing it is undone."

I squeezed her hands. "Lenya, not now, not here."

"I will call you." *She sounds... determined.*

Just because I "finished" Kiss Me, Kate *does not mean I'm the go-to guy for completing unwritten musicals! I'm producing Weill's comedy, but Leo and I are swamped with our show. Tryouts in New Haven in March. One thing at a time...*

#

All Broadway is celebrating the biggest hit in years, Lerner and Loewe's *My Fair Lady,* about as perfect a musical as could be. I can't praise it enough. I don't need to. It will run for 2,717 performances.

On Our Shores, with songs by Leonard Spinelli and book and direction by J.D. Taylor, opened last night...and will probably close in a few months. If *MFL* is the apotheosis of the classic book musical, *Shores* breaks nearly every rule in the book. Leo wanted what the servicemen went through "front and center," so we abandoned fourth-wall literalism. The characters get in the audience's faces, uncomfortably so. We don't even have a true linear narrative. It's not quite *Company,* where Sondheim, Prince, and Furth toss that entirely, but we used Eddie Stowbridge, our mentally ill Marine, as a linking theme, weaving his unsettling way through the other characters' lives. Yes, there's even a little Joe Gould in him. "Red Sky At Morning" fit beautifully, its grim final verse restored, as Eddie—the brilliant young Jerry Orbach—eats his gun.

Potent material in any era, but it doesn't match the general attitude of mid-fifties America, when most musicals—though not all—were lighthearted fun. Tired businessmen expecting an evening of escapism won't get it here. Leo quipped to one reporter, "If they're looking for gorgeous gams, they're at the wrong theatre. Hey, some of our chorus members don't even have legs!" But it's the show we wanted to do.

Leo, Jeanette, and I paced the back of the Winter Garden through the first act. The house was still, so still...except when patrons scurried up the aisle, fleeing.

Jeannie gave them the evil eye. "You'd think they'd at least wait until intermission!" she hissed.

"Hey, babe," said Leo. "I am never, ever going to do a show that won't piss off some of the audience. That's what aisles are for."

Jeannie was right: more people left at intermission. But we had our supporters, both veterans and Broadway insiders. The lobby buzzed. Lots of folks told me they'd never seen anything like it before. The people whose opinions mattered most to us appreciated our efforts. "I've never been so uncomfortable watching a musical," Gershwin told me. "But I've never been so riveted, either. Either you two are geniuses or the biggest damn fools in New York."

"Depends on if I'm wearing my director's hat or my producer's hat," I said. "It's not exactly a commercial property."

"David Taylor, master of understatement," George said, laughter crinkling his dark eyes. "This makes my latest project look silly in comparison." George, Ira, and Dorothy and Herbert Fields were adapting *It Happened One Night.* I feel funny every time I hear about it, remembering that moment when I first arrived in this world and that truck driver mentioned Claudette Colbert—and I blanked on her name.

But for once, Gershwin was wrong. "Bullshit, George! We need good musical comedies and musical dramas. And while I love your serious work, nobody writes better comic lyrics than your brother." That pleased him. He smoothed his mustache, almost preening. He'd grown it two years ago, but I'm still not used to it.

The second act barreled relentlessly to the finale. Stowbridge killed himself at the top of a jagged, black and gray abstract construct Jo Mielziner designed. I get shivers just walking past it on stage; it looks ready to devour you.

The audience gasped. Somebody shouted, "No!" Then Leo's gorgeous music, muted at first, began to build. Stowbridge isn't the only story here. The other vets, damaged though they are, reassure the audience that they—and their families—will find ways to go on. For the most part, the house cheered at the curtain.

But not all. In the lobby, an angry woman approached me. "Mr. Taylor, I am deeply offended by what I just saw! A suicide, on stage! Disgraceful!"

"Did you see *Death of a Salesman*? Or *Romeo and Juliet*? How is this any different?"

She wagged a finger in my face. "It's a *musical*!"

I pointed to the tall figure of Oscar Hammerstein. "I guess *Carousel* didn't work for you, either. Please see Mrs. Prouty at the front office for a refund, ma'am."

Oscar Levant flipped her the bird. "Taylor, if a show makes everybody happy, then it's *nothing*. It has to have a point-of-view. By God, this show's got one—even if it sticks in old biddies' craws."

The right-wing press said we were unAmerican—fuck them. The theatre critics either loved us or hated us. Walter Kerr's tin ear didn't appreciate Leo's score, but he praised our leads—Orbach, Jack Cassidy as a blind G.I., and Joel Grey, who spends half the first act with his left leg wrapped behind his thigh: "There is little to smile about in Spinelli and Taylor's *On Our Shores*, but the infectious joy Grey displays when he dances after being fitted with his artificial leg fills the Winter Garden. Unfortunately, the good feeling doesn't last." *Idiot.*

Brooks Atkinson surprised me with a rave. But, as a veteran of the first war and a correspondent in the second, he got it. "The American musical has officially come of age. J.D. Taylor's productions have long stood out for unorthodox subject matter and daring stagecraft. In *On*

426

Our Shore, his fourth show in collaboration with young songwriter Leonard Spinelli, he takes the form to another level. No mere entertainment, it is an uncompromising comment on the human condition, a reflection of harsh realities. As such, it is not always easy to accept. But it lingers in one's mind far longer than more casual, comfortable fare."

Atkinson is right. This is liable to be a show Broadway insiders cherish long after it closes—a cult show. A later generation may rediscover it, when cultural attitudes can appreciate its content better.

Off to our usual "day after" meeting, to start planning our next one.

#

From the diary of J.D. Taylor, April 21, 1957

Back from the Tony Awards, empty-handed. *My Fair Lady* clobbered everybody. *On Our Shores*, which eked out ninety-nine performances, got three nominations: Best Actor for Orbach, Best Supporting for Grey, and Best Director for yours truly. Not even a Best Musical nod, though *Shores* ran longer than *Candide*, which snagged one. Can't complain about Leo getting snubbed, as there's no Tony for score yet. I'm not disappointed; this is a great show in a wrong era.

I'm keeping busy. While Leo, Jeannie, and the kids are in L.A., supervising the film version of *The Ghost and Mrs. Muir*, I'm finishing the libretto for our next show. It's inspired by the great American acting families of the mid-nineteenth century—the Jeffersons, the Warrens, the Booths. Our family's fictional, but we're pulling things from history. Nate would be proud of my research. We're shooting for an opening in early December.

427

It's an exciting time on Broadway, with more experimental shows (like ours!), more expansive use of music and especially dance. I'm backing two upcoming musicals that will become classics: *West Side Story* and *The Music Man*. They'll help our finances. I also convinced Lenya to let Marc Blitzstein finish the last three songs on Weill's *The Doctor In Spite of Himself*. Not an ideal match—French farce isn't Blitzstein's forte. It's still limping along at the Music Box, despite Bert Lahr as the Doctor. Not Marc's fault, though. As they say, dying is easy, but comedy is hard. Maxwell Anderson's a talented playwright, but he's no Molière.

But I want to keep an eye on Blitzstein. Seven years from now, he'll be the last part of my Broadway Revival Project.

#

From the diary of J.D. Taylor, August 28, 1957
Joe Gould, in and out of hospitals and institutions for the last five years, has finally gone to hit St. Peter for a contribution to the Joe Gould Fund. Even his best friends and the writer who did that *New Yorker* profile on him have no idea where his massive *Oral History of the World* is stashed. Whatever he scribbled about me in those black composition books will never see the light of day. I'm sorry for Professor Seagull's passing, but I'm relieved about the missing *History*. After almost twenty-five years here, I'm still hinky about people investigating my background.

Work on our acting-family saga, *The World's a Stage*, is going well. We'll be casting soon; I have a reputation for insanely long rehearsal times. It's worth it, especially when you're doing something complex. Not that the actors mind. Rehearsal pay is guaranteed. How long they get a paycheck after the opening depends on the damn audience.

One possible glitch is Jeanette Spinelli. She's expecting in early December, the week we open. Four-year-old Davey has asked for a brother. Little Elizabeth, just turned two, has no clue she's about to be dethroned as the baby of the family.

I still miss my nieces and nephew, but watching the Spinelli brood grow has been a joy.

#

January 13, 1964

Nate had been in his brother's Splinterverse for only five days, but each brought new discoveries. Even before the bus took him from sleepy Oakhurst (looking much as it had thirty years earlier) to Fresno, he glimpsed a movie marquee: NOW PLAYING! THE GERSHWINS' "IT HAPPENED ONE NIGHT!" At M and V's Music Store in Fresno, he pawed through piles of sheet music. He found Gershwin tunes not only from the shows mentioned by the clerk in Kee Randall's Dallas hotel, but many others. He bought them all, plus as many albums and vocal scores he could find. His Ripperglasses recorded the titles he didn't buy; he spent hours in his hotel room noting the ones unique to this world. Rose had prepped him, but he was a labor historian, not a musical expert. *Leonard Spinelli's* Disputed Passages— *that's new to me. But so is* Bravo Giovanni, *a forgettable flop that actually ran in my era. I've got to check every single title, no matter how long it takes! The Foundation will kill me if I came back with stuff we already have.*

That meant stopping at Cal Berkeley's library before heading for New York. He spent a day buried in the stacks. The post-1937 Gershwin output alone was staggering, but this Splinterverse was clearly packed with other musical anomalies. His strangled cry of surprise drew concerned looks from a pretty undergrad with her hair in a huge beehive. "You okay, sir?"

Nate swallowed hard. "Yeah, fine. Just came across something I didn't expect." *In my world, Lorenz Hart never wrote a show based on* The Canterbury Tales. *He only worked with Rodgers, but here he's teamed with this J.D. Taylor fellow and Vincent Youmans, too. And Youmans didn't adapt O'Neill's* Ah, Wilderness! *in 1941; Bob Merrill did, in 1959. But here, Merrill's 1959 show was called* Adam and Eve on a Raft, *a comedy set in a diner, with young Bobby Morse as a lovelorn busboy. And there are at least five shows by this Leonard Spinelli, who never got to Broadway in my era.*

The more Nate studied, the weirder things got. Shows opening at different theatres. Slightly different cast lists. Larry Hart dying in 1949 of cancer, not from pneumonia in 1943; Youmans dying from a Nazi buzz bomb, not tuberculosis. A prickle ran up his spine. *It's possible David was behind all this. Which makes Rose's idea quite plausible.*

It was getting late. Nate gathered as much data with his Ripperglasses as he could before the library closed. He grabbed a stack of theatre books and began flipping hundreds of pages, working like an automaton. *I won't get much sleep tonight.*

A copy of *Theatre World*, covering the 1962 season, brought him up short. Among the photos from familiar shows like *How to Succeed* and *Carnival*, was one of "Leonard Spinelli, J.D. Taylor and stars Ronnie and Glenn Walken of *Gemini*."

Spinelli—forty, short, dark, with an eye patch. The Walkens—fresh-faced, eager brothers. J.D. Taylor—black-rimmed glasses, thick beard (shot with silver), towering over the others. David Greenbaum had been thirty-two the last time Nate saw him. J.D. Taylor was in his early sixties, but he was the same man.

Chapter 17

"Where or When?" —Lorenz Hart

From the diary of J.D. Taylor, January 13, 1964
"**Y**ou're taking a vacation? *You?*" Leo said through the pencil clenched in his teeth. Jeannie's been trying to get him to break that habit, but he's done that since he was a kid.

"Don't sound so shocked," I said. "I've always wanted to visit the Caribbean."

This world doesn't say "multi-tasking" yet, but it fits Leo. He removed the pencil, scribbled a line, and turned his single brown eye on me. "You haven't taken a vacation since I was a boy. You brought me Mexican jumping beans. My pals were jealous."

"Don't I deserve a vacation every twenty years?"

He kicked Lizzie's Chatty Cathy aside and stretched out his feet. "Sure, boss man. I'm just surprised. You hardly ever leave Manhattan." White teeth flashed in a grin. "Unlike me!"

Leo, for whom a childhood trip to his Jersey cousins had been an event, loved traveling with his family. Not as far as the globe-trotting Gershwins, but they've met their Sicilian and Scottish relatives, built sand castles in Honolulu, and gone down the Grand Canyon. The

European jaunt, though, was a working vacation: Leo supervised the London production of *The World's a Stage* in 1961. The Brits have their own tradition of actor-clans; I assumed they'd sneer at our provincial troupers, but they loved it.

But he's right. I don't take vacations. I saw enough of the world with Ramon. I'm happy here, seeing shows. But I can't tell Leo: "Sorry, but I'm seeing Eartha Kitt in *Shinbone Alley*, since it's only gonna run two months." Besides, the off-Broadway choices have been especially interesting, with shows that never existed in my timeline— daring offerings, based on unusual subjects. I suspect I've had some influence there.

We mounted *Eclipse* back in 1959, at the Gate Theatre on Second Avenue—a hit, to my surprise and Leo's delight. Two decidedly dark shows opened the following year; one a blatant copy of ours, the other an intriguing, through-sung adaptation of Mary Shelley's *Frankenstein*, filtered through Cold War worries about technology run wild. A critical success that wouldn't have found backers without the example of *Eclipse*. I looked up *Frankenstein*'s creators on my Ally. Couldn't find him; looks as if she taught at a small southern college, but no theatrical credits for either. This fall, another newcomer is planning a musical *Desire Under the Elms*. I'm having more unintended consequences in this world.

But if my presence here changed the fortunes of those writers, I also may have altered circumstances enough to turn the final step of the Broadway Revival Project into a wild goose chase. Which could be good or bad, depending.

My last target is Marc Blitzstein. Aside from backing *The Threepenny Opera* in 1953, I've had little to do with him. My time-traveling here hasn't changed his track record—interesting, original shows that all failed—but this Broadway is a different place, thanks to J.D. Taylor.

So that had me wondering: would Blitzstein's movements in the last months of his life be different? I've been keeping an eye on him, asking his friends (Lenny Bernstein, for one) about his plans. Their answers match my research: he's writing an opera based on Sacco and Vanzetti and a musical adapted from Bernard Malamud's stories. As in my timeline, he's using some grant money to rent a villa on Martinique through the winter. In my world, he died there. Of course, he may not do the *exact* same things that led to his death, but I'll try to make sure he doesn't die. If nothing happens, I'll have a Caribbean vacation.

"I figure I can take a few weeks off without disrupting our schedule for *Selkie*," I said, sipping my tea. Our latest show's kind of an anti-*Brigadoon*, adapting Scottish tales from Jeannie's mum. Damn, those Scots have some freaky legends. "I'm leaving after the *Dolly!* premiere."

"Yeah, the new Thornton Wilder musical. Think it will do better than our *Skin of Our Teeth?* Herman's a nice kid, but I didn't like his first score."

I tried not to snarf my tea. "Oh, it will run. I guarantee it." *Over twenty-eight hundred performances.*

Leo had begun gnawing his pencil again, half his mind on me, half on his lyrics. "Huh, the famous Taylor guarantee, backed up by the famous Taylor money. Well, have a great time, David. Send the kids some postcards."

#

From the diary of J.D. Taylor, January 19, 1964
I should rethink vacations. Snow covers Manhattan, but here in Fort-de-France, Martinique, I'm in shorts. Vines cover the iron grill balconies of my rental home, with purple

and blue hummingbirds buzzing about the blossoms. A mulatto granny named Anita fixes wonderful dinners—usually octopus or mackerel, smothered in spicy tomato sauce. In her striped dress and knotted kerchief, she's a walking rainbow. She even sings. I'd cast her in *Once On This Island*—if only it were written! My French is lousy, but between my Spanish and her bits of English we manage. Her grandson, Henri, keeps my place stocked with fresh fruit (bananas, pineapples, mangoes), and I get bread at the bakery. The coffee's good, too. That's important, since I have some late nights ahead.

I've rented a gray 1955 Citroën 2CV—I took driving lessons last year, to refresh my memory and learn a stick shift. I've made other preparations, too. I haven't played a role since the adventure of Jerome Kern's piano, but, as I did then, I've shaved my beard and ditched my glasses. Running into Blitzstein isn't a concern—I know his daily schedule—but I don't want to be recognizable from the street. After so long, it's eerie seeing David Greenbaum—an older, weathered David Greenbaum—in the mirror. I've been J.D. Taylor almost as long as I lived under my real name. Weird.

I'm too tall to pass for a Martinican, even if I hid under a cone-shaped straw hat. I'm not Gallic enough to impersonate one of the *metros* from France who dominate the government here. So I'm just another American tourist. Fortunately, Taylor's a common name. Today I wandered the dockside, sampling *planteurs* at bars, peeking into side streets and alleys. My clothes and camera give me an armor of status—at least in the daylight. The locals fall over themselves, hoping for tips. No wonder Marc wrote his mother about the inequities between classes and races here.

Of course, he's living pretty well himself. His villa, near Le François on the eastern side of the island, has a lovely ocean view. I've also scouted the road between his place and the capital. Blitzstein takes those fourteen miles like a bat out of hell. I've seen his black Peugeot zoom past. When he died, the first reports said it was an auto accident. Far from the truth, but people believed it. It's what Marc *wanted* them to believe.

I'm writing this by flashlight. My Citroën's parked off the street, shielded by an abandoned *carbet*, a small straw shelter, just outside Fort-de-France. There's only one road from Le François; if Blitzstein drives into the capital, he has to come this way. He'll be easy to spot. During the day, workers stream in from the countryside, but Fort-de-France is deserted at night. The only ones on the streets after seeking late-night pleasures ... or mayhem.

While I wait for a confrontation that may or may not happen, I'm researching *Zorro* for Gershwin. He got the idea from his son, Sammy, who liked the television series. George wants to use some of the music from our long-ago trip that didn't make it into his "Aztec Ballet."

Gershwin's continued work is one of my greatest pleasures, and that includes the next generation. Eldest son Morey isn't eager to take up the family calling; he's a crack shortstop with dreams of playing for the Yankees. Ruth, however, has her father's sense of rhythm and her uncle's gift for language. She's looking forward to college, even if Morey isn't. (I'm urging George and Sylvia to *make* Morey go; I don't want him in Vietnam.) Thirteen-year-old Sammy is a fine artist, like George. I'm not as close to them as I am with the Spinellis and Finkelsteins, but I'm excited for their futures. I'm excited they *have* futures. I did a few things right, anyhow.

Back to watching the dark road and reading pulp tales of old Mexico.

#

January 17, 1964

Nathan Greenbaum was tired. He'd spent days digging through books, working out how his brother had affected this Splinterverse. No wonder the readings were different every time the techs checked. From April 1934 on, changes came fast and furious. Now, with the address of Taylor Productions in hand, he hoped to see the man himself. *Unless, as Rose suspects, he's off on another mission.*

He was striding down 45th Street when a harsh voice called out, "Hey, David! What happened to the fuzz? You look years younger, you *alter kacker*. Oh, my mistake. You look like a *doppelganger* of a friend." A short, troll-like man grimaced. "Sorry."

Nate managed a weak smile. "That wouldn't be J.D. Taylor, would it? I'm his cousin, here for a visit." *I think that's Oscar Levant, but he looks ghastly.*

The man lit a cigarette with shaking hands. "Tough luck, pal. He's vacationing in tropical Martinique. God, *I* gotta get back to L.A." He glared at the cloudy skies through enormous dark eyes.

He's high. "With luck, I'll see him before I head home."

"Heh. Take a number. Between Gershwin and Spinelli, your cuz is in demand." With a curt nod, he continued on his way.

Martinique! You're right again, Rosie! Nate reversed course, heading back to the Ritz for his suitcase and passport. *I could sit tight and wait for him to get back, but I want this too much.*

#

From the diary of J.D. Taylor, January 20, 1964
No sign of Blitzstein last night or tonight. Anita teases me about sleeping all day. Tomorrow night's the critical one, if things go the way they did in my world.

#

January 20, 1964
Right after talking to Levant, Nate booked a flight to Puerto Rico, with a puddle-jumper to Martinique the next morning. *My brother's after Marc Blitzstein. Find Blitzstein, find David.*

He'd done his homework. He knew where Blitzstein was staying, knew his routine. At half past eleven, the composer took a swim. From the shade of a pear tree, Nate gazed down at the turquoise water: a skinny man in black trunks was spreading a towel on his private dock. *He looks older than fifty-eight, nothing like the youngster who played the piano at* The Cradle Will Rock.

While Blitzstein sunbathed, Nate planted a tracer inside the wheelwell of his car. A special Ripper device, it was good for only a few days. Then it would fall off and an acid ring would fuse its innards to a useless glob. Until it did, Nate could trace Blitzstein's movements on the tiny island.

He drove back to the capital to survey the dockside—the bars, the alleyways, the Place de Stalingrad—once Pont Démosthène, but recently renamed by the city's Communist mayor. As he cased the run-down plaza, he wondered if he'd see his brother doing the same. *We both know how to do research.*

437

No sign of David, but he chatted with local dockworkers about their jobs and their unions. *Maybe I'll get a monograph out of this. Now for a nap. Could be a late night.*

#

From the diary of J.D. Taylor, January 21, 1964
I'm awash. Coffee keeps me awake, but I'm always afraid I'll miss Marc's car when I get up to pee. Though it's nice to stretch my legs. Citroëns aren't built for guys my size.

Back to *Zorro*.

11:45 PM—Marc's car!

#

January 21, 1964
Full of lobster salad, Nate waited in his room. About eleven-thirty, the tracer pinged. Nate slipped on his coat, headed for his car. He parked next to a shuttered shoe store, while the tracer's tingle increased. Nate wasn't sure which bar Blitzstein would choose, but he had an idea. Three likely dives were right across the street.

Blitzstein's Peugeot soon screeched to a halt in front of the first bar. Fort-de-France didn't have much night traffic, but two vehicles followed the composer. The first, a red pickup with chickens in the bed, pulled up beside Blitzstein. The driver shouted French curses before roaring off. Another car, a gray Citroën, parked half a block behind the Peugeot. Its lights shut off, and the darkness enveloped it. The truck kept Nate from seeing its driver leave; when a short black man walked into one of the bars, he took him for the Citroën's driver.

His focus was on Blitzstein, who hurried through the open door of the first bar. As he entered, he called out,

"Un ti'punch, s'il vous plaît!" Nate could not hear if the bartender responded in the traditional Martinican fashion: *"Chacun prepáre sa propre mort."* Each prepares his own death. It meant the bar had the fixings for making *ti'punch,* the national drink—rum, cane syrup, and lime— to personal taste.

Nate shivered. *I'm glad I didn't hear that phrase, not tonight.*

Blitzstein would drink there for another two to three hours. Nate shifted his seat and popped a caffeine pill. Tree frogs peeped. *Are you out there, David?*

It was nearly three when Blitzstein and a lithe young Martinican stumbled out of the doorway. The teenager, his white dungarees picking up the light from the window, gestured. Blitzstein nodded; the pair disappeared into the alley separating the bar from its neighbor, one Nate had checked out before.

This isn't the same world as mine. Maybe nothing will happen, and I'll find David in Manhattan... oh, shit.

Two swarthy seamen banged out through the bar's door—older and tougher looking than the youth. Laughing nastily, they too vanished around the corner.

David or no David, I can't let this happen. The three men would rob and beat Blitzstein, leaving him half-naked. He would die of a ruptured liver. Rippers had strict rules about intervening in events, no matter how horrific. Nate had seen many deaths in past eras, from brutal attacks in labor strikes to Dillinger's gory end.

But this was a Splinterverse. His own brother had changed this timeline again and again, from curing Gershwin onwards. *Hell, what's one more saved composer?*

As Nate reached for the door handle, a man pelted down the street from the opposite direction, long legs chewing up the distance to the alley. Nate's breath caught. *Damn! He looks like Dad!*

Nate got out of his car, listening for noises in the alley—low, angry voices, but nothing more. *If things do get dicey, let's see how these bastards like tag-team Greenbaum. Assuming David doesn't drop dead seeing me.*

Then two figures emerged into the hazy streetlight—David, supporting a wobbly Blitzstein (clutching his undone trousers), heading for that Citroën. Nate quickly hid in the shoe store's doorway, feeling a wave of relief.

David and Blitzstein never made it to the car. As Nate watched, a chunk of rock flew out of nowhere, hitting his brother in the side of the face. Blitzstein shrieked as David collapsed. The three toughs popped out of the next alleyway, ready to finish their assault.

But they hadn't counted on Nate, whose Ripper program required regular self-defense lessons. Despite his pudge, he was a third degree black belt in *hapkido* who worked out every week.

He charged down the street, shouting for help. The first seaman was savagely kicking David's prone body, but Nate's own double-kick combo flattened him. The teenager spat at Nate and swung a haymaker. His eyes widened in shock as Nate blocked it, caught him in a wristlock, then threw him on top of the first man. The third, who had been shaking down Blitzstein, decided to run as the locals streamed out of the bars. They might well have sided with the seamen—Martinique was *not* a gay-friendly island—but they realized that the angry, rich American standing over the fallen was in charge. Suddenly outnumbered, the thugs weren't getting up until the cops arrived.

David wasn't, either. The rock had sliced the cheek open, but that mess was the least of it: the impact had shattered the jaw. He gurgled horribly. Nate gently opened his brother's mouth, extracting two teeth, keeping the unsupported tongue from blocking his airway. *So much blood!* A bartender appeared with wet rags and ice to help Nate. "The ambulance comes, monsieur," he said, a cool veteran of many brawls.

Blitzstein, however, was gibbering, staring at the brothers. "I don't understand." He was visibly shaken: drunk, assaulted twice, and puzzling how a fellow Broadwayite—with a near-twin—materialized to rescue him.

Nate wasn't in the mood to be kind. "Mr. Blitzstein, it's simple. My, uh, cousin and I just saved your miserable hide. There's the ambulance. I'm taking him to the hospital. The name's Nathan Newton. Hotel Saint Germaine."

The medics quickly got David on a stretcher and took off for Clarac Hospital—the one where Blitzstein died. As the sirens blared, Nate gazed down at his little brother, now older than he was, with silver threads in the wavy brown hair. *I've imagined this reunion thousands of times, but never like this.*

David's hazel eyes suddenly fluttered open, revealing uneven pupils. He flinched as the medic cleaned gravel from the wound. Then he recognized Nathan. Terror overcame pain; he looked like he wanted to bolt, IV and all.

Oh, God, David. It's not like that. Maybe for an instant, an eternity away, I wanted you dead for what you did. But no. You're my kid brother. You just saved another man's life tonight. You damn well better not die! Nate swallowed. "Hey, it's all right. You're going to be fine. I guarantee it."

#

January 22, 1964
While David was in surgery, Nate talked with Blitzstein to get their stories straight. The composer still couldn't work

out what happened, but, desperate to keep his reputation intact, he agreed to whatever Nathan said. The short version: the "newly reunited cousins" broke up a late-night mugging. No mention of sex.

The wire services picked up the story: PRODUCER-DIRECTOR J.D. TAYLOR ASSAULTED IN MARTINIQUE. Blitzstein, with his recent flops and HUAC investigation, rated just a line or two. Nate knew his brother had become a Broadway big wig. Reality was another matter. Phone calls overwhelmed the hospital and the American consulate. Reporters gathered in the lobby and cafeteria. Nate sat by his sleeping brother's bedside, watching the stack of telegrams on the nightstand grow. *The Gershwins, Joshua Logan, Gwen Verdon, Richard Burton, Jerry Orbach, Richard Rodgers. Damn!*

A noise distracted him. David's jaw was wired shut, the left eye swollen to a slit, but he was awake. His right eye focused on Nate, disbelieving.

"You're not hallucinating," Nate said. "Rose figured out your plan. Calm down, you idiot. It's okay."

David grunted, then mimed writing. Nathan handed him a pad and pencil. His brother scrawled *Marc* in wobbly letters.

"He's fine. I clobbered two of the punks."

David took in the bloodstains on Nate's shirt. He scribbled *Thanks.*

"If I didn't let Lewis Sidhow beat you up in sixth grade, would I watch while you're kicked to death?" Nate described the cover story he'd concocted with Blitzstein. "You need to get back to New York. These doctors—*oy!* Speaking of fans, you've got plenty. Anyone special I should contact for you?" *Have you found someone to share this other life?*

Adam Finkelstein, office mgr. Writing even four words was taxing.

Nate nodded. "I'll call him." *Professional, not personal. Huh.*

A nurse came to take David's vitals. She gave him a sip of water and admonished him in French.

"She wants you to rest," Nate translated. "I'm going to change and shower, but I'll be back." He rose to leave, but David clutched at his arm with a strength beyond his battered condition.

David wrote: *Kids? Isis?*

"All good. Rose is doing Tennessee Williams in Brooklyn."

Year?

"2084. Details later. Sleep."

The hazel eye closed, but not before a tear trickled down onto the white pillowcase. *That's got to hurt in a different way. Thirty years here, six back home.*

Back at the hotel, Nathan called Taylor Productions. Finkelstein sounded distraught over David and relieved (though surprised) that Nate was there. "Of course, Leo's already on his way," said Finkelstein.

"Who?"

"Leonard Spinelli. Gee, doesn't everyone know 'Taylor and Spinelli?'"

I'm sleep-deprived and saw my brother nearly murdered. "Uh, of course. I'm a little slow today."

"That's all right, Mr. Newton. Anything else we can do here?"

Nate explained his desire to get David back to New York. Finkelstein said "Mabel" would arrange funds for airfare and medical care. *Good. I'd need time to raise that much money.*

Two hours later—changed, clean, and fed—he returned to the hospital. David was still asleep. Nate was reading the newspaper when a nurse beckoned him to the desk.

"*Monsieur* Newton, a man is on the lobby telephone. He says he is Taylor's partner and *must* see him. He sounds quite mad, I fear. Could you talk to him?" She handed Nate the phone.

"This is Nathan Newton."

"Who the *fuck* are you, pal? Where'd you come from? I've known David Taylor since I was a kid; all his relatives are *dead*. Cousin, my ass!" The rage in his voice was enough to melt the wires.

Mr. Spinelli, I presume? "We're not all dead," Nate said mildly. "David's sleeping now, but I'll come down to meet you."

"Yeah? I'll be here. I'm not leaving until I see David!"

Nate hung up and trotted down the stairs. A short, dark-haired man in a travel-rumpled suit stood ten feet away, his back to him, his fists clenched. He whirled about at Nate's approach, angry enough to take a swing, then did a double-take. "Who the fuck are you?" he repeated, this time in a whisper.

"I'm Nate. You're Leo, I guess." *A one-eyed Italian in his early forties. Yup. I've seen your photos.*

The songwriter shook his head, as if bedeviled by bugs. "I figured you were a con man. But you could be his brother. Hell, you're the spitting image of this old photo he has— only that guy would be in his eighties, I guess. Crazy. Sorry if I sounded upset." His voice wavered. "It's just... he's been like a father to me. *More* than my own father. I don't know what I would have been without him—a janitor, probably. But he was in theatre, so I wound up on Broadway. A scrawny, no-account dago." He trumpeted into his hanky.

Little brother, you've been busy. "Let's go upstairs. He looks like hell, but he'll live."

When they looked into the room, David was awake. The unbandaged side of his face quirked upwards in a smile. "Hi, guys," he said. He couldn't move his jaw, but his training let the words come through the clenched teeth. *He was a decent ventriloquist, back in high school.*

"Hey, boss man," Leo said, "just 'cause the Japs mangled my mug doesn't mean you have to copy me. The kids made you get-well cards…" He faltered, laid his head on David's shoulder, and wept.

#

From the diary of J.D. Taylor, February 7, 1964
My first entry since the attack. I can keep this notepad with me until I'm discharged tomorrow. I'm lucky many times over to be alive: that the seaman decided to kick me instead shooting me with my own gun; that Nate thrashed the punks and saved me from choking to death; that he dosed me with Minarcin when I got a post-op infection. I was pretty feverish, but I remember Nate sending Leo on an errand, then producing a vial. He smashed the yellow pills to powder and put them in water, since I'm on a liquids-only diet.

"Haven't seen those since I gave some to Vince Youmans," I croaked. I must have been delirious; I never said *anything* about the Project aloud.

Nate just rolled his eyes. *"Such* a troublemaker."

Minarcin's good stuff. Five days later, Marc, Leo, and Nate had me transported to Mount Sinai in Manhattan, where I had a second surgery. My beard's coming back in; not sure if it will cover the scars. Ramon loved tracing his finger along my jawline. I suspect it will end up bumpy. When the choice is "alive, but dinged" or "pushing up daisies," bumpy is fine.

With Leo here all the time, I've had little chance to talk with Nate, but his reaction to my visitors has been priceless.

When George Gershwin walked in after Alfred Drake, I thought *he* needed a sedative, not me. "It's like Sardi's come to life," he said.

"We're in Sardi's," Leo said, grinning. "Upstairs and to the right."

Nate gulped. "Aw, ya-whoo, as my son says. I'll, uh, have to see that."

It wasn't just the stream of celebrities that impressed Nate. He blinked when George mentioned Sylvia and the kids, realizing this world had Gershwins our world didn't. Leo's enormous clan, however, really got to him. When all six clambered onto my hospital bed and Nicky pointed at my face and said, "Owie?"—the old softy teared up. Then I introduced them in reverse order, ending with, "My godson, Davey." Nate's expression was a blend of surprise, respect, affection, sadness. Whatever he expected me to do in this world, having a surrogate family wasn't part of it.

Obviously, I've committed more crimes against the timeline than just affecting musical theatre. Trouble is, I *still* don't know what my big brother the Ripper intends to do about it, once I'm out of the hospital.

#

February 8, 1964
Nate suspected Taylor Productions' musicals had nothing on their latest production, *Getting the Boss Home.* The Finkelsteins' daughter, Sadie, minded the Spinelli children with her own toddler, while the elders settled the patient in his modest Village apartment—very like his twenty-first century place. *I walked past the Seville Studios twice, looking for David in the thirties. So like him to stay here instead of getting classier digs.* Nate found Leo's Scottish wife Jeannie warm and witty, while Mabel Finkelstein reminded him of

Isis, capably handling a swarm of details. Frannie Spinelli had stocked the kitchen with casseroles for Nate and soups for David. He'd eat through a straw for another month.

Though David's friends were delightful, Nate couldn't wait for them to leave. His brother looked anxious when the gang finally said farewell. He sat on the couch, his face still discolored, his long fingers tapping rhythms on its arm. "So?" he said through his teeth. "What happens now?"

"You mean, do I drag you back home? Even the way you are, I suspect you'd give me some trouble between here and that rock pile in Yosemite. You dope, I'm not here to bring you to justice, though a few years ago that's what I wanted most."

David sank deeper into the cushions. "You did come after me, didn't you? I saw you at *The Cradle Will Rock*, and a friend spotted you hanging around the Alvin during *Anything Goes*."

Nate was fixing himself a drink. He paused while measuring the gin. "Shit. You saw me at *Cradle?* I missed you, but Rose picked out your dulcet tones on the recording I made. You were with the light guy, right?"

"Clever Rose. Yes." David shifted his seat, leaned forward with that inner intensity that Nate remembered, even if the exterior was older—and battered. "But if you're not here to take me back, why are you? Not that I'm complaining. You saved my sorry ass."

"Well, Ramon always approved of it." Nate raised his glass in a mock toast.

"Heh. It's old and saggy, like the rest of me. Answer the question."

Nate sat in a comfy chintz chair opposite his brother. "First, I have to explain about Splinterverses..."

#

447

Nate's technical details went way over my head. I gather Splinterverses happen when something affects a timeline. "See, the French meddled on June 28, 1914, to create their Splinterverse," he said. When I stared blankly, he gave me that Nate-glare. "The assassination of Franz Ferdinand, the first World War. You came here to save composers, and made this world veer off-track in mid-April 1934. Those changes just kept on coming. They're _still_ coming, these weird fluctuations in the coordinates. I have a theory about that."

I frowned—which hurts my cheek worse than smiling. "But I didn't meet Gershwin until the twenty-seventh; I remember, 'cause that's Isis's birthday. I'd just moved here, met my neighbors, started teaching Leo piano..." I looked at my brother, who looked infernally smug.

"You didn't make the rift with Youmans or Gershwin; you made it with Spinelli. But everything you've done since then—saving lives and creating musicals—has caused those fluctuations. But Leo was the big break—maybe even more significant than the others." He got out his Ally—_ooh, 2084 tech!_—and showed me incomprehensible squiggles, then overlaid a chronology of musical theatre openings on the chart. They kind of overlapped. Nate was excited, but my head throbbed. _Splinterverse theory be damned._

"I've known for years I changed Leo's life as well as Broadway history. If you're not dragging me back in chains, then _what's going on?_"

Nate dragged his eyes away from the screen. "Sorry, I only confirmed this last night; the tech crowd will go zak-bak with excitement, as Bertie says. Why am I here? To find out _exactly_ what you've done to musicals. Everything that's different from our era."

"The techies want musicals? Which of us lives in a Splinterverse again?"

Nate drained his glass, smacked his lips. "Not them, idjit. The Save Our Standards Foundation funded this trip, a scheme your brilliant niece concocted. I'm here for unheard Gershwin and whatever else there is."

I did *not* expect that answer. I felt woozy beyond my pain pills. "You're bringing the music of this… Splinterverse back home?"

"That's right. I've spent days in the library trying to make a list. With your help, I'll know just what to look for in the music stores."

Oh, my God. A second world will hear those songs. Rose will hear those songs!

My eyes began welling up, so I pointed at my bookcases. "That's the most wonderful thing I've ever heard. Everything's there—my Broadway Revival Project. Scores, libretti, records, sheet music. From Youmans' 1935 'Caribbean Concerto" to Gershwin's *Around the World in Eighty Days* to Spinelli's *Isabelle*. I've got bootlegs on my Ally, too. My shows and other stuff."

"You still have a working Ally, after thirty years?"

"I had two; one died. I hardly ever use it, except to record maybe a dozen shows a year."

Nate wasn't listening, didn't notice me quietly sniffling. He was pulling out everything off the shelves, like a kid opening presents. "God. It's all here. Unbelievable."

#

February 8, 1964
Nate knelt by the crowded cases. The Gershwin alone was amazing, but seeing sheet music and cast albums with his brother's pseudonym—producer, director, librettist, songwriter—staggered him. "Look at all these shows! Man, what was it like collaborating with Larry Hart?"

449

David winced with a pain his wounds didn't cause. "Wonderful. Terrible. I kept him alive six years longer, but it was Ramon all over again." At Nathan's incredulous look, David nodded. "We were more than collaborators. I started trying to save him from himself and we ended up a pair—as much a pair as two gay men could be in the forties. We broke up because I was stupid and only got back together at his deathbed."

"David, I'm so sorry. There's been no one else? The Rippers have their own concerns, but the Greenbaums want to know if you've been happy."

A shrug. "A couple of flings. After spice like Ramon and Larry, most guys seem like unsalted oatmeal. Besides, I've got this deep, dark secret; it was part of the bust-up with Larry. So I'm unlikely to get close to anyone again.

"But am I happy? Hell, yes! I'm on fucking Broadway, in a bigger way than I ever would have been in my timeline. I've worked with geniuses, I've let them create works fate didn't. And I'm even Uncle Davey again."

"I noticed. You always were great with kids."

David tapped the couch beside him. "Speaking of kids, I demand to see yours. A real update, not the sketchy one you gave when Leo was around. Come here. Those LPs aren't going anywhere."

Nate stood up, an album in his hand. "A compromise. We'll listen to this while I catch you up." He walked over to the stereo and put Gershwin's *Lights of Lamy* on the turntable.

#

From the diary of J.D. Taylor, February 27, 1964
Over the next two weeks, Nate scanned everything (including my diary, with details of exactly *when* I

450

altered events), recorded the albums, and copied my bootlegs. In exchange, he put photos and vids of the family, as well as all the latest Broadway cast albums, on a mini my older Ally could read. I went through a ton of Kleenexes, seeing how much the kids had grown: Rose, a beauty getting her career started; quiet, serious Hannah, a biology major at Johns Hopkins ("Dean's list," said her proud papa); and high schooler Bertie, the most changed of all. "Good lord, puberty!" I said, feeling ancient.

"Good lord, our grocery bill," Nate said, passing his hand over his head.

I recorded messages for each of them. If Rose's ended up the longest, well, it just did.

The day before he left, we had lunch at Katz's, for old time's sake. Nate naturally ordered pastrami. I had a milkshake and soup. He was amused to learn the truth about Nine-fingered Mort. "A terrible musician. *Nana* had a a better sense of rhythm," I said.

"Ouch," said my brother. He bit into the sandwich and made happy noises. I was jealous. He waved it in front of me, teasing like we were kids again. I smacked him.

He laughed, but soon turned serious. "It's *so* good seeing you. Can't I talk you into coming back with me? Though you'd probably have to stand trial for something— the fucking bomb threat, if nothing else. God, I was mad at you."

"It seems ages ago," I said, twirling my straw. "I never could have done it without Rose. She killed that scene with your techs. I miss everyone, but especially her."

Nate put the sandwich down. "What's stopping you? You said your project ended with Blitzstein's rescue."

"If I could have got my hands on anti-lung cancer meds, I might have saved Frank Loesser a few years from now.

451

The Chinese wanted more money than I had. But yeah, Blitzstein's the last."

"So come home, bro. We'll work something out about those charges. Shit, everyone's going to be so thrilled with this music, they're as likely to give you a medal as a jail cell."

I looked deep into his hazel eyes, the ones that looked like Dad's, like mine. "Nate, I *am* home. I have a career. I've got a show going up this fall; *Fiddler on the Roof* will stomp it, but I love the work. Leo and I are an amazing team. I'm researching a project for George Gershwin, for God's sake!" I slurped my shake. "I miss you all more than I can say, but I've made a life here. If it's lonely on the personal side, it couldn't possibly be better professionally."

Nate put his hand on my arm. "I understand. I'm being selfish."

"Besides," I said with a smile, "who needs a medal when I might get a Tony? I haven't yet, but it's possible."

#

February 28, 1964

"Do you think I'll ever see you again?" David asked as Nathan packed his bags. "Any chance at all?"

"What was that lyric, in your show about the actors? 'I won't say never again, since never's a long, long time.' I'm hoping the prospect of more Gershwin will tempt the Foundation to open their wallet again."

"Well, tell them about *Zorro,* early 1966. Romance, warmth, humor, buckled swash. I've produced George and Ira lots of times, but this is the first time I'll have directed one of their shows since *Young Man With a Horn*. I'm really looking forward to it."

Nate snapped the locks on his suitcases. "That's got to be the understatement of the year."

"No, that was when Marc and I thanked you, back in Martinique. Because there's no way we could say that enough."

Nate smiled, crinkling the little scar by his mouth. "I would have saved him, even if you hadn't been there. See how you've corrupted an honest Ripper?"

David struck a dramatic pose. "I'm such a bad influence."

The taxi sounded to take Nate to the newly renamed JFK Airport. The brothers embraced. "I hope I'll be back in a few years," said Nate. "I want to see how many new shows you've done."

"Oh, there'll be some. I guarantee it."

They headed for the taxi. After stowing his bags, Nate said, "One last surprise. I added another folder to your, uh, files." *Not that the driver knows what we're talking about.* "You'll enjoy it."

"Safe journey, Nate. My love to all."

"Stay well, David."

#

From the diary of J.D. Taylor, February 28, 1964
It was hard to watch the cab drive away—too many tears in my eyes. But that was a trickle next to what followed. Rose had sent hours of footage of every show she'd been in, from her last high school production to her latest Williams drama. I settled on the couch with a Bronx (and

453

tissues!) and watched my niece tackle the complicated lead of *The Serene Ones.* Not many seventeen-year-olds could do justice to that role, but she did. I couldn't wait to see the rest, but I decided to ration them. I put the Ally back in its hidey-hole.

I've always regretted not seeing Rose honing her talents, but here's a glimpse of that. What's more, soon she'll have the chance to know what *I've* done here. Her whole world would.

Epilogue

"Our Time" —Stephen Sondheim

May 12, 2089

"**D**r. Greenbaum! How are you feeling tonight?" Reporters, paparazzi and net-loggers don't usually target academics, not at red carpet events. But the opening night of *Young Man with a Horn* wouldn't have been possible without Nathan Greenbaum's tracking down his brother in the altered past and bringing back music that never existed in this world. A story so thrilling, there were plans for a movie. Bertie thought that was hilarious and Rose embarrassing.

"We're fine," said Nate. "Very excited."

"Any word on Germany's Mozart project?"

"I know what you know: they've created a Splinterverse where he doesn't die at thirty-five. They're monitoring the changes before they send anyone back there."

"Any other interventions in time planned?"

"No comment." *As if a mere Ripper could discuss those in public!* The Council was considering proposals centered on the Brontës, Stephen Crane, John Lennon, and Indian composer Navya Badami, who died in that fire in Mumbai in 2049, among others. But they were moving slowly, cautiously; all existing Splinterverses were under scrutiny. *With the entertainment world salivating at the prospects of new stuff from dead geniuses, for once funding isn't an issue.*

Nate and the family headed inside the Majestic Theatre and settled in their orchestra seats with the other elegantly dressed first-nighters. Before long, the house lights went down and the unmistakable sounds of a Gershwin overture filled the house.

The Greenbaums knew the score from the Splinterverse's cast album, but this was the first live production here. The courts had finally worked thought the licensing issues. A stellar cast, led by the multitalented Aleck Hirson as Martin and jazz great Jermaine DeWitt as Smoke.

But the family's attention was focused on the slim young woman in the silver sheath dress, making her Broadway debut as Smoke's sister. Nate squeezed Isis' hand as Rose Greenbaum moved downstage, flashed a dazzling smile at Hirson, and launched into George and Ira's newest classic, "Big Apple Rhythms."

In the roar of applause that followed, Bertie whooped, "'What could be better than that?"

"Well, Uncle David could be here," Hannah said.

Nate glanced around at the enthusiastic crowd. "Oh, he's here all right. In every line, in every bar, in every single note. He's here."

#

<u>*From the diary of J.D. Taylor, October 8, 1964*</u>
Selkie was struggling late in tryouts in Washington. I was using my red pencil when Leo entered my hotel room. He had a funny expression and was holding some magazines.

"Hey, boss man, remember old Joe Gould? He used to call you 'Bronko,' right? Well, there's a new feature on him in the *New Yorker,* about how his Oral History was a big lie. 'Joe Gould's Secret.' He kept writing the same pieces over and over in those black composition books—about tomatoes and Indians and his parents' deaths." Leo paused dramatically. "And *you!*"

"Me?"

"Yeah!" Leo threw himself on my bed and began flipping pages. He still moved with youthful energy. "Mitchell—the writer—doesn't give details, but he says among the chapters Gould constantly rewrote was 'The Man Out of Time.' He calls you 'Bronko, a famous denizen of the Great White Way, and a fine pianist, to boot.' Unquote. Oh, and you're not from here. Or anywhere. Isn't that a riot? I remember him saying things like that, like you were from Mars."

I put down my pencil. Whenever Joe made freaky statements like that, I panicked. Now that his posthumous comments were in print for thousands to read, you'd think it would upset me. If a drunken bohemian—or even an insightful, alcoholic lyricist—could probe the secrets of my background, would *New Yorker* readers start asking questions, too?

I don't know. What's more, I don't care. I'd accomplished my mission here—more than accomplished it, since the music has made its way back to my original world, where those lights were dimmed far too soon.

"Poor crazy Professor Seagull. I'll read it later." I waved the script at him. "Two notions: let's move 'The Loch Morar Monster' to after the brawl between the Orrs and the Walkers. And we should tighten the opener. Ockie Hammerstein always said, 'Musicals are made in the first five minutes.' Let's not lose the audience before the seats get warm."

"I'm game, boss man. Show me."

Rest in peace, Joe Gould. I'll raise a glass to your memory later. Right now, we've got a musical to stage.

Author's Notes

This is a work of fiction. While I've done my best recreating the theatrical world of the past, I've compressed events for brevity. The details of the opening of *The Cradle Will Rock* are one example; yes, I'm familiar with the Second Piano Theory. Other areas include some of David's projects, like *Tom Jones* and *The Corn Is Green,* which had musical treatments later in the twentieth century. He'd have known these, but I chose not to burden the reader with details. In a similar vein, I didn't obsess over the ripple effect caused by the increasing number of David's musicals—juggling shows, theatres, and performers. If I had, this book would have been as long as *Les Misérables.* Victor Hugo's, not Boublil and Schönberg's.

Many of the new musicals the saved composers wrote were projects they had contemplated during their too brief lives, including Weill's *Moby-Dick* and *Nell Gwynn.* Youmans did contact Eugene O'Neill about a potential musical, though it's not known which play he was considering. My money's on *Ah, Wilderness!.*

The Golden Eagle was a real Greenwich Village nightspot. It really did have a pet skunk, though in the early fifties. I'm proposing my Petunia as an ancestor.

Joe Gould was another Village fixture, given to talking to birds, mooching, drinking, and rewriting his "Oral

History." See Joseph Mitchell's articles for the tragic details of his life.

Gershwin's trip to Mexico is detailed in correspondence, including the outrageous behavior of Dr. Gregory Zilboorg, who really did carry a pistol to protect him from the Bolsheviks.

My thanks to Margaret Rogers for Spanish translations; Dr. Paul O. Gulsrud for medical advice; Thonas Nackid for that great cover; Russell Galen and Ann Behar of the Scovil Galen Ghosh Literary Agency for their support; and Brenda W. Clough for a valuable contact.

Special thanks to my wonderful family for living with this project for so long, enduring endless period music and ridiculous trivia like, "Hey, did you know Cole Porter had two cats named Anything and Goes?" Extra special thanks to my husband Harry and daughter Rebecca Turtledove, who let me bounce ideas off them and helped with research and editing. Extra, extra special thanks to Harry for the cameo appearance of a certain bearded baseball player.

Any errors are my own.

This book is dedicated to Cordelia and Phoebe, with much love from Mom-Mom.

About the Author

Laura Frankos has also written *The Broadway Musical Quiz Book* (Applause, 2010); the chapter on the Gershwins' *Of Thee I Sing* in *Fifty Key Musicals* (Routledge, 2022); a mystery novel (*St. Oswald's Niche*); and short fiction in the fields of science fiction and fantasy. She is a contributor to CastAlbumReviews.com and previously had a blog on musical theatre history, "The Great White Wayback Machine." She lives in Los Angeles with her husband, novelist Harry Turtledove. They have three daughters and two granddaughters.

Made in the USA
Las Vegas, NV
27 January 2023

66355993R10277